Praise  P9-BZL-076
Jane Yellowrock Novels

"A lot of series seek to emulate Hunter's work, but few come close to capturing the essence of urban fantasy: the perfect blend of intriguing heroine, suspense, [and] fantasy with just enough romance." —SF Site

"Drives the danger to dizzying heights . . . Hunter delivers the fast pace, high stakes, and flawlessly crafted fight scenes fans expect." —*Publishers Weekly*

"Jane Yellowrock is smart, sexy, and ruthless."
—#1 *New York Times* bestselling author Kim Harrison

"Readers eager for the next book in Patricia Briggs's Mercy Thompson series may want to give Faith Hunter a try." —*Library Journal*

"Hunter's very professionally executed, tasty blend of dark fantasy, mystery, and romance should please fans of all three genres." —*Booklist*

"In a genre flooded with strong, sexy females, Jane Yellowrock is unique. . . . Her bold first-person narrative shows that she's one tough cookie but with a likable vulnerability." —RT Book Reviews

"Seriously. Best urban fantasy I've read in years, possibly ever." —C. E. Murphy, author of *Magic and Manners*

"The story is fantastic, the action is intense, the romance sweet, and the characters seep into your soul."
—Vampire Book Club

Also by Faith Hunter

The Jane Yellowrock Novels

Skinwalker
Blood Cross
Mercy Blade
Raven Cursed
Death's Rival
The Jane Yellowrock World Companion
Blood Trade
Black Arts
Broken Soul
Dark Heir
Shadow Rites
Cold Reign
Dark Queen
Shattered Bonds

The Soulwood Novels

Blood of the Earth
Curse on the Land
Flame in the Dark
Circle of the Moon
Spells for the Dead

The Rogue Mage Novels

Bloodring
Seraphs
Host

Anthologies

Cat Tales
Have Stakes Will Travel
Black Water
Blood in Her Veins
Trials
Tribulations
Triumphant

TRUE DEAD

A Jane Yellowrock Novel

Faith Hunter

ACE
New York

ACE

Published by Berkley

An imprint of Penguin Random House LLC

penguinrandomhouse.com

Copyright © 2021 by Faith Hunter

Excerpt from *Blood of the Earth* copyright © 2016 by Faith Hunter

Penguin Random House supports copyright. Copyright fuels creativity, encourages
diverse voices, promotes free speech, and creates a vibrant culture. Thank you for buying
an authorized edition of this book and for complying with copyright laws by not
reproducing, scanning, or distributing any part of it in any form without permission.
You are supporting writers and allowing Penguin Random House to continue to
publish books for every reader.

ACE is a registered trademark and the A colophon is a trademark of
Penguin Random House LLC.

ISBN: 9780451488732

First Edition: September 2021

Printed in the United States of America

1 3 5 7 9 10 8 6 4 2

To the Hubs,

Bringer of joy into my life:

The one who carefully removes the hornets and lizards from the house,

Kills the spiders and the rare roach,

Sings the songs, and

Makes sure I get on whitewater.

I write words, but there are never words enough for who you are and all you do.

You are the light in my darkness.

CHAPTER 1

A Đervish in the Đark.
Poetry with Bloody Blades.

Beast woke in big bed, tangled in Jane clothes. Sniffed soft, not loud, not what Jane called Flehmen sound, but hunter's sound. Silent. Bruiser was not in big bed. Had not slept in big bed.

Beast rolled over and sat. Put front paw on Jane sleep clothes. Wriggled out. Did not claw or tear Jane clothes. Did not want Jane to be sad. Beast was not happy to be Beast form. Knew Jane would not be happy to be Beast form.

Jane had gone to sleep in human form. Jane body turned into Beast while Jane slept. Was not first time Jane body changed shape in sleep, and not when Jane or Beast wanted change.

Had happened many more than five times since Jane was healed in waters of arcenciel rift.

Sickness that was killing Jane was gone. But much was wrong with Jane body. Jane could not hold shape for many hours. Beast did not know how to help Jane. Was bad.

Angel of Beast—Hayyel—was not helping Jane.

Mate of Jane—Bruiser—could not help Jane.

Molly, mate of Molly—Evan—and Angie could not help Jane.

Jane could not help Jane. Jane was angry.

Jane clan was worried.

Beast did not worry as stupid humans worried. But Beast feared Beast had missed important thing.

Beast studied place in Beast mind where Jane slept. Jane dreams swirled, like leaf on fast water. Jane breathed fast, as if monster chased her. Needed deep calm sleep like dark pool in forest. Beast pressed down on Jane self, deeper into sleep. Jane breathing went smooth.

Beast slid to floor. No thump sounded. Silent hunter landing.

Beast went to window. Put front paws on narrow ledge, standing high on back paws to see into dark with Beast's night vision, looking into world of silvers and greens and grays. Looked out at hills and many trees with bright leaves, what Jane called mountain forest in autumn. Beast did not want to leave mountains. Was best time to hunt—female deer in heat, male deer stupid with rut and running fast, fat autumn moon making hunt effortless, cool wind so Beast could hunt for long time.

But Jane had to leave mountains and go to place of salty water called New Orleans. Was Dark Queen need. Beast understood power in African lion pride or puma family clan or clowder of cats. Understood that Jane had to keep peace, hunt Jane enemies, swat and claw and nurse Jane clan, and do Jane things. Understood. Did not like.

Beast tilted head. No light came from place where grapes rotted into pungent stench to make human wine. Was stupid thing to do, but Bruiser said that making wine was like Beast burying carcass in snow to eat later. Bruiser was not in wine-making place. Bruiser was not here.

Beast dropped to floor. Sniffed pile of luggage on floor in corner. Was Dark Queen clothes for New Orleans. Jane had packed for big human-witch-vampire event in New Orleans, for Jodi to mate with Wrassler in what Jane called wedding. Jane had packed for fighting too. Much killing things, hunting things.

But was dangerous for Jane to hunt and fight. Jane body was wrong. Had been wrong since Jane and Beast swam back through the rift. Was not sickness Jane called cancer anymore, but shifting was not always in Beast's or Jane's control. Shifting hurt Jane more sometimes. Other times did not hurt Jane at all. Did not know why. Was bad to not know. To not always control. And Jane body was too skinny, like young cat, needing more food than she could take in. Beast chuffed sadness. Padded out of room, *pawpawpaw*. Soft. Quiet. Down stairs in dark.

Went to back door. Lights in vampire dens—cottages— were lit and bright. Beast heard Koun laugh. Was good sound. Koun was old. Older than Leo had been. Older than most vampires. Was powerful. But did not laugh often because had seen too many die, had lost much. Beast smelled Tex out in dark, watching over den. Was good smell. Clan-scent. Except for Tex-dogs-smell. Tex-dogs marked trees and left scat on top of ground. Was stupid. All dogs stupid. But Tex liked dogs and trained stupid dogs to do tricks, like sniff out enemies and bombs and track missing humans and vampires. Tex made stupid dogs smarter. Was strange.

Beast padded to office. Smelled Alex at desk. Smelled much garlic and onion and stinky human pizza food. Smelled much coffee. Smelled gunpowder from Alex at gun-range. Smelled Brute—stinky wolf-scent—in room with Alex. Stinky human and stinky werewolf, Brute, spent much time together. Smelled strange lizard-with-wings-creature that Jane would not let Beast hunt and eat. Werewolf and large lizard Jane called Longfellow were asleep on big mattress in corner, lizard tail twined around Brute snout. TV over fireplace glowed and moved but had no sound.

Beast stood in dark and watched. Waiting. Breathing scent of own breath into room.

Brute nose twitched. Brute eyes opened. Brute leaped to feet and growled.

Beast chuffed. Padded into office.

Alex did not look at Beast. Said, "Are you playing games with Brute again? 'Cause you know the rules. All fights, even mock fights, go outside."

Beast chuffed. Padded to Alex. Put paw on table.

"You swat my hardware and tablets to the floor," Alex said, much patience in voice, "I'll swat your nose." Alex held up rolled papers. Still did not look at Beast. Was like cat action.

Beast liked Alex. Beast chuffed. Sat. Paw still on desk.

Alex said, "Okay. Am I talking to Jane?"

Beast moved head side to side as humans did. Felt stupid on Beast body.

"You want something?"

Beast dropped muzzle in nod as humans do.

"Do you want to know where Bruiser and Eli are?"

Beast nodded.

"Out hunting with Lincoln Shaddock. They heard about a small nest of vamps who might be building a food herd of unwilling humans. Could be Legolas's heir, or his secondo heir, and his followers, or it could be another group they haven't swept up yet. It's just a reconnoiter, not a battle."

Did not wake Jane. Jane would be angry. Beast was angry too. Beast growled.

"Jane was exhausted. They thought she might sleep all night for once, so they went without her. Their right as Jane's Consort and her second."

Beast snorted and shook head no. Felt anger for Jane. Jane's place in clan stolen by males. Jane would want to be at fight.

"The team doesn't need Jane's help. They'll either kill the vamps, or Bruiser will take them over and give them to Shaddock."

Beast snorted. Did not sound like re-con-o-i-ter. Sounded like battle. Pressed claws into Jane spirit and Jane part of brain. Jane came awake. Beast told Jane where mate and brother had gone.

Jane cursed in human thoughts. *This isn't the first time they left us at home to twiddle our thumbs. Or paw pads. I'm healed.* Jane looked at paw on table desk. *Except for this pesky shape-changing thing. And they're still treating us like I'm dying.*

Beast thought, *Teach males cat lesson?*

I don't know. What do you have in mind? Jane-thought sounded suspicious.

Beast is alpha. Beast will teach cat lesson. Beast held Jane down, pricking Jane thoughts with claws. Padded to kitchen. To cold-place, what Eli called com-mer-cial fridge. Slid paw under handle and pulled. Door opened.

Do not, Jane warned.

Beast chuffed.

Back door opened. Beast whirled, holding cold-place door open with haunch. Snarled at door.

Koun stood in open door. Cool hunting air blew in. Koun was good-smelling vampire. Smelled of woods and winter wind. Had strange pelt-skin, pale and black and blue, what Jane called *Celtic tattoos*. Was most beautiful vampire with much magic. Strong magic danced from him across Beast pelt like sleet in air.

"And what are you doing, little cat?"

Beast chuffed, showing killing-teeth. *Am not little cat. Am Big-Cat.*

"Are you going to wreak havoc and release the hounds of war?"

Jane tried to speak to Beast. Beast shoved harder with claws. Jane made mouse squeak of pain. Beast turned back to cold-place and sniffed raw cow meat inside plastic. Grabbed meat and pulled onto floor. Landed with thud. Beast pulled meat to middle of kitchen, dragging same way Beast pulled dead deer. Cold-place door closed.

Beast stared at Koun, holding Koun in place with hunter-killer eyes. Ripped plastic with killing teeth. Water-blood spilled everywhere.

Koun chuckled softly, his magic tickling across Beast pelt. "You are making a mess on purpose, aren't you? You are angry with ... Ahhh. They went vampire hunting without you. And they didn't even tell you."

Beast growled low, showed killing teeth again, eyes still on Koun. Sat with cow meat between claws. Ripped cover off meat and spat to floor. Tore meat off. Ate. Swallowed. Ate chunks. Water-blood ran across floor.

"So, the kitchen is a lesson for Eli. What are you going to do to George? Hack up a hairball onto his pillow?"

Beast chuffed. Ate more meat. Belly was full. Dead cow meat was gone.

"Tell me, Vengeful Cat. Would you like to join the vampire hunters? The Chief Strategist of Clan Yellowrock would be happy to follow you into battle."

Beast ear tabs perked high. *Venge-ful Cat. Was good name.* Beast nodded as human does.

"Do you go in cat form, or do you shift into Jane?"

Most vampires and humans in Winter Court of the Dark

Queen did not know the I/we of Beast was not always Jane. Most did not know how to talk to not-human-forms. Koun knew how to talk but did not always act with knowledge. Koun asked two questions at one time. Could only ask one. Beast waited. Stared at Koun.

Koun pursed lips, thinking. "Do you hunt vampires in cat form?"

Beast licked paws and muzzle free of blood, rough tongue getting all blood and meat-bits from paws and toes and off pelt. Shook head no.

"Shift then. I'll weapon up." Koun turned and left kitchen, closing door softly.

Beast looked at office area. Met Brute eyes, blue as sun on ice. Brute shook head and went back to big mattress in office corner. Turned three times and curled into ball with lizard. Beast raced up stairs and into sleeping room. Went to place where Bruiser kept clothes. Nosed open door. Found Bruiser best shoes for dancing. Carried one to empty room and hid in empty closet. Could bite holes in dead-cow-skin-shoes with killing teeth, but did not want to make Bruiser sigh. Hiding shoe was enough. Chuffed. Padded back to bedroom, to bathroom, and leaped into place where humans lay in hot water. Was cold on Beast belly. Took claws off of Jane.

What the heck are you doing? Jane shouted at Beast.

Beast reached into Jane skinwalker magics and thought about Jane half-form. Did not know what would happen when shifted. Did not know what form I/we would be. Most of Jane people did not know of Jane shifting problems. Some knew secret. Beast liked secrets. All cats liked secrets.

Silver mist rose, shot through with dark motes of skinwalker power. Let muscles go limp on cold white tub. Pelt shivered hard as magics rose. Pain quivered through Beast. *Painpainpain* . . .

I don't cuss out loud. Mostly never. But if anything in life deserved cussing, shifting deserved cussing. There were times when shifting was painless, but it didn't happen often. I figured that was because I learned to shift by trial and error instead of over years with a teacher. This time the pain was so bad that when the shift ended, my lungs were stuck in the exhale position.

Panic clawed at me, and I fought through the pain, forcing my lungs to expand. Air whooshed in with a sucking judder. I gasped in several breaths.

"Dang cat," I wheezed. "This tub is freaking cold!"

Inside me, Beast whistled with laughter. Which was a new sound. I had a feeling it portended nothing but trouble.

I reached a hand to the tub's edge and saw my knobby knuckles. I was in half-form. Which was pretty brilliant, actually. I could stay in half-form longer than human. My belly gripped my insides in hungry claws and growled. I patted it. "Gimme a minute," I said to it.

I pulled myself out of the tub and into our room, closing the bedroom door. Bruiser and I had this wing to ourselves most of the time, but I was fairly prudish. Nudity was not one of my comfort zones.

I opened my closet and turned on the light. Smart lights had been an option, but if we wanted to move around in the dark, with bad guys outside, then smart lights were stupid. The bright lights illuminated the mirror and the hanging rack for my brand-new armored leather. Seven sets, four in different shades of matte black, and three sets in colors. There was more armor in New Orleans, with and without leather exteriors; I had an extensive armor wardrobe. I chose a charcoal camo set. The moon was nearly full, making pure black foolish.

I held the armor up in front of me and studied myself in the cheval mirror. I never turned out the same way twice when I shifted into half-form. This time I was a six-foot-tall monster with human-looking amber eyes, furred cat ears placed high on my head, a half-human / half-cat nose on a cat snout, extralong canines, and my black hair to my waist. I had a mixture of skin and pelt on my face, human boobs with skin, pelt down my back, thighs, lower belly, and legs. I'd never win a beauty contest, not even in a cat show. I grinned at my reflection, and I was horrible to look at. Yeah. I was enough to make even a vamp pause in fear. I was the shapeshifting, skinwalker, Dark Queen of the Mithrans.

I dressed fast and pulled on the special boots that expanded to the sides to fit both human and half-form paws. I strapped on the Benelli spine harness, a double-thigh holster rig in case I shifted back to human and needed the nine-mils, and slid my blades into the blade sheaths. I debated on the sword, but I still sucked at swordplay, even with the last six months of practice. I braided my hair and twisted it into a sloppy bun. If an enemy got close enough to grab my hair, I was already dead. Into a pocket, I stuffed the Glob, a magical thingamabob that sometimes did things to protect me. I was scary and armed to the teeth. Literally. I snarled, seeing my fangs. I was at war, and I needed every weapon I had.

My warlord, Grégoire, aka Blondie, and my primo, Edmund, who I had started calling Eddie the Great on cell calls just to needle him, were taking over the European world in my name. They were pals of mine, as much as fangheads can be pals. Eddie was also the emperor of Europe, the Blood Master of all the European territory, and my vamp primo. It was complicated.

In my name, Grégoire, Edmund, and my warriors had defeated the last powerful vampires who were still active in Europe. Not that I had planned all the vamp bloodshed, but to keep European humans and witches safe from marauding bloodsuckers, and to reassert peace, I had let it happen. Yeah. In my name. I hated vamp politics.

Unfortunately, the dregs—and some of the remaining most powerful vamps—of Europe had escaped to all points of the globe, the strongest heading here to take my position. Leo had been fighting European vamps for centuries, and things had only gotten worse when I arrived on the scene.

I loped downstairs into the kitchen to find three vamps and a human, Koun, Tex, Thema, and Alex. And that was an amazing sight—a blue-and-black-tattooed Celtic warrior in modern night camo armor, a gunfighter from the Old West wearing six-shooters on each hip and an ARGO Benelli shotgun like mine strapped to his back on top of buckskin-toned armor, a black warrior in matte black armor, a woman so powerful she sometimes wore silver in her ears as a warning to others—silver being a dangerous, burning, sometimes even an incapacitating allergen to vamps—and Alex, a mixed-race human . . . not teenager. He was an adult now. A very pretty adult with curly ringlets, slightly greenish brown eyes, muscles, and a sense of self-confidence that oozed from his pores along with the garlic stink. The four of them were standing around the bar, checking comms and weapons. Lots and lots of weapons.

I walked around them and stopped, seeing the mess on the floor. "Dang *cat*!" I found the Clorox cleanser and sprayed the dried blood. The vamps watched, still as statues, until I grabbed the paper towels and started to clean the floor.

Tex grabbed my arm. "No, Janie—My Queen," he amended.

"Why not? My cat did this."

"We weren't sure if you wanted the floor left this way. But you ain't cleaning the mess. It's not, uh, *seemly*. For a queen."

I wanted to argue. I wanted to stamp my feet. My clan were working hard to make me act like a queen, like the Dark Queen of the Mithrans, which I was but which I hated. So far, I pretty much sucked at it.

I blew out a frustrated breath, placed the roll of paper towels in his hand, and walked between the vamps, muttering about dang cats. Opening the fridge, I took out a stack of well-marbled steaks, turned on the stove grill, and switched on the fan above it. I tossed a steak onto the grill and waited. Behind me, Tex and Koun cleaned up my mess. Thema was above cleaning up after a cat. She lounged against the wall, polishing a blade, her black eyes on the glinting steel. Not that she missed anything happening around her.

The steak began to sizzle. When it was slightly brown on one side, I salted it and flipped it and salted that side too. When it was mostly no longer raw, I turned off the burner, opened a package of oversized naan, which was the best bread ever made on the face of the earth, and tossed the steak into the middle. I bit into the steak sandwich. Nothing in this world was as good as ultrarare beef. Except maybe oatmeal, and there wasn't time for that too. I needed the calories that I had used up shifting. My skinwalker magic helped power my shifts, but there wasn't enough magic inside me to do it all, and I was once again skinny as a rail, so I had to eat, a lot, to make it through a shift. And when shifting multiple times, like in the middle of the night, I needed to eat a huge amount of food. "Let's go, then," I said, chewing. "We got enemy vamps to behead."

"For this alone, I would call you queen," Thema murmured happily, her accent rich with her African heritage.

"Hey, Alex," I said, grinning around the macerated steak. "Put away the queen's raw steaks and clean up the grill, wouldja?"

He narrowed his eyes at me, so much like his brother that I burst out laughing—which sounded like a cat growling. I was still laugh-growling around the steak and bread as Koun pulled the SUV along the winding drive. Behind us, four more SUVs followed. Koun was deeply focused on the task of negotiating mountain turns, but I realized that he was smiling. A harsh, stoic man, a warrior to a Celtic queen, a Roman slave, soldier, fanghead for nearly two thousand years, he smiled too seldom.

Watching him from the corner of an eye, I leaned the seat back, propped my funky-looking boots on the dash, and licked the steak grease from the fingers of one hand. I ripped more meat and bread off and chewed noisily. Licked some more. My tongue was part cat, and its rough surface cleaned things up nicely.

Koun's smile spread slightly. "My Queen should perhaps know that modern manners are relatively new in the world, that her lack thereof is not shocking to me, as it was to Leo Pellissier and his ilk. In *my* day, we ate with our fingers and licked them clean. It is an efficient method of eating, allowing a hungry person to get all the fat and nutrients from their skin."

Ilk? I grunted, wondering if I could make him laugh. "Squatting over an open fire, meat on a spit, and then you rubbed bear grease and ashes into your skin as grooming?"

Calmly, a strange light in his eyes, Koun said, "Ashes are efficient topical antibiotics, as is rendered animal fat. My Queen is deliberately attempting to insult me?"

"I'm tribal. My ancestors probably did the same at one point. But yeah. Goading you. Being difficult. Seeing where the chinks in your armor are."

Eyes on the road, Koun lifted his eyebrows, his pale eyes twinkling. "I have no *chinks*. I am perfect."

I snickered. "Yeah. Okay. Glad you told me. I musta missed the announcement."

He laughed, and his shoulders relaxed beneath the armor. Bingo. Mission accomplished.

I knew a lonely redheaded witch-vamp who might like Koun if he was happy more. Not that I was going to matchmake. Nope. No way. Especially not from within my clan, where my interest could be considered by some to be an order. Ick. However, I *could* do things to make Koun feel like smiling more often, though so far, the only things that seemed to get a rise out of him were battle, me goading him, and me being crude—the Leo comment to the contrary.

I finished my sandwich, used premoistened handwipes kept in the glove compartment to clean up, and pulled up the address on my tablet so I could study the area where we were headed. Time passed.

"How many people are we bringing to this fight?" I asked.

"Us, three other Mithrans, and six humans," Koun said. "And, as you might say, a buttload of weapons."

"The humans are not to engage the enemy," I said.

"My Queen will leave all such decisions to the chief strategist of Clan Yellowrock and the Dark Queen's Executioner," he said mildly, giving me his official title.

I grinned, showing my extralong canines. "You gonna make me, you blue-skinned Smurf-boy?"

Koun burst into laughter for two full seconds before clamping off the amusement, his rock-hard abs shaking just a bit. I was making progress. His wide eyes said that he didn't hear his own laughter often, and never twice in one day. He swallowed and forced his face into its usual emotionless, unreadable expression. "Yes, My Queen. I will tie you to the back of the SUV and leave you behind, to keep you safe, while the human warriors and your Mithrans secure the house and grounds."

"You can try it, but I'll beat your butt, Elmo."

Koun's breath shook with silent laughter. His tone

heaped with sarcasm, he said, "My Queen. I am happy to be either Smurf or Muppet, should it please *Your Majesty*, but *Grover* is the blue furry creature. Not Elmo. And if we have an accident whilst your feet are on the dash, the safety balloon will break both legs, likely your pelvis, and possibly your spine. You can shift to heal, I know this, but we have insufficient steaks for that."

"Airbag, not safety balloon."

"My *deepest apologies* for my error, *My Queen*." Yeah. Definite snark in the "my queen" part.

I called that progress. "Direct route," I said. "And speed it up, slowpoke. You may consider that an order, Smurfy." He maintained his leisurely pace, but I elected not to swat him with my claws. Instead I went back to the sat maps.

Our target was a small house on East Avon Parkway, up near Beaver Lake. I went through sat pics and street-to-street Google cams, getting a feel for the topography. A block out, I closed the tablet and checked my weapons. Put the special cat-ear comms set on. "Testing. Yellowrock."

Into my ear, Alex, back at the inn, said, "Got it, Janie."

Koun stopped a half block out, and I opened the door. We were downwind. I caught the scent of battle. "Blood. A lot of blood," I said.

"And silence. We are perhaps too late."

I snarled. Bruiser might be injured. Or dead. Adrenaline shot through me.

If he was dead because Koun didn't drive fast enough, I'd behead my self-appointed chief strategist of Clan Yellowrock. I pulled on Beast speed, her night vision, her stealth, and raced into the darkness. Not that Koun would lose me, not with nighttime vamp vision and vamp speed. I pulled the Benelli and vamp-killer blade. Leaped over the back fence. In midair I spotted people lying in the dark under the stars, everything looking green-gray-silver in Beast eyes. Dead vamps. Dead humans.

Beast leaped to the front of my mind. *Not ours,* she thought. She was right. The scent patterns said that some of our people were wounded but suggested that none of the dead were ours. I/we landed silently in the grass.

Bruiser was standing in front of a post, where a vamp was secured with silver-plated zipties, his right hand on the vamp's head, his left on the fanghead's neck, holding him stretched up high. My honeybunch was alive. Relief shot through me until I realized he was draining and force-changing the vampire, binding him, compelling him to give up all his secrets and loyalty.

I knelt on my toes and one knee in the shadows, watching, still downwind, breathing in the stench of vamps and blood, flowers and spice, death a sickly sweetness. Breathing like a cat, the air pulled over scent sacs in my mouth.

The vamp beneath Bruiser's hands twitched, shook. His mouth opened, and his fangs clicked back into the roof of his mouth. His eyes bled back to human, changing from vicious killer to drug-happy in the space of seconds. "My master," he said. "I am yours. May I taste your blood?"

I didn't react. Not where anyone could see it or smell it. But I hated this. Bruiser was different—not *less* human than ever before, yet not *more* human. He was silent more than usual and most often did winery chores alone. He claimed to be only introspective and a smidge melancholy, as if that definition and explanation made it okay. Eli said Bruiser was depressed but had a right to deal with it in his own way, at least for now. The scent wafting from Bruiser on the night air was determined and yet full of self-loathing. He was doing this to keep me safe. To keep his people and my people safe. But he didn't take joy in it. He hated what Leo had made him and hated even more what he was becoming. I feared that, eventually, he would begin to hate the person he was doing this for. Even though he disagreed with my opinion, I feared that protecting me might drive him away from me.

I looked away from my Consort and found Lincoln Shaddock leaning against the house. The tall man's eyes were on me. A lot of thoughts raced through me, formed into understanding, and settled.

The Master of the City of Asheville had been feeding my Consort. Not often. Onorios weren't vamps and didn't have to drink often. But they had to have some vamp blood to survive. Shaddock would know exactly what Bruiser was feeling. Would know how conflicted Bruiser was about mentally draining and chaining vampires to his will, and even how he felt about drinking blood to make his physical powers stronger, blood he desperately needed because he had tried to live without it in the *fame vexatum* method of blood-starvation practiced by Mithrans. Bruiser had hoped that he would grow more mentally powerful, but the starvation had left him physically famished.

While he was weakened, we had been attacked in Asheville on Shaddock's titled hunting territory. Bruiser had tried and failed to drain our most recent enemy's Onorio, Monique Giovanni. That powerful Onorio had been working with the Flayer of Mithrans and would have defeated Bruiser had their mental battle not ended when it did. Monique was still around and would eventually come after him to finish the interrupted battle. So Bruiser was training hard to learn to do something he hated: binding the minds of vampires with the power of his mind.

Bruiser's emotions were twisted and distorted, a coiled mash of love and protective instincts for me, and miserable memories of Leo's influence—Leo who had made blood-servants bound to his will and desires. Bruiser's history and his new powers often left him shut down, emotionally distant, deep in thought, and trying to hide all that.

Eli said Bruiser would be fine, that he was watching my Consort, and that Bruiser had a handle on it all. I trusted the elder Younger to read Bruiser and keep him safe, but this period of emotional healing was hard.

To the side, Eli appeared, directing a large group of unwashed, smelly humans from a garage to gather beneath the porch roof. "You're safe now," he was saying softly, gently. "You can go home. Your torturers are dead." He directed two of our humans to pull the dead enemies face-up. "See? Dead."

Eli swiveled his gaze my way, frowned to see me here, but nodded, a single thrust of his head, as if acknowledging the inevitable. "We haven't finished clearing the house."

"Copy that," I said.

I adored my adopted brothers. Eli was battle-worn, tired, stretched thin both mentally and physically, but gentle and kind enough to worry about others, like the people he had rescued. Working with me had made the Younger brothers way more than just "financially comfortable." It had made them kinda rich and had given them a purpose they had been looking for. They were my co-heirs of Clan Yellowrock, and all the properties and monies that entailed. They would protect me with their lives. But in return, I could never keep them safe. Being the Dark Queen was a two-edged sword, and the people I protected always ended up cut and bleeding.

Feeling Eli's eyes on my retreating form, I turned and leaped back over the fence. Sheathed and harnessed my weapons. Stalked back to the SUV.

Koun's armored butt was against the SUV's grill, his booted feet crossed at the ankles. *He was in armor.* Yeah, I should have paid closer attention to that. Koun fought naked, more or less. Or he used to. Everything was changing. I stopped near him, taking in the armor, which I had thought was camo but was matte black, swirled with midnight blue dye in the colors and patterns of his tattoos. *Nifty.* He was alone; Tex, Kojo, Thema, and the humans were elsewhere. Koun was studying the area on satellite maps, his expression back to its usual hauteur.

"My Queen," he said by way of greeting. But he didn't look up and he didn't sound happy. In fact he sounded really ticked off. "My *Queen*," he said again, "hurdled an eight-foot fence alone, without backup or intel."

"I'm armed and armored. Bruiser and Shaddock won. There were humans inside. They're okay."

"How many of our enemies are dead?" Koun asked.

I thought back to the bodies as I opened a bottle of water, put it to my mouth and crushed it, the contents shooting into the back of my throat, and swallowed it all down. "Three vamps. One is still alive."

"And how many humans did they hold captive?"

"I dunno. Maybe forty?"

Koun tilted his head to me and pocketed the tablet. "And *My Queen* did not find the numbers disproportionate?"

My half-form nose caught a scent. I pulled in air over my tongue and into the scent sacs in the roof of my mouth with a loud sucking breath. Inside me, Beast growled and so did I, smelling vamps approaching in the night. Six? Eight? More? "Vamps."

Koun's weapons were instantly in his hands. He leaped to the hood of the SUV and searched the night.

"This was a trap," I said. "They were waiting for me."

Koun sniffed the air and scowled, his pupils widening slightly, beginning to bleed black. "You should not have come."

"Gloat later."

Koun touched his comms. "Alex. Bring Eli and the others onto this channel."

"Done."

Identifying himself, he said, "Koun, speaking to the Consort, Shaddock, and the Youngers. Vampires approach by stealth. Six from upwind. Likely more from downwind. Our people will engage from outside the fence."

I added to Koun's summary, "I smell Monique Giovanni, the *senza onore*. They want Bruiser and me both."

"Keep Jane safe," Bruiser ground out.

Koun vamped out, faster than a heartbeat, eyes going from almost human-looking to solid black pupils in rings of scarlet sclera, his jaw unhinging, fangs clicking down in a fraction of a second. "You will wait here," he demanded of me. He stepped forward.

Beast does not wait, my cat thought. She took over our body and rammed her power into me/us.

I/we raced forward, cat silent, redrawing my weapons, silvered vamp-killer blade in my left hand, Benelli in my right. A vamp in black, his face covered, leaped from behind a tree.

Battlefield awareness kicked in hard. Time slowed, everything around me glowed crystalline green and silver in Beast's vision. As if I had all the time in the world, I swung the blade back and leaped to the right. Arm out, long and horizontal, swinging low to high, I spun my body. Rotating forward and away from my opponent. Whipping my spine. Putting momentum and weight behind the swing. Aiming midline, transverse cut. The blade sliced through flesh. Starting just below the waist. Hit the vamp's spine and stuck there. Jarring up my arm. My body continued the spin. Pulling on my shoulder. Pulling the enemy revolving after me. Blood gushed everywhere.

Still in the air, I hit the vamp in the face with my fist, holding the Benelli. His head snapped back and my vamp-killer came free.

The body began to fall.

I landed and danced back on my toes. Still spinning.

Fired the Benelli point-blank into the torso of a vamp racing in to attack.

Danced to the left. Fired the Benelli again. Missed. Whirled and took off a vamp's arm. She screamed that piercing ululation of a vampire dying.

I was fifteen feet from the fence when Koun hissed a soft sound near me, a sword in each hand. He took off the shot vamp's head, then the one-armed vamp's head. Then the head of the one with the navel cut, though I was pretty sure that one was dead anyway.

"You left their heads," Koun snarled at me.

"I wasn't finished," I snarled back.

More gunfire sounded. Flashed bright in the night. Near and distant, upwind and down. Shotguns and small arms fire.

Monique Giovanni was just ahead. I could smell her, could make out her form in the darkness, her honey-colored hair shining in the low lights.

"There. Her," I said to Koun.

My warrior at my side, I raced toward her. She vanished through a gate I hadn't seen into the backyard. She was going after Bruiser.

Again, I leaped the fence. Koun said something in a language I didn't understand and one-handed his body up and over, after me. As I landed, I swung the bloody blade and took down an enemy vamp.

Eli said, "Jane." Battlefield tone.

I gyrated on my toes and saw him. He was shoving the humans toward the house, toward safety. Several were wounded. Two on the ground. They were in the line of fire. *Eli* was in the line of fire. He'd never take cover and leave them.

So many humans. So much collateral damage. *Eli*. A vamp raced toward him.

Lincoln Shaddock flew in the air from out of the night and beheaded the vamp. Landed. Whirled to strike another. He was using two dueling swords. A dervish in the dark. Poetry with bloody blades. Racing to another target, Lincoln said to me, "Get to George," and darted into the dark.

Koun took on more vamps at my side and behind me. With him there, I was safe. Had time to reconnoiter. Eyes darting and scanning. I spotted Kojo, Thema's mate, and several more of our best warriors. Most injured.

Weapons out, I turned in a circle. Searching.

Koun said, "There." He slung the blood from his swords, pointing.

Bruiser was in a death stare with the *senza onore* who once worked with the Flayer of Mithrans.

Koun said, "You were correct. This was a trap, ready to be sprung with or without you."

"And without us, our people would have lost."

Koun made a soft sound of agreement.

Gunfire sounded. Comms crackled. "We got encom inside the house," Eli said, warrior-speak for enemy combatants. "Take out all the staked vamps."

"Copy that." "Copy that," Thema and Lincoln said in concert, accents dueling.

I raced for Giovanni but stopped just short. She and Bruiser were locked in silent combat. Staring at each other. As I watched, her hand lifted and touched Bruiser's shoulder. Onorio powers worked much better when the aggressor was in contact with the defender. I didn't know what to do. How to help. If I beheaded her while she was in his mind, would that scramble his mind, like most *anamchara* when one of them died? Would it kill him?

From the corner of my eye, I saw Thema's sword rise and descend with finality, beheading a vamp on the ground.

Bruiser was sweating. Monique Giovanni said, "Yes. Tell me about your love."

I muttered, "Stupid staring contests." I stabbed my bloody vamp-killer into a true-dead body so I could find it easily and, with my off hand, pulled a nine-millimeter semi-automatic handgun.

I shot her.

CHAPTER 2

I Kinda Suck at Royalty

I took it all in, in an instant as Bruiser fell beside her, shaking, confused, and exhausted. The physical battle behind us seemed to be over. Already. Real battle is seldom as long or picturesque as Hollywood makes it. It's usually fast, bloody, and over with, too late to change anything.

Lincoln pointed to two of his vamps, saying, "Feed the Consort." No one addressed Monique's wounds. Onorios were made of stern stuff, and though she was gasping and bleeding, she wasn't dead yet. Around us, other vamps were healing themselves by feeding upon healthy humans, others feeding injured humans, including some of Lincoln's blood-servants.

One injured and dying human was hauled off to the front of the house, a vamp's fangs in her throat, the forced change to Mithran already beginning. Meaning I had been wrong. Some of Lincoln's people had died or were nearly dead, and his people were having to save them the only way they could, by turning them into vamps.

"Crap," I muttered.

I checked on Bruiser, who was feeding from a vamp's

wrist. There was a trickle of blood in his beard, which made Beast perk up. *Good mate. Good pelt on face.* I kinda liked it too. Especially when—

At my back, the fence crashed to the ground. I felt Koun step between the downed fence and me. His voice fierce, Koun said, "Blood challenge. Here. Now. You will not escape me again." That sounded personal. He and a female vamp met in the middle of the backyard, swords flashing in the dim light. Battle wasn't over yet after all; there was a second wave. Or the first wave was just a feint. Whatever was happening, Koun needed to take a head to clear past grievances.

More vamps came through the gap in the fence. *Goodie.* I needed to hit something.

Into my earbuds, I heard Bruiser gasp something, but his mic cut out. All I heard was, "There's . . . house . . . -ap."

Alex chattered, trying to reestablish contact.

Kojo and Thema took out three more ambushing vamps and raced for the house. Moving Beast-fast, I stepped into cover provided by a narrow column, and slid the shotgun into the spine holster. Changed out the left nine-mil's magazine for a fresh one, color-coded to show it was loaded with silver-lead composite hollowpoint rounds, which would shred inside a vamp's body and poison them from the inside. The weapons were too small for my big fingers, but I could make do if necessary. I holstered it and removed the vamp-killer from the headless body, cleaned it on the dead vamp's clothing, and sheathed it.

As I worked, Lincoln's vamps took out several more attackers. Again it looked as if the attackers were finished, but Bruiser had said something about the house.

I wrenched a sword from a dead vamp's hand and tested it. "Not bad," I muttered. My sword skills sucked, but I could stab a vamp in the back with the best of them. Blades instead of bullets meant that there would be no collateral damage. As Koun finished and beheaded his enemy, I slipped quietly toward the house and took down two vamps from behind, first with the vamp-killer, then with the sword: stab, behead, stab, behead. It was messy and bloody but efficient. It also ruined the wallpaper and the rugs.

I raced indoors. Ducked behind the counter and pulled

the nine-mil. Shot a human who came around the corner, raising a weapon at me. Another. I was hyperventilating, hiding behind the counter, under halfway poor cover. I slowed and sucked in breaths. Stood and dashed through the house. Shot two vamps, young ones, based on the way they fell with the silver shot, and beheaded them. Whirled. Sought the corners. Listened. Sniffed the scents on the air. Everyone was down. I was alone.

The light seemed too bright, too sharp. Everything had taken on a strange, muted silence—muffled moans and gasps, barely heard, distant conversation. For my human form, I had micro-gated headphones that kicked in at the first soundwave to preserve my hearing, but since my ears were all over the place in half-form, they didn't fit my various ear positions. I was deaf from the firefight, short as it had been. I took a slow breath of the stench of open wounds and death. Was it really over?

In my earbud, Alex's tinny voice was demanding that all our people check in.

"Yellowrock here. Inside. Safe," I said.

Eli and a human woman were kneeling over a downed man, an injured human. Eli, who had somehow beat me inside, shoved a tampon into a gunshot wound. That meant he was out of XStat syringes to stop bleeding.

"You okay?" I asked him.

"Younger. Clear. In kitchen with injured humans. Call medic," he said, though I was halfway reading his lips. To me, he added, "We got DBs everywhere, twelve more freed injured humans, none of whom signed papers to be blood-servants, and, if I understand Bruiser right, we also have four vamps in a hidden room in the basement with more human hostages." He indicated a door a few feet away. "Down there. We need some vamps alive to find out who and where the clan Blood Master is. And we need someone up here who can cover me while I stabilize the injured."

"Okay. Got it. You keep the humans safe. And you stay safe. Liz will kill me if you get scratched." Liz Everhart and Eli had hooked up and somehow stayed hooked up for months. They were officially an item.

Eli chuckled, snapped off his gloves, and pulled on a fresh pair, applying pressure to a different human's wound.

"She won't kill you, but she might turn you into a toad. My girl is freaky powerful, and she thinks I'm adorable."

I raised my voice. "Shaddock? Tex? Eli needs backup at my location! Koun? Kojo? Thema? To me!" With little puffs of air displacement, my vamps were instantly at my side. I told them what needed doing, and before they could bubble-wrap me and make me stay safe upstairs, I kicked open the basement door. I could have turned the knob, the door wasn't locked, but kicking it felt so good.

Inside me, Beast screamed with joy. She shoved her gifts into me, and I/we leaped out in a controlled fall down into the dark. Cat leap. I/we landed at the bottom of the stairs on a small concrete pad. Took it all in. The basement was finished with a low, dropped ceiling. Carpeted floor. Once white walls with rust-colored swirls.

I took a breath. The air reeked of blood. Blood on the walls. Blood on the carpet. Beast-fast, I changed weapons again, holstering the smaller handgun, pulling the Benelli. Nothing attacked. Kojo and Thema dropped to my sides. Somehow Koun ended up in front. *Dang vamp.* "We need them alive," I growled.

Koun grunted in disagreement. He wanted to fight to kill. With him in front, we moved slowly through the darkness.

The attacks came from all sides.

Silvers and grays and brilliant shades of greens. I whirled to the rear and fired the shotgun point-blank. The attacking vamp fell, the silver fléchette rounds ripping through her.

My new sword swung as if self-guided. Buried itself in a vamp's shoulder. Cutting deep and down, at an angle toward the center, slicing arteries. Blood spewed. He fell. All the attackers were down. Once again, combat was over.

"I have two alive-ish here," I said. "Make sure they survive." I wiped my sword clean of blood on the clothing of a dead vamp. The blade came away just as bloody. I shook my head and sheathed the Benelli. "Save the humans," I said.

Into my comms, I said, "Eli, Alex. Premises are secured." I turned on a toe and raced back up the stairs.

In my comms, I heard Eli say, "Alex. I just found another batch of injured humans. We're overwhelmed. We need medic."

"Roger that, already called," Alex said through the comms.

Medic meant human ambulances and human law enforcement. And since we hadn't been invited here and had killed lots of people, that meant legal trouble, a weeks-long investigation. I initiated a conference call with Alex and Brandon Robere, in France. Brandon led my legal team. *Holy crap.* I had a legal team. I walked outside for privacy as the conference call initiated. As it went through, I watched the mess in the backyard. Lincoln called Kojo over for something, and the vamp turned his back. It was a vamp snub, one that said Kojo did not answer to Lincoln and that Lincoln wasn't strong enough to make him do so. Something had happened between Shaddock and his guest, but that was something to deal with later.

When I had Alex and Brandon on the connection, I said, "Alex, will you provide my current location to Brandon Robere?"

"Got it. Done," Alex said.

I never felt like talking all vamp-proper, but I sucked it up and did my job, recollecting and using some of the formality I had learned working for the Master of the City of NOLA. I said, "This is an official announcement from the Dark Queen of the Mithrans. This property, its dead and wounded, are hereby claimed as property of the Dark Queen, whose people suffered an attack while rescuing humans kidnapped by a group of rogue Naturaleza. Brandon, feel free to put in all the legalese and send it to me for my e-siggie if needed. Then you can put it under whatever pending, potential, or otherwise legal mumbo-jumbo wrangling you can cobble together. I'll reimburse the owners for the loss of the property and provide a settlement for their heirs if they died here."

"Yes, My Queen," Brandon said. "I'll contact the State Department and get our emissary on-site as quickly as possible."

"I'm calling local law enforcement," Alex said. "Tell everyone to put down their weapons."

Brandon said, "If Koun is with you, get him to put your

banner in the front yard. Brian and I will be home tomorrow, in New Orleans, for the wedding and to correlate the Mithran legalities for the coronation, so we will both be on hand to assist with any fallout."

"And I'll trace the financial trail and confiscate all monies used to finance whatever this was."

I looked around at the dead in the backyard. "Yeah, yeah. Whatever. You two chat. I'm out." I removed myself from the call. My ears were getting better. I heard sirens in the far distance.

Koun appeared at my side, having heard the conversation. Vamp hearing was even better than my half-form's. "You should leave the premises before the humans arrive, My Queen."

I made a noncommittal sound.

"I have placed your banner in the front yard." Before the call. I got that. I hadn't had to tell him. Koun was good at his job. "The media will arrive the moment word goes out that you are here and you have fought another battle. Your Consort should speak with the press and deal with the officials. And you should not be seen, My Queen. You are bloody and . . . not human."

I tested my snout with big knobby fingers. Still mostly cat-faced. "Yeah. I might scare the babies. I'll slip out in a bit."

Koun followed me to the woman on the ground. Monique Giovanni was being held in the arms of one of our female vamps, was being fed and healed. I couldn't remember the vamp's name, but I said to her, "Stop feeding and healing this woman. She's my enemy."

The vamp didn't stop. She didn't even look up.

"Monique, if you take over the will or loyalty of my faithful servant, or try to take her from me, you're dead meat." I grinned and showed my fangs, which were really impressive, even by vamp standards. "You be a good little girl, and I'll let someone heal you."

She raised a hand as if to claw me or try to take me over. I snatched her hand and broke her wrist. That pain and the not-quite-healed gunshot wound should keep her busy and unable to concentrate enough to use her powers. Koun pulled the lethargic vamp away from Monique, lifted her into his arms, and carried her into the darkness.

Bruiser and another one of the vamps I sorta recognized stepped to my side, the vamp yanking Monique's arms back. Bruiser was holding a pair of silver null cuffs, a device developed by law enforcement or the military or maybe witches working for both. The cuffs stopped witch prisoners from generating magical power, making them easy to transport or keep in prisons, and the latches were difficult to remove unless a prisoner could get hands up to them. The cuffs worked on were-creatures and other paras too, or so I heard. Bruiser slapped a pair on Monique's wrists and twisted a second pair until they formed a headband. He locked them across Monique's head and then secured her hands with regular handcuffs so she couldn't get to the latches. She tried to bite the vamp who was restraining her, which for some reason, made me laugh out loud.

I was still laughing when Thema, Kojo, and Koun escorted me to my SUV, put me in the back seat with Kojo, and Koun drove us away from the approaching sirens. I looked back and saw my banner in the front yard of the massacre scene brought by my enemies. A small voice inside murmured, *This will be the legacy of your war. Betrayal. Ambush. Murder. Death.* I hadn't designed the banner, but it was fitting that the banner was a bloodred background centered with a gold laurel-leaf crown, a pale whitish Glob, a feather, and a puma fang.

"Just freaking ducky," I said aloud.

Thema, riding shotgun, swiveled in her seat and stared at me, her black eyes glistening in the dim interior lights. "Your people left you at home in your bed sleeping and went to hunt without you. They did not tell you they were going. They did not allow you to share in the glory of battle. I would behead them for such insults."

His voice mild, Koun said, "The Consort explained to me that tonight was supposed to be a simple reconnoiter, to determine if rumors in the Mithran community were correct: that a small group of Melker's followers had escaped the Dark Queen and were regrouping. The rumors suggested that Melker's new heir was possibly on the premises. No combat was planned for tonight, solely reconnaissance, though of course, everyone came heavily armed and prepared for battle."

"Of course you did," Thema said. There was a hint of snide in her tone, which made me smile.

"Who is Melker?" I asked, the name familiar but not tied to a face.

Koun glanced at me in the rearview. "You called him Legolas. Or Lego."

"Oh yeah," I said. "Pretty hair. Super-duper dead."

Koun's eyes returned to the road. "While you were changing and shifting, we learned that when your people arrived, they saw a Naturaleza draining and killing a human. Eli intervened. That resulted in combat."

"They left you at home," Thema said to me again, her tone deliberately accusing. "It was an insult to a warrior."

Ah. Thema had been left behind too. A warrior not called upon. I squashed down on the anger that wanted to rise. I knew the real reason I hadn't been invited. My body doing the uncontrolled flip-flop shape-shifting-change thing wasn't well known. Thema wasn't included in the small group that was privy to my little problem. The guys and Molly, my witch BFF, were all worried about what would happen if I changed shape in the middle of a battle and what would happen if I shifted too slowly and died. I could practically hear Eli's pedantic, cool voice in my head. *You haven't died since you were healed. We don't know what's happening with your body or your power. You could get people killed trying to protect you.*

And on top of his mental voice came Bruiser's. *You are more than just a rogue-vampire hunter. When you killed the first Son of Darkness, the Flayer of Mithrans came to revenge him and kill you. When the Flayer died, others came to power. This is the way of life among Mithrans and Naturaleza. There is always an Heir. When you became the Dark Queen, you became the most valuable target in the world. You have political value and significance at this moment. You are the only thing keeping the Mithran world in balance. You need to stay alive so we can fight this war.* He had laughed then. *All that political reality aside, where you*

*go, there I am, Jane. We can run away together and say to
hell with all this, or you can stay, can choose war to protect
all paranormals and humans. A war that will seldom allow
you to fight. But you must choose.*

Eli and Bruiser were both right. I had rushed in to help,
probably making things worse by triggering a trap set for
Bruiser and me, one that might have ended early had I
stayed away. But if I hadn't come and the trap had been
sprung anyway, my people would have been dead. "Well,
crap," I said.

Koun's cell phone buzzed. He answered and put the cell
to his ear. "Koun."

Bruiser's voice said, "Shaddock bled and read two human blood-servants. There's another house also being
used as a nest, and the important Mithrans are there. Tonight was supposed to be an ambush that drew out and
killed the Consort and the MOC of Asheville. And if they
were very lucky, also the Dark Queen. With or without
you, we would have been attacked by the second wave."

In an instant, I put it together. When I became Dark
Queen, I promoted Shaddock to master of the city status,
and most vamps—any who had never seen him in action—
would think that meant the recently upgraded MOC was
an easy mark, his territory easy pickings. Shaddock was
more than he appeared, but had they succeeded in taking
him and Bruiser out . . . that might have destroyed me. The
trap was an excellent political ploy for them, a win-win.
And then of course, I raced to the scene, giving our enemies all the eggs in one basket. *Crap.*

"Someone set this trap," Koun said, still talking to
Bruiser, "and made certain that the intel got back to our
people. We have a double agent or spy in our midst."

"When don't we?" I leaned forward and plucked the cell
from Koun's fingers. "Send us the address of the other nest.
Send us fighters. We'll make sure this ends tonight."

Bruiser said, "Local law enforcement received a call
from the governor of North Carolina, and they ceded control of this site to the Mithrans, pending a state court ruling on Friday. We may not remove any of the dead humans.
We may not remove any Mithrans. The State Department
has not returned my calls. It appears that the long-expected

but hoped-against clash of the United States and the Dark Queen's Court of Mithrans has begun."

I hated politics. And I sucked at the sneaky finesse they required. "Call the governor back and remind them that vamps burn up in daylight, and they'll take all the other bodies, and the premises, with them. Tell the powers that be to stop being stupid, or I'll kick their collective asses. Except. More polite."

Koun's shoulders relaxed and my honeybunch chuckled. I'd been fighting political battles from afar for months. Having taken part in a real battle and having the love of my life still with me was the best thing to happen in all that time.

"I shall endeavor to remind all law enforcement and political powers," Bruiser said, "that My Queen is most generous with her financial support in all elections and that she has also been generous with Mithran blood to heal their children and their families."

"Way more polite," I said. "Don't forget the address." I ended the call. The address popped up on Koun's screen with the words "Keep her safe." *Good.* They were going to let me play, this time without an argument, which meant they probably already knew it was safe, but I could pretend that wasn't the case. I still needed to hit something.

Unfortunately when we arrived, there were no vehicles in the drive or the carport. The doors to the house were open to the summer night. Lights blazed through the windows.

When our party of ten stormed the house, no vamps were present. There was nothing to hit. Just a ransacked house that stank of vamps and old blood.

Still, we cleared the house carefully and discovered five humans in a back suite. I watched as Koun questioned the one who seemed the most mentally coherent and discovered that they had been unwillingly taken, bled repeatedly, and blood-bound. They were blood-slaves. They knew nothing. All they wanted was a vamp to drink from. My fists clenched. I needed to punch something. Or someone. Making human blood-slaves was one of many things about vamps that brought me nearly to rage. Most vamps called them cattle. Food. Toys. Under my rule as DQ, humans couldn't be treated as cattle. Making new blood-slaves was no longer permitted, and though (according to the Vampira Carta of the Americas) I couldn't outlaw it, I could tax it, and making blood-slaves was now a big financial drain on suckheads.

A lot of vamps who had sworn to me probably hated that, and if they had made slaves, they hid it well around me and members of my court. Blood-servants were fine. They could contract for and make all the servants they could take care of. Slavery? Nope. No more.

A few vamp pharma businesses, including Leo's lab in Texas, had been researching treatments for humans who had been blood-bound, with some success but also with some failures. For now, these slaves could opt for the experimental treatment or be brought over to blood-servant status if a vamp was willing, had the funds to care for them, and could find a job for them.

I stood in the open garage and dialed Bruiser.

"My Queen," he said, a caress and a warning in his voice. Others could still hear us.

I took a deep breath and blew out my fury and frustration. I breathed in the calm of night and gave him a down-and-dirty debrief.

Bruiser listened with the intense concentration that had made him the best primo in Mithran lands and the best Consort I could ever have. When I finished, he said, "We've learned that the remaining vampires from this nest are among the last powerful vampires from Europe."

Formal words and tone. So maybe the chief of police or the sheriff was standing there listening, and he was informing them as much as me. Bruiser continued. "From the information gathered in the bleed-and-read, their plan was to ambush and kill us all, and if they failed in that, to kill as many of your followers as they could, leaving you crippled. Then they would kill and disable local law enforcement, travel to New Orleans, and take over there, while the Dark Queen was rebuilding her court."

And grieving my Consort, my brother, and Shaddock. Yeah. Those deaths might have brought me down all by themselves.

I heard Shaddock's voice in the background. "My Queen, your position is under threat, about to be usurped."

"Yeah, I got it. Those powerful vamps are on the way to New Orleans."

"One presumes," Bruiser said.

"Just in time to screw up Jodi and Wrassler's wedding. For which Jodi will kill me."

I heard Shaddock laughing as I ended that call to dial the Council Chambers of NOLA. Thankfully Wrassler himself didn't answer, but one of the original Tequila Boys, the security team put together when I first took over vamp protection there, did.

"Antifreeze," I said. "This is Jane."

"Yo. Legs. How high you kickin'?"

"Nobody lets me kick lately," I complained. *Except for tonight.* Maybe they knew I needed the release.

"Yeah, being rich and powerful must suck. Hang on while I curtsy."

I had missed this kind of insulting banter. Dear heavens, I had missed it so much. "You guys are rich, dude. I made sure you got an increase in pay. You even got dental and visual plans."

"Legs, there's comfortable with purdy teeth and nice specs, and then there's *rich* rich." Before I could reply, he shouted off the cell. "Hey guys! It's her majesty, Legs."

"Legs!" another guy shouted in the background. I was pretty sure it was Sweaty Bollock. The Tequila Boys were named after tequila cocktails. I had never asked what the ingredients were in a Sweaty Bollock, for fear they might tell me. "When you coming home, girl?" he yelled. "I have a deep and abidin' need to spar with a royal."

I glanced up and spotted Thema watching me, standing in the shadows, vamp-still, silent as the grave. *Haha.* "I might hurt you," I said to Antifreeze and Sweaty. "Send you to the hospital for weeks. You'd be out of work, lose your house and car."

Antifreeze said, "Come to think of it, we need a long-term care package with an 'injured on the job' clause."

"Yeah, yeah, take it up with Raisin," I said, referring to Ernestine, Leo's *very* elderly human accountant. "Meantime, we got some big bads on the way."

"Girl, when do we not?"

"Initiate Cowbird Protocol at HQ and all the clan homes."

"Roger that, Legs. Hold on."

I heard typing and clicking in the background as he activated the security measures based on the real cowbird, which meant a traitor on premises. I said, "Antifreeze, I want additional cameras integrated into the system, even places formerly off-limits. Cameras outside the bedroom doors, cameras showing the entrances to public restrooms. And would you mind letting my housekeeping service know I'll be home sooner than expected? I'd like to get my house and Yellowrock Clan Home ready for visitors, ASAP."

"Already done, Fang Queen. Report: HQ is on high alert with two special units gearing up to roam the halls and grounds. No one has been allowed out alone without a hall pass, just like high school. Other units will be deployed to back up each of the clan homes and outlying properties, including the currently sparsely occupied NOLA Yellowrock Clan Home and your private residence. I've sent a message to Wrassler notifying him of your orders, and so he may call you and tell you not to fu—ah, mess up his wedding."

I smiled. Tequila Boys were all former military, and their jargon was always military-oriented. And they all knew how I felt about cussing.

"Perfect. Thank you, Antifreeze. Remind me that I need to include Christmas bonuses come time."

"You da best, Legs. Later, woman." He ended the call.

Legs. Woman. Fang Queen. Wonderful snark. I had missed it so much.

Thema was still watching me when I pocketed my cell, the moonlight shining on her dark skin, her eyes narrow with . . . suspicion? Curiosity?

"What?" I demanded.

"You have servants to make such calls, yet you make them yourself. You did not demand respect from your underlings. They called you names about your legs."

"So?"

"You are a strange ruler. People with power most often spend their days trying to take more power. They have nothing without the mantle of royalty."

"I kinda suck at royalty. And I have my own mantle."
With an index finger, I drew a circle in the air around my
furry face.

"I see this. I could teach you how to be decorous and
genteel and royal, but I will not. The lack of propriety suits
you. And it makes me laugh."

"Yuck it up. Poop will hit the prop soon enough, and no
one will be laughing. At least that's been my experience."

"What is this poop prop?"

I laughed and walked off. *I kinda suck at royalty.* No
kidding.

It was nearly dawn when Lincoln Shaddock arrived with
three vehicles. His people escorted blood-slaves into two
cars and let them snuggle down with vamps. They would
share blood, and that would calm the humans' anxieties, at
least for a while. As the sun began to gray the sky, Shaddock took up a position near the front of his own vamp-
mobile. They all had super dark tinted windows and heavy
armor, toys he needed for the MOC position. He drew two
swords and pulled on his power as master of the city. I felt
the energies shiver through the ground, a cold wave of danger. "Thema! Kojo!" he shouted. "Attend me!" The power
rolled out. A *summons.*

The two vamps raced in, popping into place directly in
front of him. They both looked shocked to be *summoned*
and *compelled*, and instantly they drew dueling swords.
The two were facing Shaddock, swords up, in a stance that
meant impending combat.

Shaddock vamped out. Fully. Black pupils in scarlet
sclera, fangs too long for his actual vamp-age. He was seriously ticked off, his power a frozen sizzle on my exposed
skin, like nothing I had felt from him before. Thema and
Kojo vamped out too. Fast, that immediate instinct-
vamping that meant their human selves were lost beneath
bloodlust and violence. Both of them were wearing silver
earrings, a show of power that they hadn't paraded since
they first came to Asheville.

"Crap," I said. I wasn't a vamp but I could *move.* I pulled
on Beast's speed and my own skinwalker gifts, and skidded

to a stop between the three, my weapons sheathed, arms out to the sides, feet and head moving to keep them all in sight. They spread out around me. No matter how I maneuvered, I had two vamps mostly behind me. Adrenaline shot through me. They began to circle me. *Crap. What was going on here?* "Easy. Easy there, boys and girls."

The smell of vamp was astringent and floral and heated. They stared at one another. No one looked at me. Which was strange enough to prick my predator warning system. Something was about to happen between the three vamps.

"Get in the cars. Care for the cattle," Shaddock said to the two vamps. *Cattle.* I hated that term for humans.

"We will not," Thema said.

Softly, speaking slowly, I said, "I don't know what this is, but no blood challenges. Not here, not now. And Linc, especially no duels with your guests." Or whatever they were. They hadn't sworn to Shaddock, and I didn't know why. And I hadn't cared. Until now.

The master of the city slowly took his predator gaze off his guests and put it on me.

Koun popped in from the dark. Barreled into the two vamps behind me, sending them flying. He stood at my back, swords drawn. Thema and Kojo dashed back to us, their swords out at Koun. "Do not make me kill you all," Koun said calmly, as if the possibility of him dying wasn't on the challenge table. Idiot man would get himself killed fighting against multiple powerful vamps.

My powers were different from a master of the city; I couldn't *summon* people like Linc could. But I had the power of my office—not that I knew how to use it yet. But I knew how to use the power of the skinwalker. Power was power. Right? Maybe? Sorta?

I took a slow breath and thought about *le breloque*, its magic, its purpose, its meaning, and I wrapped myself in the mantle of the Dark Queen. My head went up, my nostrils flared. The paranormal power that came from the Dark Queen's position threaded through me, strengthening my bones, rooting me to the earth. I reached out with that magic. "Put down your weapons," I said, my voice cold and demanding. *"Now."*

They lowered their swords. I was so surprised that I didn't know what to do next. And it hit me. They had obeyed *me. Holy crap.*

Shaddock ignored Koun, speaking to me in his old-fashioned country accent. "I took in the broken humans just like My Queen demanded, just like all the others left in my broken city when her enemies came here searching for her, destroying everything I had built, and killing so many of my scions. Every human will be attended to and cared for and healed as best my people are able. These two? They drink from my cattle and give back nothing."

"We fight your battles," Kojo spat. "Our swords have been yours."

"I got plenty of warriors. What I need are Infermieri."

I had never heard the word before, but it sounded like a title.

Shaddock turned his eyes to me, trying to roll me with his mesmerism. Like the vamped out state, it was a challenge. I wanted to stick my tongue out at him, but unlike Leo, Shaddock wouldn't find me amusing. "You can't roll me, Linc," I said, my power brushing across him. "Don't even try."

He blinked slowly, as if he hadn't known he was trying something wrong and now had to get himself back under control. His pupils constricted slowly, and his sclera pinkened to a watery blood shade. But his fangs stayed down on their little hinges.

"What's an Infermieri?" I asked.

"Infermieri heal the broken cattle and heal Mithrans in danger of true death. These two are old and their blood would be potent. When they came to kill the Flayer of Mithrans, I accepted their swords at my side to defeat him. But that danger's long gone, My Queen. They drink from my cattle but don't feed or heal them. They leave 'em half drained and blood drunk. And beyond the use of their swords in war, they ain't bothered to swear to me."

"Bad guests who outlasted their welcome?"

"Something like that, Queenie."

"Okay. But this sounds like a long-term problem. What happened that made all-a y'all get so bent outta shape tonight?"

"I am not *bent*," Thema said.

"Their blood is powerful as all get out, while my best healer scions are worn slap out. You created a problem, and I don't have enough healthy healers to deal with it. They know how stretched my people are, yet they refused help to heal the new broken cattle from tonight's battles."

It was common knowledge that the two didn't want a blood-family, but I hadn't known they were abusing the humans they drank from by not sharing blood in return. "You two got a reason for this?" I asked. "Or are you both just buttholes?"

The two glanced at each other, probably saying dozens of things in that one glimpse. Kojo said, "Our blood is old. It can be dangerous to those unaccustomed to it. It is not wise to share it."

I'd had blood from vamps two thousand years old. They weren't telling the full story here. "So that's why you hang around Shaddock's place and my place. So you can move back and forth, hoping no one notices that you drink but don't share your blood. That's—" I almost said *mean*, something left over from a childhood spent in a Christian children's home. I changed it to "unacceptable."

"Their belongings will be removed from my clan home," Shaddock said, "and delivered to the Winter Court of the Dark Queen."

"Fine," I said. "I'll have my people look for an un-aligned Infermieri, which I'll be happy to share with you and your scions."

"I once had such a Mithran. If she will come home that will help greatly."

I tapped my mic. "Alex, you got that?"

"On it now."

Shaddock inclined his head, telling me he had heard. He took two steps away and sheathed his swords, jumped into his vamp-mobile, and it pulled away fast.

"It is nearly dawn," Koun said. "The Consort is on the way to pick us up. You two will curl up in the trunk." Koun looked at me. "The Consort will drive. I will be your pro-tection, with you in the back seat. There will be no argu-ment, My Queen."

"Okey dokey."

Koun's head tilted to one side. "You are never going to act like a monarch, are you?"

"Nope." A black SUV pulled up, Bruiser driving. There wasn't a trunk. Too bad. I really wanted to see the two malcontent love birds curled up in one. Instead they crawled to the floor behind the back seat and pulled a heavy-duty tarp over themselves, just in case of an accident that resulted in a stray sunbeam. Koun and I got in the back seats.

Moments later, we were still forty minutes from the inn, and the sun rose behind the morning's clouds. Koun and the travelers were old enough to stay awake if they had to, but the two in back fell asleep, a sign of trust maybe. I pulled a reflective tarp over Koun, who grumbled that he was awake, and he was, sorta. I patted his arm soothingly. Satisfied that I wasn't going to damage the expectations of my scions and guests, I removed my weapons and headgear, crawled into the front seat, and snuggled with my honeybunny. He slipped an arm around me and nuzzled my head near my furry ears, all the while not taking his eyes off the road. Now *that* was a queen's life. Not that it would last.

At the inn, we backed into the winery fermentation room—which had several huge steel fermentation tanks, two filled with table wines—a white and a red from this year's very first grape harvest. There was a small windowless room just inside the door, nominally a lab to test when the grapes had high enough sugar content to pick. Bruiser also used it to taste and test the wines at various points in the fermentation process and to combine various types of grapes for different sugar content and tastes. Bruiser's winey stuff. And to dump vamps when sunlight made it necessary.

He waved away the new manager, Josue Gagne, a French winemaker he had hired to run things while we were in New Orleans. He backed the SUV into the narrow room, easing in beside the long workbench. Together we dumped half-snoozing vamps onto the concrete floor, leaving Kojo and Thema in a tangle of arms and legs as they twisted themselves into more comfortable positions, and Koun slumped against a wall. We disarmed them, just in case they woke up testy and wanted to fight some more.

"Thank you," Koun murmured as he curled to his side.

"We need an underground garage," I said, not for the first time, "so we don't have to keep dumping our friends here."

"Yes, My Queen," Bruiser said, again, not for the first time, sounding serene.

"Will you do me a big?" I asked as we got back in the SUV. "Don't challenge Giovanni to a duel today, okay? Get some rest? Eat a meal or two? Drink some vamp blood?"

Bruiser pulled me into a one-armed hug and kissed my fuzzy ear, his fuzzy chin scraping me. "I have already been fed by Linc." He kissed my other ear. "You can ask me anything, my love."

I could think of a lot of *anythings* I might want, but not while I was furry. That would be just—ick. So I hugged him back, liking that even in this form, he was still just a little bit taller and a lot broader than me.

Bruiser maneuvered the SUV out, closed and locked the door to the windowless room, parked the SUV, and we walked toward the inn. Thirty feet out, the skies opened, and a cold fall rain shower inundated us. At least the rain washed the vamp blood from my armor, which had begun to stink.

CHAPTER 3

This Idiot Man Has Your Back

I woke alone again, in Jane form this time, and checked the clock. I had slept three hours.

I climbed out of bed, did all the girly things I had to do after I shifted shape, and pulled on comfy sweats. The bedroom hadn't changed a whole lot except for the rugs. The floors were now covered with tribal rugs, primarily ultra-antique Tabriz and Hamadan rugs in all the shades of the color spectrum. Bruiser had a collection he had stored for decades with a family of rug collectors and brokers, and he had begun bringing his possessions out of storage to actually use, live with, and enjoy together with me and our extended family. I figured that was a good sign, that it meant he was getting over losing Leo, losing his job, losing his place in a changing society and culture. His whole world had been turned upside down when he left Leo and came to me. And then Leo, who had been his entire life for decades, ended up dead.

I liked the rugs. They made me want to walk around in my bare feet no matter the season, sliding my soles over the different nap depths and designs, some of which had a feel of magic to them, though why that might be so, I had no idea. The wool rugs were especially nice on rainy, chilly days like today.

Barefoot, I padded out of the bedroom wing, down the stairs to the kitchen, which smelled wonderful. Inside the ovens, I saw three big loaves of bread cooking in one and several quiches in another. In the quiche oven, I counted shrimp, mushroom and spinach, four cheese, and a meat lovers that had bacon crisscrossed on the top of the eggy mixture. The kitchen—the entire lower floor, actually—smelled heavenly.

I rinsed out one of Bruiser's whistling kettles, poured in water to heat, and rinsed out a teapot to prepare tea, opening a tin of lavender black that was a little too floral for me but that some of the vamps particularly liked. As the water heated, I studied the kitchen, which was strangely empty of people for the time of day.

Bruiser had received more deliveries, and his stuff was piled on the island: an antique French coffee maker, two old carafes, a twelve-piece set of Spanish-looking fancy gold utensils, a new stack of china that matched the original blaze orange Le Creuset cookware, and some in a post–World War II color called Élysées Yellow that had come early on. Bruiser was nesting, building a home of his own for the first time in his life. With me.

The water was taking its time, so I wandered the inn, snacking on beef jerky and PowerBars, seeing more rugs, tables, shelves, couches, and chairs in the various seating areas offered by the sizeable inn that had become our mountain home and my official winter court. Bruiser had put original art on the walls and art objects on the shelves, some bronze statues of naked women and bucking bulls and little children squatting, looking at flowers. I stopped and wrapped my arms around me, my toes buried in colorful wool, and turned in a circle, studying the house from the central area. All this stuff . . . Stuff Bruiser loved. Modern stuff he had wanted and never bought until now, or stuff he had bought long ago and never used, because he had lived in Leo's house. I didn't give a lick about stuff, except a comfortable bed, squishy sofas, and a nice shower. Bruiser liked stuff. But he had been Leo's and never his own.

Now he was his own man for the first time in his long life. He was making this place *home*. This once-an-inn, tucked away in the mountains of Beast's hunting territory, was *his* home, giving Bruiser space to put out all the stuff he had collected and never used. Tears gathered, hot in my eyes. His very first home. I breathed deeply and pushed the tears away. This was good stuff, not girly cry stuff.

Maybe someday Bruiser would bring his collection of motorcycles here, though I was pretty sure they would be harder to transport from New Orleans than the smaller items.

I stepped into Alex's office, which was empty of people, programs running in the background but the screens black. I was curious, but I'd never touch his stuff. I valued my paws. And my fingers. In the corner was a large memory foam mattress where Brute and two of Tex's dogs, Martha and Jangles, were sleeping, Brute snoring mightily. The flying lizard was nowhere to be seen. I'd once found it sleeping in a teapot, and after that, we had all been careful to check inside the pots before pouring in boiling water.

The kettle whistled, calling me and waking the dogs. Tex's two raced past me and outside. Brute's claws clicked across the floor, and he nudged my leg. Looked at me with those crystal blue eyes for long enough that he might have been trying to tell me something. Then he turned and went out the cat-dog door into the rain. He'd be soaked when he came back in. No way was I bathing and drying that big hairy werewolf.

Making sure it was still empty, I poured steaming water over the leaves in the strainer into the teapot. While the tea was steeping, I found mugs and set up a proper tea tray. I'd been watching Bruiser's ritual, and though I couldn't tell the difference in tea made by my usual methods and Bruiser's fancy-schmancy one, he always seemed quietly pleased when I noticed what he liked and how he did things. And he swore he could tell the difference in taste. So few people ever did a kindness for the Consort, the former primo, without wanting something in return, without it being a way to get to Leo (and now to me), to receive a favor, or to obtain power. This small thing with tea made him happy.

*   *   *

I got a fire going in the big central area fireplace. I can make a fire from dry wood and matches if needed, but natural gas and a remote made it so much easier. Sitting on a big comfy sofa in front of the gas fire, I tucked my bare feet under a cushion, enjoying my solitude, sipping my tea from a big mug. The cup was bloodred on the bottom half and white on the top half. There was a drawing of a vamp on the top half, his head half off and his blood appearing to spurt into the bottom half of the mug, as if still filling it up. The vamp had a bubble over his head with the words "You vant to drink my blood."

I had no idea who brought in the mug, but I had claimed it. Between sips, I replaited my hair into a sloppy braid. Tied it off with a string I pulled out of my sweatshirt hem.

Alex and Eli came in the back, stripped out of rain gear, and made matching cups of espresso. Eli tested the quiches and left them cooking. The rain softened to a slow patter.

Both men joined me on the big couch. Saying nothing. Not a word. It was comfortable and pleasant and calm, the way things used to be when we lived together in the freebie house in New Orleans. A shaft of longing stabbed through me. I wished things could always be like this.

But they stayed silent a little too long, sipping their extra-strong brews, and that was weird. It hit me that they might be ticked off at me. I glanced back and forth between them. Yeah. Matching expressions, somehow neutral and disappointed at the same time. I had done something bad. *Go me.*

I sipped the cooling lavender tea, thinking through my night and morning, figuring out why they were unhappy with me and then trying to decide how I wanted to address the issues. When my cup was empty I said, "You two planned a reconnaissance mission that turned into a rescue, an attack by our enemies, and a defense against incursion."

Eli tilted his head the barest hint to show he was listening.

I said, "I showed up. The vamps hiding in the woods then attacked. That initial reconnaissance mission went south. You think that it's possible that if I hadn't shown up, the vamps in the trees would have left and attacked another time. But I think that's a fallacy. Linc says they planned to take whatever they could get, meaning that they would have killed or captured the MOC, my Consort, and my brother of choice, knowing that would be enough to draw me out. To make me go after them. Without you to back me up."

Eli frowned ever so slightly and nodded again, that bare hint of movement.

"Our enemies think. They plan ahead. Multilayers of plans. Plans that take decades to come to a finale. They have a plan A, plan B, plan C, D, and E. They incorporate one plan into other plans. They refine and restructure. And I'm the wild card. Leo knew that. He put me in place to be the wild card that would keep them unbalanced and uncertain."

"You can't be a wild card if you're dead, babe," Eli said softly. "And here's the thing. We know some layers you don't. One in particular."

"Holy *crap*." A bunch of crazy stuff came together like magnets attracting and pulling in filaments. It was so clear I could almost hear clicking in my brain as they snapped into place. "*Leo* talked to you before he died. *He told you stuff*," I accused.

"Pretty much," Alex said, shooting me a side-eye grin. "He called us into his office at HQ once, while you were off—ah, um, *canoodling* with Bruiser."

That could have been anytime in the last few years. Bruiser and I canoodled pretty often, and the boys were often at NOLA HQ together while the aforesaid canoodling took place. Easy peasy for Leo to get them together. "Could you narrow it down some?" I demanded.

Eli chortled, a soft burbling sound. It didn't last long, but it made me feel good. He gave the side-eye too. "Early on, after you first achieved half-form, Leo told us we had one job: to keep you alive. He said the SOD hanging in sub-five basement had been bitten by a dangerous creature, and that bite gave Joses the ability to see bits and pieces of the future. This was before we knew much about the arcenciels."

I went cold as stone. An arcenciel—a shape-shifting creature of pure energy from another realm—had bitten the eldest Son of Darkness (aka Joses Santana and a few more akas) and made him insane. Other arcenciels had visited him in subbasement five, where he had hung on a wall for decades, starved and sucked on. I had no idea why they had shown up there.

Leo had drunk Joses's poisoned, tainted blood for decades. Leo had been partially nutso too for all those decades, but he kept drinking that blood. Why?

Because with it, he could see parts of the future.

I had been fed healing blood from vamps who might also have drunk blood from the poisoned vamp.

I had been bitten by an arcenciel on two different occasions.

We had postulated that timewalking was latent in my skinwalker genes.

Or maybe the venom had changed my magic, making me able to see future possibilities and giving me cancer all at the same time.

"Holy crap in a bucket," I breathed.

Had Leo seen me in his futures? He hadn't recognized me when we first met; I was sure of that. But maybe later, after the half-form manifested. Maybe he only saw my half-form in his futures. Maybe only after Bruiser left him. Had Leo seen that I had a chance to . . . what? Rule the vamps? Kill all the vamps? Keep the arcenciels from plans of their own? What? And what if I did the wrong thing? Would all humans cease to exist? Would the vamps cease to exist? What would that do to history?

"We never told you," Alex said. "But we *have* to keep you alive."

"Huh?" I asked, dragging my thoughts back to this conversation.

"But we can't do that if you don't trust us," Eli said.

"We need to be able to talk to you. Tell you what we're thinking and discuss the potential problems, refine plans like you and Leo used to do," Alex said.

"And then you stay out of the way and let us do our jobs," Eli said.

"Keeping you alive," Alex finished.

I nodded and tucked my mug between my thighs. "Fine. You want me to stay out of the way, right? You want to tell me what you know and let me help with the planning. Then my stupid crown and I will stay safe and sound in my little queenly castle and let my friends and brothers and family go out and die in my place. Right? Like last night? That about it?" I smacked the back of Eli's skull. Then Alex's skull. Both men looked at me with astonishment and some bewilderment. "How 'bout I knock some sense into your heads? I suck at twiddling my thumbs. We do this all together, or we don't do it at all."

Getting up, I clinked my mug into the kitchen sink hard enough to crack it, stuffed my bare feet into my mudders, and yanked on a thin green slicker. I walked toward the door and yelled, "I'm hungry, and the quiches smell like heaven. So not fair!"

I may have stomped, and stomped some more as I headed into the rain. It was possible. I'd miss that mug.

I strode away from the house, letting the cold rain patter onto me, trickle down my collar, letting the slow fall of water cool me off. "Idiots," I said.

I heard a doggy chuff and spotted Brute watching me from the overhang of one of the cottages, still and silent. "Men are stupid," I said.

Brute sat up tall and raised his eyebrows as if considering my statement. He lifted a paw, touching his head. Then he looked at the cottage near him. There were footprints in the soft, rain-wet ground leading to it. They had been there long enough to be full of water. They didn't belong to Eli or Alex. Worry whispered through me.

Bruiser?

Stepping slowly, as silently as I could in the mucky grass, I approached the cottage window. I heard his voice and a woman's voice. I didn't like her cajoling, suggestive tones.

I backed away, raced back inside, toed off the mudders, and sprinted up the stairs to the closet where I kept my own toys. I slid out a plastic container and rummaged around for the Glob, but it wasn't there. I found it in the pocket of the armor I had worn to the vamp battle and raced back down. Downstairs, I slapped my crown on, felt it adhere to my head, too tight, as always, and patted my pocket where the Glob rested.

Eli was standing at the back door, a nine-mil in one hand, a machete-looking blade in his other, a water resistant pouch cinched at his waist. "What?" he said.

"Don't know. Brute's out in the rain, staring at the second cottage." I pulled on the mudders.

"That's where we put Monique Giovanni after Shaddock finished healing her gunshot wounds and relieved her pain from the broken wrist," Eli said.

From the office, Alex called out, "I have footage of Bruiser entering the cottage. Forty-two minutes ago."

"Too long," I muttered. "Looks like I may have to slap the back of my Consort's head too. I'm surrounded by idiot men."

"This idiot man has your back."

I looked at Eli, his dark eyes calm and steady. "We okay?" I asked.

"Babe . . ." His tone called me stupid. And loved. And family.

I laughed once, but it was a sad tone, not real laughter. "I shot Monique. And broke her wrist. She heals up nicely with vamp blood, but if she's messing with his brain, I'll end her."

"Roger that."

Together we stepped from the back door. I spotted Brute, who was standing, four-pawed, beneath the window of the cottage. I bent slightly forward and crab-raced to the cottage, Eli behind. He sped to my left and disappeared around the cottage, making sure this wasn't an ambush.

I leaned close to the building but couldn't hear a thing. Eli joined me from the right and mouthed, *Clear*.

"Wish I had cat ears," I whispered. I glanced at him and grinned. "Never thought I'd say that."

From his dry bag, Eli pulled out a tiny black rubber suction cup and pressed it to the lower corner of the window. We waited a moment to make sure no one inside had seen the tiny cup appear, but there was no reaction from within, the voices talking on without change. Eli snapped in a small plug and unwound three black wires, two earpieces, and one micro video port, which he plugged into his cell. He handed me an earpiece and took one for himself.

Just that fast, we had ears and eyes inside. I loved tech. "Mr. Prepared."

"Always."

I worked the earbud in and could hear just fine, Bruiser's voice and Giovanni's, hers all seductive. I wasn't jealous of her tone, so like a vamp in mesmerism. She had no idea what Leo had put my sweet-cheeks through. No way she could roll the former primo, especially not with the silver cuffs on her wrists and head. I took in what I could see of the room. It was the back bedroom of a two-bedroom cottage, decorated in leaf green with charcoal gray walls and white trim. Giovanni, wearing dark purple pants and a sweater, was sitting in a captain's chair in front of a gas fireplace, which was not lit.

"I am not the Firestarter who attacked the Winter Court of the Dark Queen," she said. "Look at my hands. At my face. You saw that one. The Firestarter . . ." Her voice trailed off and she bowed her head. The woman was facing away from the window; Bruiser was sitting in a second chair, facing slightly away from her, at an angle from me.

I had to wonder why they were talking about Aurelia Flamma Scintilla, the Firestarter sorta-Onorio who started out a witch-in-the-closet nun and made burning vamps to death her reason to live. Who picked her as a topic? And why? Aurelia was dark haired, dark eyed, and was neither vampire nor blood-servant, but a rarer creature, similar to Bruiser and the B-twins, but a dark type of Onorio called a *senza onore*. We saw an illusion of the former nun last March as we fought a losing battle.

"I am not Aurelia," Monique whispered, so softly I nearly missed it. "I did not burn the mausoleum in New Orleans."

And then I understood. They were talking about Leo's death. It all came back to Leo. To his death. His burial. The burning of his mausoleum. I had assumed that all those blasted layered political threads he had woven together over the years had come apart when he died. But clearly there were threads I didn't know about. It seemed Leo had woven me and my entire family into his final tapestry.

"The Firestarter," she said, "is in New Orleans once again. It is said that Aurelia burned the outclan priestess to a crisp, that the priestess was true dead. But the Firestarter doesn't believe this. She is hunting for Sabina."

That figured. Aurelia tried to burn Sabina to true death, hoping to find and steal the relics guarded by the outclan priestess. Monique shook her head as if she was sad, her dark blond hair moving on her shoulders. She raised her bound wrists close to her face, as if scratching her nose. Eli said that Linc had healed her, but clearly only partially. Someone had splinted and wrapped the broken wrist and let her clean herself up. I wouldn't have bothered. But then I'm not a nice person. Niceness was saved for friends, and we didn't really know what Monique wanted or the extent of her power.

She was right about the Firestarter and Sabina, useless as the reports were. Gossip in vamp circles touted both versions, a dead Sabina, and sightings of the blackened husk of a woman, hunting humans, leaving them happy and alive but much lighter on blood. It was possible for badly burned, very old vamps to survive, and if she did, Sabina had the last piece of the Blood Cross in the United States. And probably other stuff too. Possibly even the last ingots of the iron Spike of Golgotha. Along with the wood of the crosses, the nine spikes of the crucifixion had been found all in a pile, collected, and re-shaped into a single spike, a dark magic amulet called the Spike of Golgotha. Then ingots had been cut off of it: they were used in time-magic, dark magic, and the creation of amulets of power.

Mate is in danger, Beast said.

Yeah? I thought to my furry half. *I don't see it.*

Beast sees. She showed me her vision, as thin smokelike tendrils of purple and green magic swirled lazily in the air over Bruiser's head. Magic, even though the *senza onore* was wearing null cuffs. That shouldn't be possible.

But Bruiser wasn't blind to her antics. Woven through the strands of her magic was Bruiser's own power: red, blue, green, and a soft golden yellow knotting off the purple and green strands. This convo was a verbal and magical duel of sorts, as if Bruiser was using the cuffs to figure out how strong Monique was. He was fighting back, but with defensive magic only. I had asked Bruiser not to challenge Monique today, so . . . right. He was defending only, not attacking, because I had asked him not to. I scowled.

And then I saw the silver null cuff on Monique's head slide through her hair and dangle in the fingers of her broken wrist as she lowered them to her lap. She had gotten the head cuff off. Bruiser stared at it in her hands, even as the one on her wrists clicked and fell to her lap.

My Consort smiled. He had known it was coming free. He had let it happen. And he was wearing gloves. I hadn't even noticed. They were nearly the color of his skin, and in Beast's sight, they glowed with power, different from the cold energies of the null cuffs. *Hedge of thorns* energies.

I tightened, not sure if I should intervene. Eli shot a look at me. I shook my head, mouthing, *Not yet.* Bruiser had known what she would do, what she was doing. He needed this mental combat. Needed to overcome this woman and her power. He needed to *win*.

Seduction and wile in her tone, Monique said, "Sabina, if she lives, knows where another relic is. I will leave Jane alone if you help me find it. There is rebellion brewing, Onorio and *senza onore*, and also against some of the ancient Mithran overlords. You could stand beside me. Work with me. We could lead this together."

Bruiser's magic lashed at Monique's, stabbing and twisting, pulling the strands apart. He murmured, "Ancient Mithran overlords?" He chuckled. "I am loyal to the Dark Queen. I am not interested in joining an Onorio rebellion. Your service to the Flayer of Mithrans—an ancient overlord himself—changed you in some fundamental way, Monique. Your magic feels unclean, tastes vile against mine, lacking in life and joy. No human exposed to that noxious combination of ancient evil and irrationality could stay sane."

Monique said, "I am more than I once was. As you could be too."

"Again, not interested."

"And what of Leo Pellissier?"

"My master is dead."

"Death does not end love. You still love Leo. What would you give me to get him back alive? What would you give if his master could give him back to you?"

"Holy crap," I murmured.

Bruiser said nothing, a pause that lasted heartbeats too long. "Nothing. I would give nothing to revive the dead. And his master is dead at the hands of my own Lady Mother."

My Lady Mother was what Bruiser called his titled mother, who died killing the vampires who were using her body and taking her blood. I knew the story. She killed Amaury Pellissier and numerous other vamps by drinking silver-laced alcohol before they attacked her.

Monique breathed and raised her hands, putting them on Bruiser's face, cupping his cheeks and stroking his lips with her thumbs. The fingers of the broken wrist were still bruised and swollen, but she seemed not to notice. "Not his maker. His *master*."

"Who—" Bruiser jerked back, breaking the touch. He was holding the null cuffs. She hadn't noticed he had taken them off her lap. The *hedge of thorns*–imprinted gloves glowed in my vision.

Monique's purple strands attacked. Bruiser stood, his hands laced together in a single fist holding the cuffs. Using their magic. His arms thrust up. Knocked Monique's to the side. Stepped back. Kicked her in the chest. Pivoted into a rooted stance. All in one smooth motion, a basic martial arts move, breaking a hold, kicking, twisting away.

Her chair tilted back on two legs. Her hands threw magic like dark purple lances. The chair tipped farther. Her attack magic was absorbed by the gloves and the null cuffs except for a single strand that hit Bruiser in the chest. He threw his entire body at her and rolled her out of the chair. Across the floor. Latching the null cuffs around her neck so tight they cut her flesh.

Her blood landed on the metal, and her magical attack slowed to a trickle, choked off. Her mouth opened in gasping silent rage.

Bruiser inhaled, catching his breath. Latched the wrist cuffs back on her, accidently bending her broken wrist through the splint and tape as she sucked in a pained breath. He almost apologized for her pain, but stopped himself, his mouth tight.

Monique was still reeling as he righted her chair, picked her up, and sat her in it. He stretched behind her to the mantle and grabbed a roll of duct tape I hadn't noticed. Moving primo-fast, he stripped off a length and wrapped it around her wrists on top of the cuffs and then around one chair arm. He secured her ankles together and then to a chair leg. It was a well-made solid oak captain's chair, and though it was possible to break the chair apart and get away, it couldn't be done silently.

Bruiser stepped away from her. Touched his chest the way people did on TV when they've been shot, and looked at his fingers. There was no blood from the place where Monique's magic had hit him. He turned and left the room. A moment later, Eli and I heard the outer door close and the lock turn. Bruiser's footsteps moved toward the barn-like fermentation room, sounding somehow dejected.

Even wounded, Monique had bested him again, using guile and mesmerism, and my Consort had been forced to resort to physical means to defeat her. When he was gone, Monique started crying silently. Besides reinjuring her broken wrist, it was clear that Bruiser had hurt her magically too. Good for my sweet-cheeks.

"What did she mean, 'Not his maker. His master'?" Eli whispered.

"I got no idea. Follow him?" I asked. "Make sure he's okay. She hit him with a spear of purple magic. Right in his chest."

"And what are you gonna do, Janie?"

"There's blood at her neck. I can use that blood."

"Don't get yourself killed."

"Copy that," I said, as Eli gathered up his equipment and followed Bruiser.

He glanced back. "Don't forget your appointment. Noon in the sweathouse."

"Yuck," I said. He gave me that not-really-there smile and loped after my honeybunch.

I was alone except for the white werewolf. "Hey," I said to Brute. "You're standing in the rain."

He chuffed at me.

"Wanna go inside and roll all over a mean woman who tried to hurt my boyfriend?"

Brute's mouth opened and his tongue lolled out. He panted into my face and wagged his tail. His breath was a dreadful combo of salmon from his last meal and mint from the chewy he gnawed to keep his teeth clean.

I faked a gag. "Yuck. And I'm taking that as a yes."

I made my way around the cottage and inside, opened the door to the bedroom, and let the werewolf in. I closed the door after him without Monique seeing me. I pulled off *le breloque*. It wasn't always agreeable to being removed, but it didn't clamp down this time. I set it aside, puttering around the kitchen, which was kitted out with all the necessities a visiting vamp might need. I started a pot of coffee and turned on the kettle. Placed a few Irish Breakfast silk tea bags in the pot. Banged around a bit. Found some commercial bakery lemon cookies in an unopened brown paper sack. They were still fresh enough, and I poured some into a small bowl. I set up a tray, sorta the way Bruiser might, coffee carafe on one side with a mug, teapot on the other with a mug. I added stirring spoons, creamer, sugar, and some stevia stuff. The mugs were all white and bland, with no catchy sayings on the bottom. I needed a mug about Onorios. Something pithy. I tore off and folded paper towels instead of napkins. Classy.

As I worked, I heard squeals and shouts and various phrases repeated: "Get away from me, you stupid dog! Stop! Horrors! Someone get this dog off of me! Ahhh!"

I placed *le breloque* to the side of my teapot, opened the door to the bedroom, and snapped my fingers. Brute bounded out, happy as a puppy. I let him outside and closed the door. Lifting a small serving table, I carried it into the bedroom, placed it near Monique's chair, then brought in the serving tray. It looked nice.

When I had it all set up, I pulled a chair over and sat, crossed one ankle over the other knee like a guy, and leaned forward, cupping my chin in my palm and that elbow on the bent knee. I stared at Monique Giovanni for a while, taking her in and not hiding it. She had dark honey-colored hair with professionally dyed blond and brown streaks. Bluish eyes. Good bone structure. Small weak chin. Right now it was covered with dog spit, and her clothes were wet and well crusted with dog hair. Other than the spit and dried blood on her clothes from when I shot her, she was attractive in the way humans got when they drink a lot of vamp blood over the years—excellent skin, all glowy. Onorios don't have to drink much blood to keep the effects up, and unlike regular humans, they didn't become blood-bound.

I checked to be sure there was no werewolf spit on her abrasions, and mentally congratulated Brute for saliva placement. She wouldn't get were-taint and he wouldn't get sliced and diced to death by a grindylow for turning her. *Good werewolf,* I thought. And then I wondered if Onorios could actually get were-taint. Vamps couldn't. An interesting thought for another time.

I rummaged around in my brain for what little I knew about them. They couldn't be bound. They could drain a vamp's power unto true death. They could take over control of a vamp from a stronger master, creating a scion who was little better than a slave. They could drain vamps of magical power, leaving them defenseless. They had improved healing and much longer lifespans than humans, though less long than vamps. On the negative side, in a battle with another Onorio, they could be drained of their own magical power, which could lead to death. There was probably more, but that was all I really needed.

"You know who I am?" I asked.

"You're Jane Yellowrock. The bounty hunter."

She meant it as an insult to the Dark Queen, and I wanted to laugh. You have to know someone well for an insult to take, and bounty-hunting rogue vamps was a way better job than this queen crap. I kept my reaction off my face and went for crude. "You need to pee?" I asked.

Monique's eyes went wide. Clearly, my unladylike question was vulgar.

"You been here a while, all tied up, so I wondered."

She studied me back now, blue eyes not giving much away. "I do need to use the facilities."

"Hope you don't have a shy bladder. I can't let you have privacy." I removed the duct tape from the chair and her ankles but left it attached to her wrists, holding the null cuffs in place, her hands together in front of her to give her some use of them. Hauling her to her feet, I gave her a little push toward the bathroom, looking her over. There were no zippers in her clothing. It would be difficult for her to get it all back in place, but she'd manage.

I followed her in and watched her do her business, clumsy but workable, her wrist clearly in a lot of pain again. Her clothes were half tucked, rucked up on one side when she was done, but she was covered. She washed her fingers and face at the sink, patted herself dry with a guest towel, and tried to smooth down her hair, which clearly the wolf had licked. A lot. She shuddered as she worked, and I had a feeling she didn't like doggie kisses. Good to know.

I followed her as she retook her place in the captain's chair and knelt in front of her with the roll of tape. "You try to hit me, roll me, or make a run for it, and I'll make sure you don't live to regret it. Capisce?"

She gave a stiff nod, and I strapped her feet to the chair legs. I left her arms free, though still attached together at the wrists.

"Coffee or tea?" I asked, taking my seat.

"I'd rather have a ginger ale."

"Going dry then." I moved the coffee tray away and strapped her bound arms to a chair arm.

"On second thought, I'd like tea."

"Too late. You had your chance. I don't negotiate. I just bust skulls, break arms, and collect vamp heads." That was Jane Yellowrock's rep, so I'd use it. I poured myself a cuppa with a splash of creamer and one sugar. Stirred my tea, making little tinks. Sipped it. Settled back in my chair with the mug in one hand. "Just out of curiosity, can you feel magic? Yours, mine, Bruiser's, a vamp's?"

She seemed uncertain where this was going, but she finally said, "Yes."

"With the cuffs on?"

"It's more distant, like listening with earmuffs on, but yes."

I lifted the crown of my reign. "Can you feel anything from this? Don't grab. It might kill you. Just extend a finger."

She uncurled an index finger, and I let the crown touch her fingertip. She shook her head. "No. Why?" She was staring at my nice mug of tea.

I set *le breloque* aside and raised the mug to my lips; her eyes followed it. I made uncouth slurping sounds, watching her face. She wasn't disturbed by my lack of manners, unlike the ancient vamps, but she was thirsty. "How about now?" I slapped the crown onto my head, and it adjusted to fit, snugging down tight. I felt tingles all down my body, like green ice that warmed and was gone. It was a new effect, and I wanted to see if she—

Monique's face did this weird thing. It seemed to shout, *Rattlesnake!* Or *Quicksand!* Or *Acid!* Her eyes landed on mine, and she clamped her mouth shut. She saw me as dangerous. She saw the crown as dangerous. *Coolio.* I could use her fear.

"Ah. Good. Then you'll understand why I'm doing this." Not that I understood why I was doing it. Since there was no one to teach me how to use the crown, flying by the seat of my pants was my only option. But vamps and blood went together like hands and gloves, and *le breloque* was at least partially vamp crown, so . . .

I set down my mug, leaned over her, and tore the duct tape off her neck where Bruiser had taped the cuff in place over her scratch. It had scabbed over beneath the tape, but it opened up fresh with the adhesive pull. I swiped my fingers through her blood, shoved the tape back in place, and sat back. I didn't pull out the Glob. No point in giving away all my secrets, and it wasn't working exactly the way it used to anyway, so it had to be kept in reserve.

Meticulously, I wiped some of the blood on a paper towel for possible later use, stuffed it into the pocket holding the Glob, and while in the pocket, wiped the blood onto the magical thingamabob. The Glob went red hot, fast, and then cooled to an icy temp that probably had frost on it. I also probably had a blister the size of my fist on my hip and several on my fingers. Note to self: find a padded bag to hold the Glob and wear oven mitts when I test stuff. Testing things taught me a lot, but some of the things I learned were painful.

Being more obvious about it, I withdrew my hand,

touched my bloody fingers to *le breloque*, leaned back in my chair, and half closed my eyes, bloody fingers pressing on the gold. The power of the Dark Queen had to be worth something, and if I lived long enough, I might learn what. The crown warmed slowly beneath my fingers, and unexpected sensations and reactions swam through me.

To the crown, the blood felt nasty, slimy, dark, a close cousin to treacherous and evil combined. But inside me, something was happening, something different from my skinwalker magics, Beast's own power, or the crown magics. This power was also mine, but it was prism-bright, the colors of the rainbow and the sound of brass gongs, like light through stained glass and cathedral bells ringing. This new magic was warm as sun on a summer beach; it smelled of night-blooming jasmine; it had texture, like thrusting my hand into a basket filled with skeins of brightly colored silk yarn. This was something I had brought back from the rift and from contact with the Angel Hayyel. It wrapped around my skinwalker magic, and if power had emotions, I'd have said that it blazed with delight at the melding. I focused all that magic, all my own power, and all that power of the Dark Queen onto the blood drying between my fingers and the crown. Through her blood, I focused that power on Monique's magic. I looked at it with Beast's eyes.

Monique had shields, layers of them, Onorio defenses, light and shadow, sound and texture, taste and scent. Protective magical armor. The kind of thing that would absorb and dissipate the energies of a *binding* working, whether it originated with witch or vamp powers.

Beyond the layers was what felt like a membrane, rubbery and slick and rough all at once. And below that was a great open space. I pushed through the membrane and slid free on the other side to hover in a long, dark room with a curved floor, like the hull of a boat.

It was dank and rank and foul. It rocked, like a boat on the sea, back and forth, side to side. In the bottom of the hull, old blood sloshed gently on the wood and partway up the rounded walls. A slow, clotted sloshing.

There was a semifamiliar feeling here, and I realized that my mind was looking down on some version of Monique's soul home, though her home was wood and rot and blood, and not the clean stone of my own. I was in the center of her being, and I almost retreated, but I steeled myself and stared down.

In the sloshing blood were the bodies of beings she had bound. They were tied and gagged, rolling back and forth, eyes closed. Four of them. At least two were vamps, and the others were definitely not vampy, but I couldn't tell what kind of paras. As I watched, a thin purple tendril of power rose from the pool of blood. Without knowing *how* I knew, I knew it was intended to harm me.

CHAPTER 4

This Ain't My First Rodeo

Without opening my eyes, I said, "Stop or die."

The rise of magic stopped. I had a feeling that without the cuffs binding Monique, I'd have seen that power rise like smoke from a green-wood fire mixed with steam from a boiling kettle and scald me dead.

I slid my hand back into my pocket and touched the Glob with a single finger. Images, sounds, visions came clearer.

I had known that Monique was not *just* Onorio. She was more. A mixture of twisted things I couldn't identify, except that her bound captives were still alive somewhere, and she was using them. It was as if her rotting slave ship was full of a dark magic of destruction that sucked the life from the bound beings trapped there. Blood magic was one way that demons worked, yet Monique wasn't a demon.

Demons had a unique feel, a distinctive stench. And they were aware and discerning of watching eyes far more than Monique was.

But she was something different.

And she was very, *very* powerful.

I wondered . . . if I could stop her magic? A spiral of curiosity curled through me. What was blood magic without blood?

Le breloque warmed again, and in the vision—or potential ultra-dimensional reality?—of Monique's soul home, I lashed out with my prism of light. Fast as a lightning strike, the blood boiled and scorched dry. In moments there was nothing left but the rotten wood of the hull and the bound bodies of her captives.

The light of my magic spread out and began to thread through the grain of the wood, braiding, knotting, whirling as my crown and my office sought to bind the binder. It wasn't actually happening, but it was clearly something I had the power to do.

The Glob offered images of various other possibilities. My weapon just wanted to drain her and set the ship on fire. It sent me visions of the captives screaming. The Glob was more than just a tool. It was half sentient. And the crown was a tool I wasn't sure how to use just yet. So I held both amulets back, reining in their power. Needing to learn more.

On the floor of the hull, one of the bodies rolled over, straining against Monique's bindings and the floor itself. Smeared in blackened, scorched blood, she stared at me. Seeing me through my own magic, inside my own vision. The woman staring at me was the Firestarter, Aurelia Flamma Scintilla.

Monique wasn't alone in her soul home, and the Firestarter could see me here. Which meant that in some way, all of the beings lying on the hull were actually *here*. And so was I.

I had killed another spiritual presence in my own soul home once, and the body, in real life, had died too. It was possible that I could die in Monique's slave ship soul home if I wasn't very careful. I flattened myself against the flat ceiling above and behind me.

Once before, I saw Aurelia up close and personal, or at least her illusion. Dark haired, dark eyed, skin like milk but with a faint, pale olive tint. She had been wearing black nun's robes, and might be now as well, though here they were stained in old dark blood. Beside the Firestarter was a bloody vampire female, her dark hair clotted with filth. She turned her face away, as did the others bound in the hull.

But the Firestarter. That one didn't turn away. She stared at me.

Monique murmured, "Join us, place your power with the Firestarter. Together we will drain and rule all the vampires in the world. With you and the primo-Onorio, we have the Rule of Three needed to govern and control."

The woman couldn't count, unless the Rule of Three meant something besides the total, which was way higher.

"Why would I volunteer to be shackled?" I asked, watching the trussed bodies.

"We are not master and slave," Monique said. "We are friends. We have willingly wrapped ourselves in chains, all working together."

The others kept their faces turned away, hiding their identities, but they pushed up to sitting positions in slow concert. The actions were either choreographed, or it was the same kind of control used by the Flayer of Mithrans. A chill started in my fingertips and raced up my body. Monique Giovanni had worked for the Flayer. He had the unusual ability to bind and control and use the bodies of the people around him. Either he had taught her how to do that, or she had figured out how his power worked and made it her own.

An Onorio who could use uber vamp mesmerism was a new thing. And that was scary enough to make me mouthy. "Yeah? I don't see you in the blood and the rot. That's convenient." I didn't try to hide the sarcasm.

Monique was Onorio and also more than Onorio. She had bound the others, and I was pretty sure she had convinced them they were there willingly. This vision had meaning, each element both a spiritual reality and a symbol of the physical world. These bound paras and Monique were sowing violence among the vamps, building discord and fear and war between masters of the cities. That violence was the rot and the blood. They were working together, willingly at first, but now bound; that was the meaning of the vision of the captives in the soul home of Giovanni. They didn't have enough willing helpers. Or perhaps willing sacrifices. They needed more. They wanted Bruiser to come to them willingly. They wanted *me*. There were other Onorios in the Dark Queen's retinue and territory, and if they got me, they probably got them—Bruiser, the B-twins, all the vamps sworn to me, the outclan priestess, just to think of a very few. Taking me would leave very few slots to fill in any combination of the Rule of Three. And there was a *senza onore* in the NOLA witch null prison, a woman named Tau. A very dangerous woman.

And . . . Thema and Kojo were creating strife in Lincoln's clan. I needed to keep a careful eye on them. *Crap.*

When I entered the vamp world, I was a wild card. I had somehow managed to rearrange everything. Monique was perhaps another wild card. She was a warrior Onorio with access to magic and mind tricks. She could take over the world.

The boat-hull vision began to fill with smoke: purple, charcoal, deepest black. I flattened myself even more and reached for my body. I had learned a lot, but it wouldn't be worth it if I got stuck here. The ceiling, however, felt solid even in my amorphous form.

Pain lanced along my forehead. I jerked, trying to get out.

"Give me the relics," Monique said.

The pain along my forehead grew, something digging into my scalp. "Give them to me," she said, spittle hitting my face. *Monique was attacking me.* My hands shot up and caught hers. I stood. Wrenched my body hard left. Shifting her over my bent knee, rotating my frame from toes to scalp. Using the bound wrists of the woman, her own weight, and the chair her feet were still taped to. Throwing her to the floor. My motion was so fast, so hard, her chair broke into chunks and sharp splinters that went flying. I landed atop her chest, a knee in her solar plexus.

Breath whooshed out of her. She grunted with pain.

I flipped her facedown, the chair slamming into the floor again. I pulled her arms up and her body back into a bow. Her bones cracked. She grunted.

I hadn't even opened my eyes. I stretched her harder,

one knee now in her spine, her head bent back over her butt. I leaned toward her ear and whispered, "Try that again, and I'll burn your slave ship."

She stiffened under me. Or she started fighting for breath.

I was suddenly back in her soul home.

Purple clouds rose from the bloody floor. Magic like a fine mist and smoke lifted toward me.

My mind filled with images of death. Me dying by exsanguination, my blood being collected in a big blue bucket.

A vision of Grégoire dancing with a sword against three opponents. Beheaded. Blond hair flying.

A vision of Tex bound in silver as someone killed Martha and Jangles. As his dogs howled and called and he raged.

Edmund trapped in a deep pit, mostly filled with water. Silver chains weighing him down. Silver needles stuck into the flesh of his neck, which was purple-black. Poisoned. Dying.

Is not real, Beast thought at me.

Monique was using these images to keep me out of her mind while trying to bind me.

I said, "This ain't my first rodeo, you little bitch." Beast's claws ripped through the images of the people I loved being tortured. Beneath them was the bloody floor and the four bound helpers. I couldn't see what they planned. I needed to know—

Monique slashed at me, her power like hot knives.

In the clouds of purple energies, I caught a glimpse of vampires. I saw Monique with *le breloque* resting loosely on her head. A vision of Bruiser being killed, stabbed with blades.

"We will kill all Onorios who refuse to align with us," one of her prisoners said.

Ah . . . I pulled back on her body and leaned away at the same time, my body weight doing the work.

From her rotting soul home, from the faces in the clouds of her magic, I heard French chatter, too fast to follow. Commanding tones.

Monique and the others were working with European

vamps, ones not bound, not present in the soul home. With magical assistance, the bound ones were watching the vamps. Monique planned to betray them. Especially one of them. Male. Old and powerful. Faces swept by in the rotten hull of her soul home as I searched the vamp faces. Which one was her ultimate target?

I saw a face I knew. Legolas. Melker. He was true dead. His former scions, the main new vamp in charge of his blood-family and clan had planned and carried out the attack at the house near Beaver Lake. Why was Legolas's face here? Had we killed the new leader, or was his replacement vamp still out there ready to do harm? As the questions swirled, I saw yet another face. It tore at my memory, the name not coming clear. Then . . .

The purple magics stabbed at me as they had stabbed at Bruiser. Part of Monique's power was *senza onore* magic and dark energy. Magic that drew on and used power that wasn't hers, power that belonged to the bound bodies on the bloody hull.

Black and purple clouds of smoke, boiling and raging, reached for me. Reached for my mind. *Le breloque* flashed with light. Blinding prisms of the Dark Queen's power shoved back against the bloody darkness. The Glob sucked the darkness down into the place where it stored energy. A pocket world. I saw it, the barest glimpse of a maelstrom of energy, a black hole of magic in the Glob. It sucked her soul home dry.

Something inside Monique's mind snapped with an audible popping sound. The purple energies whipped at me and away. I eased her to the side and stood over her, panting with exertion, watching her as the minutes crept by. She lay there limply, breathing fast, sweating, as if she had run a race. She said nothing. She didn't turn and look at me.

I tried to see and think through all the layers of her plans. I had never deliberately set out to bind anyone to my own will, never tried to create a mental slave, but I understood why people like Leo did, just as I understood why I killed. To get and maintain control. Because without control, there is chaos. And because, once upon a time, deep down, I had believed I knew who should live or die.

Trying to exert control over my life without killing, I

had accidently bound Ed to me. I had bound Kemnebi to Rick LaFleur as his slave. Mistakes in judgment. The kind one makes with good intentions and not enough knowledge or wisdom, and then stupidly continues to make them.

That pretty much made me one of the monsters.

I hated that I had made mistakes, had killed humans who were bound and not acting under their own wills, had beheaded newly risen vamps when they might have been healed by Amy Lynn Brown's miracle blood, or taken into a scion lair by a master vamp to wait through the decade-long curing process. So many of the people I had killed might have been saved. That knowledge made it hard to just lop the heads off my enemies, except when they attacked me or mine. Defensive battle was different. It meant death, but a death different from judgment and execution. This mental duel had been combat.

Yet I had not bound Monique. Whatever that snapping sound had been had happened in her brain. But it wasn't my fault. She had attacked me. Right?

As a queen, I understood that Monique deserved to be executed for the crimes she was trying to carry out. I might be the only one who could stop this woman, and if so, then I had two choices: bind her the way Bruiser bound vamps and Monique bound everyone, or kill her.

But if I bound her, would that free her captives to continue to work their magic? Would the unknown European vamps just keep coming? Yes and yes. I needed to know the identities of the people she was conspiring with, where they were, and who they planned to betray. For now, Monique as my prisoner would have to be enough.

She was Onorio. She'd probably heal in a few weeks, but she wouldn't be out in the world with her conspirators, fighting or binding anyone.

I stepped away from Monique. There was snot on her face where the wolf spit had been before. Her bowels had released. Her feet were still tied to the chair pieces, but her wrists were free, the tape bitten through where she had freed them. I stood guard between the schemes this woman and the Firestarter had in play. Because she couldn't bind me, Monique would kill me if she could.

"I'm the Dark Queen," I said, touching my crown, and poking at the tender places in my scalp where she had tried to pull it off. No blood, so that was good. No one could peel it off of me. And with her here, I could monitor her and stop her the moment I discovered the names and locations of the people in the vision, especially the French vamp whose voice had been so infused with power that it had caused Monique's stolen energies to spike and cut, and the other one's face, the one that was tied to Legolas/Melker. The memory of the man, someone I had seen in the past, someone I had met, was already fading like a dream after waking.

Until they all started to betray one another, the beings in her soul home were a real danger.

I added more duct tape to Monique's bindings and re-wrapped her wrists together, behind her back this time, so she couldn't bite through the tape again and take off the cuffs. They seemed to work, but only if she couldn't remove them. I also retaped her ankles and gathered up the chair pieces, tossing them into the other room. I texted Alex to have someone rinse the poo off Monique. I didn't envy that person.

I had a lot to think about. I left the room, the silent, probably unconscious, maybe brain-damaged woman on the floor.

It was full daylight when I closed the cottage door behind me and leaned against it. Guilt wormed through me for the way I had treated Monique, but I quashed it. I was a monster, and monsters weren't supposed to feel guilt. Besides. She was alive. She might heal. I took a breath and smelled smoke. Which was the only thing that reminded me. I pulled my cell and checked the time. I had company. I was late.

I still had the crown and Glob. I had Onorio blood on my hands and in my pocket. I was feeling uncertain and a little bit mean. I was also still in human form and might shift to another form at any moment. "Dang," I muttered.

"Whoof." It was a kind of doggie sound of *Look at me*, or *I have to go out and pee*, or *It's supper time*. Brute was standing at the bottom of the cottage steps, staring up at me, his crystal blue eyes intent. He turned and looked at the cottage door and back to me.

"What? You think I shouldn't have broken her brain?"

Brute, the three-hundred-plus-pound werewolf, showed me his fangs and snapped at the air, telling me I should have killed her and let him eat her.

"Not yet. She has friends in low places, and she isn't working alone."

Brute chuffed and wagged his tail.

"Do we have company in the sweathouse?"

Brute blew out a breath through his nose, a disdainful sniff that meant yes, and he didn't like the people inside.

"I'm not fond of them either. And this means I'm gonna have to eat cold quiche."

I walked through the lawn and into the woods down toward the creek. Eli had built my sweathouse early on, and I had used it several times lately to try to stop the unexpected shifting. It hadn't worked, but then, I had been trying to force my magic on half-understood sweathouse ceremonies, and that wasn't the way *Tsalagi* ceremonies worked.

Eli had set up this meeting last week. I hadn't fought it very hard. Admitting I needed help was awkward and embarrassing, but not as bad as continually waking up in a different form and shifting unexpectedly from human to half-form or Beast form in public or in the middle of a fight. And since there were only two other skinwalkers that I knew of, getting help meant asking family. They had ignored me for decades. I hadn't been particularly nice to either of them once they showed up. Yet Eli had asked and here they were. In my sweathouse.

I stepped behind the new privacy wall, removed my clothing, crammed it into a paper grocery bag, mudders on the bottom, and showered off beneath the icy water. Fighting the shivers, I opened the big plastic bin of supplies, shook out a towel, dried off, pulled on a linen shift, and tucked the Glob in the pocket. *Le breloque* was still stuck on my head when I opened the sweathouse door.

The fire in the firepit flamed bright and high and threw sparks. Heat and steam rushed out, the scent of rosemary strong on the air. Light flooded the darkness for a moment as I stepped inside and closed the door, thinking that rosemary was odd, not a traditional herb, but one brought over by the Europeans. *Why rosemary?*

The fire settled. My eyes adjusted to the dimmer light. My Beast was interested, peering through my eyes.

Most ceremonies I'd taken part in started at sunrise or sunset. Not midmorning. Most involved fasting and drinking herbal stuff that tasted like rotten spinach. All involved fire, smoke, herbs, and lots of listening. I don't really listen well. I've been told I'm confrontational.

Standing in the shadows, I studied my brother and the woman I called grandmother, fighting down the desire to be rude and combative. When I entered, Ayatas FireWind had been sitting in the guru position, knees crossed, and he stood slowly, his bare legs unfolding gracefully. It was really unfair. We were both skinwalkers, and he was graceful, while I was more often a klutz. He was also a senior special agent and the regional director of the Psychometric Law Enforcement Division of Homeland.

"Igidoi," he said softly. *Sister*, the possessive form, as in *my sister*. It set the tone for this meeting. He was here as a brother, not as a cop.

There were many ways to respond, many different ways to say *my brother*. I had been studying the proper forms of address for the last week, but hadn't been able to decide on one until now. I chose *"Agidoi,"* which literally meant *my sibling of opposite sex*, and was also possessive. No combative words here. Nope, nope, nope.

He nodded at my choice of address, and his braids swung forward. He wore two, both of them neat and spare and perfect. I wanted to toss my braid behind me to hide it. For the Cherokee, the state of one's braids was indicative of many things, and mine was sloppy and careless. But I held still.

Ayatas was dressed in a breechclout, which he must have brought with him, because it was colorful and not the undyed cotton of the ones in the bins. It was also a traditional Cherokee covering and was more conservative than the one he wore the last time I saw him wear one. This breechclout was a length of bright red woven cloth that passed between his legs, draped over in front to the knees, and was tied around his waist with a second piece of rust-colored cloth that also secured his medicine bag at one hip. It left his buttocks mostly bare but covered the essentials. It was appropriate attire for hard work, fishing, or hunting in hot weather, and for ceremony.

The flames flickered over his bare chest and face. Like me, he was yellow-eyed, tall, too lean, his musculature clearly defined. He was also beautiful, while I was . . . interesting. Striking sometimes. Never beautiful.

I transferred my eyes to the old woman sitting on the log seat in the place of honor, more or less at the point of north. It was low to the ground, and her knees were bent, relaxed. She was heavily wrinkled, her braided hair a mix of intense black and steel gray, streaked with pure white. Her yellow eyes sparkled in the firelight, her gaze tight on me.

The memory of the last time I saw her flashed through my mind and was gone. She looked older than the night the white man had tried to kill me on the Trail of Tears. To save me, she had forced me into my bobcat form and shoved me into a blizzard to live or die. To the child I had been, bleeding and broken, she had always been old, but that had been over 170 years ago. Now she looked ancient.

Like me, she was wearing a linen shift, one from the plastic box outside. Beside her was a small, traditional drum, a pitcher for water, and a basket of dried and fresh herbs with mortar and pestle. I would not be drinking anything she made for me.

"Enisi," I said to her. It meant *my grandmother*, the possessive implied, though not stated. Cautious, informal, respectful.

"Vgilisi," she said. It meant *my daughter's child*, but was less specific as to relationships. It wasn't *my granddaughter.* *"Jaladi."* A polite form of *sit down.*

I sat across from her, at south, folding down as gracefully as I could. Aya sat as well, and there was an empty wooden cup at his knee. We studied each other. "I thank you for coming. I don't remember much of the speech of The People. Do you mind if we speak English?"

Enisi, better known as Hayalasti Sixmankiller, gave a single nod, but her lips went hard and flat. "I understand you have adopted two men into your family." She threw a fresh branch of rosemary on the fire. "You should have spoken first with tribal leaders. There may be disagreement with this decision."

Ahhh. That was better. Provocation was something I could deal with. I gave a tiny shrug. "There may be disputes," I agreed. "The elders have cared nothing for me for a hundred and seventy plus years. Tell me why I should care what they think now."

"You want help."

"My brother," I hesitated and looked at Aya, "my *adopted* brother, not you, believes you can teach me to manage my skinwalker magics better."

"Your shifting is uncontrolled," she stated.

"It has become more difficult to control," I hedged, which was true enough.

"We will go to ceremony—the ceremony of Full Circle—to heal families. You will participate. You will yield to me as did Tsu Tsu. I will teach you and govern you."

Aya's eyes shot to his grandmother. His expression didn't change, but his fingers tensed the tiniest bit. Yeah, got it. Not acceptable language around a Full Circle firepit. Not a *Tsalagi* concept. And I didn't know what a tsutsu was, but I had a feeling I wouldn't like it.

"Full Circle is always voluntary," I said. "My elders, Aggie One Feather, her mother *uni lisi*, and Savannah Walkingstick, would tell me that you can't command me in this."

"You would disobey me?"

"In a heartbeat."

Hayalasti Sixmankiller's eyes flashed again. My nose, which was better than human, caught a faint scent beneath the rosemary. Unpleasant. Then it was gone.

"You. Will. Yield," she said.

Inside me, Beast hissed in displeasure, showing killing teeth.

I stole a sound from Leo Pellissier and laughed softly, letting the sound ripple along my skinwalker magic. Inside me, Beast's ears perked up high. Outside me, silver and charcoal skinwalker energies scattered through the air, all laced with hundreds of darker motes of power. The magic

of I/we. The magic of the creature we were together—
Beast.

As my magic rose, so did my grandmother's magic. I
could only see magic with Beast's vision, not my own,
which meant Aya and Grandmother likely didn't see energy at all. If she did, she would have hidden her power.
Her energies were black, shot through with motes of red.
The feel of her lightless energies sliced along my skin like
tiny knives. Black magic . . .

"No," I said. "I will not *yield*. I will, possibly, work with
you. But I will not be ruled." I touched *le breloque*. "And
not just me. The Dark Queen will not yield."

Hayalasti's eyes flashed again, and I got a good look at
them this time. The strange light in her eyes was the reflection of fire, but not the fire between us. In her eyes was a
roaring fire that spoke of battle and war. I caught a whiff
of the stink again, tantalizingly familiar, and then it was
gone. Her power shaped into a long-fingered hand. It reached
for me.

The Glob in my pocket heated, red hot and fast. Its energies were clear, crystalline, and spread like a net, like a
flower opening. The energies met between us in a sparkle
of light that even they could see. The black power spiraled
out of shape and into a tiny black tornado, heading for my
pocket. The Glob sucked down the power like flushing filth
down a toilet.

Grandmother jerked back, pulling on her power as if it
was a rope in a game of tug-of-war. Her power began to
fray, split, fine threads breaking. The red motes whirled in
a circle around her head.

She made an inarticulate sound, too loud for Cherokee
speech, like "Dladladla!" She grabbed at her chest as if the
loss of power hurt her there.

Aya looked back and forth between us, his eyes wide
with shock.

"I yield to no one," I said.

"*Gigadanegisgi* tried to buy you. I should have sold you
to her," she spat.

Aya jerked, a loss of control I never would have expected. "*Gigadanegisgi?*" he whispered.

I started, "Somebody tell m—"

"*Gigadanegisgi* means blood taker," Aya said. "She would have sold you, her granddaughter, my sister, to a *vampire*."

It should have surprised me. It didn't. "Crap on crackers," I said.

Grandmother stood in a single fluid motion and leaped over the fire at me.

CHAPTER 5

Spear Finger, Liver-Eater, and U'tlun'ta

As always, the world slowed, a strong battlefield readiness and that weird time shift of war. The world around me thickened, as if time itself had turned to cold molasses.

There wasn't time to stand and meet her attack. Beast did . . . something. I raised my left arm in defense. Pain shattered along my spine, across my shoulders, arms, and through my hands. My fingers burned. My body shifted. *Fast.* To half-form.

She was still midleap.

I rocked back to my butt. Away from her. Caught her foot in a knobby hand and threw her over me, past me. She crashed into the east wall.

Beast screamed her challenge. I stood on my/our wide paw-feet. "I do not yield!" I shouted.

Grandmother twisted to her feet, limber as a teenaged gymnast, her linen shift pulled to the side. She stopped. Her yellow eyes were on me. Her mouth hung open. Grandmother had never seen such a thing as I had just become. We faced off, me hesitating, Grandmother frozen in shock.

I took a breath to speak and caught the strange scent,

unmasked by the rosemary. Once before, the old woman smelled very faintly of witch magic. Now it was stronger. And beneath that, she stank of—

U'tlun'ta. Liver-eater. The creature skinwalkers became when they—when we—did black magic and took the life and the flesh of a living human.

Rancid as a battlefield littered with the fallen and the burned.

That was why the potent rosemary. To hide the stench.

There was an amulet tied around her neck, visible where her shift had twisted.

From the corner of my eye, I saw Aya slowly rise to a crouch, but he didn't stand to fight. He wasn't reacting to his grandmother smelling like a burning rotten corpse. It was as if he couldn't smell the rancid reek. As if he was frozen in indecision and confusion. Or frozen in Six-mankiller's power.

Grandmother's magic attacked again, blacker than a starless night, cold as the depths of hell. The Glob heated. It wasn't skinwalker magic. It wasn't *u'tlun'ta* magic. It felt and looked like black magic, which was witch magic. Six-mankiller was not a witch. The power had to be stolen. More black power shot out, countered by the Glob in my pocket.

The attacking energies came from the amulet resting on her breastbone, tied around her neck. It wasn't a medicine bag. It was something else.

The Glob sucked the attack down like a white shark swallowing prey. The amulet on Granny's neck began to glow a dull red, like heated steel, then brighter. The Glob drained down the light too. Grandmother screamed. I smelled burned, rotten flesh.

The old woman dove at me again, shoving off with her right foot.

There was a knapped stone blade in her left hand.

She stabbed forward.

I ducked back and blocked her knife hand with my left, shoving up and around in a whirling motion.

She snapped at my exposed arm. Biting at me. Her teeth grazing my skin.

U'tlun'ta. Liver-eater. The evil of the skinwalker, to eat the living and take their form.

She wanted to be Jane Yellowrock.

She wanted to be the Dark Queen.

The Glob sucked the last of the amulet's power away. *Le breloque* did . . . something. Grandmother froze.

I swiped her face with my claws. They caught the edge of her jaw. Down her throat. Caught the thong around Grandmother's neck. I ripped away her charm. Her blood splattered across me.

The stench of *u'tlun'ta* filled the sweathouse. Grandmother dropped, curled to her knees, and shifted. In a second and a half. She simply *became Bubo bubo.*

The shift falling away, she flew at the door. Her claws and body battering it. I hadn't latched it. The door opened, and she flew into the daylight.

Bubo bubo. The Eurasian eagle owl.

I stood still, Grandmother's amulet hooked into my claws, swinging. The owl was not native to this continent.

When I had to fly, the eagle owl was my bird of choice, even though it wasn't a bird native to the western hemisphere. It had been hard to get the bones. Not impossible, just freaking difficult.

Bubo bubo eagle owls were part of a prophecy told to me by Sabina, the outclan priestess. The one burned by the Firestarter. I'd once had a vision of grandmother leaping at me and calling me a rabbit. Rabbits were choice food for owls.

I had always assumed the owl in the *Bubo bubo* prophecy was me, but . . . this and the memory . . . I had a memory of Sabina and Grandmother in a Cherokee war council. Sabina was a *gigadanegisgi.* Blood taker. Had Sabina tried to buy me when I was a toddler?

"Jane?" Aya whispered.

Aya was an officer of the law, working with PsyLED. He had to know that we had a real problem here, and not one that his department was equipped to handle. I lifted the amulet in my oversized, half-form hand and studied it. It was a rough diamond, big as a pecan-half, knotted with hide thongs.

Diamond.

Things came together.

Diamond. Like my Glob. It too had been a diamond, a reddish blood diamond, filled with the magic of the sacrifice of witch children. Had Grandmother been using the diamond to direct her magic, or had the energy been coming from the diamond itself? Was this one of the amulets the fangheads were always searching for? How had Grandmother gotten it? Had she stolen it from Sabina when the vamp tried to buy me? Was this the blood price for a skinwalker child?

"Holy crap," I whispered as the amulet cooled. My voice was Beast-low and growly.

"Jane?" he asked again. "I couldn't move. How . . . What did she do?"

I looked from the amulet to Ayatas. I was going to have to explain, and I didn't know what words to use.

Something about his body posture changed, and I was suddenly seeing Ayatas FireWind, cop, not Aya, brother. "Did you see the magic?" he asked.

"Saw it, smelled it. You remember the stories about spear finger, liver-eater, and *u'tlun'ta.*" Aya nodded. "And you remember that I killed one." He gave a small cop nod. "That *u'tlun'ta* . . . He smelled like Grandmother."

Aya breathed in and frowned fiercely, making long grooves from his nose to his chin and two sharp lines between his eyebrows. "Is that what I smell? Like rotten meat cooking on a spit?"

"Yes. And the stench is worse than the last time I met an *u'tlun'ta.* She did black magic—black *witch* magic—with this"—I indicated the amulet—"and she's changing, Aya. Changing into *u'tlun'ta,* the cannibalistic evil creature that our kind all seem to become when we get old. She's hiding that change behind spells she bought from witches. And she attacked me with this." I held up the dead amulet in my knobby fingers. "It's a diamond. Or it was. Now it's black and"—I stopped. I pulled the Glob and tapped Sixmankiller's stone with it. The diamond cracked and its internal matrix shattered in my palm—"dead. Still intact, but cracks running all through it, ruined down to the cellular level."

"What is that?" Aya demanded about my ugly weapon.

"It's the blood of sacrificed witch children, a piece of the Blood Cross, a round ingot melted from the Spike of Golgotha, one of the vampire blood diamonds, and my flesh and blood sealed together by me being struck by lightning."

Aya's frown vanished and was replaced with a scant smile. "You have lived a long and fascinating life, my sister." It could have been an accusation, but it wasn't. It was spoken in that tone that cops use when speaking to one another.

"I figure you have too, little brother."

Aya's eyes went wide, and his posture shifted again, the cop falling away. "You called me *little brother*, and not in insult. And . . . earlier you called me Aya."

"Yeah, yeah, don't get all weepy on me. Our liver-eating gramma claimed she wanted us to be family." I shrugged, a *Tsalagi* lifting of the shoulder blade, but which now was part uncertainty and part discomfort. "But we already are. Family. You know, now that I'm over being upset that I got tossed into the snow to live or die."

"Elder sister," he said, his tone and eyes formal and yet amused, "I grew up listening to tales of your exploits when you were merely a child of five. Growing up in the shadow of a superwoman was difficult. My heart never doubted that you lived."

"Huh. Why would you think that?"

"How could you not still live, with such a history? But when we finally met, I had to recognize and resolve my long-forgotten childish jealousy."

My discomfort grew. "Whatever. Back to Gramma. You brought her to me, wearing this." I shook the internally shattered diamond at him. "Why? It's obviously a magical amulet. You're an ass, but not a total jerk."

Ayatas touched the ruined amulet with a fingertip. He shook his head. "I never saw this before. After I first learned of the *u'tlun'ta* you killed, and after I saw the security footage of you fighting the half-man, half-saber-tooth lion and defeating it, I watched the footage with Grandmother to see if she knew what the creature was. She claimed she didn't, but she was . . . let's call it *overly interested in the footage*."

"Cop talk," I said. It was the same kind of comment

Rick would have made, back when we were dating. "You really mean to say that she knew what it was and she was lying."

He tilted his head in acknowledgment. "I've been a law enforcement agent for over half of my life. She watched the video dozens of times, and she asked for a copy. I told her no and saw something flash in her eyes like fire. She couldn't hide her intense reaction to being refused. A day later, my flash drive was missing, and someone had tried to get into my computer. I began to watch Grandmother. Something was different." His eyes were still on my hand, holding the ruined amulet. "And you had told me that you possessed a gift for seeing magic, which I do not have. I wanted you to look at our grandmother and her magics." He looked back up at me, the too familiar yellow eyes, big nose, like looking in a mirror that showed a prettier, more refined me. "I wanted you to see her magics, did not think she would try to harm you. And I *never saw this* until now."

"Maybe she kept it in her medicine bag. I'm pretty sure it contained a mixed cluster of spells. An illusion or glamor spell calibrated for scent, probably an *obfuscation* working, and several rounds of a big mama attack spell."

Aya said something in *Tsalagi* that I didn't understand. Cherokee didn't curse, but it sure sounded like it. He reached out and stroked my jaw once, as if curious if the cat fur was real. I was fully pelted there, the sensation of his skin on my fur a shock. "I have loved and feared the old woman for decades," he said. "She saw you shift into this, your half-form. She will want that ability, that power. If she is *u'tlun'ta*, she will try to take it from you. She tried to bite you."

Like a sucker punch to the jaw, it hit me. "It would be easy for our grandmother to take my body. We are already genetically linked." The transition using the snake in the center of all things—my DNA—would be child's play for an old skinwalker like her. I lifted my claws close to my face. Her blood was caught there, stinking badly, now that the spell hiding her scent was gone. Softly, so quietly that Aya had to bend close to hear, I asked, "Is she still the woman you knew as a child? Is she still Hayalasti Six-mankiller?"

An expression like a steel veneer dropped down, replacing his grief and horror. Just as quietly, Aya said, "No. She is not." His voice changed, taking on a cadence that was similar to the way tribal storytellers talked when imparting ancient tales or wisdom. "When I came back for a prolonged stay on the remains of the Indian Territory in Oklahoma in 1985, she was different. Colder. More cruel. She has been different for a very long time—" He stopped, his words cut off sharply, as if by a knife, and his face wore an expression of grief, as if he was accepting the changes in his *elisi*, his grandmother.

He didn't speak again and when enough time had elapsed to make me uncomfortable, I asked, "In any of the old stories, is there any mention of a way to reverse the changes in *u'tlun'ta*? Any binding, forced ceremony, maybe a vampire could reverse her?"

Aya blinked and looked at me, seeming himself again. "No. Not in the old stories. Vampires killed our kind, killed skinwalkers, because we couldn't be bound. Becoming *u'tlun'ta* is a choice. A decision. Once the first step is taken on that path"—his voice hoarsened—"the old tales tell us that there is no way back. Of course, the old stories didn't have access to the weapon you carry."

"It's called the Glob," I said, my mind on other things. *Bruiser* . . . What if he could bind her? Could I magically drain a liver-eater using the Glob? Force a skinwalker to reverse paths?

"The Glob. Of course," he said, slightly amused. Then the pleasure faded.

My brother's eyes held mine, already grieving, as if knowing what I was about to say.

"If we can capture her before she eats another human," I said, "another sentient being of any kind, there are some things I can suggest." Bruiser . . . Did I dare ask him to try? "If Gramma was a vamp, it would be the Dark Queen's job to make certain that she was neutralized. I'm not sure what I'm responsible for with our particular paranormal species. But once she kills . . . as a law enforcement officer, it's your job to find her and bring her in and make sure she's kept away from humans."

Aya lifted his head to me, his jaw forward, an aggressive

stance. He seemed to steel himself, and when he spoke, his words were toneless. "No other paranormal is likely to be effective against her. The old stories tell us that the *u'tlun'ta* is the responsibility of the family and clan elders. It is their responsibility to render judgment. That would mean me, outside of my job."

"I'm family and clan too, little brother. I am eldest. I am a war woman, whose job it is to deliver judgment. If I can't capture her and stop her, then *we* will have to do it. And soon."

"What will you—" He stopped and started over. "What magical methods of manipulation and restraint would you attempt?"

That was an interesting way to phrase things. Null cuffs were a military and law enforcement tool, and I wasn't supposed to have access to them, and cops all had a love-hate relationship with null prisons and scion cages, which existed outside of human law and human control. I threw caution to the winds and said, "First, physical restraint and null cuffs. Then maybe, if the witches allow it, a room in the null prison. If that doesn't work, then magical binding, like what a vampire does to a human but on a greater scale." Like what Bruiser did to vamps he bound. And I had the Roberes too. Three Onorios working together might do what no one imagined.

But there were lots of things that no one imagined.

The vision of the bloody hull of Monique's soul home blinked onto the back of my eyelids. Yeah. That's what Monique was doing. Putting together a cabal of Onorios to fight a battle of her choosing and betray the vamps.

"Greater scale," Aya said, not quite a question.

"Yeah." I forced my attention back to the present. "I have friends and scions in high places." And I have the Glob and my crown. At the words and the thought, *le breloque* warmed on my head.

Aya took my knobby fingers in his, staring at the half-form knuckles and retracted claws. "You asked about the old stories. They say, 'It is a rare but necessary thing for skinwalker elders to shackle one who has lost her soul, and take her to the top of the mountain and throw her off.' That is what the old skinwalker tales say."

"Well, that sucks."

He smiled sadly.

My baby brother was an Elder of The People. Though I was technically older, I had spent around 170 years in Big-Cat form. By comparison, and considering my lost years, I was a child. I needed to remember that and, according to the old ways, ask his counsel. I drew on the formality of vamps and said, "Little brother, Gramma can shift to an owl and fly away. She has amulets and spells you don't know about. How do you catch a spirit in the night?"

"Mmmm. Perhaps we will need a plan B."

"You think?"

He smiled a full, real smile.

"Did you both fly in?" Because if she flew in, she had to deposit mass on a stone somewhere to become so small.

"No. She was here when I arrived. I came over the mountain as *wahya*—black wolf—and I carried enough beef jerky and snack bars to tide me over."

"So she deposited mass somewhere. If we could find that place and wait for her, we could take her while she was starving and weak." *Or we could destroy the missing mass before she shifted back*, a small voice in the back of my mind suggested, *and she would likely die.* I didn't say that.

Aya nodded. "It is unlikely that she deposited her mass nearby."

I tilted the hand he still held and extended my claws, cat-like. "But not impossible." I stepped away, lifted the pitcher, and poured water onto the fire. It sizzled and smoked and spat as it went out. Aya followed me into the afternoon sun and watched as I stepped into the small alcove with the shower and the bins of clothes, where I wiped my claws on a washcloth. I pocketed the rank blood. There were spells that could track people by their blood, and my BFF was a witch. I put Gramma's shift into a bin and sealed it, washed my claw under the icy water, and stepped back and away, indicating my hospitality. "As my guest, please use the facilities first."

I walked toward the creek behind the sweathouse. The shower came on, and I heard him take a shocked breath as the cold water hit him. I left him there to dress, and, wearing my sweaty gown, the washrag with my grandmother's rancid blood in my pocket, I walked to the creek. It was fall yet not cold. With climate change it was often warm-ish into early November.

It had rained briefly while we were communing, and my odd, square-looking paw-feet squished in the mud. Ahead, I saw the rounded tops of stone, nothing that was broken or shattered. No indications the stones had been used to give her human form mass, and then that mass deposited back as more broken stone when she returned to *Bubo bubo*. Aya was probably right that Grandmother flew in and was flying back to pick up the original mass she had left hidden and far away. She had deposited and retaken mass from a long distance, which suggested the old woman had power and magic way beyond what I had. She had probably tied herself to a stone as I did with my gold nugget. I reached up and touched the nugget at my neck, hanging on double strands of gold chain. I seldom noticed or thought about the piece of gold that tied me to the rock of my first shift into Jane. It was as much a part of me as my hands or my teeth. Not noticed until they were gone.

Leaves had begun to fall, golden, red, dull brown. I made no attempt at stealth. This was my land, my home, as much as any place was. In my sweaty shift, I stood looking down at the creek more than ten feet below. It was sluggish and chuckling, not full and roaring as it had been in winter and spring with snowmelt and heavy rain. The trees were still taking in rainwater, and there was little runoff. All sorts of animal tracks were pressed into the sand on the beach across the way. When Beast hunted, she often started here at the closest watering hole. Above me, the sun peeked through the clouds, reflecting in raindrops on leaves and branches, casting shadows. The world smelled alive and clean. Part of me almost thought I could hear bells in the distance. I put the Glob in my empty pocket, waiting.

A moment later, I was joined by a huge black wolf. He wore a gobag strapped around his neck, and his breath smelled of beef jerky. He looked up at me, his eyes glistening, and made a soft chuffing sound.

"Is that dog for 'See you later'?"

He chuffed again, nose-bopped my hand, and turned upstream. I watched my brother trotting along the creek away from me. His shape-shift had been fast, not as fast as Grandmother's had been, but less than my usual long minutes. I was jealous. And then I remembered I had shifted into half-form in two seconds or less. Beast had mad gifts. *Thanks*, I thought to her.

Beast is best hunter. Jane is hunted.

I kept my breathing slow and steady. *Oh? Like right now?*

Light dragon is watching. Above Jane in trees.

"I do not understand what is happening," a musical yet petulant voice said. "Why are so many of the walkers in one place?" The voice came from my right and about twenty feet overhead. It was Storm, arguably my responsibility, her presence gifted to me by the head arcenciel, Soul.

I didn't look up or indicate surprise, but then, arcenciels might be able to read heart rates and a spike in blood chemistries, for all I knew. The gold corona around my head was warming. *Le breloque* was also called *la corona*, and it had some importance to the rainbow beings. I didn't know if it was reacting to the presence of Storm or just planning to burn my head off. With one finger, I pushed at the gold laurel leaf crown. It remained firmly attached and didn't get hot enough to scald me, so that was good. *Le breloque* was different since I went through the rift and back. It was either less powerful or biding its time.

"Are you listening to me?" she demanded.

"I heard you. We're . . . The walkers are . . . family." One of whom I might need to kill. My stomach suddenly felt acidic and empty. I had shifted and eaten nothing. Adrenaline had kept me going, but now I needed to eat.

"Family is an earth concept where human women carry young in their bellies. Eggs are much more efficient."

"Yeah. I happen to agree. Childbirth can be messy."

Kitssss, Beast thought at me.

"I have asked many questions about you," Storm said. "The elder ones say you are the Giver of the Rift. They say the corona is yours for now. I have registered my complaint that a *walker* should possess the corona."

"Registered with who?"

"With She Who Claims the Rift."

She Who Claims the Rift was Soul. "Yeah. Aren't you sweet." I wondered if Storm had been on earth long enough to understand sarcasm.

"I have no sweetness," she said. "I taste of saltness."

I looked up to see her sitting in the tree in human form, her gauzy gown all shades of gray and lavender, her hair lavender too. She was a shape-shifter, a being of pure energy, who could achieve a state of matter and any form she wanted. Many with big teeth and claws. She was also immature, unsure of her place or her boundaries, yet full of opinions, and aggressively sullen. Like I had been as a teenager.

I had never been able to resist yanking her chain. "Salty. Good to know. In case I get hungry."

Storm reared back as if insulted. I laughed and glanced upstream for any last sign of Ayatas. He was gone, so I headed back to the sweathouse. I double-checked the fire and picked up the plastic bin containing the undyed gown Grandmother had been wearing. In it I tossed the bloody cloth from my pocket. I wondered if Grandmother knew what could be done with DNA these days.

After I showered, towel-dried my pelt, and redressed, I put my own shift into a separate bin, Monique's scorched bloody cloth went into a zippy, and I carried them inside the inn, heading to Alex's domain. On the way, I grabbed leftover quiche from the fridge and munched it down. It hadn't been there long and was still warm from the oven. I bit in and chewed. *Heaven.* Next slice would be shrimp.

Alex was sitting at his desk, yawning, a cup of espresso at his elbow.

"Alex, will you send all these to Leo's lab in Texas for DNA testing? Three samples."

"Your lab," he said. "Leo's dead."

"Fine. The one with the scorched blood is Monique Giovanni's. The unscorched one with the blood is to be listed, 'Unknown.' It's Gramma's."

He looked up, startled. "Hayalasti Sixmankiller? That gramma?"

"The one and only." I tapped the one on top, adding, "This one is mine."

Alex met my gaze, speculation in his. "You sure you want to do that, Janie?"

"No. But we need a comparison, and my brother didn't leave his loincloth behind."

"Not a problem." He pushed my bin back to me. "Wash that. We have your DNA and Ayatas FireWind's DNA already." He turned back to the screen.

Carefully, in my best Christian children's home manners, I swallowed and said, "I beg your pardon?"

Alex ducked his head, his eyes on the screens. His fingers shifting between three of five keyboards. His dark skin carried a greenish tint from the screens, and his spiral curls bounced into his eyes.

"Alex?"

His fingers faltered. "So fuuu . . . reaking not fair." He blew out an exasperated sigh. "You remember the first day Ayatas showed up? After you coldcocked him, and once he was able to breathe again, we ate a meal?" He stopped.

"I'm listening."

"I collected your spoon and Ayatas's fork, and . . . Well. We sent them to this doc at Leo's lab. He ran both of them. So we have a record of you both already."

"And you didn't think that sharing this with me was important?"

"It wasn't urgent. We didn't tell Dr. Northern whose it was. So he just put them in with the others, and the tech ran them with the next batch. It took a while. And then you had the Sangre Duello and the cancer and . . . ummm." He blew out a breath, and the little spiral curls fluttered. "And we got the results. But they didn't tell us anything we didn't know. Ayatas is your biological brother, and you both have fuc—messed-up DNA."

I knew for a fact he had just dumbed down the report for me. "I've been in the Rift. Run mine again and get them to run a comparison between my new and my old, as well as against Gramma's and Ayatas's." I slapped the back of his head, and he resisted the grin that wanted to pop out. "No cussing. And this time I want to read the comparison report."

"Yes, Mooom," he said, drawling out the word as if it was an insult. "Just so you know, it will take weeks to do a comparison unless we send it as urgent or send it to a specialist genetics lab."

"Call it urgent. Keep it in-house. And stop treating me like I'm dying."

"Hard habit to break. You had us terrified."

"I love you too, bro. I'm grabbing some more leftovers and getting a nap in. See you in a bit."

I didn't nap well, and I didn't need much rest in this form, though I did hope falling asleep might allow my body to shift back into my human form. No such luck. Late afternoon, I woke and was still in half-form, but the uncomfortable crown had come off, so that was good. Bruiser's scent was on the air, letting me know he had checked on me while I slept. A peaceful warmth spread through me. "Coolio," I murmured, rolling out of bed. I wasn't used to being loved or having people to care about. I was still practicing all that and experiencing the joy of family.

I had showered at the sweathouse, so I was fast, brushing my fangs, pulling on clean yoga pants and a long-sleeved tee in a washed denim blue color. Makeup, even lipstick, was impossible with a partially pelted face, and I still sucked at putting the stuff on. I checked myself out in the mirror. I still had pawed feet, so shoes were a waste of time. I shrugged at my reflection. "Good to go," I said to myself.

Beast is good to go. Where are I/we going? Hunting? Beast wants to hunt! Have never hunted in this form. Claws are short. Jane has kit-fangs. Jane should take white man's gun and knife. Can shoot and cut flesh from prey and eat. Jane will like raw meat.

Erp. No hunting. No raw flesh. "Good to go" is just a saying.

I got the feeling that Beast was disgusted by my response, but she didn't reply. As I padded down the steps to the main level, I heard Alex saying, "Texted George and Eli. Texting Janie now. Hang on." My cell in my thigh pocket buzzed just as Eli strode in the back door, pocketing his cell. His body mechanics were all battlefield alert and ready for action. Bruiser entered through the front, also pocketing his cell. This couldn't be good.

I reached the office first.

"Hey, Janie. Where's—never mind." He tapped a button. "Gang's all here, Wrassler." To us he added, "HQ security is on FaceTime. You need to see."

The guys stood behind and to my sides. On the screen, a pixelated image began to form, flickering pale cream and black with a splotch of green in one corner. The video cleared and stabilized, revealing a cemetery, New Orleans style, with mausoleums situated along a white shell drive. The frame scanned around slowly, revealing the vamp graveyard, easily identifiable because all the mausoleums had been scorched in the fire that burned Sabina, the outclan priestess, and sent her into hiding, and also because I had studied this scene often over the last months. The warrior statues on top of each small building had become brittle and fractured, missing arms and hands and one without a head, the base metal of their swords and adornments melted. The videographer paused at the chapel or, rather, where the chapel had once been. It was gone now, just a foundation, blocks blackened and cracked. No one in New Orleans had heard from Sabina. Her last words had suggested that she was burned so badly as to be true dead, even though she was extremely powerful and very advanced in age.

I leaned into Bruiser. He smelled of the winery, the sweetness of grapes he had harvested, pressed, and mixed with other kinds of grapes from other mountain vineyards and now were fermenting in huge stainless steel vats. By the sweetness of new wine on his breath, I deduced that he and Josue had been tasting the red, Bruiser giving the younger man instructions. Bruiser's arm went around my middle, and he hugged me close. Even after all this time, it was still odd to be close to a man taller than me.

On the screen, the view changed, sweeping slowly back to one mausoleum, the Pellissier crypt, blackened and so heat-damaged the stone was cracked and fragile-looking.

Wrassler said, "This is why I contacted you, Queenie." The screen changed as he walked around the small building to the side that was hidden from the road and the chapel. The wall had a hole in it, one not caused by fire. He walked closer, focusing on the damage, and said, "It's about three feet by two. It appears it was knocked down from outside, maybe with a short battering ram."

"Why not use the door?" I asked.

"The fire sealed it. The flames were so hot they heated differing materials and fused them together. The result means the door is stronger than the walls."

I thought, *Someone busted in. No one clawed out of the caskets inside and got away. Leo wasn't alive.* Not that I hoped he would rise from the dead again. That was where revenants came from, and they were dangerous as rabid wolves and had to be put down by rogue-vampire hunters. Like what I used to be before I got stuck with the Dark Queen gig. "When?"

"The guard makes a round every six hours. It was like this at noon and she called me. I wanted to check it out before I notified you."

"Without messing up the debris," I said, "can you hold the phone inside and let us see the caskets?"

There was some fumbling as someone else turned on a cell flashlight and both cells were held inside the hole. Inside, the caskets were all blackened by heat that had penetrated the walls from outside. Based on the wreckage, there had been five superheated cement vaults, the caskets inside pulled out and dumped onto the floor. The vaults had been busted into chunks and dust; the caskets were ruined, blackened, pitted charcoal, and most were open, empty. There were bits of vamp remains here and there, not much more than pieces of charred skeletons. I'd have expected the bodies to be less intact. Vamps burned easily.

As the cells scanned around, Bruiser's hold on me had tensed. In the carefully controlled tone of Leo's primo, Bruiser asked, "Is there any way to tell which one was Leo's?"

"His was on top," Wrassler said. "The caskets on bottom were less burned than the ones higher up. So this one," a finger entered the field of view, "or that one. I can go in and be sure." He meant be sure that Leo was burned, not taken.

"Don't go in," I said before I thought. "We'll be there before morning." I didn't want Wrassler to touch anything. I wanted to see for myself.

Still in the same tone, Bruiser said, "We'll be there two

days early. Make certain that Yellowrock Clan Home is clean and aired out and Jane's personal residence is also prepared, including the new rooms upstairs."

"Yes, Consort. Sending teams to prepare."

"Put two full-time guards on-site at the cemetery, silver ammo, wood stakes, silvered blades, and a silvered cage," Bruiser said. "They have orders to shoot and stake any Mithran who might approach them, burned or not. Should that occur, they are to toss the body into the cage and contact me directly with photos of the Mithran. I will give orders. Those orders might include a beheading. Make certain the guards understand that."

"Even if—"

"My master is dead. But even if that isn't true, he was beheaded. He would rise a revenant. We will not dishonor him by allowing him to continue in that state."

"Yes, Consort. If a trespasser is human?"

"If it's the Firestarter, execute her. For any others, the guards may use their own discretion. Make certain they're also armed with nonlethal weapons that might disable humans."

"Yes, Consort."

The video ended and Bruiser stepped away from me. "My Queen, I will finish the packing and have your jet prepped for flight."

Packing. All the suitcases piled on the floor for Wrassler and Jodi's wedding in just a few days. *Right.* And I hadn't said a word to Wrassler about the wedding. I'm an idiot. "Yeah. Sure. Thanks."

Without looking back, Bruiser walked from the room, his footsteps tapping up the stairs.

Eli was watching me. I could feel his eyes. When I didn't look his way he said, "He called Leo *my master.*"

"I heard," I said, staring at the screen where, only a moment ago, there had been a view of Leo's desecrated tomb.

Eli said, "Grief is a peculiar thing. It can hit out of nowhere and knock you off your feet. Take you back to another time and place. Another part of yourself."

I nodded but didn't reply to his wisdom, instead changing the subject. "I read the Onorio's mind. Monique's, not Bruiser's."

Eli tilted his head the barest fraction, visible in my extreme peripheral vision. "How?"

"I rubbed a little of her blood into the Glob and onto my crown, and I touched her."

"Guesswork? What if she had taken you over?"

I shrugged and said, "I'd have broken her neck."

"Good answer. Still. That was stupid."

"Yeah. Next time I'll make sure you're there. But she was secured with null cuffs that I duct-taped in place. And I got info."

"I'm listening."

I turned to face Eli and told him what I had learned from our prisoner. With a battle-worthy smile, he said, "We should take Monique Giovanni with us. She might be enough of a lure to bring out the Firestarter."

I chuckled, and though it sounded tired and worn, I managed to add, "Make it so, number one. Oh. You may need a stretcher. I think I broke her."

Eli gave me that rare, full grin, flashing pearly white teeth. "Good. We got this, babe. It'll be fine."

I didn't believe it. Not with the words *my master* falling so easily from Bruiser's lips. Silently, I climbed the stairs and entered our suite. Bruiser wasn't packing. He was staring out the windows at the hills, arms crossed over his middle. I stood in the doorway, watching him, the tightness of his shoulders, the angle of his head, looking out and down.

"I want him to be dead," Bruiser said, his voice laced with the softness of grief that Eli had mentioned. "I want Leo to be dead because if he is not, and if he has risen as a revenant, I will have to find him and kill him."

It was much the same thoughts I'd had about Grandmother. But I wasn't sure why *Bruiser* had the "kill Leo job." That was my job.

I crossed the room to him, standing with my shoulder touching his. Together we looked out over the quiet, peaceful vineyard and the hills beyond. I didn't know much about the way love turned to hate in people, but I had seen it often enough. I let him talk.

"His death as a revenant would fall to me as his former primo. That responsibility was assigned to me when I accepted the position and was part of my contract with him."

"And if he rose sane?" I asked.

"If Leo is twice risen, thrice born, and if he rose in his right mind, he would have gone directly to the Mithran Council Chambers, where he would likely have challenged you to take back his city." Bruiser let go of himself, turned, and pulled me slowly into his arms. "Yet he has done nothing. He has not appeared. There are no reports of feeding massacres. He has not shown up at the place of his power in the city." His arms tightened around me.

"I don't know what to think. I don't know what to do. He was my friend." He massaged his temples with one hand for a moment, as if he had a headache, before he put his arm around me again and dropped his head to mine. "I loved him once, but that was a long time ago. I will end him if I think he is trying to harm you. I will drain my former master into my slave. And that might . . ." He took a breath that quivered softly. "That will either break me or make me just like him."

I hugged him tightly.

CHAPTER 6

Whoopie Đang Đo

An hour before sunset, Bruiser and Eli loaded the luggage into a suburban, readying clothes and gear to be taken to the airport. As they sweated and grunted, I watched and twiddled my thumbs and ground my teeth. I really hated the Dark Queen's official jobs and lack of *real* jobs. I wanted to be hauling luggage. Which was stupid.

I realized I was bored. And that made me grind my teeth even more. I was the DQ. I should be able to do what I wanted. But I couldn't. I watched them drive away to the airport, leaving me safely in my quarters. Frustrated, I decided to eat a snack. A dozen eggs and big bowl of oatmeal sounded good. I needed the protein and complex carbs. Maybe I'd put a pile of sugar on the oatmeal.

They were back at the inn by the time the vamps woke at sunset, and we loaded everyone into SUVs and headed to the airport. There were hungry vamps in the two leading Suburbans—Kojo and Thema, Koun, Tex, and their human breakfasts. I still had to deal with the whole "Kojo and

Thema drinking but not sharing blood for healing" thing. In the middle SUV were Bruiser, the Younger brothers, and me, all of us heavily armed in case we were attacked on the way to Asheville. Monique Giovanni, still unconscious and securely shackled, and her guards rode in the fourth vehicle. In the last vehicle was the remaining luggage, things everyone forgot to pack and just *had* to have. The five-vehicle caravan wove down the hilly roads. It would be a miracle if the Learjet didn't fall out of the sky with the weight of us and all the stuff.

Except we didn't board the Lear. When we stopped, it was in front of a bigger aircraft.

Bruiser said, "It is a PC-24, Pilatus charter jet. It's big enough to carry us and all of our luggage. And it is almost as fancy inside as your Lear," he added. "Go on. Check it out. We'll wait."

I climbed the outside flight stairs and stepped inside the hatch. A human met me there and flinched only a little when he saw my furred and muscular self, all broad shoulders and knobby knuckles. And all the weapons. I did look kinda scary, so I didn't fault him for it.

"Dave Hines," the man said, bowing his head slightly— probably in lieu of a handshake with weird-looking me. "I'll be your captain on this flight." He was about five eight, with straight black hair all of an inch long, dark skin, and almond-shaped eyes with epicanthic folds, likely of a mixed ethnicity. I liked his self-contained calm. He seemed like someone who would handle himself well in an emergency, which was a good thing. Pilots on my jets tended to meet danger in firefights. "I'll introduce the flight crew to you when you are all assembled."

"That works," I said, and then I drew on my children's home background and said, "Pleased to meet you."

He gestured me into the cabin, where there was beige leather everywhere, plush carpet, multiple video screens, and fold-down tables. "There are two sleeping cubicles in back," Hines said, "and a full kitchen and bath."

"Okaaay," I said, drawing the word out. "I'm impressed, Captain."

"In that case, we are fueled, preflight checks have been

done, and we are ready for the last of the luggage to be stowed and for passengers to board." He stepped into the cockpit and closed the door. Hatch. Whatever.

I looked around again and saw the fully stocked bar, Russian-style samovar teapot, and espresso machine. "Perks," I murmured to myself. I had to remember the perks of the DQ job. Money didn't buy happiness, but it did let me have pretty things. And I'd get back to NOLA way faster than I would have on my bike, and not be crowded into the Lear.

Do not want to fly in belly of metal plane bird, Beast thought. *Do not like to fly at all. Will make Jane regret flying. Will wake Jane in mud with al-li-gator.*

Yeah. I figured. But if you're really nice, we might hunt boar while we're in NOLA.

Beast perked up. *Big-boar?*

Sure. Why not.

Beast is best hunter. Will fly, but will sleep when flying.

I was laughing softly when I stepped back down the flight stairs toward the ground and the group standing there. I spotted Monique on the ground piled with the last of the luggage. Halfway down, I met Bruiser's lovely chocolate-brown eyes and said, "Nice. Very nice. I claim one of the beds in back. Captain Hines says we can board."

Monique moved. *Vamp-fast.*

Everything went slow, like cold honey.

The night shot through with the green and silver of Beast-vision as she thrust my cat sight into me. Bright. Crystalline.

Monique lunged at Bruiser. Her hands went around his shoulders. She wrapped herself around him. They started to fall.

Eli dove for the falling two. Thema and Kojo sprang at Monique.

My hand moved before I thought. Drew a nine-mil. Aimed. Squeezed. The sound of gunfire echoed in the night. Monique fell and rolled away from Bruiser. Head shot. I shot her body again as it dropped to the ground. And again. Eli, Thema, and Kojo had stopped in midcharge. The vamps were preternaturally still. Eli turned to me.

No one else moved.

Beast is best hunter, Beast said in the back of my mind.

She had drawn the weapon and fired.

We'll be chatting about this, I thought back.

Beast does not chat. And she was gone.

Bruiser spun to his feet in a crouch and scuttled back, his eyes wide and shocked.

Eli was laughing slightly, a battlefield laugh, all mocking mirth. "Go Janie."

Kojo and Thema rushed to feed and heal the Onorio. I holstered the weapon. "This is getting old," I said. "Let her die."

"But she is necessary to finding the Firestarter," Thema said. "The Consort explained all to us."

I reached the ground and toed the body. Monique wasn't breathing or blinking, her open eyes to the dark sky, her skull misshapen at the exit wound. It seemed that three silver composite rounds were all it took to kill an Onorio. Her bowels and bladder had relaxed again, and she smelled like filth to my enhanced nose. TV doesn't show the really gross parts of death.

Beast had done this, taken those shots. I never would have. There had been zero margin for error. Too high a likelihood of killing my own people. Belatedly, adrenaline gushed into my bloodstream. My heart raced.

"Another set of silver null cuffs," I said. "Everything we have. And zip ties strong enough to chain a water buffalo. And hose her off before you put her in stowage with the luggage. She stinks from losing bowel control."

I met Bruiser's eyes and could see in them an awareness that Monique had been stronger than he was. He couldn't have won a battle against her. Monique was the bigger monster. Dead monster.

Brute, who had not been in any of the vehicles that drove down the mountain, appeared at Monique's body. On his head was a striped lizard with red wings, and on his back was a neon green grindylow. He bent over Monique and sniffed little bursts of breath, nose fluid snorting across her. He turned to me and growled a warning before bounding up the stairs and into the plane.

"How did you get here, and who invited you?" I called after him. He didn't reply.

*   *   *

I woke in the small but fancy sleeping cubicle when we landed with a soft bump, engines roaring as we slowed. It wasn't yet midnight; I was human-shaped and alone on the memory foam mattress, the room small, dark, and comfy, like a puma den with silk sheets. The jet was taxiing from the runway, the vibration steady, the jet engines still noisy. Voices could be heard through the walls.

I rolled over and thought about my shifts into Beast form and half-form. Once upon a time, I had shifted forms only at specific times. Well, usually. There were one or two times when Beast had changed how and when I shifted. And now, I shifted when I was sleeping, and the pain never woke me up. When I slept, Beast was often in control. I let that thought settle inside me. Was Beast controlling the seemingly accidental shifts while I was asleep? That would suck.

Beast had given me the ability to move faster than I used to be able to. Fast enough to draw my weapon when we were boarding and fire at Monique before she and Bruiser hit the tarmac. Before the vamps and Eli could invade my field of fire. Fast and steady enough to not miss my moving target and accidently hit Bruiser. Vamp-fast.

Beast likes vampire blood, she thought.

You took and used the DNA of vamps, didn't you. Vamp blood to make me faster. Vamp blood. *Just like you took the canine DNA to get a better scent-nose.*

Jane cannot take the snake that lives in the center of all things, things that still live, without becoming u'tlun'ta. *Liver-eater. Beast is not Jane.*

Holy crap. I sat up, silk sheets *shushing* across me. *You did. You took vampire DNA. And you can . . . Can you shift at will? Can you?*

Beast cannot control sleep shifts. Beast did shoot Monique person. Beast loves Jane. Beast's angel loves Jane.

So the angel did something to us. Figures. I rolled out of bed and dressed in the same clothes I had worn onto the jet, except I put on normal battle boots. *Have you been practicing on me? What about the short time limit on staying human?* I asked her.

Beast and Hayyel tried to fix this in the time that was past, she thought, *and we failed.*

Oh goodie. A busybody but relatively unhelpful angel was helping a sentient mountain lion to *fix* my latest shape-shifting problem. *What could go wrong?*

Jane needs weapons. Killing claws and white-man guns. Jane is in danger.

Which was a different kind of answer to a different situation entirely.

I debated on the effect I wanted to have on my people. Subjects. Whatever. I was landing in possibly hostile territory, so I still strapped on the weapons I'd worn on the trip to the airport, enough to start my small war. Eli's previous instructions and comments on commanding warriors flashed through my mind. He was right. It would never be easy for me.

In the tiny lavatory, standing in front of the miniscule mirror over the small lavatory shelf, I brushed my teeth and smeared on red lipstick. I rebraided my hair. It was long and black, and this time the plait was neat and uncomplicated, a tight, fine tail that fell over one shoulder to my hip. Before I left the small lavatory, I texted Aya and told him I was in NOLA, wondering if he'd offer any info about grandmother.

He sent a one-word reply: "Thanks." Ayatas FireWind wasn't chatty with me. I wondered if he talked to his team at PsyLED or kept them at arm's length.

I had to get the vamps to safety from the morning sun and get everyone else where they belonged. And tour HQ. First time since I killed the Son of Darkness in HQ's basement. And because Wrassler and Jodi's wedding was so close, I had to make sure none of my problems would overshadow their festivities.

Looking badass in jeans, tee, and denim jacket, my chest strapped with blades and three semiautomatic handguns in a harness, I left the sleeping nook. The main area was empty, smelling of vampires and anxiety. The jet's door was open to the night. We had landed at the commercial airport instead of the private one, where we kept the Lear and the helicopter. A bigger plane needed a longer runway. Right. Warm, sticky-wet air blew in from outside.

It smelled of burned jet fuel, auto exhaust, and the salty water from the Gulf of Mexico. And that distinct, old-city scent of urine and spices and coffee and people and sex and urgent energy mixed with the slow lethargy that was New Orleans.

This city wasn't truly home, not like the mountains. But still. It was another kind of home. I stood in the open doorway, watching as Eli and Bruiser directed the vamps and the humans into specific vehicles and loaded the luggage according to some plan they seemed to understand. Without my input.

It hit me. This was a trip not only for a wedding, and to discover what we could about Sabina and Leo's body, but for discovery and introspection and friendship. And to establish that I was the Dark Queen, Blood Master of Clan Yellowrock, and interim Master of the City—all jobs I had tried to get out of but that no one I considered trustworthy wanted. Eli looked up at me, standing at the top of the stairs, a perfect target. He frowned, and I started down, out of the silhouette of cabin lights, while he scanned everything around us.

My feet rattled the metal stairs as I descended. I might have to fight here. I might even die here. But I would never do it alone. I'd be with the people I loved. And this time I was healthy and whole, and had hope that my funky shifting problem might have a solution, some secret that Beast and her angel might have firmly in hand. Paw. Whatever. I'd have Bruiser, Eli, and Alex. And my clan. This could actually be fun.

Seven vehicles were parked nearby, all armored, all belonging to HQ. Without discussion, Bruiser had taken over as if he was my primo as well as my Consort, and was directing how everyone would travel. This stuff was vital decision-making but boring, and everyone here knew I hated the tedious stuff. Not having to be in charge of vital minutiae was another Dark Queen perk. Go me, seeing the positive.

Eli and Bruiser tossed a heavy bag into the back of an SUV. I had ordered her to be hosed off, but even from here, the bag smelled of blood and feces. Monique in a zippered duffel. Brute growled at it, and Bruiser stopped and looked from the werewolf to the body bag.

When I reached the tarmac, I held myself high and with confidence. I was, after all, the Dark Queen. It was time to start acting like it.

"Tex, Alex," Bruiser said, "please take the dogs, the were-wolf, the lizard, and the majority of our gear to Janie's personal residence." That was my freebie house. "Secure the premises and verify channels of communication. Then I would like Tex to join the rest of us at HQ."

Eli said, "With Alex at our house and me at HQ, we can verify and secure channels, can look over current protocols, run a scan for surveillance, and make sure all electronics there are up and running and integrated with HQ and the other clan homes." He glanced at me in my human form, my belly growling from the unplanned shift. "There's plenty of meat at our house, Janie."

My mouth watered. "Bacon from Cochon?"

"I ordered a delivery of andouille, tasso, bacon, and a couple of capicola."

Capicola were whole pork shoulders cooked Italian style. Best meat ever.

"And the usual roasts and steaks and some smoked salmon," he said. My mouth started watering, and Eli chuckled. "And normal groceries for the less carnivorous."

Bruiser said, "Kojo and Thema, gather your gear. You are guests at HQ. I have issued orders for Wrassler to find you a safe room there."

"We would prefer to stay with the Dark Queen," Kojo said.

"You are not her scions," Bruiser said. "You chose not to swear to her. We could put you up in Acton House, the Mithran boarding house, but you have no blood-servants to feed upon." Bruiser's tone had gone from primo precise to the compassionless tone of someone bringing down the full weight of truth and the result of lifestyle choices upon their heads. They were unwanted guests. We were being nice, but on our terms. "In the Mithran Council Chambers, there are a few masterless humans who will likely offer themselves to you."

Kojo's face fell. Thema turned black angry eyes on me. Once upon a time, I might have smiled at her or shrugged to show at least a little caring. But I was the DQ. Their fealty and loyalty had been temporary, and that time had passed. They were currently unsworn. Living in my territory. Drinking from humans who were sworn to me. They were tolerated, not welcomed.

Plus, I thought, at HQ, there would be someone to keep an eye on them, and they would not be close enough to present a danger to the rest of us. Unsworn guests, guests who had not been bled and read by my most trusted Mithrans, would not be allowed to live with me.

"Koun," Bruiser continued, "take the body in the bag to HQ. You will place the body, with the null cuffs and strips still in place, in the scion room, lock it in a cage, and train a security camera on it. There is something about the body that made Brute uneasy, so I'm not taking chances. Then you can ride back with My Queen to our home. There are two safe, windowless rooms in the attic for you and Tex."

"And who will feed us while we guard our queen?" Koun asked. "There is no room in the house for our blood-servants."

Bruiser glanced sidelong at me. "While we were vacationing, we arranged all the necessary permits with the Vieux Carré Commission, and we have created a gate in the brick wall between the former Katie's Ladies Bordello and Jane's personal residence. With the permission of Katherine, the Master of the City of Atlanta, our humans will stay there and will have a chef and a housekeeper to look after them."

Tex shrugged easily in agreement. "Good by me, hoss."

Koun inclined his head. His pale skin and black and blue swirling and geometric tattoos made him look dangerous, but it was the expression in his pale eyes that told the true tale, a violent and primitive hunter and warrior who loved war and fighting. And because he had lived so long and lost so many, he no longer had anything left to lose. Yet, he had appointed himself Chief Strategist of Clan Yellowrock, a battlefield promotion that I had confirmed. And he had sworn his loyalty to me.

"This is acceptable to me," he said. "But we will need more Mithrans and therefore more blood-servants to protect the houses, the grounds, and the Dark Queen." He

gave a small smile. "Our queen is strong-willed and difficult to control. She will inevitably get herself in trouble."

"Say what? Me? Get myself in trouble?"

Eli said sadly, "Babe . . ."

Koun, that small smile still in place, bowed his head formally. "With your permission, I will choose an additional
number of Mithrans, their blood-servants, and human warriors from headquarters to stay temporarily in the old bordello."

"As the chief strategist suggests," Bruiser said, still in
primo mode, but this time with an answering small smile.

"Consort." Koun bowed low. "My Most Royal Queen,
Your Majesty." He stood upright, his pale eyes glinting
with sly amusement. "You have my thanks, my loyalty, and
my service."

Clearly he was messing with me. I snorted, got in the
SUV Bruiser directed me to, and strapped myself in, the
Benelli across my lap. I stared out unseeing across the air-
port, a plane landing as another taxied for takeoff.

I wasn't very likeable. Or charming. Or beautiful. I sure
as heck wasn't very royal. And yet I had all these great
people around me. I must be doing *something* right, however small. So maybe . . . Maybe I could do this. And if I
did everything just right, I might get to kick some vamp
butt, and that might make it all worthwhile.

With Kojo and Thema trailing us, Eli and Koun preceding
us carrying the body-duffle-bag, dripping a little, and Bruiser
at my side, we climbed the steps toward the bullet resistant
airlock at NOLA vamp HQ. At the top of the stairs, I turned
and looked back over the city that had become mine. My city.
Because I was master of the city whether I wanted it or not.

A dense fog was rising from the Mississippi close by. It
haloed the street lights, blurred neon lights, and obscured
the low buildings of the French Quarter. The low clouds
muted the sounds of traffic, the strains of jazz and blues
from the bars and restaurants. Moving car lights were magical little globes of glowing fairy mist in the heavy air. The
smells here were water, water everywhere, coffee, liquor,
fried food, heavy on the spices. Yeah. A different kind of
home from my mountains.

A small, snowy white owl, like something out of Harry Potter, soared along the street, wings flapping once, silent as death. A moment later it disappeared. A small animal screeched in agony. NOLA didn't have snowy owls. It wasn't cold enough here, especially in the fall. It felt like a portent or an omen. "That's not creepy," I said. "Not at all."

Eli chuckled that dry, emotionless sound that meant nothing funny and nothing good. Together we turned and went on up the stairs.

The front entrance system of the council chambers was unassuming on the surface. We stepped through the first "glass" airlock door and faced the second set of glass doors, more glass to either side. All of the glass was far more than it appeared. It was triple-paned polycarbonate bullet-resistant glass. It was strong enough to stop most ammo up to a small rocket. It would now take a lot more ordnance than most gangs, rogue vamps, and blood-magic witches had around to get to us.

The outer doors locked behind us, securing us in what amounted to an airtight, see-through cage, with steel supports and structural armor in the ceiling and floor. We'd been bombed here once. We'd learned from our complacency.

Thema and Kojo, not knowing what to expect when the doors whooshed shut, tensed and crouched, hands on weapons. The scent of vamp, floral and herbal, rose from them on the air. Neither was breathing; neither was moving but for the flash of dark eyes. Not vamped out, but ready for anything.

I watched through the glass into the foyer, recognizing the security measures as Cowbird Protocol was carried out. Cowbird meant that we weren't just worried about attackers from outside but were possibly in danger from bad guys already inside HQ, and I was bringing more unknowns in with me. Four security guys approached the airlock doors, forming a semicircle with small subguns drawn and pointed directly at the doors. Wrassler peered out from the secondary video and security control nook off the foyer and met my eyes, assessing not just expressions and weapons, but body language and those subtle indicators of trouble. I lifted a single finger to him, and he ducked back into the small room.

When he and the other guy watching the entrance on security cameras were satisfied that we were welcome, were present under our own wills and not compelled, the inner doors would open. If security wasn't satisfied, we would be asked to remove all our weapons, empty out all pockets, lift our shirts, and remove our shoes. As it was, the doors swished open, and we were allowed to walk through high-tech metal detectors built into the walls. A silent alarm went off inside HQ, registering the total amassed weapons as we were each scanned.

Despite the alarm, Wrassler left the alcove, limping slightly on his prosthetic leg toward us. He was dressed in a dark charcoal suit and dress shoes, not the dove gray suit of Leo Pellissier's blood-servants. He approached Thema and Kojo and said, "All guests wear trackers while in HQ." He held out black silicone bands, each with a small crystal face. "Your left arms please."

Someone must have warned them of the procedure because both of the guests extended left arms. Wrassler locked the tracking bands into place and moved back. Twelve feet away, he stopped and stood still as if waiting for something.

I started to move toward him, but Bruiser took my hand, stopping me. "Wait," he whispered.

I took in the foyer, which was different now from before. There was still a lot of white and gray marble and ornate woodwork. But now, instead of the Pellissier crest inset in the gray marble floor, there was a simple six-foot-diameter brass circle with laurel leaves like my crown, an image of the Glob in quartz, a brown marble feather, and a puma fang in white marble. The emblems were the same as on my standard and said everything there was to know about me. My crown. My power. My city. *Whoopie dang do.*

The armed guards stepped backward into shadows. From all the open hallways in every direction, and down the curved stairway leading to the next floor, vamps and humans began to arrive, walking slowly in step, almost like some kind of dance. A dozen of them. More. And behind them even more. They gathered in the foyer, shuffling feet, clearing throats.

Vamp scent gathered with them, hanging on the air,

spicy and hot like peppers and allspice and cloves mixed with the floral of funeral flowers. A top note of sex and blood rode above the scents, cloying yet bright and sharp. I saw my clan members, people I loved and trusted, and others I kept closer than friends because their trust was questionable. So many people, every single one in party gowns or tuxedoes or black suits, which made me clench up with something unexpected and unfamiliar—a sense of being woefully underdressed in my jeans.

Wearing dark red to match her hair was Shiloh Everhart Stone, a vampire witch and my BFF's niece. Shiloh's primo, Rachel, wore a matching shade. Jodi Richoux, Wrassler's fiancée and her partner at NOPD, Sloan Rosen, wore NOPD dress uniforms and black dress clothes and stood beside Wrassler. Deon, Katie's former cook, and now one of the Council Chambers chefs, wore a green spangled tux. He blew me a kiss when he entered. Katie's former ladies from her vamp bordello entered: Christy, Tia, Ipsita, Rachel (with Shiloh), Indigo, Najla, and even Bliss—aka Ailis Rogan—who was learning how to be the witch she had always denied being. All of them were my scions, my clan members, and my friends to one extent or another. All of them were people I was sworn to protect.

Behind them pranced Gee DiMercy, my Enforcer, a less trusted confidant. He took a place at the far left. He was a glamoured Anzu, and he had Longfellow perched on his shoulder, the flying lizard's striped tail wrapped around the man's throat. Brute stood at Gee's knee with a grindylow on his shoulder—Pea, or Bean, or maybe Sprout. They were impossible to tell apart.

Standing to the right of Gee were members of NOLA's other clans, vamps and humans I knew. I totally had not expected this, whatever this was.

There was Bettina, the leader of Clan Laurent, a woman who exuded sexual attraction. With her were two of her scions and several humans. Innara and Jenna, the *anamchara* Blood Masters of Clan Bouvier, were present with Roland, their heir, two scions I vaguely knew, and six humans. Brandon and Brian Robere, the Onorio B-twins, both wearing black tuxedoes, looking like sex on sticks, were clearly standing in for Grégoire, the master of Clan

Arceneau. Blondie was currently fighting duels in my name
in Europe, but he'd be here soon. Entering last was Clan
Master Ming Zhane, her black hair up in a braided ornate
bun I could never hope to replicate, wearing a black-gold-
and-scarlet robe. She was petite and delicate and beautiful.
Ming had been declared true dead, had been found, rescued, and brought back to full health. Her clan had been
reinstated by Leo and funded by me before I left. In vamp
terms, that meant she owed me not just fealty but an ongo-
ing boon, which in vamp terms meant anything I wanted or
needed.

Behind the clan Blood Masters stood Ernestine—
Raisin—who ran HQ finances. She shuffled in, looking irritated and sour as always. The ancient blood-servant was
so wrinkled she looked a bit like a mummified Shar-Pei
puppy. Behind her came the working staff that kept the
chambers running: cooks and cleaning crew, security
guards, IT guys, the eight remaining Tequila and Vodka
Boys, Derek Lee's security teams recruited directly from
the military. There was Larry, Leo's former valet, and
Quesnel, Leo's wine steward and sommelier. There were
people from housekeeping, groundskeepers, kitchen help.
Humans who had been sworn to Leo and who had stayed
on here after he died, keeping the place running until the
city had a new MOC who wanted to do business out of
NOLA again.

Dozens of my people walked into the large foyer, slowly
assembling. Thema and Kojo faded behind us off to the
side. My first thought was that they were cowards. And
then the energy of the crowd rose, biting and sizzling,
sharp as frozen knives. My skin crawled and jumped, muscles quivering. I had felt this before. It was . . . *Holy crap.*
This was a *gather,* and not one a Blood Master had created.
I had no freaking idea what to do. Bruiser's hand was the
only thing that held me in place. The word *coward* wasn't
lost on me. I glanced at him, and his face was solemn, made
more so by the dark beard.

Except for Wrassler and Bruiser (and Kojo and Thema
edging to the back of the foyer) all the people crowded into
the huge foyer looked at me. They bowed their heads and
knelt, dropping in waves. Koun and Eli dropped the bloody

body bag and knelt. Brute, the werewolf, stretched out on the cool marble. Gee gave an elaborate court bow, his head nearly at the floor. The sounds fell away, apart from the shush of fabric and the breath of humans. Silence spread through a space that had always felt too large and drafty and now felt entirely too small and claustrophobic. This was why the foyer was so dang big. It was also a greeting room. A *gathering* room.

When he was sure I wouldn't bolt, Bruiser released my hand and accepted a small gobag from Eli. From it, Bruiser pulled out *le breloque* and placed it on my head. Instantly it did that snap-into-place thing, but this time it was so tight and hot against my skin that it was close to blistering me. Bruiser handed me the gobag, and inside I felt the energies of the Glob. He may not have expected this, or planned for this possibility, but he had my gear with him and he knew the proper protocols. He knelt at my side, and I pulled the magical weapon from the bag. It was vibrating in a way it never had before.

Inside me, Beast purred with delight at the *gather*.

Wrassler was still standing. He said, "Blood Master of the City of New Orleans, Dark Queen of the Mithrans. Welcome to the Mithran Council Chambers. We are yours to command."

Crap in a bucket with toe jam.

All the confidence about me being able to do this fled. I thought I might hurl. My palms were sweating. And then Derek stepped out of the security nook. He didn't kneel, and his face wore an expression that said he'd shoot me before he knelt to me. I didn't blame him, not one bit. And that look helped to steady me.

I could try for vamp formal, but I'd fail. So I would be myself, probably breaking some long-standing vamp protocol. I was best at being a little offensive. "Holy moly, y'all. Stand up. Really. Stand up. I want us to see each other."

Totally confused, they stood. Wrassler looked across the gathered, and I realized he had probably been making them practice the etiquette of the *gather* for weeks, knowing I was coming back. As usual, I had messed up the planning committee's arrangements. Ming of Mearkanis lifted a black, well-shaped eyebrow as she stood. Beneath the white face paint, she might have been smiling ever so slightly.

"Okay, here's the thing," I said. "Grégoire or Katie or Edmund Hartley should have been your MOC. One of them *would* be if this hadn't happened so fast, if there hadn't been war in Europe, if EuroVamps hadn't come here to fight, and if Katie hadn't been sent to rule Atlanta. So you're stuck with me until Eddie, the emperor of Europe, makes up his mind about being the ruler of NOLA as well as emperor. Between now and then, I'm honored to be the DQ and the MOC. But"—I took a deep breath, feeling oxygen deprived—"as you know, I got no idea what I'm doing."

Everyone laughed as if in agreement. My reputation of hitting first and talking later was well known. With the laughter, the energies rose and the Glob was suddenly so hot I had to shift it to my other hand, back and forth.

"I'm just Jane Yellowrock. The same person I've always been. I'll be depending on each of you to do your best job and to handle problems according to procedures already established. If you have problems, you know who to take them to. If you need something, you know who to ask. So just go on like you always have. I . . ." I stopped and looked around at the earnest faces, male and female, all races, and all united by blood that I couldn't share with them. Of them all, I was the outsider. And then Ming smiled, a human smile, small and . . . *holy crap.* Kind. Tears pricked at my eyes. "I thank you for the energy, the power you have shared tonight. I am energized and full of hope. I honor your faith in me. I honor each of you and the job you do keeping NOLA up and running and vamp central open and safe."

Someone snickered. I had said *vamp central*, not the proper title. And meanwhile, the Glob was even hotter, absorbing the energy in the room. Bruiser held up the hanky he always carried, and I wrapped the Glob into it like a potholder.

I had a rep to uphold. I should get back to that one.

"We all have jobs to do until Edmund and Grégoire get back home for the coronation. Until some vamp becomes the new fanghead MOC." I grinned at them and said, "Until then, if anyone needs their butts beat, we'll be sparring in the gym at some point in the near future. I may not be a vamp, but I'm fast, I'm sneaky, and I'm powerful. And I always win." I let them think on that one for a while as I met eyes and watched people react.

"Wrassler," I said, "we need a quick security meeting ASAP. Extra guards on the grounds. Deon, if it's your shift in the kitchen, I am *dying* for a real New Orleans fried shrimp po'boy and a good local beer."

"You got it, Queenie," Deon said, his island accent deliberately stronger. "One of the best po'boys ever made will be delivered to wherever you are in twenty minutes." He looked around and put a hand on a hip. "And heavy hors d'oeuvres will follow for everyone else. We have been cooking . . . *food* . . . allllll day. Bismark and Coco? To the kitchens, ladies." He snapped his fingers, both hands, the sounds sharp as blades clicking. "We have a feast to get out."

I smiled when Deon winked at me and sashayed away. Two men followed him, and I had a feeling that Deon was making new friends. That was good.

"That's all, folks," I said. "Ummm. As you were? And all that stuff? And maybe someone should open the bar? I see you got all dressed up for this, sooo . . . let's have a party?" That felt right. I raised my voice, *"Laissez les bon temps rouler*, people. Turn up the music and let's dance!"

And with that, the energies fell. The *gather* released its hold on all of us.

I tucked the Glob into the gobag and turned to Koun. "Toss the body into a cage in the scion room, quick update and debrief in the security room." I pointed at the mess on the floor below her body bag. "You might want to call housekeeping for a cleanup. She's leaking. Then let's join the party."

Koun had a strange spark in his eyes, something I hadn't seen before. Softly, he said, "As *My Queen* commands." It was an unusual emphasis on the words, but not something that seemed to matter to anyone but him.

CHAPTER 7

Leo Had Been Playing the Long Game

The music pumped through HQ's speakers, starting off with NOLA favorites, the Neville Brothers, homegrown musical heroes. It was good music, even when Eli turned the volume down for the quick security briefing. He gave an update on what we were facing and the security changes expected for the upcoming wedding. I got a chance to hug Wrassler in congratulations of his nuptials, and though I wasn't a good hugger, he was. Bone-cracking good.

When the meeting was over, I let Eli help me off with my weapons—because a queen never did that sort of thing alone—and I was ready, way more ready than I even knew, to party.

While I was still being deweaponed, Deon entered with a wooden tray covered with newspaper and brown paper napkins. As if it was an offering to a queen, I sat and accepted the po'boy and a beer. I bit in. Flavor flooded my mouth, spicy, greasy, shrimpy, the best spicy mayo, and—oh my gosh—Louisiana had the *best food ever.* I was in love. I chewed and swallowed and ate some more. After months of worry and uncertainty, I began to relax. Eli turned up the volume, the music going louder, thrumming through me as I ate the entire po'boy and finished off the beer before wiping my hands on the warm damp towel Deon offered me. I stood, grabbed Deon, and kissed the top of his head. "Dude, that was a tiny bit of heaven."

"I live to make you food," he said, his face soft and full of joy. "I'll make you another. You're too skinny." He started to leave, and Joe Bonamassa riffs slammed through the speakers so loud that they vibrated the walls. Deon stopped and looked back at me. "Wanna dance?" His hips shot to the left and he spun, one hand out.

Without looking back at Eli and Bruiser, I said, "I *always* wanna dance." I took his hand and thrust my hip forward, dropping it twice, belly dance moves I had practiced often while trying to control my shifting, hoping that physical activity would help my lack of control. It hadn't. Dance was just for fun, it seemed. I danced after him, letting him lead me out of security and down the hallway, toward the party, and also toward the kitchens, where he left me with a kiss on the back of my hand before wrapping my fingers around a fresh beer.

I drank the beer and wandered into the crowd in the ballroom. Alcohol did nothing to or for me, most of it cleared out of my system by skinwalker energies, but dancing? Dancing did what beer never could. Dancing freed me.

I *moved*, my whole body like a snake on steroids. I had missed this, the roar of voices, the smells of food and party. I was dressed for travel, not dancing, and at some point in the next few hours, I removed and lost my denim jacket and my boots. I ate another sandwich. Or three. I drank another beer or three. I danced until the misery was gone, boogying to Roddy Rockwell, gliding to the raw tones of Joe B. and Beth Hart. People were dancing in the hallways, the foyer, the reception rooms, the gym, everywhere I went. I danced with multiple partners in small groups, in big groups, with Ming and then with Bettina, with Wrassler and Jodi; the man had eyes only for the woman he loved, and Jodi was glowing. I even danced with Derek, mostly by yanking him into a Latin beat—and that man could *move*. And I danced alone.

Mostly, I *danced*.

I caught sight of Eli and Bruiser from time to time, checking to see that I was safe. Other times, a security guy would wander past, smiling and nodding, keeping an eye on Queenie. It was cute, since in half-form, I was pretty sure I could take them all. Of course, in human form I was too tall, too skinny, and had too few muscles to fight fairly and probably would have to resort to sneak attacks.

Arms over my head, doing chest lifts and hip figure eights, I danced into the scion room to check on the dead body of Monique Giovanni on the floor of the silver cage. Dead. Deader than dead. I danced into Leo's office, which was empty. Not something I needed or wanted to see or think about. I danced into the reception room and ate some smoked salmon on toast points. When I was sweaty and tired, my legs quivering with fatigue, my muscles loose and exhausted, I danced back into the security room and up to Bruiser, my arms up, my hips popping and swirling, my spine and belly a continuous roll up and down. He was sitting in a swivel chair, his beautiful hands curled on the arms. I took his left hand and pulled him upright and close.

"Dance with me, Consort," I murmured into his ear.

His arms went around me, pulling my own hands back behind me in a move from a tango.

"As My Queen commands. As my only love demands." He drew me close, and his free hand splayed across my spine, pulling me against his hips. He was aroused, pressing into my belly.

"Yes," I whispered.

Together we danced out the door. My eyes closed, feeling the beat of the music, the demand of the rhythm. Bruiser's lips touched mine. I wrapped my arms around him and pulled him tight to me.

Somehow we ended up at the lower entrance. And inside a limo. Hands and arms and bare feet and tongues and naked flesh. And then we were in the freebie house, wrapped in a blanket I didn't remember seeing and inside my bedroom, the door locked behind us.

We fell on the rug beside the bed, a new rug I didn't remember, the pile so deep it was a pillow.

Mate, Beast thought. She pulled Bruiser's Onorio magic out of him and into us, a sex magic that smelled of jasmine and oranges and cloves. It quivered through me, through us, and lit up the world.

And Bruiser was inside me. And the world outside of us disappeared.

I woke around five a.m., in the bed, after a too short nap. Oddly, I was still human shaped, which made this the longest time I had been human in quite a while. Six hours? That was excellent. I was alone. Sated. Satisfied. Hungry. The crown was loose, thank goodness. I rubbed the bruises on my skull from sleeping in it. Rain was a soft patter on the windows, and it was still very dark out, the rain and heavy clouds holding off the dawn.

I slid from that splendid mattress, my head hitting the antique boxing gloves Bruiser had given me, gloves so stained with ancient sweat that they would forever smell of my love. My feet hit the rug we had rolled around on. And I remember the unimportant words he had spoken.

"The rugs are like the rugs at the inn, Tabriz tribal rugs, from my private collection, in perfect condition."

"You own rugs and wine and Harleys."

"And I am owned by you."

"I like rugs. But the sheets feel better."

"As my love wishes."

After that, we had finished the night on the bed. I was tired and sore and felt fabulous. The sun was graying the night through the windows. On the air, I smelled bacon and other wonderful meat. I stood and stretched, muscles aching in ways they hadn't in ages. I hoped housekeeping figured out they needed to change the sheets again. I smiled at the memories.

It was time to meet a new day. New problems. I opened the closet to see that all my clothing and gear had been unpacked. Hanging there were the work clothes I had left behind when I ran away. Black suits. The clothing Leo had paid for . . .

The joy of the night fell through my feet into the floor with a crash. I had a trip to a cemetery to make. To Leo's grave. I had been to the mausoleum once before, not too long after he died, hoping to feel something—anything— from Leo inside his coffin. There had been nothing. He had died, and nothing in the timelines had shown me a different possibility.

I took a deep breath and forced myself to think that through clearly. *I am going to Leo's grave.*

I put my crown on the closet shelf and stumbled to the shower to wash the dancing off my feet and sweat off my body. While we were in the mountains, someone had remodeled the bathroom. It was all sleek white marble and mirrors and lighting that made me look fabulous even without makeup. The shower water was strong and hot, and I leaned back against the cool tile, letting the water beat the soreness out of me and wash the dancing sweat from my hair.

I didn't look to see it, but the water reminded me of time suspended in water droplets, showing me options and possibilities, a timestream of the future and the past. The potential results of every move, every decision. A liquid minefield of failure with few droplets showing success. And I remembered the timestream where Leo died.

I had hated him. I had feared him. I had respected his abilities to hold his violent people in a static form of peace and weave a future that might bring true peace between all the paras and the humans. Some small part of me had respected that ability to instigate and then keep all the machinations and loyalties and games straight.

And he had died. A million times in every water droplet. And in reality.

When I opened my eyes, the water was just water. No timeline. A memory.

I hadn't tried to bubble time or slide around in it, changing the outcomes of actions. I didn't know if I still had that ability. I hadn't tried to see the future since I came out of the rift, healed from the cancer that timewalking had brought me. It was better this way.

When I left the shower, wrapped in a soft black robe someone had hung on the shower door, my hair twisted up in a towel, Bruiser was sitting on the foot of the bed. While I showered, someone had changed the sheets and made up the bed. The room smelled fresh and all Bruisery. I smiled at him, and he smiled back a little uncertainly.

From the closet, I pulled out a black suit, a black nylon

tee, and a gold top that wrapped left and right and would be perfect to hide all the weapons I wanted to wear today. I kicked a pair of waterproof fancy leather boots with straps and buckles and ties up the sides into the floor space and held up the clothing. I said, "Whatcha think? Queenly enough? 'Cause I'm not ever gonna wear boring heels and a dress to my calves and a pill box hat."

Softly, that odd expression still on his face, he said, "You will look beautiful and frightening, as you should."

Thinking about his expression and his tone, I turned away and hung the clothing on the small hook on the door-jamb, one that hadn't been there before. Inside me, Beast padded away. Hiding. I frowned, shoved my fists into the robe pockets, turned back to Bruiser, and leaned against the closet door. Something was wrong. "What?" I demanded.

"Last night was wonderful." Carefully, he added, "Magical."

"I was there."

"I used Onorio magic. On you. Onorio sex magic. And I didn't even realize it until," he made a waffling motion with one hand, "after."

"I was there," I said again.

He smiled, a sad faint little twitch of his lips. "Onorio magic binds people to me."

It hit me. He was feeling guilty. Shamed. There was something in his body language that said he was about to bolt. About to leave me for my own good. I recognized it because I did that too; I ran away when things hit the fan. "Have you ever tried to bind me?"

His head shot up. "No. But last night—"

"Last night Beast pulled your magic out of you."

His eyes drifted away, unfocused, remembering. "Is that what happened? Is that why I don't remember?"

"Yup. I think you should try to bind me. Right now."

Bruiser's head shot up. "No. Never."

"Why not?"

"That is what Leo did. What Leo wanted me to do to you. I am *not* Leo. I will never try to own you."

"Monique wants—wanted—to bind you. Wanted to bind me. What if an Onorio can succeed where a vamp couldn't?"

"How do you know she wanted to bind us?"

"That little talk I had with her in her cottage?" I had fessed up during the night of dancing. Bruiser hadn't been happy with me talking to Monique, but he hadn't been unhappy either, so that was good. Of course, I had left some stuff out. "She tried then."

Bruiser's mouth tightened.

I gave a helpless shrug. "She was wearing null cuffs, which limited her power, and I broke her before she could get a mental grip on me. But what if she was at full power and got to me when I was the weakened one? We need to know."

He shook his head. "No."

"And if Beast tried to own *you*? The way Leo did? If Beast tried to take over and make you do what she wanted?"

"As she did last night?" His eyes fell to the floor where we had . . . His smile spread. "I suppose there are worse forms of slavery."

"No. There aren't. That would be the worst kind. So try to bind me." I crossed the room and sat beside him on the bed, taking a hand in mine. He had amazing hands, well-groomed nails, and long fingers, like the English gentleman he had been brought up to be. "Try."

"But—"

"Try. And I'll try to bind you."

"Why?"

"I discovered last night that I could participate in a *gather*. That should only be possible if I was a vamp and had shared blood with all the people there. We don't know what powers the Dark Queen really has, and so far as we know, there's never been a Dark Queen with an Onorio Consort. We need to know. Like seriously. *We need to know*." And I needed to know if Bruiser might be capable of binding Grandmother. So much I didn't know, and there was no one to teach me now that Leo was gone. Except Bruiser. And for the skinwalker stuff, Aya and our loony, flesh-eating granny.

His eyes, which had not looked at me except for swift glances, rested on my face. "You're sure?"

"You're my Consort. So yeah. We need to know what our strengths and our weaknesses are. What if, together,

we could hold off multiple mental attacks all at once?"
What if, together, we could bind Grandmother?

Bruiser slid his arms around me and kissed me. His
magic rose, this time smelling of catnip. A deliberate attempt at allure. My own magic—mine, not Beast's—rose to
meet it. The energies twined together, a warm brew of scent
and taste and happiness. They met, equal in power.

Bruiser pushed against my skinwalker defenses. It began
as a gentle pressure, then grew harder. His hands tightened,
pulling me closer. His tongue plundered my mouth. He
pulled back, his teeth nipping at my neck. But the magic
didn't pierce me. Instead our powers wrapped together.
Merged. Became stronger. He pulled away, his eyes wide. He
laughed, a rare, joyous sound. "I can't bind you."

"And I can't bind you. Feel better?"

"So what happened last night?" He patted the mattress.

"I think Beast can draw out your magics and use them
for what she wants. And last night she wanted me to have
sex. Lots of wonderful sex."

"But she didn't attempt to bind me."

"No," I said ruefully. "She used you to get happy, but I
think we were both well on the way to that anyway."

"I am your servant in bed, Jane. Never your master."

"Ditto. Now," I threw the back of my hand to my forehead like an actress in an old movie, "if you don't feed me,
I may swoon."

Bruiser gave a well-mannered soft snort. "Get dressed.
Eli has made quite the spread."

Bruiser left me sitting on the bed. "Beast?" I whispered,
knowing I hadn't told Bruiser everything. "How much of
this nonbinding thing is you and how much of this is your
angel?"

Beast didn't deign to reply. And I had a feeling that
might be a bad thing.

Leo had tried to bind me and partially succeeded, except that I had bound him as well. Eventually, I had figured
out how to throw him out of my soul home and out of my
life. Or Beast's angel, Hayyel, had given me the ability.

I wondered if Aya and my grandmother could be bound.
If not, then the *Bubo bubo* prophecy might be about *all*
skinwalkers because we can't be bound. Skinwalkers might

be all that stands between the Onorio / *u'tlun'ta* / *senza onore* / Naturaleza plan, whatever it was, and the loss of our world. I wondered if outclan priestesses knew this about skinwalkers and if that ability, that defensive mechanism, was why Sabina tried to buy a skinwalker child from my grandmother.

I dropped the towel from my hair and finger-combed it, pulling it back from my face. I tried to think the way vamps did, with layers and motivations and intents that made no sense to normal humans. It was like trying to play 4D chess: up, down, back, forth, and also through time.

There had been another skinwalker in NOLA, pictured in a now-burned mural in Grégoire's home. Ka N'vsita. Who had really brought her here? It was supposed to have been Adan Bouvier, the weather-witch-vampire who was enslaved and forced to try and catch arcenciels in a geode to work time. But . . .

Fear whipped through me like electricity. Could Sabina have found Ka N'vsita and brought the child to Adan? Had Grandmother sold a skinwalker child after all? If so, Ka? Because Ka was more pliable? Or had my father or mother refused? Had the vamps found a way to bind Ka because they had her from the time she was a malleable child? What had really happened to her?

I didn't know enough. About anything.

Maybe just as important as how she got to NOLA, had Ka and Immanuel's liver-eater met? Had they known what each other were? Had Sabina? Vamps worked and laid plans in layers, with twisted timelines, so it was possible that Soul and the arcenciel old ones did too. Somehow, someone had arranged for there to be three Onorios in New Orleans. And Bethany had made all three of them. Had she been planning for there to be three Onorios in the city? Had she planned that far ahead? Of course she had. Until Bethany died, there had also been two outclan priestesses. And Edmund and Grégoire, two of the best swordsmen in the world. And me. *The gang's all here,* I thought. Too much power in one place for someone, or many someones, not to be pulling strings. Leo. It had to have been Leo.

I stood and went to the bath, where I combed my hair and left it loose. I did my toiletries and applied a little mascara and blush, saving the lipstick for after breakfast. Back in the bedroom, I dressed and wondered where my boots and my jacket were. And my weapons. Eli had taken them at the party so I knew they were safe.

As I dressed, a final strange thought hit me. Adan Bouvier had been kicked out of New Orleans and sent back to Europe in disgrace. Later he had been working for Le Batard because some of his people were being held prisoner. Cold shivers crawled over me. Adan had owned Ka at a time when slavery had been legal. Ka was supposed to be dead. Everyone had said so. But . . . But what if she wasn't? What if she was in Monique's hull-shaped soul home?

That was stupid hope talking. But. What if that stupid hope might be true? What if Ka wasn't true dead? And . . . what if Adan Bouvier, who had been turned over to Leo for punishment for creating a magical storm that nearly swamped NOLA, was still here, doing someone's bidding?

I signed in to my laptop. Typing quickly, I created a timeline for Immanuel, Ka, Sabina, and the Trail of Tears. I had a photo somewhere of the mural painted on Grégoire's wall before the clan home burned. Ka N'vsita was the only skinwalker I ever heard of who lived as a blood-servant in NOLA. But if skinwalkers can't be bound and the vamps think she died and maybe she didn't . . . What happened to her? The local vamps said she was sent away and died. But that was gossip, not fact. Did Ka have any impact on what was happening today? Had I missed something when Adan Bouvier was trapped by a EuroVamp and forced to try and change time? Was Ka still alive and still a prisoner? Monique's prisoner. Had I missed that?

On the laptop, I found the photo of the mural and studied the vamps, all in a state of undress, some now true dead. And Ka, her face sad and lonely and closed in, as if she existed in a cage of herself.

Everything that had happened in New Orleans since I came had started with Immanuel, Leo's supposed son, who was really a skinwalker turned *u'tlun'ta*. But the layered history of Immanuel and skinwalkers and vampires had begun long before that. It had started with a Spaniard, an invader named de Allyon, who was turned and became a vampire and slaughtered the Cherokee skinwalkers by the hundreds, drinking their blood. He took over Atlanta and hid there for centuries, a secretive evil vamp.

When I killed the insane shape-shifter posing as Immanuel in my first few weeks in New Orleans, de Allyon had left the city of Atlanta to try and take over NOLA and had attacked Clan Pellissier. He'd had possession of small iron discs. I killed him. Then soon after, I went to Natchez and came into possession of pocket watches created with iron disks that had been made from the iron Spike of Golgotha. There had been skinwalker blood on the ingots. I still had some of the bloody discs. And skinwalker blood, my blood, went into creating the Glob.

The timeline was chilling. I just had no idea what it meant or what to do about what was essentially history with seemingly little bearing on today.

I texted Alex for the translation of *La Historia de Los Mithrans en Los Americas*. It told the tale of de Allyon, of his exploits, his evil, and had drawings of de Allyon and piles of skinwalkers dead and dying.

The long game.

Leo had been playing the long game against the Master of Atlanta. And because of me, Leo had won. That time. But that win had set others free to work on their own long game. 4D chess for real, with living, breathing humans, holy people, castles, knights, kings . . . and queens.

All those players included Monique and the Firestarter. I'd had an illusion-to-face meeting with the Firestarter, Onorio Aurelia Flamma Scintilla. I was almost certain Aurelia was one of the women from Monique's soul vision, but there had been others. Could one have been Cherokee? That frisson of fear expanded inside me.

Was it possible that Ka was still alive? I hadn't seen the eyes of the people in the bottom of Monique's bloody-hull soul home. Ka had eyes like mine, the yellow of a skinwalker. I hadn't thought the bound creatures in Monique's mind were important, but they might be the most important ones of all. And if Ka had been there, then skinwalkers, some skinwalkers, could be bound.

I was an idiot.

I had left NOLA when I was dying and walked away

from the game set in place centuries ago. Now I was behind, and reconnecting to New Orleans's life wasn't easy. I had to play catchup and figure out what was going on and fast. I added a request for Alex to track down Adan Bouvier's location. The nutso vamp and I needed to have a frank discussion. Once upon a time, he'd accused me of not yet tracking down his blood-servants and saving them from captivity. We had tried but never found them. So if Ka had been one of those captive blood-servants, and Monique had her, that made freeing the bound people in the hull-shaped soul home even more imperative.

Finally the smell of bacon drew me away from my research, and I went to the kitchen for breakfast. I had dithered so long everyone else had eaten, and so I was alone with my thoughts, sitting at the table, eating a feast meant to pack some pounds back on me. As I ate, Eli washed dishes, keeping an eye out the front window as an armed guard walked along the sidewalk close by the house. It was so strange to see armed security walking by, keeping us safe. Eli was also armed. Always armed.

I was guarded. That was my life now. I could accept the restrictions and the power and make something good come from them, or I could whine and run away again.

I was done with running.

As I ate the last of the pancakes, my cell rang. It was Jodi Richoux's number. I sat back in my chair and answered. "Good morning, Jodi."

"Thanks for the party last night. I had no idea you could move like that." I started to speak but she rushed on. "You screw up my wedding, and I'll skin you alive. Got it?" Before I could answer, she hung up.

As I processed that, Bruiser walked in and took the seat across from me. "Wrassler called. Two Mithrans out for a near-dawn walk near the Garden District were attacked and killed in Lafayette Cemetery Number One. Do you want to come?"

"Oh," I said, staring at the cell with Jodi's contact info on it. "That's why the threat."

"Someone threatened you?" Eli demanded.

"Jodi. Not to screw up her wedding." I pushed back my

chair. "Okay. Let's go see the crime scene, and then we can go to see Leo's tomb."

In a slow rain, water shushing all around us, Bruiser and I pulled up near the cemetery in the Garden District. It was odd how many vamp things seemed to happen in or near graveyards, but when you're mostly dead, maybe you feel at home hanging out with the other dead people.

Our security parked around us, blocking the street, and when we got out, a human met me with an umbrella and a soft-spoken "My Queen." He held the open umbrella over my head, protecting me, as if I was too weak to do it myself and might melt in the rain. Or too important to be allowed to get wet.

I held in the irritated sigh and smiled at him. "Thank you."

Bruiser joined me and took the umbrella, gesturing the armed man down the cement pathway before us. In most places in the U.S., burials were accomplished below ground, but in a few locations, like NOLA, the water table was too high to allow for the typical six-feet-under burials. Here, the graves were often above ground, making for an old-world feel in the graveyards.

Silent, we walked between family crypts, the rain puddled everywhere. It was dreary, dark, and I asked, "Is it still dark enough for us to have bodies, or have they crisped in the dawn light?"

"As I understand it, they are still intact. The cleanup crew is in a van down the street, awaiting our arrival, and we hope to get the bodies out of the light before the rain lets up and the clouds clear."

Ahead was a blood-splattered mausoleum, scarlet spray up along one sidewall, where it was protected from the rain, and down into the puddles, where it had turned the water the color of cherry Kool-Aid. The colorful water was running along the pathway and into the grass to either side. The bodies were between two crypts. Their heads were nowhere to be seen.

Bruiser and I walked up, and the HQ security who had been guarding the site stepped back.

Together we studied the bodies in the dim light. Headless vamp bodies were not a surprise, but usually the damage was caused by a sword or a vamp-killer. Here, it appeared as if their heads had been torn off. There had probably been a lot of blood on them, but the drenching rain had washed the flesh clean and pale, the bloodless hue of most Mithran vamps. The neck tendons had retracted, the blood vessels too, as their hearts pumped out the last of the blood. The only indication that they were vampires were the claws at the ends of their fingers. They had been vamped out when they died, and the nails hadn't retracted.

"It looks like they were out for a stroll," one of the guards said. It was one of the Tequila Boys, Blue Voodoo, and I was pretty sure we had danced a wild samba last night to something loud and Latin. We exchanged nods. "No visible defensive wounds," he said. "We haven't searched the bodies. Shall I check their pockets?"

"Yes," Bruiser said.

Blue Voodoo did a thorough search, handed Bruiser the cells, and laid out on the ground two nine-mils, extra mags, four ash-wood stakes, credit cards, all in the name of John Smith, and a package of breath mints. He checked their collars and said, "Brooks Brothers, both of them."

Bruiser knelt and checked all the fingers against the cell's fingerprint button. None of the fingers worked.

A voice called out, "Found a head!"

Bruiser and I followed the voice through the falling rain and met one of the new security guys a good hundred feet away. He was standing over a head. It was pretty banged up, but there was no doubt it was a vamp, even with broken-off fangs, torn lips, and a broken nose.

"Anyone recognize him?" Bruiser asked.

No one replied.

"I had hoped facial rec on his phone would allow us access," Bruiser said.

"Got the other head!" a woman called.

This one was away from the bodies at a different angle. I was glad I was wearing my waterproof boots. My feet were covered with diluted vamp blood, and my pants were soaked.

This head was also a vamp, but it had taken all the damage to the back of the head. "Anyone know him?" Bruiser asked. Again no one replied. "Do you have a plastic bag?" Bruiser asked the guard. When she nodded, Bruiser said, "Bag it and bring it to the car, please. And alert the cleanup crew they can get in here."

Back in the SUV, I scrubbed off my boots with sanitizer wipes and dried off my pant legs with a cloth the driver handed me. As I toweled myself, Bruiser held the first cell over the dead head, and the phone came on. "Modern security measures," Bruiser murmured, appreciative, flipping and tapping through. "Not much here. Burner phone."

He stopped, staring at a photo.

"What?" I asked.

He turned the screen to me. It was a pic of a parchment scroll, the kind that very old, hidebound vamps used for official proclamations, demands, and invitations. There was a smear of red on the bottom that looked like a wax seal. With two fingers, he made the photo larger to read the calligraphy-style writing. I leaned over his arm and read. It was a list of addresses. The top three were the old Rousseau Clan Home, now the Yellowrock Clan Home, Grégoire's rebuilt Arceneau Clan Home, and my freebie home. Below were the rest of the vamp clan homes in NOLA.

I could smell Bruiser's fury rising. "This is an assault list," he said, his voice vamp-soft and vamp-silky.

Beast thought the power and emotion was sexy. She rolled over and showed her belly at the tone.

Down, girl, I thought to her.

She chuffed in amusement. *Is strong mate. Beast loves Bruiser.*

I went back to the scroll. At the bottom were the words "Blood Master of Melker Clan," followed by three initials that didn't show up well on the photo of the curled scroll. "Melker," I said, remembering. "Legolas's real name."

"The seal and the style of the letter itself tells a great deal," Bruiser agreed. "The initials could be SML or SNL, or even SNQ. Whoever it is, they're a Blood Master, one strong enough and old enough to use handmade paper and a wax seal for orders. He or she is ready to attack you. They are here planning against you, initials on a scroll of command. I doubt it's the ultimate power behind everything that's happened, but even an underling could be a powerful vamp." Bruiser took a pic of the pic with his own camera and sent it to Alex before calling the IT wizard.

"What?" Alex demanded. It was the snarly tone he used when he was being interrupted.

"George, here. Alex, do you have any footage we can view?"

Alex had scripted supersecret programs for hacking into private security camera systems, and I had no doubt that they were all going at full speed. "I'm in four different security companies and scrolling through as fast as my programs can. Searching for visuals of the men on any of the streets that bordered the cemetery. So far I got nothing."

"We're bringing you a vampire head and his cell phone. We need access."

"Yeah good. Bring it on."

"On the list Bruiser sent, at the top," I said, "is the address of the newly remodeled Arceneau Clan Home. It's near where the fangheads were killed." Alex didn't answer. "Alex?"

"Sending you something," he said. "It's security video. Grainy as heeeeck."

"Got it," Bruiser said when his cell vibrated. On the screen, we watched as the two vamps stopped at an entrance to the cemetery. They stood still, not talking, not moving at all. A charred, burned, skeletal creature scuttled up to them on three limbs. They didn't move. The creature reached up with its free arm and drew one down. Almost casually, it drank down the vamp. Then the other. The creature leaped the fence and so did the drained vampires, following. They disappeared.

Bruiser replayed it, both of us watching closely. "Male or female?" Bruiser asked.

But what he really meant was, was it Leo, risen as a revenant, or was it Sabina? The outclan priestess had been burned in the vamp cemetery fire. "Watch it again," I murmured.

But even after three more viewings, I didn't recognize the jerky movements of the vampire. Couldn't prove or rule out anyone, of any gender. The vamp drank down two bloodsuckers, ensorcelled them to follow, and ripped off their heads. Killing one's dinner in such a violent manner was a revenant action.

Except that the victims were not humans or clan vamps. They were enemy vamps on New Orleans hunting territory. That suggested choice and reason, not things revenants demonstrated.

As if we had shared that thought, Bruiser whispered, for my ears only, "What if it's Leo? What if he is risen and is *not* revenant? What if he is simply confused and is going to war against his enemies?"

"That assumes the crispy critter is Leo and not Sabina. And if so, what is he? Something better? Something worse? He drank SOD blood. And he was beheaded, or close enough to not matter."

"I don't know. He always played the long game," Bruiser said, echoing my own recent thought.

"So did Leo assume he would survive? Or assume he would die?"

"Both, I'm quite certain."

"We need to see the vamp cemetery," I said to the driver.

A van pulled up behind us. The vamp cleaning team had arrived to sanitize the site and send the bodies for full ID at the vamp funeral home. The rain began to let up. The cleanup crew, wearing white uniforms and face masks and gloves, raced to beat the sun. Our driver pulled away from the curb and wove through morning traffic, wipers working against the sprinkles and mist.

We stopped at a drive-through coffee shop where they made an adequate chai latte for me, and Bruiser ordered a coffee with chicory. The driver took care of the transactions. Despite the direction of our travel, I could get used to the perks of having paid servants.

Silent, sipping, we wended across the river and to the vamp cemetery.

I had never wanted to come to the burned fanghead graveyard, the charred mausoleums, the scorched destruction. *Tsalagi* of my time had not revered the resting places of the deceased. We didn't go sit at the grave and talk to the dead. But the scope of the fire that had taken place hit me hard as our vehicles rolled slowly up the road in front of the cemetery. The inferno had burned so hot that the walls of the crypts were crumbling. The metal on the statues had melted in long black streams; the marble cracked and split. The scorched ground was sprouting new grass, wild things that had self-sown. The original grass had charred into the roots, the heat glazing the sand here and there. The white shell walkways that wove among the mausoleums had been baked into quicklime by the heat of the fire, caustic and potentially dangerous. The chapel was burned to the raised foundation. Nothing was left of it except the foundation bricks and the steps.

The gate was open, and we rolled closer to the Pellissier crypt and the two SUVs parked there. Wrassler was waiting at the side of the small building where he could see us and the damaged side of the crypt. We parked and walked up to him, moving as if we were attending a funeral. For me it *was* the funeral. I had missed the real one with all the pomp and circumstance and bloodletting. It had happened while I attempted to recover on the island where he died. My short visit to his grave, later, hadn't been the same.

Wrassler greeted us with an unsmiling nod, which I returned before walking around the crypt.

This mausoleum had received the brunt of the heat. The walls were blackened char, the once-beautiful stone pitted. The door had expanded with the heat and had curved, wedged tight. The walls were intact, except the one closest to the next crypt. It was damaged. I stepped into the narrow space and dropped into a squat.

Just like Wrassler's video had shown, the blocks of the wall had been knocked inside the hole recently, long after the fire was out. Had Leo escaped, they would have been pushed out from the inside. I looked over the nearby crypt wall. There wasn't room to wield a standard battering ram. So maybe fist power, vamp-style?

I stood, pulled off my jacket, handed it to Wrassler, and accepted a heavy-duty flashlight from him. The beam was blinding. This sucker was a big, heavy, well-balanced weapon, enough to decapitate a zombie with one good blow. I almost smiled at that thought.

Bending low to the ground, I duckwalked across the rammed stones and inside, shuffling my feet through the debris on the floor to stand. There was room for only one person in the mess.

There were ashes on the floor where yesterday there had been body parts. The sun had been enough to burn them, and the smell of smoke, scorched stone, and bone dust hanging on the air brought on a sneeze. Then a few more.

When they passed, I shined the light around. Wooden coffins had been pulled from their vaults and dumped. Amaury's, two child-sized coffins, three against the far wall. I searched for the coffin with Leo's stone nameplate and found it in the corner near the warped door. The lid was closed. I shoved the coffin around, and the rank stench of scorched rotten blood hit me as the light beam played along the surface. The wood had once held a beautiful grain; now it was raised and rough where my fingers touched it.

"Jane?" Bruiser asked from outside.

"In a minute," I said.

I didn't really want to open the casket, but I had to know. I slid my fingers around the crack and found gouges in the wood, as if someone had used a crowbar on it. The lid was no longer sealed. I lifted up on it, bent, and aimed my flashlight and my left eye into the crack. The stench boiled out. The wood casket was lined with seamless metal, and there was no fluffy satin stuff for the body to rest on. There was a layer of scorched blood and char.

But there was no body. A faint shudder of shock cascaded through me.

Before Leo was interred, his casket had been filled with the blood of his enemies, forcibly bled as some kind of weird vampire tribute. That blood was supposed to give a vamp a chance to be thrice born—raised from the dead a second time—so why waste it on fabric. The blood in the bottom was dried, cooked, and so rotten that Beast shied away from it.

There were no ashes. No bones. No body.

Leo's body was missing.

I wasn't sure what I felt about that, my emotions frozen and contained, as if I held tightly to them. I opened the casket fully and inspected it with the light and with my fingers, gingerly, not touching the old blood, but moving fast, before the sunlight could set it aflame. The char in the bottom wasn't scuffed, as if Leo had moved around. There was only the impression of a body in the bottom layer of burned blood.

On the inside of the casket was a long slide latch, a way for the thrice-born to get out of the coffin if they came back with sufficient strength. This one was still latched, though badly damaged by the crowbar.

Something caught my attention. Scratches on the metal, all along the length of the slide latch. I touched them with my fingers. They were fresh, with no blood caked in them.

Something in the back of my mind whispered that vamp fingernails were tough enough to scratch metal. But Leo had been completely covered in the pooled blood. It would have been all over and under his vamp claws. These scratches were clean.

Had someone stolen his body and then staged it to look as if he had come back from the dead a second time? I went back over the entire casket and found nothing significant. Satisfied that I would accomplish nothing more, I laid the casket lid down and duckwalked back out.

The day was much brighter than when I went in, and I squinted as I handed Bruiser the flashlight. "Better see for yourself," I said.

He hesitated, then crawled into the dark hole. I could hear shuffling and Bruiser moving around. Wrassler questioned me with his face, eyebrows going up.

I shook my head. "Let him make up his mind what he's seeing."

Ten minutes later, Bruiser crawled back out. There was dust and ash all over the knees of his pants, smudged across his face. His fingers were coated with a grimy, oily, rank layer of old blood. As he stood in the sunlight, the blood flamed and was gone. His skin seemed unharmed, which was weird because I could feel the heat where I stood.

Quietly, Bruiser said, "If this is real and not staged, then Leo was awake and could not pull the latch. But I have my doubts."

"Me too."

"No blood in the scratches?" he asked me.

I nodded. "Yup. Come on. Let's check out the chapel before we leave."

Sabina, the outclan priestess, had either lived in the chapel or used it as a storage place for the relics she kept hidden in her crypt. Now, however, there was nothing left of the chapel or the crypt. The Firestarter had destroyed everything.

Like a punch to the gut, I remembered the first time I had come inside the chapel. I had been with Rick LaFleur, and we both came close to being dead. The memory of that event bled through me.

The chapel had been one long room: white-painted walls and backless wood benches in rows. It had been nighttime, and moonlight had poured through red-paned stained glass windows, tingeing everything with the tint of watered blood. At the front was a tall table with a candle and a bowl of smoking incense filling the air with the scent of rosemary, sage, and bitter camphor. There was a rocking chair beside the table and a low stone bier carved with a statue lying face-up, marble hands crossed on her chest. The stone woman was Sabina.

Bending and drawing on Beast's strength, I pushed the stone cover, and it moved with a heavy, grating sound, stone on stone. It weighed several hundred pounds, and it took work to move it even a few inches. Behind me, Rick lit the candles with his cigar lighter. Holding one, he joined me, and we looked through the narrow opening into the crypt.

There was no coffin in the bier; the stone was lined with tufted white silk and boxes. I pulled three boxes out of the narrow crack I had made, exposing a bit of parchment from a scroll. It was so old it crumbled, flaking away. I closed the box and opened the next one. Inside the velvet-lined interior was cradled the largest pieces of the Blood Cross in the Americas, the ancient wood sticks wire wrapped, shaping them into a cross.

"You would dare to steal from me?" Before I could turn, Sabina was on me, fangs at my throat. Claws tearing my flesh.

Even now, my heart was pounding. I had never met such an old, powerful fanghead.

"Thief," she'd hissed. Rick had drawn his weapon and prepared to fire. But the outclan priestess had immobilized him with her mind. He couldn't even breathe. I knew what it felt like to be held like that. The adrenaline-spiked terror.

We had survived. Barely.

I pulled myself away from the terror-memory and stared at the space where the chapel had once stood. I swallowed hard.

Then I recalled the front porch. When Rick and I had walked across it, had our boots sounded a little more hollow than the rest of the chapel flooring? I leaned over the foundation and looked into the muddy mess of standing water within the low walls. The area where the porch had once stood was wetter and sloppier than the rest. "Wrassler? You got a shovel?"

"I do. But the Dark Queen won't be shoveling this muck."

"I need the exercise," I said. "Shovel."

Bruiser and Wrassler exchanged glances, and both shrugged.

I pointed to the foundation and said, "Sit."

Amused at the dog-trainer-style command, they did.

I gave my nice waterproof boots a workout and ruined the fancy work clothes in the first fifteen minutes. From now on, I was going back to jeans and casual clothes. I really was not made to sit around and let people do things for me. On nonformal days, I needed to dress for who I really was, not what Leo and fate had made me. The men sat on the wall watching, entertained at me strong-arming a shovel and waterlogged earth.

The mud kept caving in, but I finally got below the surface of the water table, and my shovel hit rotten wood. Wrassler and I exchanged tools, and I hefted the pickax. I liked it. Well balanced and heavy enough to brain an enemy. I lifted the ax in both hands and brought it down on the wood. Putting my back into the blow. The wood split and parted. Two more strikes and water appeared, along with an underwater brick wall. The water was murky-muddy as any bayou. I stepped back, sweating but feeling really good. More like myself than in ages.

"Tunnel," I gasped.

"No mold, no mildew, no slime on the brick," Wrassler said, staring into the hole I had made. "Fire scorched the stone to the ground level, but not below it. Maybe this is where Sabina dug her way out?"

"I don't think so," Bruiser said, looking over the muddy area. "It doesn't look disturbed."

Wrassler said, "This looks like a water witch working, like in subbasement five. Maybe a *stasis* working and a spell to keep it dry. Looks as if it failed or was deliberately destroyed."

I tossed the pickax out of the short pit and asked, "Can we get some divers?"

In a sequence that was too fast to follow, the black water erupted. Something wrapped around my throat. Claws dug in. And pulled me under.

CHAPTER 8

You Got It, Legs

In a split second I knew. *Sabina*. A burned, charred husk, her claws at my throat just like the first time. I remembered the burned crispy critter who had ripped off the unknown vamps' heads.

Swimming strongly, she pulled me along a water-filled tunnel, blacker and colder than the pit of hell. The water felt thick and heavy, and my body moved through it oddly. I hadn't gotten a breath and I needed to inhale. My lungs burned. I tried to pry her fingers off, but I might as well have been gripping titanium.

I needed air. Panic built. I struggled, my body whipping back and forth. Though there was no way I could drown, because my throat was clenched shut. My stomach roiled. I might vomit and aspirate, drowning on my own breakfast if she didn't—

She yanked me up through the thick water and shoved my body high. She let go. I sucked in air. Rank, dank, horrible, wonderful air. My feet kicked, the water feeling so heavy it felt like treading in oil. I gripped my throat, coughing. Breathing. Coughing. Gagging. *Breathing*.

"Yellowrock," she rasped.

Sabina.

I wanted to ask how she got from the Garden District to here, but she was the outclan priestess. She had some sort of witch magic and training from before she was turned. There was some evidence she could timewalk. And there was magic in the water, sparking on my skin. Too much magic.

My body began to shift. *Nonononono,* I thought. If I became Beast, I might drown. My skinwalker magic rose, silver with darker motes of power. My bones snapped and popped, and something in my spine twisted in agony. But the transition stopped at half-form, a form much stronger than either of my natural forms. If Sabina came at me again, I might have half a chance. *Right. Sure I would.*

She lifted me by the throat and sat me on something. Like a beam under the water or a half wall. She let go of me, and I nearly fell, sucking in another gasp of stinking air. I grabbed on to my perch with both legs and one hand. With the other, I wiped water from my eyes.

"Yellowrock," she said again. Behind her head was a pale pink light inside a water-filled glass globe. The pinkish light came from an amulet in the bottom, and it waved and sparkled as if the water moved, though it appeared motionless.

Still gagging, the pain of the shift and the fight-or-flight chemicals raging through me, a different pain ripped into my belly. *Hunger.*

"Yeah," I said, my voice nearly as rough as her burned vocal cords. "Thanks for nearly drowning me." I focused on her. She was charred and skeletal, her eyes huge and black, her fangs down on their little hinges, vamped out. Hairless. Naked so far as I could see. Like bones covered with black cracked leather.

"I saved the relics," she said. "All are buried here, beneath the chapel, in the mud outside this tunnel." Her other hand rose from the water, gesturing at the walls of the tunnel and the mud-soaked earth beyond. Her claws were fully extended, black as obsidian, sharper than steel knives. Woven around her fingers was a gold chain, dangling with a dozen tiny charms. "You must protect them."

"Okay. But I have questions about *Bubo bubo*—"

She reached out and placed her palm on my forehead. Her fingers stretched along the top of my head. Her claws dug in, holding me in place. My vision changed.

My mind was filled with images, memories, something that might have been concepts and emotions, but all rambling and confused and demented. I began to slide off the low wall into the water. Sabina steadied me. Again I wanted to hurl as my brain spun around.

Glimpses of the Firestarter, Aurelia Flamma Scintilla, through Sabina's memories. A hard woman, a stone statue chiseled from a block of anger. The priestess wore black robes, a silver cross on her chest. A vision of the woman throwing a fireball at a group of vampires. Old memory. Old death. Old friends, burning. The stench of vamp flesh on fire. The piercing ululation of vamps dying.

A vision of Ka N'vsita, a child with black hair down to her hips. Yellow eyes. Ka, who was a skinwalker, like me. Ka, related in some way to Grandmother. Ka, who, rather than me, was . . . *sold* . . . to Sabina by my grandmother. The sound of amulets and money clinking into Grandmother's palm. Sabina and Ka, walking out of a longhouse and into a forest with the child's hand clasped in the vamp's. Tenderness filling the old vampire. Love. Protective instincts as old as time. Ka, dozens of memories of her, all flashing by. Ka, learning how to ride a horse sidesaddle as the white women did. How to dance while wearing a corset, petticoats, and a heavy dress. Standing in a witch circle, trying to work magic. Ka, grown, standing with Adan Bouvier, looking at him with love in her eyes, while fear grew in Sabina's heart at the thought of losing her.

One of Sabina's memories solidified. It was of Ka, standing with the Firestarter, Immanuel, and a blond man whose face was turned away. They stood in a cemetery with no crosses, no angels. It reminded me of the Jewish graveyard in NOLA. The women were talking, wearing clothing from the 1950s. Ka took Aurelia's hand. In the trees was an owl.

A Eurasian eagle owl, *Bubo bubo. Grandmother . . . Sabina. In the same place.*

The memories whirled again. I saw the images of a more

recent cemetery, peaceful, the moon hanging in the trees. Ka stood in the moonlight near a mausoleum in the vamp graveyard.

My heart leaped in my chest. *Ka.* Wearing modern clothing, jeans and a T-shirt with running shoes. Sabina walked out to the porch of the chapel, waiting to see what her guest wanted.

Ka looked up and saw Sabina. Their eyes met. The connection was electric. Unexpected. *Wrong.* The skinwalker rushed toward her. Tackled her. Fighting. Claws and fangs. Blood and speed. The stench of foul things and fury. Sabina had not fought a duel or hand-to-hand in decades. Perhaps centuries. But she was strong. She threw Ka off and raced into the chapel. Slammed the door and dropped the beam over the entrance.

Ka was alive. A wave of shock washed through me. Alive, or a really good illusion of her. Was that possible?

Through the scarlet windows, Sabina watched what happened next. The Firestarter appeared out front, standing on the far side of the cemetery. Aurelia raised her arms. I realized when this entire scene took place. It was the night of the fire in Leo's graveyard, eight or nine months ago.

Ka, as I had feared, was working with the Firestarter.

Orbs of flames roared out from Aurelia's hands and then in from everywhere. Fire tornadoes swirled high, fire devils, lifted on the rising wind. Trees exploded in the background. The stone of mausoleums charred and split. The statues on top of each one breaking and melting. One shattered, raining molten metal and shards of stone everywhere. She targeted the chapel. The heat like magma, so hot everything was afire instantly. The pews, the lectern, the small table. The rocking chair rocking as the flames blasted across it. Sabina. Her white robes on fire. Her hair on fire. Her skin burning.

Magic in the fire. Hatred in the fire. Curses in the fire.

Burning, screaming, Sabina slid the lid off her crypt and gathered all the relics she kept hidden there. Boxes and bags and books in sealed containers, all tossed into a larger fireproof bag and tossed into the back of the crypt even as she burned. Into the space she had made, Sabina crawled and pulled the heavy stone top over her. The fire in the chapel was cut off. Using something that didn't burn, she batted at the flames consuming her body.

I could feel her pain, hear her screams, the ululation of a vampire dying. Except she wasn't dead. She wasn't consumed.

But the heat from the burning building was growing. The temperature inside the stone was rising. She crawled through more stuff to the bottom of the crypt and felt along the base until her fingers found a small niche. Inside was a tiny metal ring. She turned it. Straining against the base of the heavy vault, she began to shove a hidden doorway open, across the floor. But even with her vampire strength, it took too long.

Heat penetrated the stone, fissures formed, fine cracks. The rock fractured, splintered, and exploded. Superheated stone shards pierced her. Again, her body was enveloped in flames. Sabina howled with pain, the sound drowned by the roar of the fire.

I was screaming with her. Her pain, my pain.

The crack in the floor widened. Sabina and the bag of relics dropped into the darkness. Hit the dirt beneath. She pulled the stone back over her.

Rolling in the dirt beneath her crypt, she put out the flames on her body. Rolling, rolling, the flames dying. Breathing hard, she pulled the crypt's stone floor closed until the metal ring in the vault's stone base clicked closed. She had told me once that she would not live through another burn. This one was much worse than the last. Sabina dug into the soil as if digging her own grave. Searching for a hint of magic. *It should be here. Just here,* she thought. *Four feet from the right corner of the foundation wall.* But the wood was on fire only inches above her. The floor beneath the stone vault and above her head began to give way. Heat broiled down.

And then she felt a tingle of magic and dug with all her might. Dug and pulled the bag of relics after her. Covering herself over with the dirt, she clawed into the earth. Away from the heat. Into the tunnel she had prepared centuries ago. The fire above was magical, burning hot enough to crack the stone foundation and break the last of the old water working in the tunnel. Water from Louisiana's high water table began to seep in and the dirt beneath her turned to mud.

There were only a few inches of water that night, but it was winter cool, and Sabina rolled in it, trying to ease the horrible heat in her body. Crying. She wept with pain and failure because she had lost Ka so long ago. Lost her skin-walker to Adan Bouvier amid proof of black magic. She had been unable to keep the child safe. "Ka," I whispered, one hand holding on to Sabina's scorched arm, the two bones feeling hard as steel beneath my fingers.

Sabina's memories fell into me again. The night the cemetery burned, Sabina buried the relics in the foundation and crawled away through the mud, even as water in the tunnel continued to rise. Then she was elsewhere and else-when. I saw an image of a human cemetery inside New Orleans. Broken stone angels were everywhere.

Sabina's hand tightened on my head, her vamp claws cutting into my scalp. Blood, warm but cooling, ran down my scalp and dripped into the dank water.

There was a vision of a letter written in a language I didn't know. But from Sabina, I knew what the message told her. Ka was alive. She had been found living in a chateau outside of Paris. The letter was official notification that Ka, an Onorio herself, had joined forces with a *senza onore*.

Together the two had burned down houses full of vampires in France not so long ago, hoping to kill Mithrans she considered her enemies. Ka had failed. The letter was unsigned but dated, only a year past. I knew who had been attacked by fire in France, as he slept.

"Edmund," I whispered. He had been attacked, and the house where he stayed had been burned to the ground. Edmund Hartley, who was the titular Emperor of Europe and my primo, in a complicated relationship engineered by Leo. More of Leo's machinations.

Betrayal is everywhere, Sabina thought at me, her words now booming on my brain, her claws digging in. *Ka, vengeance in her soul, filled with hatred of all the ones who had harmed her in her life. Ka led them to me to kill me and to steal my relics.*

"What does she want?"

Ka wants what you have. You, who are the first non-Mithran to be Blood Master of a clan and Master of a City. You, who are the first Dark Queen in centuries to live longer than a few days. If you can do all of these things, then Ka, the skinwalker who studied with Adan, who willingly swore her loyalty to Adan for so many years, while she was lost to me, believes that she can take all this from you. She is powerful and her anger has broken her reasoning.

Pain spiked into my head. Pain like an ice pick driven through my skull. Again I thought I might hurl.

Ka was working her own long game. But why attack now?

Another memory that was not my own sliced into my brain. Sabina hiding, watching Adan Bouvier and Ka. They were standing on a concrete floor set with a twelve-foot black square. Just inside the edges of the black square was a witch circle formed of wood and iron. Witch circles were almost never made of iron. The group were in clothes from the turn of the previous century, Adan wearing a vest and a white shirt and holding a sword, Ka dressed in a revealing spaghetti-strapped sheath nightgown.

Ka was gripping a narrow iron spike about six inches long. I knew instantly that she was holding a length of the iron Spike of Golgotha. She was . . . *Ka was trying to bend time.*

Adan stepped back once, still inside the circle. He stabbed Ka with the sword.

She screeched. Blood gushed from her. Betrayal and horror filled her expression.

Sabina, hiding in the darkness, tears on her face, watched as Adan caught Ka and the spike. Holding them both, he sank his fangs into her throat, into the carotid. He drained her even as she tried to fight, even as the life bled from her. Ka went limp. Yet Adan kept drinking. And drinking. In the lamplight, Ka's flesh went pale. Then ashen.

Adan laid her across the floor and cut her clothes from her, moving fast, his blade catching the light of candles I hadn't even noticed until now.

Bethany stepped from the darkness on the far side of the circle. She was naked. Adan did something with his hand, and the circle of power dropped. Bethany stepped into the witch circle, and Adan stepped out and closed it, raising the power again. Bethany lay across Ka's dead body.

I had seen this before. Bethany was starting Ka's transition into Onorio.

"You knew," I whispered to Sabina. "You knew what they were about to do, and you let it take place anyway. Did Ka even know you were about to put her in danger?"

Instantly the images swirled again. Pain pierced my skull, the mother of all migraines. I had a feeling that whatever Sabina was doing to me was bad for my brain. When the pain receded, there was a vision of the NOLA graveyard, with broken stone angels everywhere. It shifted again, and there was a vision of a pile of broken cherub wings and angel wings. They were burning. The stone flashing black and cracking.

And then there was a vision of de Allyon, a vamp I had killed. The vampire who had killed all the skinwalkers. But here, in this memory, he was facing others, their backs to me, all wearing modern clothing. This was recent as vamp timelines went. Maybe five years ago, before he left Atlanta and crossed into Leo's territory to kill the strongest vamp in the States. One of the vamps with him shifted position and I saw his face.

"Shaun MacLaughlinn," I whispered. He had been the mind-bound *anamchara* of Dominique, who had been sentenced to burn with the dawn. If he was alive at all, he was likely brain-dead at this point. "Holy crap."

"Holy. Yes. The most holy. This last you must see so that you will understand." Sabina shoved a memory into me. A blast of pain followed it, intense, flaring. "The moment I became undead. The moment when I was turned so very long ago. I share this with you." There was a bright light. Flashing white and green and intense blue. A man walked toward her, his arms out. *The redeemer,* she thought at me. *The moment I lost my soul.*

The vision went blinding. A feeling of utmost joy suffused through her and by extension, through me. *Heaven,* she thought at me. *Not gates of pearls and streets of gold. But light and dark and love and forgiveness. Heaven.*

In her memory, the man stopped, dropped his arms. Turned away. She was thrust back into her body. The light went out. Aloud she said, "Every Mithran sees this vision. This is why we mourn. Once turned, no vampire, whether Mithran or Naturaleza, anywhere has ever seen it again, even the thrice-born. Only at the moment of first death while being turned do we ever get a glimpse of heaven. And this, *this* is why we grieve. This is the cause of the devoveo, the grief that destroys our minds."

I remembered then the few times that Mithrans had told me about *fame vexatum*, the practice of not drinking to the full, not killing humans. They were earnest, intent, and full of . . . belief? Was that because of the way the first vamps were made, with the wood of the crosses and the iron of the spikes of Golgotha, and the blood of the sister of the Sons of Darkness? The death of the girl child who became the shadow of the Flayer of Mithrans? Fangheads always said they had no souls. This was why. Everything in their entire world was about three things: time and death and resurrection.

The Mithrans and Naturaleza did not have an afterlife. They could not be redeemed.

This was why they grieved. For that one memory of utter peace, forever lost.

I pulled away, processing what I had seen from Sabina's memories. I slid off the beam and nearly sucked in a lungful of the water. Sabina caught me again, holding me above the surface.

Ka had been sold, nurtured, and groomed to try and timewalk, and had been betrayed by Adan, a vamp she had come to love. And then Adan had been taken by a stronger vamp and put into servitude, catching arcenciels, trying to timewalk, and bringing storms to New Orleans. And I had interfered with those plans. Where had Ka been during Adan's captivity? Who had controlled her? What had she suffered?

The vamps had records of the Firestarter's life. The timelines of both women were full of huge holes, times and places where Ka and Aurelia might match up. And since Ka was both skinwalker and an Onorio, what powers did she have? How did she meet up with the Firestarter? And Monique. After I freed Adan and gave him to Leo?

Pain like a sword cleaved into my brain. I could feel Sabina drawing back. I had questions. Too many questions. Before my head split in two, I asked, "What relics are there?"

"Many. I have lived long and collected much. And this." She put a piece of metal in my hand and dove under the water. "No—" I started. But water flooded my mouth and choked me.

I caught myself on the slick beam. Felt Sabina stroke and kick as she swam away into the dark. Coughing, I stared around at the small space, placing where I was in relation to the light. I tucked the piece of metal into my waistband and pulled off my heavy, water-filled boots. Dropping them into the water, I grabbed the pinkish globe of light and ducked under the surface, using the light to determine which way was out. While under there, I searched for the bag of relics but found nothing on the block floor except a little sludge and my former fancy boots. I broke the surface. Treading hard in the too-heavy water, I took and expelled several breaths. Then I started swimming back the way I had been dragged, the globe lighting the way. Every stroke was harder than it should have been, as if I was swimming through oil.

The tunnel wasn't nearly as long as I thought when I had been choked. And—literally—there was a light at the end of the tunnel where I had broken through. I kicked harder.

The globe went out.

Darkness hit me, cold and shocking. The water, so heavy only a moment before, went liquid and soft, and I flailed before my limbs caught up with the difference. Breath tight, I kept swimming for the light. A huge splash altered the brightness ahead, and bubbles darkened the hole as someone jumped in, shone a light around, and focused on me.

Too-bright light blinded me. *Bruiser.* His body movements both strong and frantic, he swam toward me.

He was at me, one arm going around my throat in a drowning-swimmer save. I wanted to shout, *Stupid man!*

But I'd have to take a breath, and there was only water. He pulled me up into the light, and I breathed in clean air. Wrassler reached down and heaved me out of the water, still Wrassler-TV-strong even with the prosthetic leg and other damage.

"You're half-form-shaped," Wrassler said, midsaving yank. "How—"

"I talked to Sabina," I interrupted. "I shifted. There's an air pocket." I landed on squishy ground. Icky water flowed out of my clothes.

"No," Bruiser said from the water. Wrassler pulled him up too. Water went everywhere, cascading off of him. "I jumped in immediately after you."

"No way. I—" I stopped. Remembering the feel of the heavy, thick water. Remembering how hard it had been to swim until the small light in the globe went out. The way the water seemed to change, growing lighter, easier to move. I looked at the globe. Inside was a small pink stone. I twisted and slammed the globe on the foundation wall. It shattered. The pink stone fell out and hit the mud. I picked it up. Instantly I knew what it was. What it had to be.

It was a piece of the original chunk of rough, uncut, blood diamond, the stone that had been used to gather the death energies of the witch children sacrificed to bring the long-chained to sanity. Part of the same stone that made up the Glob.

"Jane?" Bruiser asked.

I held up a finger, not wanting to lose this thought, remembering the magic I had felt when Sabina grabbed me, that sensation of thick water as she swam. Sabina had been warping time with this amulet. With this, she had created a time bubble. I had to make sure it didn't get close to the Glob. No telling what would happen.

I pulled the metal thing Sabina had given me from my waistband. I had thought it was iron, but it was made of gold and other metals, long and slender and curvy. It was a tiny dragon creature with wings partially furled. Like a metal replica miniature arceneiel. A cold chill raced through me. I tilted the amulet to the sunlight and saw all sorts of tiny things embedded all over the dragon: small dull dark gray metal disks, tiny shimmery somethings tinged red, and some with little bubbles beneath. They were placed so the amulet looked striped and so it shimmered when the light hit it, just like a real arcenciel would. I turned the amulet back and forth, and the bubbles moved. Whatever was beneath the shimmery discs was liquid.

"Why would anyone put . . ." I stopped.

"Janie?" Wrassler asked.

Gently I touched a fingertip to a single metal disc. Power met my touch. I touched one of the reddish, iridescent, transparent things. It had a sheen to it, and magic tingled beneath it too, the touch sensation oddly, similarly iridescent.

Little bits of things I knew, had seen, or had heard about came together.

I knew what I was seeing, what I was feeling. The imbedded metal was from the remnants of the iron Spike of Golgotha. The shimmery things were bits of arcenciel scales. Beneath each scale was a single drop of arcenciel blood, which—the one time I had seen their blood—looked like molten glass.

I peeled down the waistband of my soaked pants and looked at my skin where it had rested while I swam. My flesh was dimpled and red in the shape of a flying lizard. I touched my skin. I didn't feel any foreign energies. Didn't feel as if anything had been done to me. But still . . .

"Holy crap," I murmured.

"Jane?" Bruiser asked.

"It's an arcenciel-based magic amulet." I held it up for him to see. The sunlight hit the scales, and it was obvious that most were red. Red scales. In stripes . . .

It looked a lot like Longfellow, Gee's lizard. The one he had taken from a dead vamp, whose blood it had been sipping for who knew how long. Under Gee's care, it had grown wings and gotten much bigger. It was as big as a thirty-pound dog now. Was there a connection? Coincidence? Me reading into it something that wasn't there at all?

Holy crap. Did arcenciels hatch small and wingless and grow bigger? Did they develop wings as they aged? Had sipping vampire blood brought on Longfellow's transformation? *Holy crap.* Was Longfellow a miniature or baby arcenciel? But that timeline didn't work. So maybe Longfellow was a species related to the rainbow dragons, in the way that burros were related to horses, or wolves were related to dogs?

Gee had called me little goddess. It was a similar title to the name he called the arcenciels, who could timewalk. I had once been able to timewalk. No way was I time-traveling again.

But maybe I was supposed to be able to use this some way? To do something? And the diamond in the globe of water?

"Holy crap," I griped again. "Why don't these things ever come with an instruction manual?"

I could feel the power in the metallic lizard—the same kind of energy that emanated from a crystal containing a trapped arcenciel. The kind that vamps used to time-jump, to bend time, to travel back or forward in time and remake history. I was betting that it could be used to assist in a time-jump, the way vamps did it. The spike was said to be able to control vampires. The blood diamond was powerful no matter what kind of energies it was used for. No wonder Sabina could bubble time, or time-jump. Remembering the bracelet with the jangly charms she had worn, I had to wonder what other trinkets and relics she had taken with her when she went to ground. I raised my eyes to Bruiser's and then out over the sloppy foundation and pointed to the far corner she had mentioned.

I turned on my Queenie voice, my tones stolen from Leo. "We dig there. By hand. No big equipment except to suck up water. We're looking for a burned gray bag about this big." I showed the dimensions with my hands. "If you find it, stop digging and call me. It's probably dangerous. But we need to find it before the Firestarter does."

"Is that bag why someone burned the cemetery?" Wrassler asked. "To get the bag?"

"Partly, yeah. And then someone stole Leo's body. And no. I have no idea why. But I'm going to find out."

Wrassler started issuing orders to the men present and pulled his cell to call for strong-backed reinforcements.

"Wrassler?" I interrupted. "Put someone you trust in charge here; I want you with us."

"You got it, Legs."

*   *   *

On the way home, we stopped at a Popeyes, and I got a bucket of chicken to pay for the underwater shift. As we dripped muddy water all over the leather seats and the floor, and I crunched my way through a ten-piece box of heaven, I told Bruiser what had happened. We studied the lizard amulet and discussed all the paranormal creatures who might want Sabina's relics and why. And what her buried icons could do.

"I need a safe place to keep them," I said, "away from the Glob and *le breloque*. I don't know what would happen if they all came in contact."

Quietly, Bruiser said, "Set the world on fire?"

"I doubt it would be good, whatever it is."

Back at the freebie house, Eli put the new amulets in the gun safe, and Bruiser and I cleaned up, Bruiser showering upstairs and me showering in my en suite. It always took me longer than it did Bruiser to shower in half-form because of the pelt and the long hair. It gave me a lot of time to think and to remember what Sabina had shown and told me.

The vision of God walking away from Sabina didn't match the God I thought I knew. Her vision was one of a God who punished people that had evil done *to* them. Sabina had been turned by one of the first few vampires, without knowing fully what life as a vamp would mean, perhaps even against her will, yet according to her, she had lost her chance for an afterlife, lost her chance to see heaven, beyond that one brief glimpse. Had vamps like Molly's niece, Shiloh Everhart Stone, lost their souls? If so, it was the punishment of an Old Testament God, not the "sinner can be redeemed" spirit of a loving God. So . . . maybe they were wrong? Maybe there was a way to give them back an afterlife. Like, maybe their souls were in a pocket universe somewhere, waiting for the power to either reunite with their bodies or move on. I had seen a pocket of time/space once, with a vamp and a witch stuck inside, caught in the moment of death, like a mosquito in amber. Maybe vamps' souls were like that. In some weird stasis instead of snuffed out.

The vamps could ask God . . . *Right. Sure they could.*
Did God hear the prayers of a vamp?

I sucked at being a theologian, but even theologians disagreed on this one.

I thought about calling Shiloh or Koun or Tex and asking
about the loss of their souls, but that was a weirdly personal
question. Would it be considered the height of offensive
disrespect? Probably.

When my hair was clean and braided, and my pelted
parts were finally dried off, I dressed in jeans and a T-shirt.
I didn't normally wear shirts with sayings on them, but
Alex had bought me a Mardi Gras T-shirt, silk-screened
with a drunk alligator wearing a party mask and beads,
carrying a champagne glass and a magnum bottle. A woman's foot wearing a five-inch red stiletto was sticking out of
his mouth. It was not queenly. Or fancy. The cloth was a
little scratchy. But it said something about who I really was
and how I felt today. And maybe how I'd continue forward.

As I opened the door, I could hear the guys talking in
the living room: Eli, Alex, Bruiser, and Wrassler. I glanced
out the windows and saw guards walking everywhere.
Good. Operation Cowbird was in full force. Barefoot—
bare pawed?—I padded into the kitchen and chose a mug
for tea. I picked one with an alligator on it. The sleeping
gator was upside down, drunk of course, and a naked
woman was sleeping beside him, also drunk. Vodka bottles
were everywhere. The caption said, "What happens in
NOLA stays in NOLA." It was crass. Kinda like me. And
the gator matched my T-shirt.

There was a fresh pot of tea in one of Katie's ancient
teapots from the tea room / butler's pantry. It smelled like
green tea, slightly citrusy and sweet. I filled the mug to the
top and added a squirt of lemon. It was delicious.

Eli laughed when I came out of the kitchen. The others
turned and looked at me too.

Wrassler nodded at me and gave a grin that was nearly
back to his normal grin, the one he had before he lost so
much. Bruiser, looking like sex on a stick in jeans and a
skintight tee, was on the phone and smiled.

Eli said, "Nice to see you back, babe."

"Nice to be back. Alex, I got a job for you. Track timelines of Ka's life and the Firestarter's life. And Adan's life. See if you can find where they align with Bethany's and Sabina's or de Allyon's timeline. And also see if any of them align with Leo's son Immanuel's trip to France, where Immanuel met his bride to be. And see if you can locate Adan?"

"Okay." Alex popped the top on a healthy version of an energy drink. "Why am I looking for all this?"

"Immanuel was *u'tlun'ta* long before he went to France. Which means he had been replaced way before that. The thing that ate Immanuel and took his place started out as Cherokee. And it occurs to me that he might have met Ka. And also, he probably knew my gramma at some point."

Everyone in the room went silent.

Bruiser said, "I'll call back," and ended the call. "You think that this—all of this that has happened in the past months and years—is part of an elaborate plan to restructure the Mithran and Naturaleza world. You think this is all tied together based on Immanuel's plans. But Immanuel was not capable of such layered timeline-based plots. The original Immanuel was indolent. Lazy. The replacement might have been focused and driven, but because Leo's true son had little interest in politics, his replacement would not have known anything about the political structures he was interacting with. He must have had a teacher."

"I think someone was pulling Immanuel's liver-eater's strings too," I said. "But Immanuel the second thought he was smarter than he was. He developed his own goals, which changed his master's ability to carry out the original plans. Then I came along and killed him. I think that the oldest vamps have played the long game for centuries, way before they even knew about the Americas. I think there are multiple layers of multiple plots put in place by multiple players. One or more may have been using Immanuel—and not just the family of his fiancée, as we first thought, but someone more powerful. I think finding a timeline might help us to figure out what's going on and who we have to bring down to make it all stop. It's like that game with the blocks that you pull out a block from the bottom and then put it on top, moving blocks and placing them elsewhere until someone finds a linchpin, and it all comes tumbling down. Leo said I was the wild card, the one who would shake up everything. But maybe I was never the *only* wild card. So let's see what lines up and then let me get started shaking things up again. Seems to be what I'm best at."

"And the thing you're worst at is swordplay, which you may need if this thing goes south. You need sword practice," Eli said. "You and Bruiser go to the sparring room and hit each other with wooden sticks. Wrassler and I'll go over the security preps for the wedding."

"Thanks," Wrassler said. "Jodi's afraid that with Jane in town, the whole shebang will go into the toilet."

"Hardy har har," I said.

But his expression told me he wasn't joking.

I couldn't remember where my feet went with each move. How high I should lift an elbow. How far I swept right and left before I lunged, lunged, lunged. I was clumsy, my mind on too many other things. My concentration was shot.

Or it was until Bruiser put on some Latin music. The beat thrummed through my paw pads, woke up my brain. And when Bruiser swatted my bottom as he passed by, I laughed.

He took up a position, long wooden stave high, short sword across his body. It wasn't a fighting position I had seen before except in the dueling ring. "Let's dance," he said, a glint in his eye that communicated we were about to have fun.

I mimicked his position.

"Left elbow higher. Good," he said. "Defend yourself."

Fun, Beast thought, purring, peering out through my eyes with a golden gleam I saw reflected in Bruiser's. He attacked.

The wood staves clacked, slow and careful, the sound reverberating off the bare walls and floor of the third story. Then louder. Faster. And I was sweating and breathing hard, even in this form. And it was glorious.

But vamp swordplay *hurt.* When I complained, Bruiser said, "It's supposed to. Bruises teach your mind to fight through, no matter what. Soreness teaches your body to move even in pain."

What it really taught me was that I sucked at this, even

with the faster reflexes and greater strength of my half-form. But seeing it as a dance made me more graceful. More attentive.

Beast is lithe and lissome, she thought at me. *Jane's words for Beast.*

Beast is a bruised cat, I thought back, as I barely blocked a vicious head strike.

Beast is best ambush hunter. She took over and dropped us into a crouch. Swiped Bruiser's knees, while also stabbing upward into his gut. Both staves landed. Bruiser oofed out a breath and danced away limping.

Okay, I thought. *Yeah. We* are *getting pretty good at this. I/we are better than Jane and Big-cat.*

We struck out again. And again. Suddenly we were fighting together as one, one creature with one blended mind on blended reflexes, the same way we had fired the weapon that killed—sorta—Monique.

We landed hits—*fastfastfast.* Bruiser oofed and oofed and danced away.

"It's supposed to hurt," I sorta quoted him and laughed. "Bruises teach your mind to fight through, no matter what Beast and I do. Soreness teaches your body to move even in pain."

His eyes lit up again. "You and Beast are fighting together? Good. Then I don't have to hold back on Onorio gifts either."

And that right there—and the attendant bruises and bangs and whacks and pain—taught me to keep my snarky mouth shut.

CHAPTER 9

Jane Needs Holy Water.
Go to Place of Holy Water.

"Aw," I grumbled afterward, trying to stretch out the sore muscles. We were all in the kitchen for a typical Louisiana afternoon coffee break, with attendant beignets and multiple hot beverages. No one had looked at Alex's timeline, though we each had a hard copy in front of us.

"Old school," Alex had called it when he placed the sheets on the table and took his seat. It was comforting, especially with the fire in the new fireplace burning merrily and the rain beating down. NOLA had nine months of summer, a month of fall and of spring (give or take) and two weeks of winter (but not all at once). The crazy temps were standard New Orleans fall: hot one minute, chilly the next.

He continued, "The info is mostly collated from Reach's old files. I never bothered to update this."

I sipped my tea, ate a beignet, and read the bullet-pointed timeline of Immanuel Pellissier, Leo's son of his body, the child reproduced by human means and born into a powerful vampire family. The vamp eaten by one of my kind, and replaced by an imposter, by an *u'tlun'ta* doppelgänger. And then dead by my hand, the first month I was in New Orleans. By the end of the first few lines, I was beginning to understand why I was the wild card in all of this, because all sorts of possibilities were skittering around in my mind, none of them good. I had originally thought Immanuel had been eaten and replaced while in France to meet his fiancée, but I was wrong by more than a hundred years.

- Immanuel: born in early 1800s, no exact date specified in Reach's files. Could have been sooner.
- Immanuel went upriver the first time that we know of in 1825.

I made a note. I was born in 1830. His liver-eater could have been alive when I was a child and still living among the *Tsalagi*. We could have been related. It was too bad I couldn't call and ask Grandmother if other skinwalkers were around at that time. But maybe Aya would know and tell me. He might even have PsyLED records about other skinwalkers. I had never asked him—point-blank—if there were others like us, if he knew other skinwalkers. I wasn't sure why I hadn't asked, except for that sibling thing we had going where we kept each other at arm's length while, at the same time, wanting the other closer. Stupid family stuff. I went back to the list.

- As per Reach, Immanuel went upriver multiple times before 1915. We considered the probability that he was turned in France, but it's possible that on one such trip upriver, the liver-eater returned instead of Immanuel. With Leo busy running the city, he might not have recognized the scent change in his son, or Immanuel might have been able to change that too. Scent-change amulets exist, so it's a possibility.
- According to best guess timeline, one provided by the outclan priestess Bethany (now true dead), Immanuel made his trips upriver before the first Son of Darkness was bitten by an arcenciel and ended up chained in the sub-five basement of vamp HQ.

- Ka N'vsita, sold to Adan Bouvier by her family or by Jane's grandmother or by someone claiming to be Ka's father when she was eleven, around 1803, entered NOLA around 1803–1804. She would have been born around 1790 or 1795? She was a mature woman when the B-twins "came to service."
- Ka became Adan's primo, but primos need to be bound. Conflict? Or something else?
- Ka could be Jane's relative back a long way. Cousin, second cousin, great aunt? Someone closer.
- Leo took charge of NOLA in 1912.
- George Dumas (Bruiser) was 12.
- George became bound to Leo at age 16.
- After he took over, Leo sent Adan back to France for some undisclosed evil, and Ka went with him. Or she died. Reports vary. Leo told everyone that Adan died. But clearly he didn't and they hooked back up, before Adan ended up a vamp prisoner, trapping arcenciels in a geode. (Which Jane destroyed.)
- Amelie (Immanuel's fiancée) and Fernand (her brother) were blood-servants, and Leo turned them both, wanting them to be tied to Immanuel. Both might have been directed to Immanuel by de Allyon. Or our mystery vamps who are pulling the strings in the background. Perhaps multiple vamps worked together to keep Immanuel's secret.
- Alex's note #1: When a liver-eater eats a living being, it gets the body and the memories, but Immanuel was never considered a political being. Not saying he was stupid as shit, but he wasn't known to be a genius either. Possibly someone pulled Immanuel's strings. One possible candidate is de Allyon, but he's dead, so there's that. Not like we can drive up and politely ask him.
- Alex's note #2: Three very strong vamps had primos or Enforcers that could not be bound . . . Adan, Leo, and Grégoire. Significance?
- Jane was the Enforcer. All of the primos (Ka, George Dumas, and the Roberes) were turned to Onorio by Bethany, outclan priestess, now true dead.

I rubbed my fingertips over the words on the sheet of paper, as if I could get wisdom from the tactile connection. It was interesting that we were thinking alike. If skinwalkers were so hard to bind, then how did Ka become Adan's primo? Was it voluntary? Forced? Or a relationship similar to the one the Robere twins and Grégoire share? They loved him, so serving him had always been a choice. I went back to the research.

- If skinwalkers can't be bound, what hold did de Allyon or a EuroVamp have on the male skinwalker, Immanuel, and why did he stay with the role of Leo's son for over a century?
- Jane (skinwalker) killed Immanuel (the skinwalker liver-eater), the agent of someone else.
- Immanuel dead. Jane working for Leo.
- Vamp who had been in charge of Immanuel lost his long game. Now pissed.
- Rick and Jane hooked up.

I glared at Alex, who slurped another of the disgusting-looking natural energy drinks. His lips twitched up, but he didn't look away from his own pages.

- The Damours took Molly's kids, making another attempt to bring their long-chained to sanity. Did we consider timewalking attempts as part of their blood-black magic?
- Rick and Jane had a few weeks together before the wolfpack came to NOLA.
- Gee kept track of Rick. Failed to stop the black leopard bite. Notified no one of Rick's location.
- Gee might have tried to get rid of Rick. Posit that Leo approved of the removal of Rick very early on and set things in motion for it to happen. If so, it changes lots of things because Rick then ended up partnered with Soul in PsyLED. Was Rick a gift to the arcenciels?
- Grindylow killed the biter instantly (who had already turned Rick into a black were-leopard) but

didn't kill the wolfpack right away. Why? Posit—the only one in this hemisphere who knew Rick had black panther were-taint. And they don't render judgment for killing humans, only for turning them.

- Gee rediscovered Rick's whereabouts after he was taken by the wolves, but may not have told Jane right away. Again, there exists the possibility of Leo's machinations.
- Jane went all badass and killed the wolfpack. The bitch who was their queen died.
- With Rick out of the picture, the field was free for Leo. (See above posit that Leo wanted Rick out of the way.)
- Jane claimed Enforcer status, giving Leo another hold on her.
- De Allyon's Enforcer is killed by Jane.
- First major appearance by a demon and then the Angel Hayyel.
- De Allyon made his move for world (or at least U.S. vamp) domination, attacking other vamps with the vamp plague.
- Jane killed his ass. Cut off his head. Whatever.
- Timewalking circle in Natchez.
- We found iron ingots from the Spike of Golgotha in Natchez in pocket watches. Bethany and Sabina mention the "vessel" that can hold blood—Holy Grail? Or were they being vampy, inexplicable, and referring to something else?
- First appearance of spidey vamps (with exoskeletons) was in Natchez.
- First time we found a timewalking circle was in Natchez, and that killed lots of witches.
- Le Batard came to town. Grégoire killed his ass. Cut off his head. Whatever.
- If Adan knew the arcenciels wanted to destroy vamp timelines, he might be willing to trap and use them to keep that from happening. Or he pretended to be imprisoned in order to obtain trapped arcenciels for his own purposes. Or—who knows what Leo was planning. He was a sneaky bastard.

- Ka was possibly a prisoner of the enemy, which forced Adan to do their bidding.
- Now Ka is back, along with others. Assuming Adan is back too.
- Suggest torturing Gee to get answers. Just kidding. Not really.

I ignored the last part. Some of this was history, some of these dates had already been contradicted by Sabina and by my own grandmother, but there was enough that felt right for me to not sweat the small things. I remembered that the B-twins, Brian and Brandon Robere, had once commented to me that Ka N'vsita was a "good kid" and that she died in the twenties. The Roberes were old enough to have known Ka, but she hadn't seemed to make much of an impression on them.

Gee had once mentioned that the old ones remembered things they had never written down. I tried to figure out who to ask about it all. Raisin, at HQ, was old enough to have been alive during this time frame. She didn't like me very much, but if I brought her a pie or some beignets, maybe she'd talk about Ka.

Or Koun. He might be even better. I checked the time. He was still sleeping. I texted Koun, Raisin, and the B-twins for any info they might have. I didn't have a number for Coreen, the oldest living blood-servant in the western hemisphere, and she didn't take calls anyway, if I remembered right.

There were so many people in NOLA vamp history, so many threads of time and power and position. How did Leo keep up with it all: all the layers and threads and the depth of the tapestry that he had been weaving? And how did I unravel it enough to see the power brokers behind the scenes?

So many had died since I entered the picture: both Sons of Darkness, Le Batard, de Allyon, Louis VII, and Charles II of Spain—all VIVs—very important vamps. The heads of countries and masters of cities all over the world. Who had taken their places? Who were their heirs? Who was left?

There was always an heir. Almost always. Leo didn't appoint Immanuel for around a hundred years, so Leo had been an outlier there. Most vamps appointed an heir the moment they came to some new kind of power or the moment the previous heir died true dead. There had to be someone to accept a vamp's power, both magical and political. But not all heirs were able to handle the power or politics the way they needed in order to maintain a balance of power or gain more power. The life of an heir was often short and ended violently.

So what did the heirs who were causing problems want with time travel? Replacing vamps took only a decade, but replacing old vamps was impossible. Once ancient vamps were dead, they were *dead* dead. A strange thought reoccurred to me, one I'd had before, but it hadn't solidified, not so concrete. What if the vamp causing problems wanted to go back and change the original black magic working at the moment their kind was created? What if they wanted a way that would allow them to keep their souls and regain an afterlife? To daywalk and live like humans? Maybe to not have to drink human blood to live?

It was that same moment, that act of black magic, that arcenciels wanted to go back to also, but their goal was to destroy the Sons of Darkness before vamps could be made. War could be on the horizon as the two paranormal groups considered timewalking back to the beginning of vamps.

My mind circled back to the scene of Sabina watching as Bethany and Adan killed Ka. They had been standing in an iron witch circle. I flipped the current page of the timeline over and drew a sketch of the black square in a concrete floor and set it with the iron witch circle. To show dimensions, I added stick figures.

When I was done, I slid it to Bruiser. "Have you ever seen an iron witch circle like this? In a black square?"

His face pulled down in thought. "No. Maybe?" He rested his chin in his palm, elbow on the table. His sleeves were pushed up, and the fine hairs on his arm made Beast perk up.

Mate . . . she thought at me.

Bruiser said, "I vaguely remember seeing a section of a black marble square tile with a line of iron in it. Somewhere. But it was just the one tile. Not a whole circle. Is it important?"

"It might be," I said.

His face pulled down more. "Let me think."

I was feeling antsy. And bruised. And I needed something without knowing what it might be. Outside, the rain had let up. It was daylight, which was an impossible time to change into human shape, at least for me. But Beast had secrets and skills I didn't have. She had changed shape in the daylight in the past.

I adjusted the gold nugget on my necklace and removed the cat tooth that hung there, just in case she wanted to get frisky and be a cat all day. Not that she usually needed it, but with my funky shape-shifting these days, I would remove any advantage she might have.

Inside me, Beast snarled and blew hard through her nose, a cat snort of disgust.

Suck it up, I thought at her.

Not caring if I got my clothes wet, I went out through one of the new narrow doors to the side porch. Bitsa, my bastard Harley, was on the porch leaning against the house. Beside it was Bruiser's Indian. One of the boys had clearly seen that the bikes were delivered, because the last time I saw them was when Bruiser and I had taken a three-day, midsummer trip through the mountains, staying in cheap hotels, seeing my world. It had been wonderful.

I touched my bike. Freedom surged through me, the need for it, the desire for it. The certainty that someday I'd be free again, not have to be the DQ, but just a Master of a Clan, able to put my own people first. Maybe have a little fun.

I pulled my hand away. That day wasn't today.

Walking into the yard, I studied the changes carried out at Bruiser's orders. The gate in the brick fence into Katie's backyard, the paved space to park a small car or turn one around. Katie's fountain had been cleaned, and the bowl was full of rainwater. There were flowers planted everywhere along the fence walls in pots of all sizes. Fall greenery had been tucked into crevices of what was left of the boulders Katie had put here when I first came to New Orleans. Most of the boulders were shattered or broken, used for mass changes when I needed them, but one was still mostly intact. Bare-pawed, I maneuvered across the rain-slippery rock, avoiding the plants someone had put so much care into, and sat on top.

I closed my eyes and went back to my earliest meditation exercises—a candle in a dark place. I took and released several breaths, each breath slower and deeper than the one before. I kept the candle before me, the only light in the darkness.

Beast? I want to be Jane.

Why? Jane is weak.

I will never be weak as long as Beast is with me. I/we are Beast.

Out of the darkness, Beast padded into the light of the candle. Her golden eyes met mine, her mouth partly open, her killing teeth showing. *We are more and not-more than we were before,* she thought.

We have a lot of things to do. Sometimes I'll need one form or the other. And right now, I need to go to HQ and check on things there.

Jane spirit is still broken. Jane needs holy water. Go to place of holy water, and Beast will shift.

Okay. Deal. But I want the shift now.

Beast reached a paw and placed it on my hand. I began to shift. Pain slithered up from her paw, up my arm, into my shoulder, and down my spine.

I woke stretched out on the boulder, human shaped, in a freezing, drumming rainstorm. *Dang cat,* I thought. But it was affectionate, not irritated. My clothes, however, were shredded, and I had really liked my alligator tee.

I got my icy hands under me and shoved up into a sitting position to see Eli standing on the porch with a blanket and towel. I squelched to him on my muddy bare human feet and let him wrap me in the blanket and my hair in the towel. "Wipe your feet on the mat. Go get a hot shower. I'll have oatmeal ready when you get out."

I nodded, pulled off my ruined jeans while wrapped in the blanket, and handed them to him so I wouldn't mess up the floors. I went inside, leaving him to wring out my pants. It felt good to hear him chuckling as I followed orders.

Bruiser and Wrassler had gone to HQ to handle some problem, and when I was dry and mostly presentable, I weaponed up over a thin T-shirt and pulled a sweatshirt over that. Beast said I needed holy water, and there were only a couple of places in NOLA where I knew I could get baptismal water. One no longer allowed me in the doors because I had befouled the pool, and the other was a new church I had never really worshiped in. I emptied my out-of-date holy water vials and tucked them into a gobag before I told the boys where I was going.

"Not alone," Eli said. "I'll drive."

"I need to do this alone," I said. "Please."

He hesitated and Alex muttered, "Bro. She's going to church, which she hasn't done in months. She doesn't even make us pray over meals anymore. Give her some privacy. Sheesh."

Surprised that Alex had noticed that, I took a set of keys from one of the hooks by the door. Out front I beeped the fob, raced through the sprinkles to the SUV, and climbed in. I waved to the security detail as I drove off. And pretended not to see Eli racing to another SUV to be my backup. He was an overprotective idiot, but he was *my* overprotective idiot.

The church I once attended had been in a storefront before it moved to a better location. A new church had taken over the site, and I pulled into a parking spot down the street. I stared at the church front, thinking, or maybe just sitting in a fog and not thinking, watching people in a line go in and come back out. I realized they were homeless, entering with backpacks and bedrolls and exiting with the same but also with paper bags of food. I left the SUV, locking it as I neared the storefront and the new little church that now inhabited it. I joined the slow-moving line of homeless people of all races and ages, and some families with kids. I nodded to the man in front of me and the old woman in a soaked winter coat who came in behind me, waiting patiently with them as we shuffled forward.

Inside, it was bustling. Where there used to be two rows

of chairs with a central aisle, the chairs were folded against one wall, making a wide area where tables were set up and five people behind them were making sandwiches and putting lunches together. At a different table, someone was going through neatly folded stacks of clothing and passing out shirts and jeans and occasionally a rain slicker. At the last table was a man with a three-ring binder and an ancient laptop going through and looking up essential services and addresses that offered showers, health testing, and dentists who helped the needy. In front was the preacher couple, praying with anyone who wanted to join, teaching scripture to a small group. Few of the homeless joined that group, but it looked like the place I needed to be.

I took a chair in the second row and laced my fingers together, bowing my head. The male preacher was talking about the nature of redemption. I didn't know if that was cosmic coincidence, God talking to me, or just the man's usual spiel. Either way, the universe had a weird sense of humor.

"Redemption takes both faith and action, and is denied to no one," the preacher man said. But I remembered the bright and blinding moment when Sabina lost her soul, and I had to wonder. After the short message and bible reading, the meeting ended and the couple stood around chatting with the participants. When their backs were turned, I hoofed it behind the curtain to the baptismal pool.

It wasn't the same baptismal pool as last time. This was a new, oval, redwood, Japanese hot tub, with the benches around the sides removed. I leaned over the edge and refilled my vials of holy water, tucking them away safely in the gobag. Where I found a fifty dollar bill. I always travelled with cash and a change of clothing in case I shifted and ended up naked and alone somewhere, but I didn't remember the fifty.

"Can I help you, sister?" a voice said from behind me. I swiveled and saw the woman preacher.

"Maybe," I said, surprising myself. "Your husband said that redemption is denied to no one. But it's been said that the fallen angels couldn't be redeemed." My brain went sideways with possibilities. "So can vampires? And are other paras cursed? What about were-creatures who were turned against their will? And what about witches?" *What about me?*

"Redemption is . . . complicated," she said gently. "Angels who fell knew beyond doubt that they were fighting a war against the one true God. Redemption isn't offered to humans who believe yet sin anyway, only to those who repent and change. Witches can be or do whatever they wish. If they desire redemption, then it is theirs. Vampires live long lives, as do were-creatures, some choosing to trade humanity for a form of eternal youth." She shrugged the tiniest bit. "The survival of them is in the hands of the Elohim."

Elohim. It was one of the earliest Hebrew names of God, the plural term for God, meaning *gods.* It was interesting that she used it. I asked, "And vampires and were-creatures who are turned against their wills? Abused against their wills?" *Like Rick?* The thought rang in my head like a gong, though I didn't say it. For all his flaws, Rick had a deep and abiding need to protect the innocent. After a slight hesitation, I finished. "Do they get a chance for heaven?"

She sighed sadly. "I've talked with vampires. Some of them suffer horribly, not knowing. And I'll tell you like I tell them: I don't know. That's in God's hands. But they can hope. They can always hope."

I didn't say it, but Sabina had been hoping to find her soul for two thousand years. At some point, that hope had to fade. It might already have. I looked back at the soaking tub. The water in it had been warm to the touch. Like blood. Which made sense in a macabre way, because it was supposed to take the place of blood. I wondered if a vampire had ever tried to be baptized and burned up in the water. I frowned, remembering the pool I had fouled.

"You're Jane Yellowrock, aren't you?" she said, her voice low. "I've seen you on TV." I nodded and she went on. "You've killed vampires. Are you worried that you sent them to hell?"

"If they don't have souls anymore, can they go to hell?"

"Interesting theological question. But a debate on theology is not really why you're here, I think."

She was right. That was a wild-goose chase and obscured what I was really here for. "My faith has been . . . lacking," I said. "It isn't that I'm antiredemption, anti-God, antianything. It's just that . . ." I trailed my fingers through the water, and it didn't smoke or spark or start smelling like brimstone. That was a good start. "I've walked away from God . . ."

"Because he wasn't big enough or powerful enough to save you and those you love?" she asked.

"No. But because he didn't bother. And because I've done the same thing vamps have done. I've killed because I thought my way was the right way, the only way, and it turns out that sometimes there's another way. I'm not sure if I'm . . . redeemable. Not sure if God would even want me, because like the fallen angels, I kept doing what I was doing even after I found out there was another way. I kept killing."

The woman patted my shoulder and said, "And you also did great things for this city. Reined in the feral vampires that once preyed on the homeless. Forced them to do better by their own blood-servants. Forbade the creation of new blood-slaves. Don't think, Jane Yellowrock, that your contributions have gone unnoticed by the Almighty. They haven't gone unnoticed by us either."

Totally unexpected tears filled my eyes. I had no idea what to say. Or how to say it. I turned my face away to hide my reaction.

"You sit here as long as you want." She patted my shoulder again, and this time it felt like a benediction or a blessing. "It's my turn to make sandwiches."

"How much does all this cost?" I asked, my voice rough with the emotional reaction I hadn't expected. I met her eyes and realized she was younger than I had somehow thought, considering her quiet, calm wisdom, and was maybe only in her late twenties, a dark-skinned woman with reddish hair. I waved at the interior of the small church. "Making sandwiches, cleaning and storing the clothing. Electricity. Rent. Salaries."

"Upwards of a hundred thousand a year. Lately more, because New Orleans's homeless numbers are growing by leaps and bounds since the vampires stopped eating them."

She smiled. "I really have to go now. But if you want to come back, we have prayer meeting every day at six p.m."

I handed her the fifty dollar bill and said, "Thank you."

Her eyes lit up. "Thank *you*, sister." She left me by the soaking tub.

I bowed my head and whispered, too quietly for any human to hear, "I'm sorry. I've doubted you were enough for me. Doubted you cared for anyone. But . . . you let me find the rift. Just buying that property so close to it was a coincidence. Or maybe the rift opened because of all the magic stuff I brought with me. Sooo. Maybe . . . you sent me there? You set all this up? If anyone could play a long game, you could. You know, since you have all that omniscient power and cra—ah, stuff."

God didn't answer, but then, he never had talked to me the way some people said he talked to them. "What am I supposed to do now?" I asked. And again, no one answered. I wondered if that meant it was okay with God if I made my own decisions.

I lifted a hand at the woman preacher on the way out the door and headed to my vehicle.

Eli was propped against my SUV door, his face unsmiling but not looking ticked off either, so that was good.

I said, "Hey, bro. You out here scaring the homeless?"

He tapped his earbud and slanted his eyes at me.

I said nothing. Didn't react at all.

"You aren't making a stink about me following you," he said.

"No. Just doing your job. I get it."

He gave an Eli smile. Sort of a twitch.

"How many others did you bring with you?"

"Only three. Two SUVs are situated at both ends of the block."

I handed him my gobag. "Holy water. Make sure it's shared where it's needed. And tell Alex to send ten K from my personal account to the church. They're doing good work on a shoestring."

"You heading to HQ?" he asked.

"Yeah. How 'bout you drive, and we chat, and one of the security guys can drive the other vehicle back home."

I got more of a real smile this time. "Sounds good."

* * *

We pulled up at the back of HQ and parked behind three box trucks, delivery guys unloading tables and folding chairs and linens and other assorted wedding paraphernalia. Between groups of sweaty men showing way too much butt crack, Eli let me out under the porte cochere, and Derek directed me to the side, where he put me through the security measures as if I was a guest or one of the delivery guys.

"Cute," I said to him.

"Dark Queen's orders," he said, with a trace of a snarky grin. He was wearing black jeans and a T-shirt and that hint of snark on his face as he clipped a security band to my wrist so I could be tracked. I didn't argue. I had, after all, helped create all the security protocols. Once I was trackable, Derek stepped back and said, "Morning, Legs."

And that just warmed my heart strings. *Legs.* Not *my queen* or something else stupid.

He indicated the ballroom entrance and said, "Check out the preparations. Wrassler's in there, nervous as a cat with nine tails. Maybe you can calm him down some more, though you were brilliant to send Deon to help. We had no idea he was a wedding planner as well as a chef."

Deon was a wedding planner? I sent Deon? Nope. My Consort sent Deon. We trailed the delivery people to the ballroom, and I stopped in the open door. The stained glass in the overhead arches glittered, casting brilliant light across the piled up deliveries, the columns, and the ballroom floor. The stained glass wasn't open to the sun. The "windows" were set into a dropped ceiling of arches, lights above them, to fake the appearance of sunlight in the vamp-safe room. There were rows of metal seats in two sections with a wide aisle down the middle. A woman in jeans and a tee was dressing the chairs in one-piece outfits and adding little blue bows. Another woman was directing the placement of the tables, ordering the men around like a drill sergeant. Wrassler was standing in the corner, arms hanging limply, a look of woe on his face.

I stopped next to him. "Prewedding jitters, Wrassler?"

"Huh. I got local and foreign fangheads in town for this.

A passel of witches. And every cop in town wants to be here too. The liquor bar I'm good with, but the blood bar is not gonna make my bride happy."

Music started up through the speakers, a waltz, and Gee DiMercy appeared in an alcove. I was pretty sure he hadn't been there only a moment ago. I kept an eye on him as we talked.

I shrugged. "Tell Deon the blood bar has to be moved to the gym."

Wrassler shot his eyes to me. "Really?"

"It's your wedding. You're pretty much in charge of what goes on at HQ anyway. Just make sure the visiting vamps understand that they have to be escorted back and forth to the bar—and that no means no. They do not have permission to consider this event a buffet or to roll the humans."

"And if one of them gets out of line?"

I considered. "I like beheading vamps who get out of line. And as the Dark Queen, I don't care if the blood shows."

Wrassler burst out laughing and gave me a massive hug. "I love you, Janie."

"Love you too, big guy."

From the doorway, a voice called, "Are you trying to steal my man?"

Wrassler let me go and winked at me before limping to Jodi and giving her an even bigger hug, tight enough that she squeaked in surprise. When he let her go, she shouted to me, "Don't you dare mess up my wedding, woman."

"I'll do my best to keep things perfect." As promises went, that one pretty much sucked, but it was the best I could do.

Wrassler was right. This particular wedding combo was rife with bad possibilities. As I watched, Gee gave instructions, and Wrassler took Jodi, who was like half his size and still wearing her service weapon, in his arms. With Gee correcting hand and arm positions, and Wrassler trying so hard to obey even when his prosthetic leg gave less than perfect balance, they began to waltz.

Tears pricked under my lids. "This is so sweet. It's going to be fabulous," I murmured to Derek, who was still standing near me.

"Yeah. You done good, Janie. The ballroom is looking great. Homer is happier than I ever saw him."

"Homer?" I said, watching the couple as they danced across the room, dodging the delivery men.

"Homer Perkins. Wrassler."

I shot him a look of surprise. "Wrassler's name is Homer?"

"Homer Perkins. Word is, he used to take all kinds of shiii . . . crap about it when he was a kid." There was a soft smile on Derek's mouth, not a smile that had ever been directed at me. "Then he got so big, and no one hassled him anymore, but he still hated his name. Dubbing him Wrassler is the best thing you ever did for him. Well. That and pushing him to go out with Jodi."

I frowned at him. Derek was talking to me. Normal human talk. Nothing insulting or mean or snide. "I need to go to the subbasement four storage room."

"I'll walk with you. I can update you on security for the wedding."

Derek was going to walk with me. Okay. Either he was going to shoot me and hide my body—there were probably bodies buried in the walls—or someone had changed places with him. *Invasion of the Body Snatchers*, Pod People, maybe. We got on the elevator, and the doors closed, me waiting for the other shoe to drop.

Derek slid in his card key to initiate the elevator and clasped his hands in front of him, standing with his feet shoulder width apart, like some kind of parade rest. I slouched in the corner, watching us both in the steel reflections. The elevator started down. He said, "I've been a jerk. I hope you will accept my apology."

I saw myself blink. It would have been the perfect time to attack because I was pretty nonplussed. I squinted at his reflection. "You hated my guts from the first time we met. One of your people had a sniper rifle aimed at my spine."

"I didn't tell him to shoot. *Hate* was too strong a word. Disliked immensely. More that." There was a twinkle in his dark eyes and a slight twist to his full lips. Almost a smile.

"Uh-huh. I haven't done anything to make you like me. At the *gather*, when I got here the other day, you stared daggers at me. People don't change, not without either a lot of work or some sort of life-changing trauma."

Derek said, "Trauma. I was run off the road, beaten, drained, and dragged myself back to vamp HQ half alive. I had a lot of time to think while I was trying not to die. I think that qualifies as life-changing trauma."

I looked away, thinking that through. Derek had nearly died. On my watch. That was terrible. And weird. And made me crazy. "Okay. Fine. But why is your life-changing event resulting in being nice to me?"

Derek snorted. "What it took was for me to stop being a hypocrite. I hated monsters. You were a monster. Now I'm one. That's what kept me alive that day. Being a monster. A human would have died. And that's why the anger when you walked in. It was power I expected you to abuse, but you didn't. And somehow that made me mad too."

The elevator doors opened on sub-four, and we both stepped out. The doors closed behind us. He didn't attack me. I said, "I accept your apology. I've been a jerk too."

"Is that an apology?"

"I'm working up to it."

Derek grunted out a laugh. Neither of us moved away from the elevator as it rose to an upper floor.

I said, "I'm sorry for egging you on and making you feel insecure and uncertain. I'm sorry for being a jerk." Taunting, guy-style, I added, "And for being a better fighter than you."

Derek nodded, considering, also guy-style. "I may be a bigger monster than you now. We should spar. And maybe put a little money on how fast I can take you down."

"We did that once. I beat your butt. Sure you want to lose to a girl again?"

"I'm a lot faster now, *girl*. So, how's it feel, being half cougar so much? Does the pelt itch?"

Serenely, I said, "*Ahhh*. Trash talk." I liked it, but I didn't say so. "It severely limits my wardrobe choices. My legs look weird in dresses."

Derek laughed as I intended. He gave my shoulder a fist bump. I gave him one back.

"How's your mom?" I asked. She had cancer, and Leo had been feeding her, hoping to help heal her.

"She's good." His smile softened even more. "Better than good. No more chemo. She's still cancer-free. Leo's blood made all the difference. Another reason to stop hating the monsters. The biggest monster of all saved my mom. Hating him would be pretty hypocritical."

I thought so too, but agreeing might be rude. I made a soft "Mmmm" sound instead.

"So what are we looking for down here?" Derek asked, leading me into the storage room.

"Books. Specifically journals, diaries, that sort of thing, preferably from the early eighteen hundreds."

I looked around. Someone had cleaned it up and organized it. There were trunks along one wall, shelves of knick-knacks and expensive objets d'art, clothing in vacuum-sealed bags hanging on racks. There was furniture arranged according to type: bedsteads in one area, tables stacked in another, chairs stacked or hanging from pegs on the walls. Stacks of rolled-up rugs. I followed Derek to the shelves of books.

"They're organized according to name, then by dates," he said. "Who are you looking for?"

"Adan Bouvier, Ka, his primo, Bethany, Sabina, Leo, and anyone from the last two hundred years you might think noteworthy. Preferably in English."

"Interesting mix. Okay." He pulled a ladder from across the room and then toted over a trunk and opened it. It was empty and the bottom was clean. From a shelf at his eye level, he removed a spiral notebook and flipped pages, making little humming noises. Seeming satisfied, he replaced the notebook, climbed the ladder, and handed me down four leather journals. "So far as I know, and so far as this room holds, Ka and Sabina, neither one, kept journals here. Adan kept them. Bethany did too, though she wasn't sane, so they may not make sense. And I don't think many of them will be in English."

I placed the journals into the trunk. He handed me down four others. "Leo's from the eighteen hundreds. He handed down six more. "Amaury's from the same century, up to 1912." That was the year Leo had taken over from his uncle as MOC of NOLA.

I placed them in the trunk too. "Anything else you think I might need?"

He looked over the shelves, climbed up and removed two more journals. On the way down, he reached into a nook I couldn't see from my angle and handed down a framed daguerreotype of Leo. In the early years, photography was all done with silver, and vamps hadn't photographed well, if at all, usually looking smudged or faceless. Until one photographer, Ernest J. Bellocq, had managed to photograph some famous vamps of the time, despite the fangheads' inability to reflect on the silver used in both daguerreotypes and the later wet collodion-process photographs. So far as I knew, no one knew how he had done it. This was one of his works, and Leo stood with Katie and another man, arm in arm. Very still, unsmiling, formal. The year on a plaque on the front of the frame was 1840. I thought that Bruiser might like it and tossed it in the trunk too, with the two last journals.

"That was easy," I said. "Who organized this room?"

"Vodka Boys. Angel Tit and Chi-Chi were in charge. They also organized the storage room on sub-three."

"Find any magical stuff?"

He looked at me as he climbed down the ladder. "A few things. They're in the safe. If you're interested."

"Not now. But would you mind sending a copy of the log to Alex in case I need something? Save me a trip over?"

"I don't know, Janie. You'd miss out on my scintillating conversation."

"It's a loss, true. I'll just have to pull up my big-girl panties and deal."

He was still chuckling when the elevator doors closed, but his face went tight, and he touched his earbud while he slid his card into the security slot. "Lee with Yellowrock. We're on the way." His face was set in a familiar expression. Battlefield ready. Something had gone wrong.

CHAPTER 10

Wrassler Was Down, Just Inside the Security Nook, Lying on His Side

I let Derek take the lead. Drinking so much vamp blood after he dragged himself back from captivity and near death had made him faster, and I didn't have to hold back much. I followed him to the main security room, and we burst through the double doors into the area. The scent of coffee, peppers, and fried seafood whacked me in the face.

The big table took up most of the room, and there were four security people sitting there with laptops open. No one looked up. The screens overhead showed the grounds and the entrances to HQ. It was dusk out. I had been here longer than I thought. My body might switch from human form to another at any time, which could be unfortunate. And embarrassing.

"Update," Derek said, opening a weapons' safe at the back.

Tequila Blue Voodoo was at the main station with a woman I vaguely recognized.

Voodoo said, "Something on the security screens. At least one hotspot on the grounds. Walls are still warm from the sun, so it isn't easy to follow."

Hotspot meant that the person showed up on infrared camera, meaning that it wasn't a vamp.

"Back corner," Voodoo said, putting up a camera feed on the main screen, "behind the garden." There was a flash of movement on the screen, reddish light, human shaped. "No indication of anyone else on the motion sensors or low light."

"Front gate locked down?" Derek asked. He was weaponed up like the warrior he was. It had taken less than thirty seconds. But he wasn't in armor.

"Like a tank," Blue Voodoo answered from the main security panel.

"Which team is ready?" Derek gave me a single nod and raced out the door, heading for the action.

"Tango is on the way down. Clearing the hallways in case one of the delivery people made it past the sensors and guards."

I wanted to go with them, but I hadn't trained with them. I'd be a liability. Which I understood but I could still hate.

On the screens overhead, I watched as the six-man Tango team raced through the hallways, splitting and converging at the intersections, separating into three minigroups, each third taking a different set of stairs, communicating through the hardwired Wi-Fi comms booster system we had installed a couple years back. Then they were at the inner stairs near the rear entrance, and there were eight of them. I realized that Eli and Derek had joined the team. I had vaguely noticed my brother, off and on, carrying out Eli duties.

Derek said into his mic and to Voodoo, "Copy. Tango in place. Lights." The lights inside the entrance and outside, under the porte cochere, went dark. Derek took off like his pants were on fire. His men and women, all human, unlike the vamp forces that he utilized after full dark, sped to the back exit. Stopped. One by one, they eased into the covered area. With the security lights off, they were visible on the infrared screens, low-light screen, and on a positional layout screen that showed the house and grounds and the trackers each wore. They spread out, communicating with Derek. I wasn't wearing a headset, and though I didn't want to disturb anyone, I said, "Audio on."

Not that anyone was speaking. It was all mic taps and hand signals when the speakers went live.

The light was fading. The vamps were rising. The cameras in the hallways showed them leaving their rooms, alone or with a human in tow. Some of them were day-stupid and had to feed to be alert. Others came out of their rooms weaponing up, and those few were the warriors among the vamps. A group of six vamps met just off the foyer, weapons trained toward the front entrance. Wrassler was in the secondary security room off the foyer, visible to them and on one camera. He gave a hand signal, and the vamps moved closer to the foyer.

A team of four vamps gathered in the main security room downstairs, congregating around me, speaking so softly only a vamp could make out everything they said. They were Clan Yellowrock vamps and visitors: Tex and Koun were actually breathing hard. They had crossed the French Quarter vamp-fast from the freebie house. Thema and Kojo were with them.

On the screens, vamp and blood-servant security worked the backyard in what was clearly a well-trained and practiced maneuver. The exterior steel shutters were still closed over the windows for the day. A lucky happenstance. Over comms, someone screamed, "Incoming!" The screens lit up. Blinding. The vamps and I jerked our heads away, closed our eyes.

The screens were so bright they faded only slowly back to visuals.

A fireball had exploded.

On speakers, there were a lot of overlapping orders and updates.

Outside, three more fireballs detonated, a second apart, each from a slightly different location. The attacker was moving and casting at once. Over the speakers was gunfire. Presumably from our side. Derek and Eli were out there. In that firestorm.

I took a step for the door, but Koun and Tex each grabbed an arm.

"I am sorry, My Queen," Koun said, his grip like iron. "No. You are no longer a grunt. You are the *Queen*."

A fireball hit the back entrance.

I jerked. Adrenaline shot through me. I made a sound that might have been a puma scream of frustration. Koun's grip tightened.

Bullet-resistant glass cracked and began to melt. How hot was this fire? It had to be magical in origin. It had to be the Firestarter.

"There may be more than one attacker," Wrassler said over comms. "The fires are overwhelming the infrared and the low light. All we have are the lasers and the normal-light security cameras."

Over the speakers, I heard Derek say, "Team Delta, out front. Firing positions. Shoot anything that moves. Alex. Voodoo, Spieth. We need to verify that this isn't just a diversion."

"Already on it," Alex said, working from the freebie house.

The exterior lights were off, and on low-light cameras I saw the vamps, male and female, as they edged out of their protected spaces and out the front airlock. Down the stairs. Wrassler and one vamp remained, and locked down the airlock before they took up position behind reinforced walls to cover the front stairs and entrance.

Out back, three more fireballs were thrown, this time more like three seconds apart. The pitcher was in a different location each time, though closer to the house. Fire devils roared upward, tornadoes of flame. One of the vehicles still parked out back was on fire, as if hit with an incendiary weapon.

"We have enemy combatants on HQ grounds," Voodoo said. "Repeat. Enemy combatants are on the grounds. I count three. See HQ plotting map for locations. Red dots are encom."

Alex said, "Teams at the queen's personal residence and at Yellowrock Clan Home are on high alert. No enemy activity at either location. Checking the other Clan Homes now."

Eli ordered people into different positions. While I stood here twiddling my thumbs.

The outdoor sprinkler system came on and began

dampening the fires. On the plot screen, I placed each of my guys. With the sprinklers, everything stopped. No fire-balls, no gunfire. No one moved.

"Our people?" I asked.

"Minor burns," Voodoo said.

"Where did the attacker go?" I asked.

"Unknown," Voodoo said. "No longer showing on sys-tem. Wait. Garden shed roof."

"Fire," I said. I heard shots.

On a tiny screen at the bottom, I watched as a fireball arched from the roof of the garden shed, up high, and out of the screen. On another screen, from an inside security cam, even tinier, a light bloomed, brightening the dark ballroom. Stained glass and fire fell, glittering as the fire-ball broke through the overhead dome. Inside, the over-head water sprinklers came on, putting out the fire.

The fireball and sprinklers were ruining the wedding decorations. *Oh crap.* Jodi was gonna kill me.

"Did you get the Firestarter?" I asked.

"Negative," Derek said, his tone like a curse.

Koun relaxed his grip on my arm, but he didn't let go. More vamps gathered around us. All of them were armed with weapons, blades, and stakes. Except me. The most recent arrivals headed up the stairs into good firing posi-tions to defend the entrances. But nothing was happening out back. Or anywhere. Except sprinkler water still soak-ing Jodi's wedding preparations.

An alarm went off, and I spotted the location of the alarm on the plotting map. It was coming from out front. On the only screen currently dedicated to the front of HQ, I saw that the "tankworthy" gates were standing open. In the center of the circular parking area, visible only by its interior lights, was a suburban, still running. Doors open. Windows seriously tinted. A vamp-mobile.

Wrassler was in the small security nook, firing at some-one I couldn't see on the big, overhead screen. Wrassler. My friend. Who had nearly died once already.

Movement appeared in a corner of the screen. Two other screens showing video from cameras out front ap-peared in the top right of the screen. There were two dead bodies in the shrubbery on a low-light cam, not showing on infrared. Cool bodies meant downed vamps. Another vamp was inside, having passed through a small melted circle in the airlock glass. She was firing at Wrassler. He was pinned down in the foyer.

Battle chemicals flooded my body. I felt the shift start. "Not now!" I shouted at Beast.

Beast wrenched our arms from Koun's and Tex's. Faster than anyone expected. She ripped a nine-mil out of Koun's hand. Rushed up the stairs. Koun, Tex, and my vamp protection unit pounded behind us.

My body began the shift. "Nononono!" I shouted.

I fought the shift. Racing the need away. Tamping it down.

At one entrance to the foyer, I rushed to the left behind one column, then darted back right, behind another, getting a full view of the foyer. Wrassler was down, just inside the security nook, lying on his side.

From behind the column, I fired three shots at the vamp pinning Wrassler down. As I fired, Koun leaped ahead, barely out of my line of fire, a sword flashing. He beheaded the vamp.

Tex on my six, I rushed to Wrassler. I was deaf from the weapons fire. I had no headset. But Tex shouted into his comms, "An asshat got in. Maybe more than one. Cowbird is among us." We had enemies mixed with our loyal.

I fell beside Wrassler, checking him over, feeling for blood.

Wrassler pushed me away, his chest jerking in laughter. Loud enough for me to hear, he said, "Watch the handsy stuff, Janie. That part of me belongs to Jodi."

"Sorry," I said. *He wasn't shot.* Relief flooded through me.

The shift rammed into me. Hard and fast as an avalanche. My hands popped and shook. My spine arched back. Snapped forward. I rolled on the floor in a writhing ball. Breathless. I threw back my head and screamed.

Thirty seconds later, I was half-form. Gagging. Retching. With a blinding headache and double vision. I pushed myself into a sitting position. My boots were off. Wrassler stood holding them. My clothes were ragged where I had clawed them, but the girly bits were covered.

He helped me up to my paw-feet, and I breathed hard,

trying to throw off the shakes. From the tiny store of edibles kept in the nook, Wrassler offered me a Gatorade, and I drank it down. He opened a new box of PowerBars, and I tore three open, chomping down with puma fangs. As I ate and the pain eased, we studied the scene out front. There was a firefight taking place out there.

"Headset."

Wrassler looked at the position of my ears, up high and furry, and chuckled. He pulled a headset out of a box on a shelf and adjusted its shape, adding two rubber bands and a bread tie to hold it on me. I put it on and let him adjust it, twisting the bread tie into my hair. There was another rubber band in the box and I put my hair back in a tail to keep it out of the way. I heard shots fired.

On the screen, two of our vamps went down. A familiar form appeared on the edge of the screen—Bruiser's body mechanics. My heart clenched. He was pinned down.

Koun shouted, "Open the airlock doors, you whoremongering goat!" He was standing outside the security nook door shouting at Wrassler.

Wrassler had seen Bruiser too. He reached for the controls.

"Wait!" I banged open the weapons locker to our left, grabbed up a second nine-mil semiautomatic with an extra-large grip, and slammed home a full magazine marked in silver for silver-lead loads. Vamp killers. Stuffed two extra mags in my jeans pockets. I handed Wrassler a shotgun, which he placed beside his Taurus Judge. I gave him a nod and led the way to the front airlock.

"Now!" I said.

The airlock doors opened, though the outer one was heat-warped, and it stuck midway open.

Koun pressed down on my shoulder and ordered, "Stay here. You will not die."

"If Bruiser dies, I'll die," I said, my voice like the doom of a funeral bell.

Koun cursed in a language probably long dead.

I raced through. Dropped off the porch into a corner, falling into the dark. I landed on top of a dead vamp. Stumbled off the body. Caught my balance. I was protected on two sides. A vamp raced out of the dark, raising a weapon at me. I shot her. Koun landed beside me and took her head.

Three vamps raced across the circular parking area from the vehicle. I knew one of them. From Asheville. From the winter war. He had attacked Eli in the snow. My brother had nearly died, hanging in a tree.

"Center," I said, claiming my victim. I took him down. It took six shots and he wasn't dead. Not yet. He struggled to his feet. Still kicking. That made him old. "No mercy," I directed. The other two vamps were already down.

"My Queen," Koun said. He raced out and beheaded the vamp.

Tex took the heads of the other two. I had three shots left and changed out the mag. Wasting shots to his chest had been stupid. I should have aimed two to the chest and one to the head. Shift-nerves.

Three humans raced out of the dark. Tex and Koun took them down.

Another vamp sprinted toward the open car. She was shot down. Thema darted out and took the vamp's head.

And it was over.

I stood in the shadows, shaking again. I remembered the feel of the holy water on my fingers. Mercy was a tenet of my belief system. And I had just denied it. "Bruiser?" I murmured.

"He is well, My Queen," Koun said.

To the side, I saw my Consort checking out the bodies of the dead. I heaved a relieved sigh that started at my toes.

Koun knelt at my feet, offering his sword. "I failed you. I allowed you to face danger."

"Nobody failed me," I said. I wasn't sure what he wanted, but I had a feeling he felt he had been insufficient in some way about the battle we had just fought. I pulled on all the vamp lore I could think of, and nothing fit. I settled on, "Koun. Put that thing away. I suck at staying safe, and I . . . I order you to stop trying. You did good, dude. Get up."

He stood and sheathed his sword, but he still looked unhappy. Tex joined us and set a dog on a leash free to scout the bushes in the dark. It made snuffling sounds and moved fast, excited at the hunt.

"Okay," I said, tapping my mic. "Is the Firestarter gone?"

Over the headgear, I heard Voodoo say, "I have cam recording from outside the grounds of a human-temperature form climbing over the back fence. And we haven't had more fireballs."

Meaning yes, she was probably gone. The Onorios, vamps, and their humans had brought war on the Dark Queen, just as I had expected after seeing Monique's bloody-hull soul home.

It wasn't the first time we had more than one group after us, but the makeup of this group was different. I pulled on everything Leo had ever taught me by example and said into the headgear, "Our vampire enemies are coordinating with the Firestarter. We are on lockdown until further notice." The dog barked, a sharp vicious sound. Tex reached to pull his weapon. Koun whirled, sword shushing out of the scabbard. A vamp rose out of the foliage. Aimed a weapon at me. Fired a three burst.

I felt the rounds hit me so fast it was like one massive punch. The vamp fell. I looked down. "Well, that sucks donkey toes."

Bruiser raced toward me.

To Koun I said, "Why can't this ever be easy?"

And I fell. Lying facedown on the mulch, I thought, *Why am I not shifting? I should shift. I should change shape and live.* Instead I was dying. *Weird,* I thought, *I've died before. And I've never seen heaven like Sabina did. Why vamps and not me?*

I woke, eyes closed, my face buried in pillows, sheets over me, topped by an electric blanket. It was Leo's bed. I knew it was his because it still smelled of pepper and papyrus and blood and sex. I also smelled Bruiser and Eli and Koun and Tex. Especially those last two, because they were cradling me, spooning me, one on each side. I was no longer in my clothes, so . . . what the actual . . . ?

"Here. Bleed on her here. It looks as if the round fragmented. She may need surgery to get them all out."

No, I said. Except nothing came out.

I felt Bruiser's hands on my head, gripping me. A weird power was shoved into me. It was green and smelled of roses and catnip. It was prickly and yet soft, like coarse wool and angora. It was a malleable yet demanding buzz of electric-hot-and-cold at once. Heavy and lethargic.

I took a breath. My lungs felt weird.

"She's breathing," Koun said. "Cut me again. Jane, drink."

I tried again to say no, but tepid blood was filling my mouth. It was easier to swallow than to argue. Koun's blood tasted different from any other vamp blood I had drunk, though I couldn't say why, maybe . . . meatier? As if his blood had more red cells in it than other vamps?

Beast rose in me, eyes glowing. *Good vampire blood. Beast likes Koun-blood.*

"I need to feed," Koun said.

"Give her mine," Tex said.

They rolled me over, and Tex's blood filled my mouth. *Beast likes good vampire blood. More. Beast hungers.*

I had changed shape in the foyer. Right. I needed more calories than the PowerBars and electrolyte drink to replace the energy use, and Beast took every opportunity to drink vamp blood. Bruiser clasped my head tighter. There was a desperation in his grasp. More power pushed through me. It was uncomfortable, too hot, too rosy. Too something. And then I remembered. I was still in half-form. I hadn't shifted to Beast or back to human. I hadn't healed. I should have shifted. And didn't. I died. Or near enough to not count. Bruiser's worst nightmare. And they had brought me back. My shifting was out of control. I had hoped this worst-case scenario wouldn't be true, but it was. I had been mortally wounded, and I hadn't shifted. I was truly a danger to everyone around me because keeping me safe just got a lot harder. If I was stupid and ran into battle again, I'd get my own people killed while they tried to protect me. And I had ordered Koun to stand down. *Crap.*

"This is why we need an Infermieri," Koun said, his tone icy and furious. "With Jane, we need a dozen."

My body felt strange. Cold.

But I remembered the attackers. I got a hand up and pushed at Tex's wrist. Swallowed the last of the blood in my mouth. Gasping, I told Bruiser who they were.

"I know," he said, his voice suffused with fear and rage. I had died. Bruiser was ticked. Really, *really* ticked.

Koun said, "My Queen. We killed them all but one. From him, we received a challenge from Melker's heir. It was a Sangre Duello request to challenge for Blood Master of Clan Yellowrock and Master of the City of New Orleans."

Tex shoved his wrist to me. I took more blood. My old self going *gack* at the thought. My new self knowing I needed it.

"This heir is a much worse creature than Melker," Koun said.

I made a rolling gesture with two fingers to keep him talking.

"Melker's heir's name is Shaun MacLaughlinn," Koun said. "I have accepted the challenge for you, in your name. The monster is mine to fight," his voice grated. "You will accede to me in this. My Queen."

I had a feeling the last two words were added as an afterthought to make it less of an order. Koun was blaming himself that I got shot.

Shaun MacLaughlinn. I knew that name. I poked into my memory as I drank. Bruiser pushed power into me.

As I drank and healed, I remembered who the man, the vamp, was. Shaun MacLaughlinn was the *anamchara* of Dominique, who had been heir to Grégoire until she was sentenced to burn to death on a beach as the sun rose. *Anamchara* meant mind-bound, sometimes soul-bound, though I was pretty sure now that vamps didn't have souls. Dominique had died on the beach at the Sangre Duello at dawn. Her death should have broken Shaun's mind, leaving him a gibbering vegetable. Instead, like a few others I knew about, the *anamchara* Shaun had survived and joined the forces who fought against Dominique's killers. Us.

And Shaun had been in one of Sabina's visions. Unlike the others who had survived the breaking of a mind-bond, Shaun had looked sane. That meant Shaun was vastly stronger than anyone had ever thought.

And it came clear. Shaun might have been one of the faces I had glimpsed in Monique's soul home. *Well, crap.*

I was curled on Leo's bed, in Leo's old bedroom in HQ, awake, mostly healed, and surrounded by my very irate subjects. I was not looking at any of them, in fact, looking at everything but them. But I could smell the stink of their anger on the air, and the body language was pretty clear.

I was still naked, covered in dried blood that cracked through my pelt when I moved. Some of the blood was mine. At least the bloody sheets had been taken away, and fresh clean cotton ones had been brought in and tucked beneath me, around me. The electric blanket was wonderful. And no one was touching me. That felt wonderful right now too.

For a vamp bedroom, it was stark—just the bed, a small sofa, three cute chairs, small tables, a two-person eating area in the corner, and bookshelves. Rugs were everywhere, though a different style from Bruiser's. Leo's were oriental, with a sheen only silk could give. I could see an en suite and a closet through the two open doors, and the clothes in the closet were mine. I was guessing that I now had a room at HQ.

I also guessed that I needed to apologize. Was a queen supposed to apologize? If I acted like a queen now to keep from apologizing, did that mean I had to always act like a queen? Did I have to be a queen twenty-four-seven, or was it something I could do off and on?

To keep from having to deal with the stink of ticked off humans, vamps, and Onorio, I said, "I want current info on Shaun MacLaughlinn. Someone send for Alex."

"We have done so, My Queen," Koun said. His words didn't say stupid and horrible queen, but his tone did. "He is in the building."

"ETA thirty seconds," Eli said, equally harsh.

"Okay," I said quietly. "Thank you."

A moment later, Alex bopped into the room. He was no longer a kid but an adult, and fully grown, though still gangly. I hadn't raised him, but I was inordinately proud of the man he had become. He stepped inside the door, stopped, and looked around. "You really fuuu . . . screwed up this time," he said to me.

"She raced into the fight without armor, without proper protection. And. She. Died," Eli bit the words off.

"Not *dead* dead, or I wouldn't be breathing," I whispered, remembering the sight of Bruiser out in the thick of things. Pinned down.

"And you didn't shift when you died," Alex said, recent terror in his voice. Terror for me, nearly dying. He continued, his voice rough, "We've been telling you this could happen, and you still had to lead from the front. *Idiot.*" His hand touched my foot through the blankets as if to reassure himself I was really there. "We had Bruiser covered. Backup was coming from the side of the house. And you had to jump in."

"Yeah," I said, fully ashamed. "Um, sorry, everyone. It won't happen again." I hoped. Beast had her own ideas sometimes.

"Well, at least we know what happens now." Alex shoved a vamp over and plopped his backside on the mattress with me. Exhaustion in every cell, I pulled the sheets and blankets up over me tighter as he opened three laptops and put three different screens up.

"Screen one," he indicated the screen to his far left, "is the bloodline. Grégoire was, and still is, Blood Master to Clan Arceneau. When he took off to fight in Europe for the DQ, Dominique, Grégoire's heir, took over running Arceneau things here in NOLA. Shaun MacLaughlinn was Dominique's *anamchara*. Dominique did a big-bad no-no at the Sangre Duello and was punished by burning to death in the sun. Shaun should have died. Weaker vamps either die or go insane, like some you knew. Instead he survived and began challenging European vamps who had come here. He managed to cobble together a long list of powerful followers and fought his way up the ranks to a position as Legolas slash Melker's heir." Alex looked at me. "Shaun knew everyone in NOLA. Knew all about the changes in HQ and our protocols. He created a huge clan of powerful, disaffected, dissociated, unhappy vamps from the U.S. and Europe."

And he was also mind-bound in Monique's slave ship soul home. Probably Dominique had been too. Dang. I hadn't seen that possibility. "What helped him to overcome the mind-break?" I asked.

"I think he came into control of an old amulet," Alex said, pointing to the screen in the middle. "This one."

On the center of the screen was an arm band in the shape of a snake, the kind that's worn on the upper arm. I had seen that kind of amulet before. In fact, I had two similar to it, though mine now contained only a trace of power. This one . . . this one had several shimmery spots trailing up its back. Just like the shimmery spots on the flying lizard amulet I had gotten when Sabina pulled me underwater.

"Ah, man," I murmured. Two amulets constructed with arcenciel blood in NOLA at the same time. Coincidence wasn't possible.

Alex turned just his head and looked at me from under his too-long spiraling curls. "Yeah, right? Continuing the timeline, fitting the Firestarter into it."

He pointed at the final screen and a bit of security footage, froze it, and pointed at the still shot on the screen. I recognized the brick wall at the side of HQ. Once upon a time, there was a not-so-secret access point in the brick that led to Leo's office. It was now sealed from the inside, but the small group of people shown gathered there hadn't known that.

"During the attack on HQ, Shaun"—he touched the screen, showing me the vamp—"who is running around not wearing a shirt, presumably to show off the amulet on his arm, was trying to get inside. I'm guessing that this"—he pointed to the other vamps—"is his primo or secondo, and his best fighters. And here"—he pressed a button, and another view took its place—"is where the Firestarter finished her attack in back and joined up with Shaun."

"The Firestarter hates vamps," I said, remembering the bound beings in Monique's soul home. I searched the screen. Ka wasn't there.

"The enemy of my enemy is my short-term friend?" Alex asked. "They seem to be working together, for now, since she was part of the attack that had been intended to draw off your forces front and back while he gained access from inside."

"Well, that sucks," I said.

"Good Lord, woman," a female voice said from the door. "You look like death warmed over and twice as furry."

I looked from the screen to the door and smiled, happiness filling me all over. "Jodi."

"Don't you go getting all nice-nice on me. I hear you let my wedding site get blown to smithereens."

"Sorry," I said, seeing by her expression that she wasn't really mad at me. Well, she was, but it was a different version of mad from all my male subjects' mad. "I need to use the ladies," I said. "All you menfolk, go down to security and update the crews. Jodi, will you stay?"

"Stay and what? Help you pee? God help me, the things I get stuck doing for you. Out," she said to the vamps and humans and Onorio. "Get out." When no one moved she said, "I may be wearing exercise clothes, but I am never unarmed. Don't make me shoot you. The lady needs a little privacy."

"The *lady*," Tex said, pointedly, "was just shot to hell and back, ma'am. If you spot bleeding, we'd be appreciative of you bringing one of her Mithrans back in to finish up healing her. Koun and I'll be outside the door." He wasn't wearing a hat indoors, but he touched his forehead as if tipping one anyway. I could feel Bruiser's and Eli's eyes on me, but I took refuge in Jodi and pretended not to know they were still really peeved.

When it was just Jodi and me and the door was shut on menfolk, she yanked the sheets off of me and shoved me to my feet. Pain shot through me, and I was suddenly too weak to care that I was naked. I nearly fell, and short, rounded Jodi caught me. I was also too exhausted to care that she got dried blood all over her exercise clothes. By the smell: sweaty exercise clothes. She hadn't been working at the cop shop when she got called in. That was probably my fault. She started me walking toward the en suite.

"You do know that the fire department and the eighth district all got called out because of gunfire and fire-fire tonight, right?"

"I'm not surprised," I whispered.

"And we're still all out there, waiting on a stand-down order, which no one will give us because of the political ramifications if this turns out to be important on a State Department level."

"Sorry," I breathed, wondering why I could apologize to Jodi and not my people.

"Are you the only one dead?" she asked.

I tried to laugh, but it hurt too much as she eased me down onto the closed toilet lid. "No. We were attacked, and there are a number of attacking humans and vamps dead."

"Any of your people?"

"I don't know yet." Dread drenched me like a cold flood.

"How many attacked?"

"One in back." I started to tell her about the Firestarter but changed my mind. "With an incendiary device. I think six in front."

"How many were humans?"

I realized that Jodi had been interrogating me, which made me tired and a little sad. "Stop asking questions, Jodi. Pretty sure this is Dark Queen stuff. If there's questioning to be done, the State Department can send someone to do it."

"Are you calling diplomatic immunity on this? 'Cause if you do, that makes it a lot easier on us."

So maybe she wanted an excuse to not ask me stuff? That hadn't occurred to me. "They called you in tonight to ask me that?"

"Yes," she said sourly. "Thanks to you, I'm the official liaison to the fangheads in this city. I got a promotion and a raise and everything." The last sentence was even more sour, nearly bitter. I figured that was because she had gotten the promotion not by skill but because she knew me. That had to rankle. She turned away and started the shower on hot.

"In you go," she said, pulling me to my feet. Which hurt a *lot*. But there was a seat in the shower, and I managed to get onto it before I passed out. Leo had a very swanky bathroom with a huge tub in the far corner big enough to fit three or four, which I remember very well from the one time I walked in on Leo, Katie, and Blondie lounging in it.

Jodi placed a bottle of water into my knobby, long-fingered hand, and said, "Drink. I'm getting you something to wear from that enormous closet. Don't die while I'm not in here babying you."

Babying me. Right. I slumped against the tile. Which was heated. *Holy crap, that felt good.* Water pounded, trickled, and steamed. I started to feel warm again and tilted up the bottle of water, draining it before my eyes could close. Because no way was I not following Jodi's orders. Jodi had always kinda scared me, if I was honest with myself.

Bottle empty, I looked down at the white Carrara marble and saw that fresh blood was dribbling slowly out of my abdomen. Something had opened up. That couldn't be good.

"Jodi," I whispered. "Help."

CHAPTER 11

I'm Not Fond of the Pelt. It Itches.

I had no idea Jodi had such good hearing, but she was in the shower with me before the plea for help finished echoing around the vast bathroom. I also hadn't known she could be the motherly type, as she turned off the water, wrapped me in a towel, and shouted for Tex and Koun. My two vamps placed me on the floor of the shower and joined me there, healing me, which involved a lot more furry and bare skin than I wanted to show and me drinking a lot more of Koun's meaty blood.

Jodi waited on the guys to finish healing me and then shooed them back out. She helped me shower, helped me into silk undies and a tunic and leggings created by Madame Melisende, a casual outfit that was soft and slightly brushed for warmth on the inside and sleek on the outside. And because it was handmade for my multiple body shapes, it adjusted to fit like a glove. In the drawer of Leo's bathroom—my bathroom now, I guessed—was a tube of red lipstick in one of my usual bloodred shades. I dabbed a little onto my pale cheeks and smeared it around, then lined my lips. Jodi combed out my hair, which had gotten terribly tangled.

"You want me to braid it?" She asked.

"No, thank you," I said. "I'll take care of it later."

"Are you going to fix my wedding site?"

"If it can't be fixed, I happen to own a mansion you can use. Will that do?"

"Yellowrock Clan Home?"

"Yeah."

"That'll do. But I have new rules." She put the lipstick and the comb away. "No uninvited vampires crashing the wedding or the reception. No undead mayhem. No hot and cold running revenants. No were-creatures at all, with the exception of Brute and Rick, if he can get away from the case he's working on, which doesn't look likely." Rick, her old partner and my former boyfriend, had been invited. "I'll be annoyed if you paranormal psychos ruin my wedding. And you don't want me annoyed."

I met her eyes in the mirror over the sinks and realized that this had to be a new addition since Leo died. Vamps never had mirrors. In the reflection, I could see how happy and afraid Jodi was.

Sudden tears gathered in her blue eyes, and she said, "Some people are only ever allowed one chance at happiness. And Homer will die working for you. He'll stand up and take a bullet. And die. For you."

Softly I said, "Wrassler doesn't know it, but he's about to be promoted to administrator of security at HQ. Eli already has the paperwork done. It's a desk job, Jodi, with an increase in salary and lots of power and pomp and circumstance. It was going to be my wedding present to y'all." Among other things. I'd had it all planned out. It was to be a surprise, but I didn't mind telling her. She needed it now.

Tears spilled out over her lids, and I realized she had panicked when she'd heard about gunfire at HQ. "So who will be taking care of you when you're here?"

"Derek will be head of my various security details, including protection at the clan home, my personal home, and all my NOLA traveling. Eli and Alex will continue to be my personal security elsewhere, as well as my partners in everything else. Koun and Tex will take over bodyguard detail. It's been planned for weeks."

She threw her arms around me. The top of her head came to my shoulder. Awkwardly, I patted her back with one hand. I so sucked at hugs.

"I hate you," she said.

"For making you cry?"

"For not telling me sooner." She sniffed, shoved her bobbed hair back, and wiped her eyes. The tears made them even bluer. "And for having all those gorgeous clothes. There must be twenty creations in your walk-in closet."

"You know I prefer jeans and a tee or a sweater, right?"

She laughed through her tears. "And you look fabulous in everything. Except for the fur." She touched the pelt where my neck and shoulder met. "That would make me nuts."

"Yeah," I said. "I'm not fond of the pelt. It itches."

She laughed some more, the teary kind of laughter. "And probably attracts fleas."

"Don't be mean," I said, a smile on my face and in my voice.

"I'm too sweet to be mean," she lied. "Let me call this in, and we can take a look at my wedding site."

I remembered seeing the fireball crashing through. And the sprinkler system coming on. It had to be horrible. "Do we hafta?"

"Yeah. Come on. "She hooked her arm through mine and led me into the hallway and through the line of assembled humans and vamps, all of whom looked unhappy, sad, or angry, and all staring at me. "And by the way," she said when we had passed the last one, "why were your people so bitchy when I got here?"

"Oh. That. Ummm. The blood in the shower? I got shot and sorta nearly died. I'm not supposed to die. I'm supposed to shift before I die."

Something hit me, hard and fast. My father had died. Midshift, he had died. Maybe all skinwalkers can die if they don't shift in time. Maybe, when I was healed in the rift, I lost my special ability to shift back faster than death could take me. That would suck. And since my DNA had been affected, it would make total sense. If vamps hadn't been close by, I'd be dead right now. Silent, I followed Jodi through HQ to the ballroom. She walked slowly, which was good, because dying can take a lot out of a girl. I was quickly winded.

The ballroom looked worse than I expected. The stained glass had been shoved to the side in a wet, multicolored pile. There were scorch marks on all the columns and a big scorched area on the floor. The row of tables were burned, leaving only metal frames, the tops blackened crisps. The ballroom stank like chemicals and smoke and, oddly, burned hair.

Jodi said nothing. She put her hands on her hips, shoving back the exercise jacket, thrusting her boobs forward. Jodi was one of the most hourglass-shaped women I knew, but when she assumed what I thought of as her cop stance, she didn't look petite or rounded or bosomy. She just looked mean. But at least she was dry-eyed and not teary anymore.

There were four uniformed staff with shop vacs and rug cleaners drawing up the black water. More staff were stripping off the unburned linens from most of the chairs to send them out for cleaning. Others were removing the ruined tables and carrying them outside into the night.

I looked up, expecting to see the worst, yet the ceiling wasn't as bad as I had assumed. Only one of the arches had been broken in, only one of the stained glass "windows" had been busted. Still. There was no way to repair the roof by the time of the wedding.

Wrassler entered behind us and wrapped Jodi in his arms. Size-wise, they looked like a silverback gorilla hugging a baby chimp. "I'm so sorry, baby," he murmured into her hair.

"We're moving the ceremony and party to the Yellowrock Clan Home," she said, steely voiced and way too calm. "We need someone to contact all the guests and let them know."

"My people can do that," I said.

"Yeah. They can. And they better." She transferred those sweet blue eyes to me, and I nearly took a step back. "And the clan home better look like a million dollars. And the fangheads are reimbursing the caterer and the bridal supply shop for everything the fire destroyed."

"Yes, ma'am," I said.

"Or," Wrassler said, "we can get the hole covered with a piece of plywood and get the NOLA coven to glamour the missing stained glass."

"Oh," Jodi said. She looked up at the ceiling and frowned. "Why didn't I think of that?"

She should have thought of it right away, because Jodi came from a witch family.

"That's perfect," she said. "And Jane can pay for it."

"I can do that," I said. To Wrassler, I added, "Spare no expense, and get every caterer and flower shop in town working to get the place up to speed. It needs to be perfect." I turned to Jodi and said, "Whatever the coven charges. Ernestine will write a blank check."

"Done," Jodi said. She made a snorting sound and turned in Wrassler's arms. They stood there for what felt like hours but was likely only half a minute. Then Jodi patted his big arm to let him know he could let go, and she walked from the room. Over her shoulder she said, "I'll tell the officials this is now a diplomatic situation. Get the Robere's on it." With that, she was gone.

Fortunately, Brandon and Brian were now in town for the wedding, and though I hated to ruin what was supposed to be a festive vacation, Jodi was right. They were the best men for the job. I blew out a breath that sorta whistled.

Wrassler chuckled, but it was a sad sound, as he looked around the room. He shook his head. "You have subjects you need to meet."

Subjects. I hated that word, now equating it with bloodservants, people who owed me something and who I had to protect. I wanted to say no, but I figured this fiasco was totally my fault, so I just nodded and let him lead the way back to a main-floor tea room, my big paw-feet silent on the flooring. "Any news from the vamp graveyard? Any sightings of Sabina or revenants or whatever?"

"No, My Queen," Wrassler said softly. "No reports of drained humans. No reports of Mithrans being attacked."

"Okay. Keep me informed, please."

"I will."

The room we stopped at was a tiny reception room, the table in the center set for tea for four. Wrassler sent me in alone. The room was empty, so was the teapot, and I was starving. Bummer. I wondered if the tea service had been set there for show, and if so, why? I had no idea how formal this meeting was, so I took the chair I would have taken had I been greeting dangerous enemies, my spine to the corner, facing the door. When I sat, my hands were shaking with fatigue. The room was small, I didn't have a weapon, I was backed into a corner, and I was hungry enough to make me grumpy.

Beast thought at me, *Is like cage. Do not like cages.*

Yeah, I thought back, trying to relax in the fluffy floral chair. Unfortunately the fabric of the clothes, the chair, and my pelt started to work against each other and ride up. And itch. Sometimes I hated my pelt.

There was a discreet knock, and the door opened, admitting two men and two women, Wrassler behind them. He closed the door and stood there, clearly my security. The other four seemed at a loss until Wrassler cleared his throat and said, "Dark Queen of the Mithrans. May I introduce Dr. Pierre Paquet, who has taken over the vampire funeral home. He and his wife, also Dr. Paquet, became doctors in France in 1939. I will arrange an introduction with Dr. Solange Paquet at a later time."

I didn't offer my hand to the doctor, but I did give a slight, regal head bow. He returned a fast up-and-down nod, but his eyes stayed glued to my cat ears, pointed atop my head. *Yeah. I'm a cat. And your queen.* I narrowed my eyes at him.

"Your majesty," he managed, sounding as if he might faint. He dropped to his knees, which made me want to laugh, but no way was I giving in to this hilarity.

"My Queen, this gentleman"—Wrassler continued to the next man—"is a blood-servant in security, second in line to Ming's Cai. They call him Long-Knife. He has been sent to us on loan from the Master of the City of Knoxville as assistance to track the Firestarter." There was something in his tone that said the man was more or less than just a gift. Either a prize or a troublemaker. Knowing Ming, I figured she had sent me a troublemaker. He had long dark hair, a wiry build, and eyes that might have come from the Steppes of Russia. He was also trying to hide a bad case of belligerence, which I decided to poke a bit.

I asked, "Who did you piss off in Knoxville?"

The Asian man stiffened. "Cai and I do not see eye to eye on security issues."

"Yeah? You gonna get along with Wrassler and Derek and Eli, the people in charge of security? Despite the fact that I'd likely insult Ming if I sent you back to her with broken bones, I'll do just that if you can't play nice. Are you capable of following orders, or are you just a hothead with no self-control?" It was an insult. I intended it to be.

Long-Knife frowned. It took up his whole face, and it was clear he wanted to be in charge of anything and everything. He wasn't a vamp, but had the look of a very old and very well-fed blood-servant. "I honor the Dark Queen," he said, after a too-long silence. His accent wasn't from an Asian country. Maybe Swedish, which was interesting. And he didn't answer my question. Also interesting.

"Yeah? We'll see. You can honor me by honoring them. Wrassler what else you got?"

"Your majesty. Florence is a nurse and Infermieri." Infermieri. A healer vamp. I wondered where she had been only a couple of hours past when I was dead. I studied the female vampire Wrassler indicated. She was about five five, slim, and was wearing white nunnish gowns, like some outclan priestesses wore. Her power felt soft, warm, and flexible, not shell-like and formidable. I inclined my head to her.

"Florence is outclan," Wrassler continued, confirming my thoughts, "one who is as independent and self-sufficient as any Mithran can be. I wish to appoint her as your personal nurse."

"Nurse," I said, deadpan. She had rich chestnut-toned hair up in a bun, brown eyes, and the kind of complexion that came from another time, another place. "Florence as in Florence Nightingale?"

"An unfortunate coincidence," she said, her voice lightly accented. Maybe Italian. Maybe something similar.

Wrassler started to speak, and she raised a hand, stopping him.

"I will speak for myself," she said. "I was turned by Lincoln Shaddock, before World War II, and left the scion lair after four years."

Most fangheads had to cure for ten years, rule of thumb, before they could control their bloodlust enough to be among humans. "That was . . . fast." That was Amy Lynn Brown fast. And Shaddock had never told Leo or me that he had turned another vamp who went through the devoveo so quickly.

"Yes, ma'am. I returned to Europe to visit my children and was trapped there by the start of the Second World War, unable to return to my maker. Following my son, a doctor, I went to work as a nurse in a mobile military hospital near the front lines. When my son was killed in a bombardment, I took over the medical care of 1,027 soldiers. My Mithran blood saved many. After the war, I sent papers to Lincoln Shaddock that I would be outclan, and I served under the outclan priestess Susanna. I was then, and I remain today, unaligned. I will save any that I can."

The fact that another wonder-blood vamp came from Linc's line was more than interesting. Of all the people in this room, this woman was clearly the most self-contained, the most headstrong, and the most useful. She was neither disdainful, nor in awe of my magnificent ears.

"So if an enemy Mithran and I were both injured," I said, "you would triage the one most likely to live and save that one."

"If My Queen accepts my service, and should I swear to her for the duration of this Mithran war, then the Dark Queen would receive my assistance first, unless she was well enough to survive on her own while I cared for another."

"Uh-huh. Triage I understand." In the years before I came to NOLA, I had taken a course as an emergency medical technician. I understood saving the savable, but I could tell from Wrassler's expression that what she had suggested was not acceptable. "But if you saved my enemy and my enemy then killed me before you could save me, what good would that do? Wouldn't that make you foresworn?"

Her head tilted and her brown eyes narrowed as she considered my question. I hadn't studied under Leo for nothing. I added, "You would be serving the Dark Queen of all Mithrans, not some"—I searched for and found a word a woman of her time might understand—"not some ragamuffin."

Her lips pursed, and I could see she was about to bargain with me for terms of her service. "I will stabilize the Dark

Queen first, followed by any humans. Then I will stabilize your Mithran enemies and will stake them to keep them paralyzed. Then I would fully heal you. In that order."

"That would take a lot of blood," I said.

"In one night, I stabilized eighty-seven humans and only fed three times. I did not drain my victims."

I looked at Wrassler and he nodded. This woman was way more than she appeared, had powerful blood, and amazing self-control. "Why are you here?" I asked her. "In New Orleans. Offering to be my nurse."

"I worked with Edmund, the Emperor of Europe, and Grégoire, the Blood Master of all of France, who is also your warlord. I saw what they were trying to accomplish, this new world of Mithrans who are bound to a new law. I read the Vampira Carta of the Americas, and I listened to them speak of this Dark Queen who would usher in a new and better time. Their war in Europe is now ended, and they will come here to be formally recognized. By the Dark Queen. I have come to serve this queen. You."

I needed a nurse because I was breakable and mortal. Right. I looked at Wrassler. "You set this up?"

"We inquired for an Infermieri. She hopped on the next flight. Edmund and Grégoire vouchsafe for her."

"Fine." I met her eyes, deep brown and calm. "I accept the service of the outclan healer, Florence. However, your maker, the Master of the City of Asheville, Lincoln Shaddock, the vamp who turned you, has been looking for an Infermieri. When the war's over, keep that in mind," I advised her. "He's a nice guy."

Her eyebrows went up, and I realized that suckheads didn't always think "nice guys" were worth working for or with. Only powerful guys.

I added, "You probably know this, but he's way more powerful than he acts, and you would be close to Amy Lynn."

Florence blinked once, as if processing that. For a vamp, she had a very expressive face.

"Last one?" I asked.

"My Queen. This is Quint. She is Quesnel's niece and an accomplished lady-in-waiting, bodyguard, and secretary."

Quesnel was Leo's sommelier. He didn't like me because I drink beer, not swanky wine, but he was necessary at HQ to satisfy the palettes of the fancy-type vamps who stayed here sometimes. My brain stopped. "What? Lady-in-waiting? Waiting for what?"

Wrassler's face looked as if he was trying not to grin at me, but not really succeeding. "She is trained in a variety of etiquette proprieties and royal conduct, and has studied for the last year to be your *most* personal assistant *and* security. Her areas of expertise include *wardrobe selection*"—his voice made a very suspicious hiding-laughter hiccup sound before he finished his sentence—"*hairstyling*, and *makeup*. She is also proficient in keeping a royal and personal calendar, handling events, taking care of onerous and unnecessary appointments and phone calls, and scheduling the important ones for your convenience." His voice steadied. "She speaks four languages, is a crack shot, and is a seventh dan black belt in taekwondo. She is a capable cook, has survival skills should you ever be stranded in the wilderness, can fish, hunt, and prepare a variety of wild game over an open fire. She knows of your various forms. She has no sense of fear."

I looked over the diminutive woman. She was the essence of ordinary. She was a head shorter than me, muscular, wore her hair in a dyed-blond butch cut, and had pretty painted nails. But her eyes were empty. Utterly empty. And she smelled of the absence of emotion.

"How well do you lie?" I asked her.

"I never lie."

"How often do you speak the truth?" I asked.

"Never."

"If I walked into the wine cellar and killed Quesnel, what would you do?"

Finally her eyes took on life and honesty. "I would kill you in a heartbeat."

Wrassler's entire face changed, and he reached for his weapon under his left arm beneath his suit jacket.

I held up a single finger, stopping him. "If you swear to me, Quint, how many others, beside Quesnel, would come before me?"

"No one."

I raised both brows at Wrassler and asked, "How many people other than Quesnel are important in her life?"

"No one." He nearly snarled.

"Good by me. You and the others swear to me. Right here, right now."

Florence dropped to her knees as graceful as a curtsy. The doc dropped again to his knees slowly, as if they might be achy. Long-Knife didn't want to kneel and dropped down slowly so I could see his reluctance. Quint went to one knee but offered me her knife. Which Wrassler clearly had no idea she carried. I took the blade. It was a nice, well-balanced, ten-inch vamp-killer, silver-plated, very sharp steel. Quint was sneaky. Probably a sociopath. But she would be *my* sociopath. Leo would have bound her to him in a heartbeat.

It was a truncated ceremony since I wasn't a vamp and had no intention of sharing my blood with them. Afterward they filed out, and I was left with Wrassler. I said, "So I have NOLA's undertaker, a loaner with a bad attitude that Ming probably expects me to fix, a nurse who might be the difference between me living and dying, should I not be able to shift again, and a bat-shit crazy wardrobe consultant. How did these people all happen to turn up here, tonight? That's mighty suspicious."

"The Consort was approached by Florence through the intercession of Edmund. He negotiated her potential contract, My Queen. She arrived in New Orleans an hour ago, and just now arrived here. Florence will remain close to you from now on. She will be moved into Katie's house with your overflow blood-servants and additional security. Long-Knife, once he's been bled and read, will be moved to another clan home because he's such a pain in the butt and no one wants to work with him. Quint . . ." He dropped onto the chair opposite me and rubbed his face as if his head, jaw, and teeth ached, leaving his hand over his eyes. "I had no idea about her."

"She smelled wrong."

Wrassler lifted his hand from his eyes. "Smelled . . . Jesus, Mary, and Joseph."

I figured I had surprised Wrassler.

I blew out a sigh, sad that the tea table was set for tea,

but the pot was cold and empty. I wasn't going to get tea. Or food. My stomach growled. I stood, which meant that Wrassler had to get to his feet too. Because I was the queen. Right. I hated protocol. I gestured to the door. Wrassler opened it, allowing me to exit. "You up for a walk?" I asked. "I want to check on the prisoner in the scion lair."

Wrassler frowned, following me into the hallway. "Why didn't you take Monique's head, Janie?"

"I thought about it. But Leo taught me to know my enemies. And . . ." An interesting thought reared its head. If Monique lived, I might be able to use my new lizard amulet icon to force a mental connection, just like Sabina did to me. I might learn who was behind everything.

In the scion lair, the Onorio was chained in the only cage for humans, one without silver plating. Monique wasn't breathing. Her mouth was open and her eyes were dried. She looked dead. But she didn't smell as if she was decaying. I needed to talk to some older Onorios and soon. We left the scion lair.

"I need a little privacy," I said to Wrassler.

He opened a door to a tiny waiting room, sparsely furnished with mismatched older chairs, a tiny table, and a single lamp. "I'll bring you tea. Sliced beef sandwiches are waiting to be delivered, My Queen."

I sat on the sofa and said, "I'm teaed out. How about a Coke? And, Wrassler? I'd like to be Janie when it's just us," I said. "Or Legs. You can save the queen stuff for when we're official."

He gave me the best grin, one I remembered from back before I was politically powerful and scary and all that stuff. "Sure, Janie."

The door closed, and I was alone in one of the tiny rooms that were scattered all through HQ. Rooms that had probably once been furnished with daybeds or chaise lounges used as private feeding rooms. Ick.

I leaned back and thought through what I wanted to say. Wrassler delivered a tray of food and slipped back out. I popped the top on the Coke, drank, ate, and thought some more. I dialed Brandon Robere.

When he answered, it was with the same title Wrassler used. "My Queen, how may I assist you?"

"Two things. One: I shot a powerful Onorio in the head. She has no heartbeat, isn't breathing, and she looks dead. But she doesn't smell dead. And two: I need to know about binding Onorios. Rule of thumb says Onorios can't be bound. But. Is it possible for a stronger, older Onorio to bind a younger, less powerful one, or maybe multiple Onorios to bind one?"

"I heard about the head shot, My Queen. Nice shooting. And no. If she isn't decomposing, then she is trying to heal. That may not work at all, or she may come back with a scrambled brain, like a revenant, or she may come back fine. No one knows. If you want her dead, take her head. If you want her alive for some reason, you must guard her well."

"Okay. And binding Onorios?"

"Yes and no. I have never heard of an Onorio being forcibly bound, but we can be drained, our power and our life force taken by another, leaving us vulnerable to death by normal mortal violence. I've also never heard of multiple Onorios binding any of our kind."

Never heard of didn't mean *couldn't happen.* "What about voluntarily agreeing to be bound?" I told him about the beings in the bloody hull of Monique's soul home. When I finished, he was silent for a time.

"I've heard about Onorios in the past who agreed to a *mutual* binding, much like *anamchara.* That may be what you saw in your vision. But when you shot Monique, the binding was interrupted. If there are other Onorios involved in this mutual binding, then they will be desperate. They will do anything and everything within their power to get her back. Even without her mind intact, she would be useful to them." He hesitated again before saying, "My Queen. My suggestion is to have your executioner address this situation."

Kill Monique. Not yet. "I want to use her to draw out the others. I'll see she's guarded well and I want you and your brother to take extra precautions too." Because Monique wasn't the only Onorio in NOLA. "Now. About the whole crowning of Eddie. Where do we stand?"

"The papers are all drawn up, My Queen. We are prepared."

                              *   *   *

I worked until close to dawn, making sure that Monique
was well-guarded and securely locked down. With Cowbird
Protocol in place, Monique should be fine. But I wasn't
taking chances. Eli and I also spent time with the security
teams, going over wedding protocols. Busy work, but urgent and necessary busy work.

I was still in half-form, and the nice soft lining of the
fancy outfit kept catching on my pelt and pulling it. The
pants rode up, the back got stuck, and I looked ridiculous.
When things seemed in place and going smoothly, I made
a trip to Leo's room—my room—and left the outfit on the
floor. I was sure someone would pick up after me, because
the bloody sheets were all gone, the bed was made up
neatly, and the shower and bath had been cleaned into
shiny spotlessness.

There were no jeans or tees in the closet. The only thing
that looked comfortable was a sweat suit, and it was an
ugly shade of white-people flesh, sort of like mayo with a
hint of peach. Not that I'd ever say that to them. I pulled it
on, and it was just as uncomfortable on my pelt.

Beast thought at me, *Ugly human clothes. Jane has pelt.
Should not cover up beautiful pelt.*

I pulled out the neckline of the top and looked down at
my hairless boobs. *Nope. Not happening.*

Beast chuffed with laughter.

I checked to see if Quint's number had been added to
my cell, and it had. That meant that Alex had access to my
cell and all its settings. I thought about lodging a complaint, but I could also just buy a burner phone most anytime. With the danger we were all facing, Alex's access
allowed him to track and find me if I went missing. Frowning, I texted Quint my clothing request. Her first job would
be to change out my wardrobe.

I texted Bruiser that I was ready to go home. He met me
in the downstairs entrance. The doorway still smelled of
fire and burned chemicals but looked better than I expected, except for the charred cement and the burned hulk
of a car. We crawled into the back seat of an SUV. It had a
limo-worthy privacy panel in place, and so I laid my head

on my honeybunch's shoulder. As we pulled out of the back gate, Beast shoved her claws into my brain. I/we saw a form out the side window. We sat up fast.

"What?" Bruiser asked. He was already holding a nine-mil.

"Something. Don't know. A shadow?" I pointed. "Another one." They were shadowing the SUV. I couldn't make them out, but I did see crotch-rocket motorcycles on side streets. I looked at my honeybunch. "You put people watching my every move."

He holstered his weapon. "Guilty, my love."

"Mmmm." I snuggled back onto his shoulder. "So when I got shot, how did you get to me so fast?" I smelled his reaction as fresh adrenaline shot through him, the scent of distress.

"I was close," he said carefully. "Alex told me the front gate had been breached."

"So you knew the front was being attacked, and you ran outside without backup. You got pinned down first. In a firefight. Then I ran outside and got pinned down too." I was half irritated at both of us, and he had to hear that in my tone.

"I was never in imminent danger," he said, the beginning of anger tinting his tone. "But you had to lead your people into battle, still thinking you are immortal. As we know now, you are not." He pulled me close, intense emotions making his English accent stronger. "You were not supposed to be there. You were supposed to be safe in the security room. *Please* do not rush in where angels fear to tread when you have been told to *stay put*."

Beast does not need help. Beast does not stay put, she thought at me. Into our shared head space, she sent images of hunting, killing, attacking a massive boar. *Beast is best hunter.*

I thought about the terror that was pumping through Bruiser's blood. Thought about what it meant to be the Dark Queen. Very softly, enunciating each word, I said, "You ran outside. You. In the face of enemies."

"This is not about me. You nearly *died*."

"Because you did *not* tell me. Without communication, I will do as I think best."

"Tell you? You did not *ask*." His scent was morphing sharply from fear into anger.

"That's a sucky excuse," I said, putting distance between us, sliding across the seat. "This is my HQ. My job. *Mine*. You will let me do it."

An inarticulate sound emerged from his throat and rose to a shout. "You could have died!" he shouted, fury in his eyes. Bruiser's fists balled, and the stink of his emotions grew. "*Died!* I could have *lost* you!"

"Yeah. That sucks. And now we know I'm mortal, unlike Leo, who was immortal and yet who is dead." And that was the problem, right there. Leo dead. His coffin empty. Bruiser facing the possibility of another loss. Me.

The car had come to a stop. We were at the freebie house, and I hadn't noticed.

"I keep trying to protect you the way I protected Leo." He forced his hands to open and placed them on his thighs, breathing through the rage and terror. "But you are not Leo. You cannot fight your enemies as Leo fought his." Bruiser twisted in the seat, opened the door, and stepped out to the sidewalk. "I could not bear to lose you," he said. He slammed the door. The armored vehicle actually shook. Bruiser stalked inside the house, rage vibrating through him.

Oddly, seeing him like that made me happy. It was like a normal human man storming into the house. Yet . . . To myself, I said, "He's protecting me like he had to protect Leo. This sucks."

The privacy panel came down. "We're all protecting you like we protected Leo," the driver said. "It's our job. If a vamp comes in and kills you, who do you think suffers? Us humans and our families, who might be put to death by a conqueror just for the hell of it."

I looked up and saw Shemmy in the rearview. I looked at the control panel and saw that Bruiser hadn't turned off the speakers. Shemmy had heard the entire thing. "Your families?"

"You're the only thing standing between us and total annihilation. If an asshole takes over from you, kills you? Bruiser and Eli and Alex will be the first to go. Then all your loyal security people. Your witch friends and allies?

Gone in the first tier. Wrassler and his human wife, Jodi? Somewhere at about the second layer of cleansing. You had to know all this. You saw the house that later became your clan home. You know how many died, and that was simply a clan battle. This will be immeasurably worse. This will be like Europe."

Where a war had raged and the death toll was over a thousand.

Shock rushed through me like an icy wind. Leo had told me that he stood between chaos and anarchy and the safety of his people. My job was even bigger than his had been. The moment I became the Dark Queen, my power placed all of my people in danger. Every single one of them. And it was my job to protect them. I had known that I needed an army and I had worked to create one. But I needed a bigger freaking army.

"And hey, Legs? You wrote our job descriptions. Dumas is just doing his job, and you're not helping him."

It was true. I had written the job descriptions, including my own. But when I wrote them, I hadn't considered that I might not shift if I died. I hadn't considered that Sabina would be burned and Leo's body stolen. I had never fully wrapped my head around the knowledge that a conquering vamp would kill my people just for funzies. That sort of head-lopping housecleaning was way beyond my understanding. A very few enemies had been dispatched when I became the Dark Queen, but wholesale killing was a baffling concept. Worse, my muscle memory always said to run toward the fight, no matter what, and Beast . . . Beast wanted to fight. She lived for it. She goaded me into the fray every single time. I had put everyone in danger trying to do things the old way, not reining in Beast, not thinking first, not staying safe.

"So I'm an ass."

"Not my words. Your words, My Queen," Shemmy said.

Okay. Lesson learned. I needed to tell them I had learned it. Show them I had learned it. And I had to apologize to my honeybunch, big time. I blew out a sigh. "Thanks, Shemmy. I needed to hear all that."

And . . . Bruiser and I might have just had an actual fight. In front of the chauffeur. In the midst of feeling like an idiot, this made me oddly, weirdly happy, and it took a moment to realize that people who are bound don't argue. This argument had just proved to me that we were normal. Just a normal couple. Laying out boundaries and figuring out how to make a relationship work, like humans, instead of typical fanghead life.

Well, aside from all the "Kill Jane" and the "Jane is stupid" stuff.

The boys were sparring on the third floor. Grunts, thumps, gasps, tiny squeals. It was noisy. I climbed the flights to the attic space, which had been converted into a gym / fighting ring / training room, two vamp sleeping closets, and a tiny bathroom. Along the walls, Koun and Tex stood, arms crossed over their chests, scrutinizing the action. Brute was sitting in the corner, watching avidly, panting with what looked like delight, his tongue lolling. Tex's dogs were snoozing in the corner.

In the middle of the floor, the focus of all the attention, Eli and Bruiser were sparring. Sparring hard. Not holding back. Bare to the waist, barefoot, fists landed to torsos and abdomens. To the face, finger jabs to the kidneys, kicks to the knees. Blocks effective about half the time. Eli was in loose workout pants. Bruiser was in his dress slacks, which meant he had walked in the door mad, and Eli had taken on his fury.

Eli was the better at hand-to-hand because he was sneaky and never followed rules, but Bruiser was faster. And stronger. And he was totally involved with this fight because he was fighting his anger, his impotence to protect me.

Fun, Beast thought at me. *Play with brother and mate?*

I had options. I could join the fray. In half-form, full of vamp blood, Beast and I might be able to beat both of them together. Recently healed, that might not be smart. Or I could take the high road. I wasn't good at taking the high road.

Eli landed a throat punch and danced back. Bruiser gagged, the punch having missed crushing his trachea by a hair.

Into the momentary pause, I yelled, "I'm sorry!"

Both men stopped, dropped their guards. They looked at me, then at each other. "For what?" Bruiser asked.

"For not knowing or thinking about being so freaking . . . killable," I said. "For rushing in like a fool. For getting mostly dead and having to be brought back with your blood," I said to the vamps. "For putting you all in danger, you and all my people and all their families. For being me and not learning a new way to do things. I suck at being a queen."

Eli barked a laugh and stepped farther from Bruiser.

"But I promise to learn," I said. "I will never be the proper protocol queen some suckheads and their servants need, but I'll stop trying to get myself and the people I love killed by not listening."

Bruiser dropped his stance, bent over, and put his hands on his knees. He was breathing hard. His face was bruised, and his lips were a bloody mess.

Eli looked no better, but he was evaluating us. To Bruiser, he said, "She's worth the trouble."

Bruiser nodded his head and managed a deep breath through his damaged throat. He stood upright and shook out his hands. "She is. Did I hurt you?" he asked.

"I'll live. A little blood might help later. You want to finish this?"

"Proper fisticuffs?"

"Hell no." Eli raised his fists and danced out the kinks in his legs. "But nothing below the belt, with knees, throats, and temples off-limits."

"Done." Bruiser attacked.

I'd be happy to be in the middle of that scuffle, but I had a feeling Bruiser would just walk away. He needed the release.

In the kitchen with a fresh cup of gunpowder green tea on the table beside me, I watched the security video of the attack at HQ. Fireballs in back. Out front, the attackers used bullets. The NOPD SWAT, uniformed members of the eighth district, and three firetrucks blocked the roads. The humans stood behind armored vehicles and barricades, waiting, SWAT team aiming through the open gates. Watching as vamps and humans raced around shooting at each other. The fireballs out back stopped. Something that might have been the Firestarter slithered like melting wax over the wall and into the darkness. Bodies were carted up the front steps, including mine. No one left through the front entrance. The gate remained open. I sped through an hour of nothing, until Jodi walked through the open front gates and up the steps, as if out for stroll.

I knew that I would be insulated from violence from now on, and it was my own dang fault. Beast and I needed to get my body and shifting back under control. I needed to be able to shift the way we used to. I needed to go to my soul home and figure out what was wrong.

Until that happened, I sipped and watched the sun rise out the kitchen window. Later I opened the trunk that Derek and I had brought up from subbasement four. I put the daguerreotype of Leo on the table on Bruiser's side of the bed and unloaded the record books.

Just as I had asked Derek, some of the journals were in English, and there was a lot of history, personal musings, often drawings and even some old photos, but there was nothing useful to the current situation, except for a small leather-bound text Derek had put in the trunk. It was titled *A Brief Treatise on Witchery and Demonic Workings*. It was in English, but nearly impossible to read, with print that used caps in weird places and mixed up *S* and *F* and other letters. I hunted for and found a heading that read *"The Uncommon and Inexplicable Rule of Three."*

It occurred to me, not for the first time, that the Onorio Monique Giovanni, the *senza onore* Aurelia Flamma Scintilla, and the other women in the hull soul home could be three Onorio types. But there were three other Onorios in NOLA—Bruiser and the B-twins, Brandon and Brian Robere. Tau, also a *senza onore* of some sort, was in the null prison, put there by me. Monique had wanted Bruiser to join her group of three. Why? Add in the Robere twins and Tau in the witch's null prison, and that made another three. Assuming Monique knew about her.

Then there were Sabina's incoherent visions and ramblings. Her visions of Ka. What was so important about Ka N'vsita? The memory of Ka, the Firestarter, and Immanuel standing together with the blond man. Shaun MacLaughlinn was blond. Could it have been him? Had Shaun been part of Immanuel's plan to take over from Leo from the very beginning? I tried to recall the fashions they wore, but their clothing faded into mists as I tried to force the memory. Sabina hadn't noticed the clothes or the time period.

What if . . . What if Ka was still alive but no longer able to change shapes. What if she was no longer an Onorio.

What if the magic Adan used on Ka had caused her DNA to malfunction as mine had, but with a different outcome? What if that was why they needed more Onorios? That made an awful lot of sense. And if Ka was no longer able to function as a skinwalker, that left Grandmother, who was definitely *u'tlun'ta*, and me. And Aya was skinwalker too. We had multiples of threes with extras if needed, plenty of paras to make use of the power of the Rule of Three. With a frisson of fear, I wondered what the Rule of Three squared might accomplish.

Where was Ka's former master, Adan? Had he known what Ka could become? Would he have cared? Even if he had understood what that meant, Adan was a vamp and a witch. He would have done what he wanted and the consequences be damned.

Fear shivering through me, I asked Alex, sitting at his desk only yards away in the living room, for Adan's location. Instantly he texted me an address in Alabama. Adan was in Mobile at last sighting. I wasn't sure what to do about that.

Vamp life was a constant jostling of loyalties and rearranging of plans. Tangled skeins of threads to unravel, broken puzzles without all the pieces needed to put it together. All this was too interconnected to be random, as if all of this was part of a weaving created by someone long ago and managed through the years.

Holy crap. Leo had expected all this. *Planned* for all this.

And that blasted fanghead bloodsucker had dumped it all on me.

CHAPTER 12

Little Brother to the Rescue

I texted Aya to beware of possible attacks and the little I knew about the Rule of Three. He texted back one word: "Acknowledged." My brother wasn't the chatty type.

I also texted Brandon and Brian Robere to beware of possible assault and abduction. Brandon replied, "We are in a safe location and are well-guarded, but we will be vigilant."

I went back to the journals, flipping through one in Spanish and two in French. They were hard to read and impossible for me to translate, but I could pick out names. I saw one area where the names Adan Bouvier and de Allyon were on the same page. De Allyon. Who killed all the skinwalkers and drank their blood. I had killed his sorry butt and taken his head. I took a photo of the untranslated text and sent it to Alex to find someone who spoke the language of the region and the timeline, and get it translated.

As I sent the text, vamp timelines begin to click together, almost audibly, in my mind. It was daylight, and my teapot was empty. I should be in bed after a long and com-

plicated night, but my brain was in overdrive. Starting a
new pot, with double the gunpower green, I made a strong
bitter tea full of caffeine.

It was possible that if Leo's liver-eater son, currently
known as Immanuel, and Adan (and by loyalty, Ka N'vsita)
were part of one group, that sometime in the 1900s, all three
somehow entered de Allyon's service. Some peculiar version of the Rule of Three?

And later they met the Firestarter, who hated vamps,
but . . . if the Onorios were going to betray the vamps and
take over from them, then Aurelia might have joined in a
relationship with de Allyon. It would have been a relationship that was destined for treachery from the beginning,
but that was vamp life in a nutshell.

But there was no proof. Unless the proof was in these
journals or other records from HQ.

I checked my email and discovered that Alex had sent
me the translation of *La Historia de Los Mithrans en Los
Americas*, so I grabbed the Glob from my closet and the
small box that contained that original version of the history text from my room. I placed them both carefully on
the table. I'd been sent a translation before, but I hadn't
studied it with the full text on the screen and the original
book open on my desk. I opened the box and looked inside at
the small, nondescript leather-bound book. The first time
I touched it, the leather had a slimy texture, even through
the gloves I wore. Now I was barehanded, but I was protected, as I lifted the book out, the Glob already absorbing
any energies that might have been woven into it. *La Historia de Los Mithrans en Los Americas* was small and very
heavy: a history of the early years of vampires in the Americas, with important stories about de Allyon's life. The paper was thick, with a heavy cloth content, and there were
drawings in the margins.

The first time I saw it, Sabina had sent word that I would
find page 134 of interest. I turned again to that page and
the drawing of a Spanish conquistador in plate armor, one
boot resting on the dead body of a naked tribal man. The
dead man's hair was unbraided, tangled on the ground, a
pool of his blood leaking from a large throat wound.

His hands were furred and clawed.

Just like my father's when he died.

Other naked tribal people were on the ground at the feet of the Spaniard, and two had yellow eyes like mine. Only one was alive, fear etched on the woman's face in stark black ink lines. Softly I spoke his name, "Lucas Vazquez de Allyon. El Rival de la Muerte." Death's Rival.

Lucas de Allyon had known about skinwalkers, had killed skinwalkers. Below de Allyon's name was a small pen-and-ink miniature of the vampire in his fully human guise, his eyes and hair dark, his forehead wide, nose Roman, wearing a Vandyke beard. The artist had captured the man's power, his domineering personality, the brutal curl of his lips. And his disdain for anything and anyone who wasn't him. I returned to the drawing of the conquistador and his living and dead prey, staring at the terrified yellow-eyed woman, at his feet.

On the next page was another miniature, showing de Allyon wearing cloth pants, a puma skin over his shoulders. The puma's head was propped on his shoulder, showing killing teeth. At his feet were more mountain lions, one with a human head, another with human hands and feet. One was a melanistic *Puma concolor*. All were bound and bleeding from many wounds, but the largest wounds were at their throats where fangs had torn them out. De Allyon, had been a vamp, and he had killed my kind and drunk their blood. The protectors of the Cherokee had been captured and slaughtered to feed the blood appetite of a Naturaleza vampire.

In the next drawing, de Allyon was vamped out, fangs down, his eyes black and scarlet. He was sitting in a gold chair holding a golden bowl, filled with blood. Blood streamed from his mouth and down his naked chest.

The last drawing had been too small to see without a magnifying glass. But, knowing what it was, I made out the image of a priest holding a sword in one hand, a blazing cross in the other. He was running, dark robes flying behind him. He was being chased by an armored man on a black horse.

Had de Allyon had access to the iron Spike of Golgotha? Had he been the one to make the disks that helped power time circles? Had he been the one to mix skinwalker blood with the holy iron? I touched the Glob. It was warm against my fingertips. There was a disk of the iron spike inside the Glob. And a lot of my skinwalker blood. Had de Allyon been trying to make a magical amulet like the Glob? If so, why?

In the years after Ka was transformed into an Onorio, had de Allyon gained possession of her? All the bad things that had been swirling around in my mind like a rancid stew came to the surface: I made tenuous connections between my own black magic in melding with Beast; Leo's son being eaten, which allowed the Cherokee Skinwalker man to fool everyone into believing he was Immanuel; and Ka and Grandmother.

I remembered Sabina's visions. Was it possible that Sabina had smelled the foul stench of *u'tlun'ta* the night the Firestarter attacked her and her chapel burned? Had Grandmother been there, watching, helping? I tried to relax so I could pull up the memory, but it was indistinct and wouldn't come to the front of my mind. It was like trying to slice fog with a knife. I couldn't remember.

I didn't have enough information.

Fear trickled through my blood like ice water as I remembered the Rule of Three needing three aligned Onorios. If my fear was right, they needed Bruiser and also maybe a B-twin, and the wedding invitations had made certain that all of the Onorios who aligned with me were in one town at the same time.

Worse. How might a very, *very* old skinwalker *u'tlun'ta* play into all this? With Ka and Monique aligned with the *u'tlun'ta*, there was considerable leeway for multiple combinations for the Rule of Three.

Grandmother was ancient. How long had she been hiding the stench of the liver-eater? And how old had Immanuel's skinwalker been? Who was Immanuel's skinwalker before he ate Immanuel?

And . . . was it even possible that Grandmother was the yellow-eyed tribal woman lying at de Allyon's feet?

Something dark and dangerous slithered through me, the knowledge that no matter what parts of my possibilities were right, I was close to putting it all together, and it was *bad*.

This was the problem in trying to think like vamps. All of the context was bound up in the past.

I/we are best hunter, Beast thought at me. *I/we do not fear predator. I/we are not prey.*

Yeah, I thought back. *Okay.*

It was too late for me to call Grandmother and ask all these things. That ship sailed long before she tried to bite me. But maybe Aya could help me put the puzzle pieces together. I'd have to tell him everything, show him the evidence. Could he keep it family and not make it a PsyLED case?

As if I had never seen one before, I studied the cell phone I had placed on the desk. And watched as my hand took the phone and pulled up Aya's number again, though I didn't tap it for the call to go through. Not yet. I turned my free hand over and flexed my fist, watching the knobby knuckles and too-long fingers as they opened and closed.

I remembered the holy water trailing through my human fingers. I hadn't befouled the water yesterday, despite being a paranormal killer. Maybe God could even use someone as violent as me to do some good.

I had been the hand of God that took down Death's Rival, de Allyon. I had taken his head.

That was good. Except God said we were supposed to love our enemies. I kinda sucked at that.

I still hated de Allyon, a flaming bright hatred that burned and ached inside me. Even dead, I hated him for the things I had read in the history book. His death would never be enough for Vengeful Cat. Never enough for me.

I tapped Aya's number.

"FireWind. How may I assist the Dark Queen?" he said as he answered. I figured that meant he was at work or with other people, and he was telling them who was calling and telling me that this was a formal discussion. So much in so few words.

"We need to speak privately."

"One moment." I heard something moving quietly, a door closing, a second one opening and closing. The soft squeak of a chair. "You may speak privately, my sister."

"Have you seen Grandmother?"

"No. Hayalasti Sixmankiller did not return to her home. No one has seen her."

"I'll be sending you a file and photos from a history book, one that's maybe part journal, part picture book, about a fanghead I killed in legal combat. Then we need to talk about Grandmother and a skinwalker named Ka N'vsita, and what might happen if two *u'tlun'tas* are working together. Grandmother and Ka. Here in NOLA."

I heard a soft tap. "Send it to my email. I have my personal laptop open. This is private. Not part of any record, correct?"

That was one good thing about Aya. He was all business, and when it came to cop stuff, not argumentative. He was willing to consider unpleasant possibilities and not hold my thoughts against me. "Yeah. You will want it private. Because it's about us. Our kind." I took photos of the pertinent drawings and sent them to his email, then forwarded the translation of the book.

We waited in silence until he said, "They have arrived."

Tsalagi didn't curse, not the way white people did. But when Aya opened the files, he cursed in English, a soft whispered word. As he read and looked through the drawings, I closed de Allyon's book, placed it back in the small box, and put the box top back on. I started talking and I told him everything. All my New Orleans years. Death and murder and betrayals and mistakes. Then I brought all the strands together: "Shaun MacLaughlinn was a midrange powerful vamp. Now he's something more because he survived the loss of his *anamchara*. He might be working with Ka, the Firestarter, and Monique. And I can't rule out Grandmother."

When I finished, he was silent. I didn't even hear papers shifting or keys clacking. I looked up from my cold empty tea mug to see Alex sitting at the table with me. Silent. No tablets, no electronics. Not even wearing earbuds to keep up with his world. He was utterly still, his eyes on me.

Aya finally said, "It will take me some time to digest this, my sister."

"I've been living it, and I'm still digesting it. What if Ka and Grandmother are both *u'tlun'ta* and are working together? Do they need the Rule of Three too?"

Aya murmured, "They may. And if so, they will want a third skinwalker. They will want you or me for an *u'tlun'ta* working. Or one of the skinwalker cousins." He stopped. "I haven't told you about them. Did you know that I . . . *we* have three distant cousins in Oklahoma?"

"No," I said sourly. "You haven't gotten around to that." Of course I hadn't told him about the two brother-big-cats I had scented so long ago out west. They had most likely been skinwalkers. "I have things to tell you too. When this is all over, we'll have an honest, frank talk about skinwalkers." Before he could reply, I added, "And yes, that includes the half-form, though I'm not sure how much I can tell you about how that happens."

Aya made a noncommittal sound. "If your conjectures are true, then the Rule of Three might require George Dumas for his Onorio power. Is the body of this Monique in a safe place? And are you certain you don't wish the dead to become true dead? The Onorio you hold prisoner is a potential threat and rallying point."

"Yes to the first. No to the second. I have a traitor at HQ. That traitor will want to free her. We're watching her body, with a full team ready at any moment to respond."

"Your call, of course. I'm in Knoxville. I'll arrange official leave and take the first flight out. I'm on my way. Keep yourselves safe."

The call ended, and I thought, *Little brother to the rescue.* I wondered if his presence would make things better or worse.

I heard a sound at the front door and felt my body tense for fight or flight. The scent hit me, that wonderful mixture of meat and spices that always heralded food from Cochon Butcher. Eli strode into the room, his dark skin sheened with rainwater; Bruiser, also rain-damp, was behind him. The sky had been spattering down off and on for hours.

Eli gestured at the table, and I gathered up my stuff and carried it to the bedroom, out of the way. When I got back, the table was full of meat and goodness. There was duck pastrami, country sausage, broiled boudin, smothered greens, mac and cheese, deviled eggs, potato salad, and two loaves of bread from a local bakery. Bruiser, Eli, and Alex were already loading up plates for an early lunch, and I joined in, putting a little of everything onto mine. Grabbing a knife and fork, I started to dig in.

I stopped. Frowned. Alex had said I didn't offer thanks anymore. I wasn't sure how a tribal chick who had been Christian-dunked in a river and then self-dunked many times as part of Cherokee rituals was supposed to pray.

"Jane?" Bruiser asked. There was worry in his tone.

"I need to say thanks," I said, staring at the food in front of me. Eli and Alex exchanged glances, as if they had been talking about just this. All three guys put down their cutlery and folded their hands on the table. I could feel their eyes on me, and with my part-cat nose, I could smell their relief. To them, this meant that I was acting more like myself. Or my old self. "I'm—" I stopped. "I'm not sure how anymore," I said more softly.

"I'll say it," Eli said, his gaze heavy. A silence stretched, and I realized he was waiting for me to *man up*, as he might put it. I gave a slight nod. Without looking down or closing his eyes, he said, "We are grateful for safety. We are grateful for bounty. We are grateful for life. We are grateful for laughter. We are grateful for each other and for family and for clan. Amen."

I thought about that statement of gratitude. It wasn't like any prayer I had ever heard. There was no *Lord this* or *Lord that*. But there was also no naming of the corn mother or the sun and moon. It was a statement of fact, of gratitude. I had a feeling it would not be enough for me at some point in the future, that I would need to go talk to God in my soul home and get my spiritual life back on some kind of track, but for now, it was a beginning.

"Amen," I said quietly. And then I grinned and added, "And we are grateful for the pig who died to give us this meat."

"Amen to that," Alex said. Irritable, he asked, "Now can we please eat?"

We ate. Silent and comfortable.

After the meal, while they all sipped coffee and I drank a chai with peri-peri peppers in it, I told the guys my theory about the Onorio Ka maybe being *u'tlun'ta*, about maybe eating the Firestarter and being the same person, about Monique not being totally dead and my plan to draw out our traitor at HQ, about Shaun aligned with the Fire-starter, and about Sabina involved with Grandmother. All my paranoid conspiracy theories. Except the paranoid were sometimes right. I finished with the information that Ayatas FireWind was heading here. The guys were silent for so long after I finished speaking that I got up and made a new pot of tea for me and coffee for them.

"Is this an official PsyLED trip?" Eli asked.

Aya had said he would arrange leave. "No. It's . . . I guess it's family," I said, uncomfortable at that word referring to Aya.

"I'll reserve him a hotel room," Alex said, heading back to his desk.

"I'll go back to the Council Chambers," Bruiser said, rising and kissing the top of my head as if I were a child, "and begin the negotiations into the rules for the Sangre Duello that Koun will fight with Shaun or his champion."

Oh. I had forgotten that part. A finger of shame wriggled around inside my brain, as he knew it would, hence the head kiss. But I knew Koun was by far the better fighter. If he died, I would lose a lot, and my friend would die. Even if Koun lost, I could negotiate safe passage for my people. If I died, things would suck. If I died, the whole city could lose.

Exhausted, the taste of roasted meat still on my lips and caught in my clothes and pelt, I left the table and the cleanup to others, crawled into bed, and fell asleep.

My last thought was the wedding. *Dang.* I hadn't checked in on the repairs to the ballroom. Then I was gone.

Beast woke. It was night. Bruiser was not in Jane bed. Had not been in Jane bed. Beast smelled burned things and felt hot air through house. This meant humans with no pelt needed warmth. Beast rolled over and pulled Jane half-form-clothes off Beast body. Sniffed for scents. Listened for sounds with ears and sniffed with nose stolen from ugly-dog-good-nose, which Jane called bloodhound. Heard protectors outside house, walking. Smelled vampires in house. Alex in house.

Eli rose from bed upstairs and walked downstairs, feet silent to humans but heard by Beast. Something had waked

Eli. Then heard very soft *tap-tap-tap*. Was what waked
Beast. Was what waked Eli. Eli would have white man gun,
but Eli would not shoot Beast.

Beast stretched on good bed, front legs out. Then back
legs out. Pulled on spine and neck and shoulders and hips.
Shook pelt.

Tap-tap-tap.

Beast dropped from bed. Padded to front window.
Raised up and shoved aside curtain with paw. On other
side of window was . . . *Leo.*

Beast heart jumped into throat. Beast whirled and raced
to door of Jane den. Could smell Eli on other side. With
both front paws, scratched onto door. Eli opened door. "Be
quiet; someone is—"

Beast rammed body at Eli legs. Eli cursed. Nearly fell.
Beast raced through house, feet and paws slipping on wood
floor and rugs. Sped to sidewall with many doors where cat
door had been created. Heard Eli give warning that Beast
was free and running. Said to shoot nothing. Knew Eli had
not seen Leo. But Eli would not know Leo. Leo was body-
changed. *But was Leo!*

Beast dove through cat door and into wet night, damp
and chill. Night smells of New Orleans were strong. Urine,
vomit, rats, stinky humans with no baths, much food, hot
fat, smelly spices, much alcohol. And stink of burned
vampire.

Sped across backyard to side yard to square block fence
and leaped. Good Beast leap. High. Caught balance at top
of wall. Fast *pawpawpaw* along fence. What Jane called cat
balance. What Beast called best hunter. Dropped body
down to ground in tiny space filled with big-leaf plants.
Landed. Stopped beneath wide leaves. Hidden. Rain made
loud noises, plopping on to leaves and ground. Was not
hard rain. Was wet. Beast did not like rain and wet. But . . .
Leo scent was on air. Was different Leo scent. Many dead
burned flowers and burned paper smell. But deep inside
scent was still Leo.

Wanted to scent deep but did not make flehmen response, did not make noise to smell. Belly-crawled to front
of side yard. Could tell Leo was not at Jane den now but
was still close. Followed stink of burned Leo on night air,

shadow to shadow, car to car. Avoided street lights and house lights and drunk humans lying in doorways.

Turned toward river. To hill called levee. Then downstream. Following burned Leo smell like dog, snout in wind. Shadow to shadow. Silent.

Saw human-shape-form sitting on park bench. Sitting human form was Leo. Sleeping human lay on ground at feet. Smelled human blood. Stopped, smelled air, and watched. Leo had been dead. Head had been removed. Then time changed, and head was *almost* removed. Beast had seen many things and beings die. Leo should not have survived, but Leo had drunk blood from great predator in HQ subfive. Leo had healing bottle of special blood from lab-a-tory. Had been buried in blood of enemies, much magic healing blood and magic string tying head to body.

Beast thought hard, trying to think as Jane thinks.

Leo had been burned in graveyard fire. Leo had been taken from Leo tomb by . . . enemies? Friends? Yet Leo was alone. Had Leo killed thieves of Leo body? Leo was good hunter.

But. Trying to think like Jane.

Was possible Leo would not be same Leo.

Human at Leo feet breathed. Leo had fed but had not killed human. Beast smelled other humans nearby, humans with no den, what Jane called homeless. They slept under plastic and boxes in slow rain. Leo had fed from them all, and all lived. Blood was needed to make Leo strong. Leo needed *much* blood to heal. Yet Leo had not killed humans. Leo was not revenant. Was still enough of Leo to approach.

Beast dropped to belly and crawled closer to Leo.

"I smell you, my Jane," Leo said. "You came to me."

Am not Jane, Beast thought. Stopped crawling. Wondered if Leo wanted Beast blood. *Would fight Leo. Beast is not prey.*

"I dreamed of you while I lay in the blood of my enemies. I dreamed of the cavern where I was once trapped, a cavern with a tall domed ceiling and rising and falling columns of stalactites and stalagmites. I was chained there by silver that I could not break, and yet . . ." Leo was silent.

His toe pushed at the sleeping human. Rolled human over, snoring. "Yet Jane set me free. Such strange dreams."

Leo made laugh that sounded of much pain. Laugh was wrong, but Beast did not know why. Needed to wake Jane. Jane would know what to do about Leo. Beast pressed claws into Jane mind. Jane mind was sleeping, curled into ball like kit.

"I dreamed of angels and demons and the Flayer of Mithrans. I dreamed of my Katherine and my Grégoire. And I dreamed of my master. But Katherine and Grégoire are gone, no longer at their lairs. Of them all, you came to me."

Beast did not move closer. Body tightened, paws close to body. Tail around hips and out of way. Was ready to leap far.

"Do you love me, my Jane?"

Beast did not answer. Jane did not love Leo. Beast loved Leo. Beast had always loved Leo. Was hard to think of love, of human thoughts for mate and kits, but Beast had always wanted Leo, biggest predator, for Jane-mate.

Jane took Bruiser as mate, and Beast loved Bruiser too. Maybe loved Bruiser more than Beast could ever have loved Leo. But old love for Leo was still in Beast heart and body. Smaller love, weaker love. But still was love.

Beast pressed claws harder into Jane mind. *Jane must wake,* Beast thought.

Jane came awake. *Holy crap, where are we?*

Beast showed Jane vision of levee. Vision of Leo. Jane peered through Beast eyes. Jane thought, like prayer of fear and amazement, *Leo?*

Is Leo. Did not kill humans he drank from. Beast showed Jane what had happened.

Is he sane?

Beast does not know. But rabid predator would have killed. Leo knows we are here. Calls us my Jane.

Yeah. He would, if he was sane. Or sane-ish. Okay.

Leo breathed. Breath sounds were strange for vampires to make. Leo spoke. "Of them all, I could not bind you, yet you served me. In your own way." Leo made strange sound of laughter again.

Shock went through Jane like arrow. Jane understood

why laugh was wrong. And now Beast understood. Leo was vamped out with fangs and wide night-eyes and claws on fingers. Was fully predator. Yet Leo laughed. Vampires could not laugh and be vampire at same time. Laughter brought them back to human selves. Should. But this time did not.

Leo breathed again. "You served. According to that blasted bedamned honor that seeps into the world from your heart and changes everything you touch. Unbound. *Unbound* you stayed with me. Me, the Monster of New Orleans. Did you know that they called me that, for a time? The Monster of New Orleans." He laughed, that odd, not-Leo laugh.

Beast did not like laugh sounds. Jane did not like sound. Human at Leo feet snored louder. Leo toed human again and snore stopped.

"That Monster of New Orleans told you of the worse monsters to come and shared the threat that you could protect your witch friends and, by extension, all of us. And you believed me. You believed when I told you. You stayed, and the monsters began to come, as I knew they would. Many of my enemies I couldn't have destroyed alone. You were the wild card in this deadly game. Because of you, many lived who would have died. Including me."

Strange not-laugh sound came from Leo. He raised his hand and looked at claws. Leo put hand on knee and tilted head to Beast. Was not-human motion. Was vampire motion, like snake. Leo looked at Beast. Beast tensed to leap, but Leo kept talking.

"You believed when even the witches themselves did not believe. My own people did not believe that I could die true dead, that I could fail to keep them safe. None of the others who drank saw the futures. No one believed that if I lost, the monsters would destroy everything and everyone. Did you see the barren, destroyed world they would bring?"

Crap, Jane thought. *Yeah, I saw all that. But how the heck did Leo know that? Unless . . . Unless a timewalker showed him. Had Sabina showed him the possible futures with an amulet of power? Had an arcenciel? Or . . . Holy crap on a cracker. Did he see the possible futures in the*

*blood he drank from the Son of Darkness, who once had
an arenciel trapped in crystal and was bitten by one . . .*

*If that's the case, then Leo was . . . Leo was expecting me
here in his city. He was waiting for me,* Jane thought.

Beast thought, *Leo attacked Jane when he saw-smelled
Jane for first time. Jane burned Leo hand with silver cross.
Leo did not recognize Jane.*

Jane thought, *Yeah. Right. So maybe his visions showed
me only in puma-form, like a were-puma, or in half-form.
Maybe his visions of the future never included my human
face, only my half-form snout.*

"And once again," Leo said, "worse monsters are upon
our doorsteps, worse monsters than I could ever hope
to be."

Leo turned head again. Beast could see Leo hair, Leo
eyes, Leo skin. Could see burned skin places. Leo wore
human clothes, with black shirt, shoes, and pants Jane
liked, called jeans. Leo was vamped out. Liked Leo fangs,
good killer predator fangs.

"I thought I had everything under control when you finally came to my city part human, part *Puma concolor.* I
thought I could use you, bind you, keep you near until the
time I needed you to kill my enemies. But they were far
closer than I had known. I did not know they had replaced
the son of my body with one of their own. I did not know
that you would kill the Mithran who was not my son."

Leo voice broke. Strange tears rolled down Leo face,
blood tears. Leo smell was changing, anger-sick smell.

Leo looked at sky. "I do not have long. The dawn is
near, and my healing is not complete. I must sleep, and
there is still much to say. The thing that is my greatest enemy is coming to this country. *My master.* He is being
drawn here because you set his plans awry, beginning the
moment you killed Immanuel and revealed what he was.
When you killed de Allyon and Grégoire killed le Batard,
a thing my dearest friend would never have done had you
not shown him a different way to live, a different life from
running and hiding from the horrors of his past. All future
possibilities began to change.

"When you became Dark Queen, my master could no
longer wait. He set his plans in motion and sent Shaun Mac-

Laughlinn to test you, to weaken you. If you survive Shaun's treachery, my master will attack. He is the last great power behind all that was put in place between the Sons of Darkness, and the power that you freed when you killed the makers of my kind. The Heir comes." The way he said *heir* sounded like a title.

Heir? Jane thought. *Melker's heir? Shaun's heir? Or some unknown heir to someone else I had killed? It is a long freaking list.*

Leo continued, "With the makers of my kind gone, there is no one to drink from who is stronger than he. With them gone, there is nothing to keep him at bay."

Except that there was a lump of flesh still hanging around to give someone power. The heart of one of the vamp creators' immortal bodies was still in NOLA in the hands of the witches. So far as I knew, Leo didn't know that the heart of one of the Sons of Darkness was being kept by witches in a safe place.

Beast's ears perked at the thought. *Good strong vampire flesh.*

Leo's eyes rested on Beast, painful. Heavy. "Except you, my Jane, my wild card."

I thought back through the silence and Leo's last words. Something about no one to keep the Big Bad Ugly at bay. *Right.*

"You are the Dark Queen, a thing I did not see in any of the visions. You hold the crown and a weapon of power. You will need the last of the artifacts to fight my master, to defeat him, for his blood is stronger than mine, and he is not blinded by hubris and a belief in immortality as the Sons of Darkness were."

His eyes returned to the sky. Leo said, "You must behead the Onorio you hold prisoner. *End her.* You must find all the artifacts, especially the last one. It is hidden in my rooms. Find it. Find it, my Jane. You will know what to do with it." Leo stood faster than Beast could follow. Air popped, hurting Beast ears. Leo was gone.

We will go to Council Chambers, Beast thought. Beast looked out over levee and saw trucks that smelled of much food. Raw meat. Raw fish. Beast had not eaten after shift.

Was hungry. Beast looked back at homeless man. Wondered if he would be stringy to eat.

Council chambers. Make it snappy, Jane thought. *And no eating the humans.*

Trucks smell of food. Can get inside belly of truck?

The farm-to-restaurant delivery trucks? No. Move it, you dang cat.

Will not run. Will ride truck. Jane was angry at wait, but Beast had done this before. Would be faster. Was like riding bison or cow to kill and eat. Beast sauntered through shadows at top of levee to wall looking down at street. When truck smelling of blood and much meat rolled past, Beast leaped from wall to top of truck. Claws out, skidded across metal, ribbed like chest of big cow. Claws caught on metal and Beast lay down, tail out, tip tapping on metal truck. Truck smelled of much meat. Beast hungered.

Two streets over, Beast leaped from top of truck to another. Soon wall and gate of HQ came into view. Beast gathered self, watching tall wall made of brick. Leaped high, over wall. Landed in front area, in grass near flat concrete. Caught self and sat on haunches, front legs straight and close together, ears high. Bright light came on. Looked away from light. When human spoke, ear tabs swiveled and folded, finding voices in night.

"Is that the queen?" a voice asked.

"You think there's another of those cats in town?" a second voice asked.

Beast chuffed. Stood and walked slowly to steps to front door. Light followed Beast.

Beast is beautiful Puma concolor. *Has golden pelt and sharp claws. Beast is best hunter. Beast is not prey.*

Show-off, Jane thought.

At top of stairs, Beast stood, waiting. Derek appeared and entered airlock, but Derek did not open door. Derek stared at Beast. Was challenge look, eyes narrow, shoulders tight. If Derek had killing claws, would be showing them to Beast. Beast chuffed with amusement. Opened lips and showed killing teeth in snarl. Derek still did not open door. Beast turned around and prepared to show human that this was Beast space.

Door opened. "Don't you *dare* spray on the windows."

Beast chuffed. Turned and went through open door into airlock. Outer door closed. Inner door was still closed. Beast whirled and raised up on hind legs, front paws over Derek shoulder, claws out, holding Derek in place. Derek hand went for gun. Derek stopped breathing. Smelled of shock, uncertainty, some fear. Licked Derek neck and face with rough tongue.

Derek jerked away, Beast claws tearing Derek shirt.

Beast dropped and chuffed. Derek started to breathe again. Inner door opened. Beast strolled into big room to stairs. Vampires were everywhere. Security teams. One team was watching Beast. Silent. Hands on guns. Beast walked slowly upstairs. Paused halfway up and looked back at Derek. Derek was glaring. Beast chuffed, twitched long tail in amusement, and trotted up long stairs.

Far below, Derek cursed.

You really are a dang cat. Jane was not laughing.

At top of stairs, Wrassler stood, waiting. "Were you kissing Derek or tasting him?"

Beast did not answer and led way to Leo old bedroom. Could smell Bruiser inside. Put paw on door and looked at Wrassler. Big human with one skin leg and one not-skin leg sighed and knocked on door. Bruiser called, "Come."

Was way Leo answered knocks sometimes. Wrassler opened door and Beast walked in. Bruiser was sitting at desk with computer and tapping with fingers. Was dressed in black. Looked like what Jane called "sex on a stick."

"Jane?" Bruiser was surprised.

Beast stalked close and sniffed Bruiser, flehmen response, strong sucking sound, pulling air over tongue and over scent sacs in top of mouth. Bruiser smelled like Bruiser, not like stick. "Do you want a keyboard to talk to me?"

Beast shook head no. Padded around Leo's old bedroom. Leo's closet. Leo's bathroom. Smelling for magic Leo left behind. Smelled nothing magic. Searched walls and floor with nose and paws. Beast found no hidden spaces for magic thing. Went to door. Waited.

"Do you want me to follow you?" Bruiser asked. Beast shook head no again and put paw on Wrassler leg.

"You want *me* to come?"

Beast nodded and left room, Wrassler following. Big blood-servant smelled of confusion. Was good. Cats must always confuse humans. Confusion was why humans loved cats.

Beast went to small cage called ele-va-tor. Raised up on hind legs and pushed button for down. When elevator came, Beast padded inside and turned puma eyes to big man. Waited. Wrassler got in elevator and put card in special slot to make elevator go. Beast pushed button for subbasement four. Beast knows numbers one, two, three, four, five, and more than five. Is enough numbers. Elevator dropped to sub-four. Beast walked out of small cage and to partially hidden scion room, place where vampires who were not old enough to be sane were kept hidden away. Jane did not keep scions here. Kept prisoners here.

Wrassler opened door. Beast walked in. Walked to cage for Onorio Monique Giovanni. Jane was silent in brain. Watching. Beast pressed nose to cage. Breathed. Listened. Onorio did not smell alive. Did not smell dead either. Onorio heart beat once, pulse in neck moving. Onorio took one very slow, shallow breath. Did not breathe again. Onorio was not dead.

I remember another creature who just freaking would not die, Jane thought. *I finally beheaded her. Leo was right. I'll need to take this one's head too. But . . . maybe I'll try to read her first.*

Beast ate vampires. Good strong vampire blood. Beast hungers. Could eat Onorio.

Let's hold off on eating people and go visit Deon in the kitchen. I'll bet he'll give you some steak or salmon.

Beast likes Deon.

You like anyone who feeds you, gives you rides in cars, or gives you catnip.

Yes.

After Beast and I ate, Beast told me about Leo. I was still getting used to the idea that he was alive and relatively sane for a thrice-born, twice-risen, and trying to process what it all meant.

When Beast found Leo on levee, vampire did not smell

same, Beast thought. *Always smelled dead. Now smells different. Smells much like Monique, but with blood and burned paper and burned flowers. Is not same dead smell but is close to same dead smell.* Beast gave a mental equivalent of a cat shrug. *But still is dead.*

Does anyone else know?

Beast cannot talk human talk. Humans are too stupid to speak / hear cat talk.

Beast scratched on a door, and I paid attention to our surroundings. Wrassler opened the door, and Beast walked in, stopped, and barred the way from Wrassler. The big man stopped and backed out, closing the door. *And we're in Leo's old office, why?*

We hunt for magic thing Leo hid here.

We walked down the small hallway into Leo's office. The office was different. There were no more rugs, no draperies, no tapestries hanging on the walls. The drinking/dinner/sex couches were gone. The low table that Leo had used for tea and drinks was gone, as were all the chairs. It was even more barren than Leo's near-empty bedroom. His desk was still there, the pretty, carved, elegant table desk. The armoire behind the desk was still there, doors shut.

So what are we looking for? I asked

Magic thing. Leo hid it here.

I thought about making suggestions, but Beast was intent—in hunting mode. I had been present when she hunted prey, but this felt different. This felt almost logical, rational. Fascinated, I sat back in our shared mind and watched.

Beast started back at the door, sniffing the walls, beginning at the floor and stretching as high as she could reach, standing up on her hind legs. Wrassler's scent moved faintly beneath the door. Guarding. Watching.

Beast moved on. She stopped at the once-hidden opening to the next office and the once-secret elevator there. No one had passed to or from the empty room. There were no fresh scents at that entrance. She moved on to the far wall. There was nothing except various weak scents from fast-moving blood-servants who removed the tapestries and the rugs. Then the scent of blood-servants having sex against the wall.

Ick, I thought.

Mating. Not ick. Mating is good. Mating was between strong blood-servants.

Ick, I repeated.

Beast didn't reply, just kept working the room. *Have scent,* Beast thought.

Beast had been through the entire room, all the nooks and crannies and hidden openings, including two I hadn't known about. Beast tightened her muscles and leaped, landing on top of Leo's desk, her nose against the desktop.

Ugly dog. Good nose, she thought. It sounded unenthusiastic, half-hearted.

Your dog-nose genes found something?

Beast kept ugly dog nose. Magic is hiding in desk. Space small as pocket.

She dropped off the table desk to the floor and padded to the door. She bumped it with her nose three times and stepped back. The door opened. Beast stared at Wrassler. Predator eyes.

Stop that, I demanded.

Wrassler likes to play, Beast thought back.

No, I thought at her.

Beast sniffed, turned, padded back to the table desk, and leaped on top. Wrassler followed, standing in the end of the short hallway. Beast tapped three times on the spot on the desk where she had smelled magic. Tapped again three times. When Wrassler said nothing, Beast chuffed, stared at the spot, and tapped again. It was cat talk for *There's something here.*

"Something's there? Hidden in the desk? Or do you just want me to get down on my knee so you can pounce on me?"

Beast dropped elegantly to the floor and stuck her nose on the table lip, right where she had been tapping, and sniffed. Wrassler walked over and pressed his thigh against Beast to move her. He bent and stared at the damp nose print, running his hand over the desk, feeling for cracks, tapping on the top, the lip, the apron, and the underside for hollow sounds. When he stood, he was frowning and pulled his cell phone. Bruiser answered. "Consort, please come to the queen's office. Her cat has found something."

Queen's office? Oh. Right. Leo's office would now be mine. Except . . . maybe not.

"On the way."

Wrassler retreated to the doorway, and Beast continued sniffing on the floorboards, where she found two more hidden spaces. There was no magic scent there, but she was curious. She was always curious. She was a cat. Bruiser arrived. His butt looked amazing, and the black clothes made his dark beard and hair look even darker. *He looks scrumptious.*

Bruiser is best mate, Beast thought back.

"Jane?" Bruiser asked me.

Beast nodded.

"You found something?"

I/we tapped the desk in the correct spot again.

"Hidden inside?" he asked, his hands mimicking Wrassler's hands as he searched it.

I/we nodded.

"It sounds hollow, Consort," Wrassler said, "but I don't feel any buttons, springs, levers, or anything else that might allow it to open."

"Me neither. Jane. Does it smell like magic?"

Nod.

"Like Leo?"

Beast thought. And gave a small nod.

"So Leo hid something magical in here. How did you know to come look?"

Beast and I stared at Bruiser, our shoulders high, head lowered. A predator stare.

"Something happened."

Nod.

"Someone told you something."

This time our nod was slow, our gaze penetrating.

"Sabina?"

We did nothing, holding the position and the stare.

Whispering, Bruiser said, "Was . . ." His voice went rough and silent. He took a slow breath, as if to calm any reaction he might have. "Was it Leo?"

I/we nodded.

Wrassler cursed. The room filled with the scents of shock, excitement, horror.

"Leo told you, in words, in English, to come here and find this?"

I/we nodded. The fact that Leo hadn't killed and eaten us was an indication that Leo was not a revenant. He was, more or less, sane.

Without turning his eyes from me, Bruiser said to Wrassler. "We do not speak of this. Not until we know more. I need a woodworker, an antiques repairer. Can you locate someone and get them here immediately? Send a car."

"Yes, Consort," Wrassler said. He was holding his cell phone and left the room, moving fast.

"Jane, can you shift to human?"

Beast and I considered one another. It was close to dawn; maybe after dawn. Except for a very, *very* few times, shifting from Beast to human in daylight had always been impossible. But I didn't know if Beast had been holding out on me all along, using the difficulty to maintain control, or if the sunlight actually was a problem. *Beast?* I thought.

She blinked. Sat. Held my mind in her predator's claws. I was poaching on her hunting grounds to ask this.

Is hard. Will need much meat and grain for Jane. Jane will hurt.

Is it going to hurt because the daytime process is so difficult or because you make *it difficult?*

Beast didn't answer, which I figured was an answer all on its own.

I looked at Bruiser and forced our head down and back up. I/we padded from the office and back along the hallways to Leo's old room. Bruiser didn't follow, but a guard met us there and opened the door, standing back as if we were a wild animal who might attack for no reason. He closed the door behind us.

Inside, alone, Beast stepped onto the bed and scratched all the covers and pillows together, making a nest, her claws pricking and pulling the fabric. She lay down in the nest and scrunched around. *Jane will hurt,* she thought. She extended the claws on her dominant paw and hooked them into her pelt at her chest. It was the exact place my wesa claws had torn Beast's puma flesh when I accidently performed black magic and stole her body and her soul so very long ago.

She ripped her own flesh. Skinwalker energies shot out, gray mist and black motes.

The pain was electric. Spiraling. Piercing. Burning, icy, slicing. I was being flayed alive. My bones popped and my spine snapped back. I screamed.

CHAPTER 13

It's Better Than Being Shot At

I woke in human form. There was blood all over the sheets. I was shivering, panting, and my muscles felt as if I had been Tased.

Bruiser eased down onto the bed and gathered me and all the bloody linens in his arms. "I'm sorry," he murmured. "I didn't know it would be this bad. I'm so sorry."

"Beast did it," I said. It came out a croak. "She shifted, and I think she made it hurt. Dang cat." I breathed for a while and tried to force my muscles to relax. When that didn't work and the muscle twitches became spasms, Bruiser carried me, sheets and all, to the shower and put me on the small, tiled seat. He stripped fast and sat on the floor, pulling me into his arms. He turned on the water as hot as we could stand it. I shivered, my teeth chattered, and I cussed Beast up one side and down the next as hard as I could. Bruiser chuckled silently at my cussing, mostly because the stuttering, chattering cussing came out all wrong.

Half an hour later, my muscles were much looser, and Bruiser and I were busy doing other things. I felt *much* better after that. When we were both dry and dressed and trying to make our hair and his beard look less like we had been doing what we had been doing, I asked, "Did you get a woodworker to open Leo's desk?"

"Yes, just before I came here. He charged an outrageous price, but he found a small locket sealed inside a well-glued wooden niche."

"And?"

"Within it are two miniatures. Tiny paintings: Ka N'vsita on one side and Adan Bouvier on the other. I have no idea what it can do, but it reeks of magic. I have had it messengered to our house."

"Okay. You want to know about Leo?"

"Yes. If you feel up to it."

"I'm hungry as a starving cat, but yeah. You need to know." Beast had let me access her memories, so I described the way Leo avoided all the security at our house, tapping on our bedroom window. I described how he looked, how he smelled. Carefully I repeated Leo's words.

Bruiser watched my face as I talked. "He was sane?"

"Yeah. He had been drinking from a lot of homeless people, but so far as Beast could smell, all were still alive. He said someone was coming, someone he couldn't defeat. He said that because I killed Immanuel, and then the Sons of Darkness, this 'my master' had come to power. And he was more powerful than Leo was now."

Bruiser shook his head. "Monique mentioned Leo's master. I've looked into Leo's bloodlines, Amaury's scion lines, and the list of still undead ancient Mithrans and Naturaleza. I could find no one worthy of the title of master who is still known to be undead. He was not speaking of Ka or Monique or the Firestarter?"

"No."

"He wasn't speaking of Shaun MacLaughlinn?"

"No. I got the impression that Shaun is here to soften us up."

"Mmmm. I wonder if Shaun knows that. Ofttimes the older Mithrans use tools who are not aware of their low status and utter lack of value." His face thoughtful, Bruiser dressed in the clothing he had tossed into the corner. They were wrinkled, but they fit so tightly the wrinkles were stretched out and invisible. He looked so good in clothes. And out of clothes. And all the time.

In the bedroom, I pulled out another of Madame Melisende's outfits and dressed. This one was a sort of old-blood brown. I hated it instantly, but it was warm and soft, and it fit perfectly. There was a pink one next to it. I yanked that one off the rack and balled it up.

"Problem, my love?" Bruiser asked, all innocent, his worry momentarily gone.

I held up the ball of fabric and shook it at him a little. He knew I hated this color.

"I think that is a lovely shade of pink," he said blandly.

Laughing, I threw it at him. "I'm sure you'll look gorgeous in it."

"I shall see that this is offered to others in the wardrobe room and a more suitable color is made for you, my love."

He tucked it under his arm, and we were still smiling when we left the room. In the hallway outside, stood Raisin. She was glaring at us. Beast was still close to the surface, and I could smell Raisin and her feelings—a mixture of animosity and fear and blood. Raisin was one of the oldest blood-servants at HQ, wrinkled like a Shar-Pei puppy but still sharp as a tack and as prickly as a blackberry vine.

"I will have a word with you Primo," she said in her British (maybe Welsh?) accent, sounding prissy and ticked off, her mouth making dozens of vertical lines on her upper and lower lips.

"I am Consort, no longer primo, ma'am, but I am your servant." Bruiser's tone was clipped and reprimanding. He turned to me and said, pointedly, "My Queen."

I knew that the "I am your servant" part was an old-fashioned way of being polite, but I didn't like it. I could tell that Bruiser didn't like the fact that Raisin hadn't called me queen. And that she said she "will have a word" versus "may I please have a word?" In the vamp world, she had been unforgivably and deliberately rude.

"My Queen," she said grudgingly.

I had wanted to talk to Raisin about old things she might remember, but I had the feeling trying to draw info out of her would be a waste of time. I also know when I've been insulted, so I ignored her. In true vamp style, and true Beast style, I turned my back on her. "I'm hungry," I said to Bruiser. "I'm heading home to see the loc . . . trinket and eat some food."

"I shall be along shortly, my most beloved queen. And I shall notify your brothers that you will be arriving shortly." He too turned his back and made Raisin wait as he used his phone.

From the corner of my eye, I saw the old blood-servant look down and lace her hands. Pretty sure she got the message.

I had no idea what time it was, but it was still daylight when I got home. I was beyond hungry, and luckily Eli knew I was on the way and starving. He had a sandwich plate prepared for me, stacked tall with thin-sliced smoked ham and cheese, with lettuce and tomato, goopy with mayo, with a side of greasy scalding fries right out of the oil. He had made plates for Alex and him as well, and we all sat down to eat together. It was a marvelous meal with dark beer, lots of salt on the fries, and neither one of the guys watched me eat, so I could stuff huge mouthfuls of food in.

When we were finished, I said, "How about the dish-washing waits, and we look at the locket now?"

Eli and Alex shared a glance that meant they had been talking about me. I gave both of them the stink-eye, but they pretended not to see me. Eli rose from the table, put his headset on, and began a reconnoiter, checking all the windows and doors. He was armed, and not just with a double-thigh rig, but with a double-shoulder holster. Four nine-mils. Extra mags were tucked here and there. And he was wearing body armor between his T-shirts. Eli was expecting trouble. Lots of trouble. I had been so hungry that I hadn't noticed.

Alex silently cleared the dishes off the table and put them in the sink. Eli and Alex were tense. Worried. I didn't know what had happened, but it wasn't good. I looked out the kitchen window to see a sentry patrol in front of the house.

Satisfied with his recce, Eli ended a sotto voce discussion with the security team, turned off his mic, and returned to the table holding a tiny box.

He and Alex sat on either side of me, protective, worried, or . . . maybe wanting the opportunity to speak very quietly. Eli confirmed that theory when he said softly, "The locket was concealed in a box. The box is carved from soapstone."

He seemed to be wanting some kind of response, so I said, "Okay."

"I'm human, and I don't want to touch it. It felt funky, so I put the soapstone box inside a wood box."

If a fully human man could feel the magics inside, that was very bad. Or maybe very good? "Okay." I held out my hands, cupped as if to drink water.

Eli pulled a weapon and pointed it at the kitchen window, a cross-body aim that only a really good shooter could hope to make. Eli was better than good. With his left hand, he placed a wooden box in mine.

The sense of magic hit me instantly. I dropped the wood box on the table. It was heavier than I had expected, and it rattled and bounced on the tabletop before coming to a stop in the center of the table. As if it knew where it was. *Yeah. Right.*

Carefully, I opened the wood box. Inside was a small round box with a nub on top, like a small stem, the whole thing carved from dark green soapstone. I rubbed my fingertips against my thumbs, knowing that I didn't really want to touch it either. But I was the Dark Queen. I had a job to do.

"Crap. Hang on," I said. I went to my room and came back, putting the Glob on the table near the small stone box. The sensation of dangerous magic decreased. "Okay. Let's do this."

I reached over and pinched the stem. Lifted it. Power rammed out of the box. I dropped the stem, stepped back, shaking my fingers. The stone lid rolled around on the table like a slow-spinning top. Carefully, I leaned over and peered inside. Nestled in the bottom was a locket.

"Holy crap with toe jam," I muttered.

"What?" Eli demanded.

"It looks like the winged lizard I got from Sabina, but it's way more powerful." It was made of the same kind of metal and was inset with powerful, clear things, a liquid droplet beneath each. I held a hand over the stone container, and I could actually feel the Glob soaking up the familiar-feeling magics. "It has arcenciel magic in it. It's made from the scales and blood of a rainbow dragon."

I reached in and lifted out the locket, dropping it on the table. With the Glob in one hand, I opened the locket. On one side was an ink drawing of Adan Bouvier; on the other was an ink drawing of Ka, just as Bruiser had said. I closed it with a soft metallic snap and placed it back in the soapstone container. I rubbed my fingers and thumb together. They felt slightly numb. Tingly.

"Okay. There are three magical thingies with arcenciel magic in them in NOLA, the dragon-lizard, the snake amulet worn by Shaun, and this locket. All have to be connected to whatever is happening between Sabina, Leo, Adan, Ka, Shaun, and this unknown master."

"We need to keep the amulets separate," Eli said. "The lizard is in the gun safe. What do you want to do with this?"

I frowned. There had been a generation of witch children that had disappeared in bursts of light. It had crossed my mind that they been stolen by arcenciels, but that wasn't a can of worms I wanted to open. Avoiding bringing up that topic, I asked, "Would an Everhart know anything about arcenciel magic?"

"I'll mention it to Liz when we talk later, but I doubt it."

"Let me know if you find out anything. I'll stick the box in my closet under Molly's *hedge of thorns* and *obfuscation* workings." Molly Everhart Trueblood was my BFF and the older sister of Eli's girlfriend, Liz. All the Everhart bloodline witches were powerful, and I knew for a fact that they had access to grimoires full of ancient magic and history. Moll provided me workings for a good price, and I took care of big bad uglies who came after her family.

I put the top back on the soapstone container and closed it all up in the wood box. The wood had to have some kind of power-dampening working in it because I could handle it now without the numbing reaction. The Glob, however, was red hot, so I left it on the table as I carried the locket to the closet, placed it on the top shelf, and set up the *hedge* amulet for the protective working. This particular *hedge of thorns* was a blood-activated, third-gen version, created to hide and protect magical thingies from thieves. I pricked my finger, initiated the *hedge* with a smear of my own blood, and the energies powered up with a faint red shimmer. It covered the box, my crown (which I didn't remember bringing home), and other, less dangerous stuff. The *hedge* might not be as powerful as a portable *null* working, but it was effective enough, and without me, it would be dang difficult to get to the locket.

I closed the doors, thinking about all the magical doo-hickeys I had collected. Wondering if anything new had been discovered in the foundation of the chapel.

In the kitchen, I saw that Eli had rolled the Glob onto oven mitts but that the tabletop was heat-damaged.

"Sorry," I said, looking at the damage.

Eli and Alex laughed as if I had said something funny. And maybe I had. Of all the horrible things that happened to and around me, a small scorch mark was one of the least important. The Glob had cooled quickly, so I carried it back to its spot in the closet, in the plastic bin with all the other crazy stuff. My life was weird.

As I was standing up from the floor of the closet, I heard a knock at the door. Eli didn't race to it, weapons drawn, but he did move fast into firing position.

From his desk, Alex said, "Front cameras show an HQ messenger. No other movement except a prostitute negotiating with a john in a Porsche down the street. Back and side cameras all negative. Katie's Ladies cameras all negative."

My cell rang softly, with HQ's main number on it. "Hang on," I said to the guys as I took the call. "Yellowrock."

"My Queen," Raisin said, sounding just a tad sarcastic.

I put it on speaker and walked to the bedroom doorway so my brothers could hear the call. "Ernestine?" I asked, pretty sure she would hate my nickname for her.

"Yes, My Queen," she said briskly. "The Primo—forgive me—Your *Consort* requested me to look over and translate a journal that the Pri—your *Consort*—gave to me. I have messengered over the journal and my translation."

Eli had ambled closer and said, "Your willingness and joy to bow to your queen and follow the orders of her Consort have been noted."

There was a faint hesitation before Raisin continued. "Yes," she said. "Things change. Often. And sometimes in dangerous ways not expected by those who rule."

Which sounded like a threat. Or a promise. But her words made Eli smile that cold battle smile that said he had an enemy in his sights. "Continue, Ernestine. And tread carefully around your queen and her faithful and loyal servants."

Raisin said, "The journal is not old, only from the 1920s. However, I found mention of a Cherokee woman and thought you might be interested. I recall this *Cherokee woman,*" she said, her tone making it a racial slur against native people.

I narrowed my eyes and glanced at Eli. His eyes were watching out the window, but his body was relaxed, too calm. Battle ready.

"She was well known as a blood-servant, though few were allowed to sip of her." Raisin's tone said that was unusual and wrong. "She had eyes like yours." More insulting tone.

Raisin had never liked me, but she had never been so totally without manners or respect. It was almost as if she felt there would be no reprisals for her attitude. We had traitors in HQ. Was Raisin aligned with them? From Eli's reaction, he had the same questions.

Raisin continued, "While I do not recall the events in the text, I thought that My Queen might be interested."

The messenger at the door. *Right.* Old vamps and old blood-servants seldom used text. The phone in Raisin's office still had a wire into the wall . . . I nodded to Eli and said, "Ernestine. Your many years of service to the Mithrans of the city, and your current manner, have been noted."

"My Queen." She ended the call without being dismissed.

I thought about the scents I had caught from Raisin when she appeared outside Leo's bedroom door. The mixture had been more than animosity and fear. It also had been strong with fresh blood, and Raisin had never smelled so strongly of blood in the past. Raisin had fed and been fed on. A lot.

Eli, weapon in hand, held down and at his side, opened the door, accepted the package from the messenger, and carried it to the kitchen table. Carefully, he inspected the envelope for mundane traps, like miniature explosives and poisons.

From his desk, Alex said, "I had Derek drill through the floor above and install hidden cameras in Raisin's office while we were in Asheville. It's not downloaded to the main security system, but to a separate system. Just in case someone talked. I've scanned it once a week for the last three months, but I'm overdue for a look-see. I'll access it and go back over the footage."

"What about her quarters?" Eli asked, shining a Wood's light over the package and the palm of his hand where he had touched the legal-sized envelope.

"No cameras there. There's some things I do not need to see. Might scar me for life."

Eli's mouth softened in his version of a smile. "Tia hasn't already done that?"

Alex didn't look away from his systems. "She's working on it, but we've only been back to NOLA for a few days. So far, I'm holding my own."

"Too much information, guys," I said.

Tia was a former member of Katie's Ladies, and she was also learning about computers from Alex, which was odd because Tia had always appeared to be . . . not stupid, but . . . slow, intellectually. Alex and Tia had been on and off again in virtual reality for months. I really didn't need to know what they had been up to in person, though if Tia and Alex were involved, that might be a good thing. She had been broken as a young woman, and Alex would be an innocent and gentle partner.

Alex ducked his head farther to hide his grin.

Oh yeah. Something-something between them. Good.

"Nothing I can detect on the envelope," Eli said, after spraying the envelope with something vinegary and then something alkaline. He went to the back of the house to the old laundry room, which he had remodeled after one of the bloodbath events over the years. He came back carrying a heavy-duty shield made of clear, thick polycarbonate, a riot shield like cops use, but this one had a sky-blue band across the bottom, signaling that it was a null shield too, giving him resistance to active magical workings.

My heart shot into my throat. Beast-fast, I grabbed Alex's shoulder and pulled his rolling chair across the living room and along the wall that placed the weapons room between us and the kitchen. It was a testament to our violent lives that Alex didn't resist or ask why. My last vision of Eli was him pulling a knife from a pocket. I heard the sound of paper being cut, slicing sounds, followed by the shush of leather and paper and the ripple sound of pages flipping. A plastic-clatter followed as the shield was placed on the floor.

"All clear," Eli said.

Alex slid back to the desk, the chair rollers whirring over wood and the fancy new rugs. I walked into the kitchen. Eli looked fine, not even a sheen of perspiration, while I was ever so slightly clammy.

Eli said, "Ernestine sent over a journal kept by a vamp named Malita Del Omo. She says to read pages sixty-three and sixty-four." Eli opened the journal to the pages and the translations to the same. Comparing back and forth, he read, "I am distraught. I shall be given to another master. The life I have lived here is over. My Ka and my Adan have been sent away by the Master of the City, the terrible Leo Pellissier. He has judged that they have performed unspeakable black arts, using Mithrans and blood-servants as test subjects. But I am still here. I still live. I am to be given away as scion to another. Given away."

"Like a slave," I murmured.

Eli slid his finger along the translation, and also along the original text. "It's some version of Spanish. Here it says, 'Adan and Ka were separated, and Ka was sent to two outclan priestesses in Europe'."

"Which ones?" I asked.

"Bethany and Edith."

"Well dang," I said mildly. "Bethany is dead, and I never heard of an Edith."

"Checking records on an outclan named Edith," Alex said from his desk. "And nothing. Nada."

Eli gave me his battlefield smile. "Puzzles, constructed from ancient mysteries and archaic riddles, bound up in antiquated enigmas." He lifted his brows, faintly amused. "It's better than being shot at."

I took photos of the translations and the journal and sent them to the B-twin Onorios who were dealing with my messes here and back in Asheville, as well as to Koun, though the vamp was still asleep for the day.

Brandon responded immediately, calling.

I answered, "Yellowrock here. Call is on speaker to Eli and Alex."

Brandon said, "My Queen. Adan was punished many times for misuse of magic and experiments into blood magic. He finally went too far, and was supposed to have been dispatched by the Enforcer of Clan Pellissier. Ka was banished and killed in a shipwreck off the coast of Spain on the way to be trained by two Onorios. Or so it was said." *Or so it was said* was vamp-talk for *it was unproven gossip*.

"Where was Bethany living at the time?"

"She spent a lot of time in Europe so she could have been there when Ka was sent."

"I see," I said, walking around the sofa in the living room, a slow circle, thinking as I walked. "We know Adan lived. And Sabina saw Ka, or an illusion of Ka, the night the cemetery burned."

I dropped onto the sofa in the living room and leaned back, pulling a throw over my feet. Eli sat beside me. I asked Brandon, "What kind of black magic would result in a magical skinwalker being separated from her master, and both being sent into exile?"

"There are few overlapping forms of black magic," Brandon said. "However, in every magical creed and practice, sacrifice, blood, and eating the bodies of the dying while they are still alive has always been the most foul of blood magic and black magic."

He was right. It was. It was how skinwalkers became *u'tlun'ta*. It was how witches went to the dark side. It was the way the Sons of Darkness, both of whom might have been among the rare male witches who survived to adulthood, created the vampires. It was indeed the most foul magic.

Quietly he added, "Many believe that is what happened between Cain and Abel. One ate the other."

That wasn't canon, so I ignored it, though it was thought provoking. "Who is Malita Del Omo, the woman who wrote the journal? And what did she know about Ka N'vsita?"

"You can ask them yourselves if you wish," Brandon said. "Malita Del Omo and Soledad Martinez are two of the more ancient Mithrans in the Americas. Both of them studied black magic a century ago, and they now live on an estate near Breaux Bridge. But I'll warn you. Though they looked fine the last time I saw them and have maintained their physical regeneration, both are mentally"—he hesitated—"unstable. They have lived mostly alone for over a hundred years."

"I could use a break," I said.

"I'll text you their address. I suggest you take the helo. It isn't far by air, but the drive will take quite some time." The call ended.

Eli's cell vibrated and he said, "The address isn't far as the crow flies, but Brandon's right. You'd have to go around the swamp. Helo will be faster. It arrived from Asheville sometime yesterday. I'll make some calls and get it ready to transport you."

Beast muttered, *Beast does not like to fly in belly of stupid bird.*

And I didn't like the way you hurt me when we shifted.

Beast had no comment to that one.

The drive to the New Orleans Lakefront Airport was ridiculous, traffic so dense it looked like Mardi Gras. I was pretty sure I'd hate Mardi Gras. I had successfully avoided the biggest drunken festival since the Roman Bacchanalia by being out of town each year, but this was nearly as bad. Maybe a soul music event or a blues or . . . whatever. New Orleans had a party every week. This one had brought out the early drinkers, the still-up-from-last-night drinkers, and the twenty-four-hours-a-day drinkers.

By the time Shemmy and I and the other two SUVs in our small cavalcade made it to the private airport, I'd had plenty of time to think about the implications of Leo being back, alive, and sane. Potential pitfalls and possible problems had played tag in my brain and left me both satisfied and uncertain. Bruiser had warned that Leo might want his city back if he rose sane, and if Leo wanted NOLA, he could have it. That one was satisfying. However, I'd still be stuck with the Dark Queen job. I'd still be the Blood Master of Clan Yellowrock. And I'd still have a primo who was also about to be crowned the emperor of Europe, and who had once sworn to Leo. That was the uncertain part, as I wasn't sure what relationship Leo and I would have, and that Leo and Edmund would have. When people's positions changed, so did the relationships forged in the past. But there were no easy answers, and until I had the chance to sit down with Leo, I wouldn't know anything.

We arrived at Lakefront to find Bruiser, who had beat us there, and the helo, waiting and ready to go.

Mate, Beast thought, and she rolled over inside me as if exposing her belly for Bruiser to scratch.

Down girl, I thought at her.

I waved to Shemmy, dashed over, strapped in, and put on headphones. Takeoff was fast. Once we were in the air, I said to my sweetie pie, "Just so you know that I know—I accept I need protecting because I have too many enemies, and if I'm killed, y'all will be too."

Bruiser pulled his mic to the front and said, "Yes. Your life, much like Leo's life once upon a time, is the only thing keeping our world stable and our people safe. I promise to talk to you more so your freedom is protected."

"Okay. For now. But we both know that Leo being back changes everything."

"And so does your inability to shift and live."

We didn't talk much the rest of the flight and set down in the middle of a deserted street at dusk. There were no other inhabited houses on the street, which was odd. As if knowing my thoughts, Bruiser said, "Amaury bought all the homes on the street. He kept them up as did Leo, but they have been unoccupied for more than a century." He took off his headphones, unstrapped, and patted the pilot on the shoulder, which seemed to be a sign that he was to wait. The helo began to power down, and I followed Bruiser from the helo, both of us doing the duck-and-scuttle move up to the twelve-foot-tall front gate.

The "estate" was really just a big old clapboard house with a tall privacy fence and a gated drive. Bruiser and I stood together as he rang an old-fashioned doorbell, a shrill three-ring-burst loud enough for us both to hear from outside. Minutes later, the helo was mostly quiet, and a blood-servant opened the door in the gate.

Her mouth fell open. "Primo," she said, sounding awed. "We are honored."

I felt Bruiser stiffen. It was too dark to see, so I pulled on Beast's night vision and made out a dark-haired girl dressed in a sixties hippie tie-dyed T-shirt and bell-bottomed jeans. She wore a bandana headband, feather earrings, her hair was pulled back and braided, and she was barefoot. And she smelled strongly of weed. *Okay. Interesting.*

Also interesting was that Bruiser didn't correct the primo comment. Instead, he said very gently, "RoseBud, I'm happy to see ʃou again. I realize that Malita and Sole-dad are not expecting company, but do you think they might welcome an old friend?"

"Well. Sure." RoseBud stuck the tip of her braid in her mouth and chewed on it while she thought. She looked at Bruiser again, and her eyes lit up. "Primo! It's so good to see you. It's been forever! Come on in. We'll have a banquet!"

"I am not here to drink from your charges, my dear," Bruiser said as we stepped into the yard. RoseBud closed and locked the gate. "I am here to ask of the old stories."

"Oh." RoseBud's face fell. "They'll be happy to see you, Primo. And I know that they'll remember you. We spoke about you yesterday, and I showed them photographs to remind them of you. But they aren't . . . they aren't real . . . *with it.* It's gotten worse in the last few months." She glanced at me, wrote me off as unworthy, and raced ahead of us to the big green-painted house ahead. Her braid was still in her mouth.

Bruiser frowned after her but led the way. "RoseBud and five other blood-servants have cared for Soledad and

Malita for over fifty years. It may be time to bring them
back to New Orleans and let others take over."

I didn't say *Ya think?* but I considered RoseBud's actions and Bruiser's reactions. I knew that drinking blood
from bat-poo-crazy vamps had deleterious effects on humans and even on other vamps, and that vamps drinking
from drunk humans also got drunk, but this looked really
odd. RoseBud had disappeared inside and left the front
door hanging open in a total lack of security. We stepped
inside. It was pitch dark. Bruiser turned on lights old style,
by pulling metal chains. The house looked as odd as Rose-
Bud had acted. It hadn't seen a coat of paint or a new rug or
refurbishing in fifty years or more. Everything was rotting.
And I started sneezing from the clouds of ganja smoke.
Bruiser took the lead and I followed, twice meeting the eyes
of heads hanging on the walls and perched on shelves—
dusty taxidermy of boar, deer, and turkey.

In the kitchen, things got weirder as we interrupted
breakfast. Two vamps were drinking from two humans, the
people stretched out on the huge farm table, a vamp sitting
at either end. Unlike most feedings, there was nothing sexual about this, but there was also nothing neat. There was
blood dripping here and there as the old vamps, each one
with three-inch-long fangs, both dressed in frilly night-
gowns, slurped. *Ick.*

The female vamps looked up when we entered, and one
waved. Clearly, neither recognized Bruiser. When they
were done with breakfast, the humans rolled off the table,
and two others cleaned up the mess, which smelled too
sweet, not quite fresh. More ick.

Bad blood, Beast thought. *Do not eat sick-blood humans or vampires.*

RoseBud said, "Senorita Omo and Senorita Martinez,
we have visitors!" And then RoseBud lit up a joint the size
of a blimp and started puffing.

Both vamp women came forward to Bruiser and stared
at him from up close. They looked young but moved and
acted like an old doddering couple. Bruiser said, "Malita
Del Omo and Soledad Martinez. It is I, George Dumas.
May we speak in the library?"

At the mention of his name, both vamps threw their

arms around him, smearing their bloody jaws all over his shirt front. There was a lot of Spanish and French chatter as they pulled him by the hand into the dark hallway nearest. I followed, yanking on lights as we moved. As dusty as the rest of the house was, the library was pristine, with leather-bound books from floor to ceiling, leather furniture, wood floors, and a tea table. A coal fire burned in the fireplace. I didn't think I had ever seen a coal fire, and I wasn't impressed at the faint heat it put out. The three of them sat on a sofa, the two vamps on either of Bruiser's sides, and since they were still fully vamped out, I positioned myself out of the direct line of sight and pulled two wood stakes. If I needed to rescue him, I didn't want to kill the old vamps.

After they chatted a while in what sounded like a mixture of European languages, Bruiser switched to English. "My dear friend, Malita. Do you recall the events surrounding the banishment of Adan Bouvier and his primo?"

As if they didn't even see me behind the sofa, the two vamps bent close together in front of Bruiser and whispered in Spanish. Bruiser glanced at me and smiled fondly at whatever they were saying. The two separated and Malita said, "We were forbidden to speak of that night. But if you will send us new blood-servants, we will tell you what we remember."

"Agreed," Bruiser said gently. "Your servants have served long. They deserve a respite."

The two female vamps launched into rapid Spanish, a back and forth, often overlapping dialogue, which caused Bruiser's fond amusement to fade until all that was left was a bitter reek of sadness. He patted their hands. He hugged them. They began to rock back and forth as they talked. They reached across Bruiser and held hands, as if seeking comfort. Bruiser murmured what sounded like, *"Lo siento por eso. Estoy triste por esto."*

Finally they fell silent. RoseBud appeared in the doorway, carrying in a tea set on a tray. She poured tea for the two vamps, ignoring Bruiser and me, which was just as well, as the tea set and cups looked as if they hadn't been washed in years.

"RoseBud," Bruiser said, "you and three of your housemates will pack and be ready to depart at dawn. The other two at the next dawn. Six new blood-servants will replace you. You have served in isolation long enough, and will be brought back to the Council Chambers. You have done well."

RoseBud threw her arms high, jumped up in the air, and squealed wordlessly. Then she sped down the hall, shouting to her other blood-servants. Moments later, Bruiser and I were in the helo heading back in the dark to the private airfield near NOLA. We didn't speak, and I figured Bruiser was processing all he had learned.

Beast thought at me, *Was sick old human blood-servants and sick old vampires. Should be pushed off of high cliff, like rabid foxes.*

Sick like the flu sick? Like the vampire plague sick?

No. Smelled of brain sick. Like old human with bad brain but . . . different.

I wondered if Bruiser had understood that. If not, our conversation was going to be a bad one. Sleep pulled at me as the vibration rattled my bones.

We landed at the private airfield and duckwalked to the waiting vehicle, which was the limo this time, not an armored SUV. Once inside, Bruiser gave Shemmy instructions and raised the privacy partition. As the vehicle began to move, Bruiser opened a bottle of champagne and poured two glasses. He sat back in his seat, sipping, looking pensive in the dim lights that filtered through the dark window tinting. As we turned away from Lake Pontchartrain, Bruiser said, "You told me about the ceremony when Ka became Onorio. You described the room with the concrete floor and an iron witch circle set into it. About Adan stabbing Ka and draining her to death." He went silent, staring into the night, his elegant fingers turning the stem of the glass around and around, the wine tilting slowly inside the glass.

I said quietly, "And I told you about Bethany beginning the Onorio ceremony the same way she began it with you."

Bruiser nodded slightly. Sipped. "According to my old friends, after Bethany began the ceremony with Ka, Adan brought in two Mithrans, bound them with silver, and Adan inserted needles into their arms and performed a Mithran-to-human blood transfusion, forcing blood into Ka."

I started to speak, stopped, and started again. "Two vamps? Which two?"

Softly Bruiser said, "Dominique and Shaun Mac-Laughlinn."

"*Anamchara*: One dead, a traitor who had been working against Leo for ages; the other still alive, sane, and in league with Ka and Monique against us." I sipped the champagne, which was probably a very expensive wine, but it just tasted winey to me. "Why did Adan give Ka a transfusion? Was he trying to turn her? Can humans or skinwalkers be changed into vampires through transfusion? I thought it had to go through the digestive tract?"

"This may have been one of Adan's experiments, a test of some kind. And Malita Del Omo and Soledad Martinez were later cut and their blood was fed to Ka, against their will. Against hers."

"I found Adan in a cage, bat-raving nutso. I broke his neck and gave him to Leo. In hindsight, letting him keep his head might have been a bad decision."

"Adan had old handwritten texts, ones Malita and Soledad insist were written by the Sons of Darkness and one of their trusted confidants."

"Who?" I asked.

"I'm narrowing that down. I received the impression that the texts were written long in the past, though I haven't been able to discover who in the Pellissier bloodline would have been considered the current master of all. And . . ." He rubbed his bearded chin, making a raspy sound. "And why he might be considered to be stronger than the Flayer of Mithrans. Leo never called either of the Sons of Darkness master."

I remembered Monique's conversation with Bruiser about Leo's master. More important were Leo's own words. *My master,* not *my maker.* Who could this master be? Was it the same person and force behind Immanuel and Ka becoming *u'tlun'ta*? Fear froze my lungs. *Could the master be Grandmother?* Had she been working with the Sons of Darkness? Or perhaps another vamp, one stronger than Shaun?

I sat up straight in the limo seat. Dominique and Shaun MacLaughlinn had been forced to give blood and forced to feed Ka, which could have created some kind of forced bond between them. And with Shaun tied to Ka, and Ka tied to Monique in her soul home, that meant that Shaun, Ka, Monique, and whoever else was still alive-ish were likely still under the control of whatever vamp had created the experiment, including the two brain-sick vamps we had just left. There was enough black magic taking place to fry the brain of any weak vamp, but Adan wasn't powerful enough to force sane vamps to his will. So who was? Shaun?

And . . . Ka had to be still alive . . .

I said all this to Bruiser and added that Beast thought the old vamps had smelled sick. "It's possible that they are still under the control of the person who forced the experiment on them. Ka was Adan's primo. Like me, Ka probably had little training, and we always thought that Adan was teaching her, but what if he was forcing her?"

Bruiser placed his champagne glass in the small wooden holder. "Your Beast found that high-powered magic locket with the pictures of them, and we have no idea what it actually does. Leo had hidden it, and we don't know why."

"Arcenciel blood was used in the construction of the locket. And in the construction of the flying lizard amulet Sabina gave me and in Shaun's snake armband. Arcenciels can timewalk better than I ever could. Leo said *someone was back*. Who? And how much power do they have, individually or collectively? And . . . what does timewalking have to do with this whole situation?"

Softly, Bruiser said, "Enough for Shaun to survive his mind breaking when his *anamchara* died in the rising sun."

"Maybe because he was mind-bound to more than Dominique," I said. "A three- or more-way mind-binding might offer some protection and strength not offered to ordinary bound vamps."

A silence settled between us, and I rested my head on Bruiser's shoulder, letting all the possibilities resonate through me. All of them bad.

Our flight and ride had been mostly silent, he had been distant, and now, clearly, he didn't plan on coming inside. He tossed the cell to the seat and opened his arms, taking my hand, pulling me closer and onto his lap. Our arms went around each other. Silent, we breathed each other's breath; I felt our heart rates, different at first, then slowly, as we sat, they synced. I lay my head on his shoulder.

"I love you," he said. "I love you, and I don't know how to protect you, how to keep you safe, how to make you happy without smothering you. You have enemies I didn't even know about. That terrifies me."

"You're going back to HQ to see who the master might be, aren't you?"

"There are journals everywhere at HQ. Sub-four. Sub-three. Leo's private belongings are stored somewhere, perhaps in the empty room next to his old office. He will have some records. I need to find the text Soledad and Malita were talking about."

"What about the library? Are there black magic texts and journals in the library?"

"Unlikely. The Vodka Boys were meticulous in finding all such items and storing them in sub-four storage," he said, "but I never directed them to look in the library, only in storage areas. Why do you ask?"

"There was one night that Bethany and Sabina called me into the library, and we had a very strange discussion. I don't remember what it was about now, but maybe it will come to me."

Bruiser breathed out a quick laugh. "Hiding in plain sight. In the library. Why not. No one looks at the books in the library, why not store things there."

"Hidden passages, hidden shelves, hidden whatever."

He laughed quietly. "It's going to be a long night."

"I get to go meet with my brother—my brother by blood—about my grandmother's perfidy and betrayal. Wanna change places?"

"Not in a million years." He kissed me lightly and slid me to the seat. "I love you. You are my love first, my queen second, and I will love you and serve you for long as there is breath in this body."

"I love you too. Be safe."

Eli stepped out on the porch. Two security vamps, Thema and Kojo, took up posts on either end of the house.

Bruiser added, "And you have plenty of security."

I stepped from the limo, muttering just loud enough for my honeybunch to hear. "Poor delicate little ol' me, needing all you big strong fighting folk to protect me."

Apparently, I still spoke loud enough for vamp ears. Thema made an indelicate snorting sound.

"Be safe, my love."

"I promise." I think we both knew I didn't know how to be safe, but for this man I would try. Inside, I crashed and slept like a log, waking just in time to check on security protocols for Jodi and Wrassler's formal nighttime wedding.

CHAPTER 14

He Made the Sign of the Cross, and No One Caught on Fire

I woke two hours before the wedding in half-form, which was unfortunate. I liked my half-form for battle or sparring, but not for fancy events with friends. I had wanted to be human-shaped for the wedding. Dang it.

Lying in the sheets, I called on Beast for help, but she ignored me.

Fortunately, I had no active part in Jodi and Wrassler's wedding. I wasn't a bridesmaid or groomsman, where my shape and pelt would call attention to me instead of the happy couple. I was a guest, which meant no one would be asking me to be all queenly, and that suited me perfectly. I could be a fly on the wall with no problem.

I got up and showered, did what few girly things I needed to in this form, and pulled on a robe and squishy slippers. Unexpectedly, without knocking, Quint was in my room giving orders. "Sit," she said, and pointed to a small chair in the narrow bathroom. I sat, and she began to tell me what I needed to know about the big event. She started with the basics. "This is a white-tie wedding. White tie is also known as full evening dress. It's the most formal, most traditional evening dress event in all of Western civilization. Put your hands down. I'm braiding your hair."

I wasn't used to being given orders, but Quint's tone had me obeying. Instantly. It was eerily like the tone used by the house mothers at the Christian children's home where I grew up. I sat, silent and unmoving, as she worked.

White tie wedding was explained to me by Quint in excruciating detail as she braided my hair into ten differently sized and differently directed plaits. Though I hated someone I didn't know touching my hair or braiding it, I would have to get used to it eventually. Might as well be tonight. I held in my sigh as she worked and tried to pay attention.

She was full of info on etiquette and protocol and the *way things must be done*. And she had said the words as if they were a title while clipping the braids into an elegant bun-type thing that I'd never have managed without her. Quint then applied my makeup, putting glittery stuff on my cheeks and mascara on my lashes. She painted my Beast-fingernails scarlet. Beast was purring at the attention. If I was honest with myself, it felt kinda nice to be fussed over. Not that I'd ever say it aloud.

While my nails dried, Quint began to pull evening wear from the closet, all made by Madame Melisende for this one event and brought here at some point over the last day or so. Because they hadn't been there before.

Careful not to mess up her handiwork, I sat in the corner chair and let Quint display and describe dresses, and tried not to sigh a long suffering note. I hated clothes stuff. But after the first red scarlet silk dress, no matter what she said, I gave the same answer.

"Scarlet silk, cross shoulder, low back," Quint said. "Slit up the leg so you can wear a thigh blade."

"Currently, I'm pelted on my back, shoulders, and my upper legs. It will show something odd, improperly pelted, will ride up, and itch. No. Next."

"Gold velvet, long-sleeved, bottomless pockets for reaching a weapon in a thigh rig."

"Ditto. No."

"Black silk—"

"Ditto. No."

"Crimson sheath—"

"No."

After the fifteenth dress, I said, "How many more do you have?"

"Your modiste created twenty-four dresses for you to choose from tonight."

"Twenty—" I scowled at Quint. "Screw all that evening dress crap. With all the eating I've done in the last few days, I've put on a few pounds, all muscle, and my shoulders will make any dress look stupid. Same with the pelt. Everything will itch. Nope, nope, nope. No dress. Pull out my scarlet leathers."

"Your majesty—"

"My Queen or Jane. I hate majesty." I crossed my arms over my meager chest.

"But—"

"No buts. Help or get out."

Quint didn't scowl or frown. Her expression didn't change. Even her scent was unchanged. Quint had no emotional reaction to my statements at all, even when I was snarly. She pulled out the scarlet leather armor, hung its hanger on a hook, and held one hand out to me, palm up. She made a little *Get up* gesture. I stood. She yanked off my robe.

I almost flinched. Fortunately I was wearing undies, but I wasn't used to anyone seeing me unclothed in half-form. I didn't like people looking at me. I glared at her. She ignored my reaction.

She walked around me, eyeing me clinically, evaluating. "You're right. No dress would do you justice." She shook her head. "You are magnificent."

A weird feeling trickled through me, uneasy, surprised, uncertain. As far as I could tell, Quint wasn't lying. *Magnificent?* Steeling myself, I looked in the mirror for more than just a glance.

Tonight's half-form consisted of the shoulders, legs, arms, and knobby hands of my half-Beast, with a more muscular human torso, tiny waist, narrow hips, and human feet. I had a long neck, my human face and head, with cat ears up high and hairy, poking through the fancy black braids like golden furry ornaments. I frowned. I looked like a cat version of Jessica Rabbit. Or a boobless and hairy Barbie doll from the fifties. Not . . .

Magnificent? Me?

Quint stretched the armor out on the bed, unfastened all the belts, buttons, zippers, and securing mechanisms, and began belting it in place on my body, cinching the straps for a perfect fit. She knelt in front and offered a new pair of convertible dress boots for me to slip my feet into. And then she began to add my weapons, mostly the ceremonial stuff, starting with my sword and the sterling and wood stakes, and ending with Bruiser's gift, the Mughal blade. Its curved scabbard rested at my hip, the shape somehow following around my side, the stone handle near my waist.

My gold gorget went on last over my gold nugget necklace and the armor, along with two matching snake arm cuffs that once had held magical workings and had belonged to vamps. Both of which had been beheaded.

In record time, I stood looking at myself in the mirror. Beast peeked through my eyes to see too, and the golden glow of her presence was . . . *Magnificent? Holy crap.*

Beast is best hunter, she thought at me. *Beast is beautiful and dangerous but needs killing teeth to go with claws.*

Mmmm. Not tonight, I thought back. *I like the human face.*

Quint and Beast were right. And . . . just . . . wow.

Quint stood on the chair I had been sitting in. Rising up behind me, she lifted her arms and placed *le breloque* on my head. It snapped into place, tight—too tight.

I hadn't planned to wear the crown, but Quint hadn't asked me. Now there was no getting it off. Every time it snapped into place, I was afraid it was stuck there for good, but when it was ready, it came off just fine. I had to keep reminding myself of that. *Stupid crown.*

We headed to HQ to probably get in everyone's way and make people stop what they were doing to accommodate the queen. Tough. I was going to stick my nose into everything.

The ballroom was stunning. The smell of smoke was gone. The magic that hid the damaged ceiling was holding up, security was on high alert to keep anyone from throwing spells or fireballs, so the room and HQ itself was likely safe. A string quartet was playing quiet strains. The flowers smelled sweet, as if just picked, the linens had all been replaced.

There was a dark rose carpet down the center aisle between the chairs. Yeah. Perfect.

The wedding was scheduled an hour after dusk, and the guests started gathering half an hour early, seated by HQ's security guys, who were Wrassler's best friends and "dudes of honor," as he had started calling them. An excited hushed murmur underlay the stately silence as the guests were ushered in.

I stood in a dark corner, Quint at my side, an unexpected and uncomfortable presence. Quint was wearing a ball gown, but even an untrained eye could see the weapons bulging here and there. Together we watched everything, my bodyguard ready for anything. At least she wasn't a chatterbox.

The first half hour, as guests arrived and were seated, went off like a charm. No one tried to drink down a human, no vamps issued challenges or cut one another to a bloody death.

The officiant arrived. Since the ceremony wasn't being held in a Catholic church, which would have allowed her to have a Catholic priest, Jodi had chosen an aging Episcopal priest, Father Juan Ramirez. He was probably the first priest of any stripe or denomination to enter the Council Chambers of the Mithrans of New Orleans without holding up a silver cross and being followed by a mob carrying torches. Father Juan was insanely curious—and nonjudgmental—about vamps, so that helped. He shook every vamp's hand, he made eye contact without fear of being rolled, and he made the sign of the cross, and no one caught on fire.

The vamps were equally interested in the priest. As they entered, their eyes found him instantly and followed his every move. If vamps still wrote journals, I guessed everything about the wedding and Father Juan would be immortalized for posterity.

I figured all that was a step in the right direction of peace and harmony between other paras and humans. Not that I wanted to use this ceremony as part of the peace efforts. That was a Leo thing to do, and even the thought made me uncomfortable. Pulling my mind away from Leo's multilayered plans, I went back to studying the crowd from my shadowed corner.

The vamp and blood-servant groomsmen were all wearing black dress coats with tails, white shirts, piqué waistcoats, and white bow ties worn around standing collars in the wing-tip style. They properly finished it off by wearing high-waisted black trousers and patent leather oxfords, or court shoes.

Some of the warriors in the crowd wore orders insignia and medals. Others in the crowd wore top hats, white gloves, white scarves, pocket watches, and orchid or rose boutonnieres.

I had spent so much time around fashion-conscious vamps that I knew what all that crap meant. Not that I admitted as much to my new bodyguard / fashion consultant.

Every single male was resplendent, especially Bruiser. *Holy crap.* He looked great in that formal getup. And when Koun entered . . . Even with my more human nose, I could smell Quint's interest. She thought he looked hot. He seemed oblivious to her interest.

The women were in full-length ball gowns or evening gowns in all the colors of an artist's palette, all wearing evening gloves past the elbow and carrying small handbags. They wore expensive faceted stone jewelry, and there were glittering tiaras here and there.

The bride's side was filled with family and cops and local witches. All the city's witch clans had been invited. The cops, both men and women, all wore full dress blues, their plus-ones in off-the-rack gowns and shoes, but just as fancy. I nodded at Sloan Rosen, Jodi's second-in-command, and took in his plus-one, a very pretty, very curvy woman who clearly had the former undercover cop wrapped around her finger.

The groom's side was filled with vamps and blood-servants. All the vamps were perfect, of course, and the vamp scents were completely pacific tonight: no blood, no sex scents, the air redolent of herbal and floral scents, and a little red-peppery with excitement. Oddly enough, even the vamps were jittery with anticipation, most of them actually breathing. Weddings were rare in the vamp world and usually made for clan or monetary purposes, seldom for love. A human wedding, a love match, in HQ was a first, and vamps who lived so long seldom got to experience new things.

Derek stood at the back of the room wearing a tux, a weapon, and a headset, talking with the security detail. He nodded at me, looking way hotter than I expected. I gave him my most regal nod back, and that made him grin as if he'd caught me playing dress-up. I sorta felt as if he had. Alex was in comms. Eli was making rounds through HQ and the grounds, keeping us all safe.

Across the room, three arcenciels in human form were dressed in silky, fluttery gowns that matched their dragon colors, the fabric moving in an unseen wind. I hadn't known the three were invited, but Storm, Pearl, and Opal sat together whispering and were quite well behaved for young rainbow dragons. So far.

And then Wrassler—Homer—entered, which meant the ceremony was about to begin. The big guy was stunning in his black tux and tails. His groomsmen and women gathered at the front in a line behind him, including Bruiser, who put everyone to shame in his formal wear. Two security groomswomen wearing black ball gowns with white collars, like the tuxes, took their places. Gee darted in and took a place at the back of the room. Not a groomsman, but I wasn't surprised he was here. He had the red striped lizard on his shoulder, its tail around his neck, and the arcenciels turned and stared at the misericord, as if they felt him enter.

Rick LaFleur took a seat, alone, on the bride's side, his face aged and his hair stark white. I reined in a jolt of shock. My old boyfriend, and Jodi's one-time partner in the woo-woo department, had been through some hard times. He had aged; were-creatures weren't supposed to.

As if he felt my gaze, he turned his head and found my eyes in the soft light. Holding my eyes, his lips quirked up on one side, and he inclined his head as if in recognition of all that had happened between us, and in our worlds, since we met. He had changed and grown, yet Rick—the player of yesteryear—had no plus-one, which seemed sad. I wanted Rick to be happy.

Deon appeared at the back of the room, a checklist in hand, giving quiet orders through a headset. He was wearing black too, though his jacket had no tails and was covered in sequins. He gave me a stern look, the expression on his face reminding me of the housemothers in the children's home where I grew up. I might be the Dark Queen, but that look still sent a shock of fear through me. He stabbed a finger at me and then pointed to my chair. I sighed and followed orders, Quint fading behind a column near my place. The moment I sat, Jodi's mother was escorted down the aisle and took her seat at the front. The murmuring voices went silent.

The quartet's music grew louder. Bridesmaids wearing jewel-toned gowns began to pace down the aisle in that odd step-pause-step gait. Some were witches, some were human, some were cops. Two were men, wearing cop dress blues. The parts of Jodi's life that she had tried so hard to keep separate and secret had merged over the last couple of years; all her friends were here to support her, regardless of job or paranormal classification.

When Jodi stepped through the doors, everyone stood. The wedding march began, the quartet amplified through speakers. I started tearing up. My petite friend looked freaking gorgeous. Her dress was a heavenly cloud of pure white silk with tiny pink rosebuds made of rose quartz sewn into the heavily embroidered cloth. She had one of those long train things in pale pink and a veil made of net; both were sewn with pearls. She found Wrassler's eyes and smiled, and he teared up too. The scents in the room were suddenly almost overpowering as Beast peeked in.

Jodi started down the aisle. She walked alone, no father or father figure to give her away, which I figured she intended. Jodi wasn't a woman who would have cared for being handed over like property.

She reached the front of the ballroom, and Wrassler took her hand. Both of their faces were glowing with happiness. They wavered in my tears.

I had never been to a wedding. It was so cool, so amazing. I hoped the house I had bought them on the edge of the Garden District was a sufficient wedding gift. It was tiny, but it was adorable and fully refurbished. No way could Wrassler and his cop bride live at HQ. And no way could Wrassler, soon to be admin head of all NOLA security, be far from the protection detail that would keep them safe.

I hoped they didn't mind me masterminding their lives. Wrassler was used to such things, but I figured Jodi would make a stink about it even with a free house to lure her in.

The wedding march ended. Everyone sat. Gowns rustled, bodies shifted on the chairs. The scent of vamp excitement rose even higher. Behind me, the arcenciels began to glow.

"Dearly beloved," Father Juan said, beginning the ceremony, which went on a long time and involved a lot of kneeling, which had to hurt Wrassler's stump above his prosthetic leg. When they spoke their vows, Homer's voice shook. Jodi's was clear and ringing. Jodi's mom cried. The bridesmaids cried. The vamps cried. The three arcenciels cried. Gee and his stupid little red flying lizard cried. The visiting witches cried. I cried. Fortunately Quint had applied waterproof mascara to my lashes, so it didn't matter. Much.

The ceremony was beautiful. The vows were passionate.

After, Jodi and Wrassler kissed and were announced as spouses.

Everyone applauded and cheered and threw rose petals instead of rice or birdseed as the happy couple raced down the aisle, the maids and groomsmen behind them.

It was perfect.

I met Bruiser's eyes at the back of the room, and my breath caught at the expression in his eyes. He mouthed, *I love you*.

I said it back to him.

And then he was swept away, and the room was quickly rearranged by the caterer and set up for dining and dancing. Deon and his staff began bringing in food. Everyone found their table to eat their weight in shrimp and lamb pops and boudin and sausages and entire tubs of steamed crawfish and corn on the cob and platters of cheese and fruit and veggies and dozens of loaves of bread. Later we all ate pieces of the cake that stood four feet tall. I loved every moment of it and ate enough that I had to loosen the waist of my armored leathers.

The vamps didn't drink down anyone, the witches didn't

turn anyone into a toad, and the arcenciels didn't make a scene. The alcohol disappeared by the buttload. And the first dance was fabulous, tiny Jodi in big Wrassler's arms.

When the waltz was over, the quartet was replaced by a DJ who had every song ever recorded on his music system. And I got to dance.

Yeah. It was perfect.

At dawn, Bruiser and I stripped and fell into bed in Leo's old room, too tired to make the drive home, so exhausted I was asleep instantly. The crown fell off during the night, but not before I had a bruised noggin. *Stupid crown.*

At dusk, when we woke, I was still in half-form, which was a pain, but at least I wasn't needing ten thousand calories for breakfast. We put on regular clothes, (jeans and T-shirts, thanks to Quint) piled our gear and equipment into an SUV, and finally made our way back to the freebie house. We held hands the entire way back, and there was something precious in the touch. Far more intense and important than making love. A quiet something that spoke of a future. A promise.

When we pulled up to the freebie house, a rental car was parked there. A familiar form was sitting in the driver's seat, watching us. Ayatas FireWind was here.

Bruiser called Eli on his cell. "I assume you know about the car parked out front. Does Jane have company?" Bruiser chuckled and tilted his eyes my way. "Eli wanted to make certain that neither of you would try to kill the other, so he made Ayatas sit in his car until you arrived."

I nodded and Bruiser disconnected.

Bruiser started to open the door to walk me to the house, but I held up a hand. "I'll go greet Aya and invite him in. Maybe this time he won't shoot me."

"And you won't coldcock him. I approve of this plan." Bruiser kissed me on the tip of my nose. "I'll go back to HQ for a bit."

I grabbed my gear and clothes and handed it all to Quint, who had followed us back in the security detail, and stood by waiting. When the limo's rear lights were far down the road, I met Aya at his vehicle. He showed no surprise when I walked up, so I knew he had been completely aware of his surroundings. My brother by blood had been in law enforcement and military for over 150 years, so situational awareness was part of his soul.

He rolled down his window and spoke in English. "My sister."

"My brother."

"You have a shadow." He tilted his head to Quint.

"Yeah. For good reason. HQ was attacked."

"I read the reports. Your team of international lawyers is excellent."

That told me he had been keeping up with the attacks both here and in Asheville. "Granny's involved with the attackers up to her neck. If I'm right, and our Grandmother is *u'tlun'ta*, then she's a danger to the *Tsalagi* in general and to us in particular. I have information that suggests she's not only *u'tlun'ta* but is also aligned with vampires, a Firestarter-witch-Onorio named Aurelia Flamma Scintilla, and Ka N'vsita who is Onorio and who was born a skinwalker." I took a breath. That might have been a lot to hit him with suddenly, so I paused to let it sink in to his cop brain, his *Tsalagi* brain, and his hind brain. More gently I added, "I'm afraid that Grandmother is your grandmother no more. She's a danger to the world."

"Succinct," he said.

"I got more. And if Grandmother gains three specific magical items that have arcenciel blood and scales woven into their magic, then not only are she and her allies a danger to this world but all the others past and present."

"The Rule of Three applies to powerful objects too," he said.

We were on the same page. Good. Remembering the Cherokee part of my protocol, I said, "You are welcome to my home. There's food on the table, beer in the fridge, and probably football on the TV. Just so you know, Alex reserved a hotel room for you." As I spoke, Aya stepped from his rental car, and I added, "Really? You're driving a Fit? How do you even get your legs into it?"

"It has not been a pleasant experience." He smiled a real smile, showing his beautiful teeth. "And thank you for the room."

A brilliant light flashed in the night. We ducked. My

body went tense as Beast shoved adrenaline into my bloodstream. Quint dropped my gear and pulled weapons, slap-
ping a nine-mil into my palm. Through the windows, I saw
Eli giving fast hand signals to the armed guards as he raced
through the house. Quint duckwalked, looking at the street
both ways. She had a headset and was talking to someone.

"That seems to have come from your rear courtyard,"
Aya said, too calmly, his head near mine below the vehicle's windows. "The Firestarter?" he asked.

"Don't think so." But I wasn't certain. I shoved off and
raced away, calling over my shoulder, "Come."

Pulling on Beast's strength, I sped across the front of
the house to the far side and leaped. Grabbed the tall gate
just to the side of its central decorative fleur-de-lis, avoiding the decorative points on the top; pulled, pushed, lifted
my body up and over in a combo track-runner / high-jump
move. Landed on the narrow drive and sprinted to the
back. Tall gates were built to keep out humans, not skinwalkers and fangheads, and Aya and Kojo, who appeared
out of the darkness, followed by the same means. Thema
raced in, popping with vamp speed through the new opening in the brick fence. Eli and heavily armed guards appeared from inside. Quint dumped my gear on the sofa in
the main room, turned off all the lights inside, and joined
us. From Katie's house, Koun and Tex materialized, Tex
with his two guard dogs, both geared up as if the dogs were
about to fight bears. Everyone was snarling.

Our guests were not who I expected, not Soul, the big
wahoo of the arcenciels. Instead it was the three arcenciels
from the wedding: Storm, Opal, and Pearl. In human guise,
they were sitting on the shattered rubble left from the boulders I used to change mass.

Overhead, lightning flashed cloud to cloud. Even in the
cool of fall, heat lightning was common here, but I had a
feeling this particular light show was more, like maybe a
gathering of arcenciels. Which meant we were either
deeply honored or in deep doo-doo. I swallowed down my
adrenaline and shaking.

Storm was sitting on the topmost stone, posed to show
off her legs, which were only marginally swathed by the
usual charcoal, lavender, and purple dress. Her hair was

long, various shades of purples, all twisted into multicolored waves and thin braids and swoops. The other two
rainbow dragons were sitting lower down on the broken
pile in some kind of position of power. Opal was trailing
her fingers through the fountain water, while Pearl was
running her fingers over the stones where I used to hide
magical objects and some of the more esoteric bones I had
used for shapeshifting. I'd had occasional visits from Storm
and from Soul, but this three-aronciel visit was new.

"Storm, Opal, Pearl," I said, handing my weapon to Tex.
"The Dark Queen welcomes you."

Storm said, "You have been named the Warrior who
Brings Peace, yet you approach us with weapons."

I lifted a hand, and all the weapons dropped. Everyone,
almost in unison, stepped back. As if they had choreographed it. *Coolio.*

Storm said, "I have been assigned by She Who Seeks
Peace, who is also She Who Claims the Rift, as emissary
to your court."

I knew that, so repeating it meant it was important. "My
court is honored."

Storm scowled like the thunderheads she was named for
and said, "Indeed you are. She Who Seeks Peace is revered.
We have been sent to learn human ways. The human ways
of mating and human ceremony. She Who Seeks Peace arranged for us to attend the ceremony of mating. We wish to
attend this thing called the honeymoon."

"No." When Storm looked perplexed, I said, "Such an
invitation is not mine to offer, and the honeymoon is private to the two participants."

"You are the Dark Queen. All bow to you."

I couldn't let them see me as weak. I'd fought one of
them before and wasn't likely to survive another such fight,
not now. But I wasn't quite sure how to keep them away
from Wrassler and Jodi.

Eli stepped forward and bowed to me. "My Queen. Perhaps I might be able to explain."

I wanted to toss him a queenly wave, but I wasn't sure
how to do it without looking stupid. "Please."

To the arcenciels, he said, "I am the queen's highest servant, called her number one."

I couldn't stop my smile at the *Star Trek* reference, but I lowered my head until I could get my grin under control.

"Such matters as marriage ceremonies are deeply personal and private," Eli said. "Only the closest of cohorts are allowed to attend the ceremony. Even the queen herself would not have attended unless personally invited. You were honored to receive the invitation. But the honeymoon is not by invitation to anyone."

All three arcenciels looked at me. I nodded, agreeing with Eli.

"We have watched the Council House Chambers," Storm said. "We do not understand why the maimed one is the choice of the powerful human witch-born woman called Jodi. The honeymoon will show us this."

Eli stepped closer, saying, "Physical perfection is of less value than strength of spirit and valor and honor. Do you understand such concepts?"

"They are human concepts. We find them peculiar. But we are here to learn. We have been ordered to learn," Storm said. She frowned at us and demanded, "You will make attending the honeymoon happen."

Pearl, whose skin held a nacre-like sheen, said, "Sister. We have not tried the negotiation of the words."

Storm said, "You are better at the negotiation than am I. I will kill them if need be. You may use the words."

Pearl stood, her clothing glowing faintly in the dim light, and said to Eli, "We have seen the weakness of the Council Chambers' defenses. The pitiful thing that throws fire has breached the defenses four times."

I felt Eli tense. We knew of one time. Not four. How had we missed so many incursions?

"One such time she threw fire," Pearl said. "There was much damage. We are capable of warding the walls and trapping the fire that she throws. This is child's play to us. And so we protected the walls during the ceremony of marriage between the strong woman and the maimed man with strength of spirit and valor and honor."

Crap. The Firestarter had tried to attack during the wedding and no one noticed.

Opal said, "We understood that dresses called ball were required. She Who Guards the Rift provided templates.

We did not appear strange or different from humans. We stood and sat together and protected with our magic. We observed only. This information is part of the negotiation of words."

Pearl said, "We did not change shape or form. We did not attack any guests even if they deserved it. We require to be allowed to attend the honeymoon."

Storm said, "I agree with all that my sisters have spoken."

I said, "You observed proper etiquette at the wedding. This will be reported to She Who Guards the Rift. However, if you disrupt the honeymoon for any reason except attack from our enemies, you will be banished from my court. And I'll call Soul and tell her you were incapable of learning and therefore unworthy."

The arcenciels didn't pale at the threat, but Opal's hands fluttered, and Storm leaned against the stones. They looked back and forth between one another, as if talking mind to mind.

"Eli, can you offer a distraction to our arenciel guests?"

Eli bowed. "Ladies. Have you ever ridden in an armored SUV?"

"No," Opal said.

"Have you ever been to the human place called the 'burger joint' for the human meal of burgers and fries?" Eli asked. "The burger joint is the cornerstone of human existence."

"No," Storm breathed. "Is this more important than the honeymoon?"

"Yes," Eli said with a straight face. "And if you negotiate with the same honor as Wrassler, and remove the request to attend the honeymoon, I'll take you to the burger joint right now."

The arceniels squealed and raced toward Eli. Moments later they were loaded up in Eli's personal use vehicle, along with Aya, and were trundling away through the busy streets. I didn't know why Aya was going but figured that Eli knew what he was doing. The human guards went back to patrolling, leaving me surrounded by vamps, Alex standing at my elbow.

Koun said, "My Queen, I have lived two thousand years and been a member of many courts, both human and Mithran. And I must say that yours is the most entertaining in two millennia."

"Never a dull moment," Tex agreed, and clicked his tongue at his dogs. "Come on, let's get you babies some steak from the queen's fridge. She always has the best food, and I have it on good authority that Deon sent over some leftover grub."

Tex, the dogs, and Koun wandered toward the house and whatever little miracles Deon had provided.

Kojo and Thema came closer. Kojo asked softly, "You do not try to capture and ride the arcenciels? Throughout the ages, all Mithrans and Naturaleza have tried to capture them in crystals and ride the past and the future."

"I don't believe in slavery. And time travel is dangerous in ways no living being can guess at." I knew. I'd done it without trapping arcenciels, had gotten cancer from it, and had made some mistakes I couldn't correct. Ever.

The two looked at each other and back to me. Without another word, they glided into the night with that disconcerting snake-like vamp grace.

Alex and I stood alone, almost eye to eye. He was taller, leaner, more muscular. And he was shaving. He had a moustache and a chin beard. I hadn't noticed. "Hey, Kid," I said. "What's up?"

"We got the DNA results back from Dr. Northern at the lab. Can we talk? Privately? Just us two?"

Something odd tickled at the back of my heart, as if something had wrapped around it. "Sure. My rooms?"

"No. Let's go for a ride around the block. No vamp ears to listen in."

CHAPTER 15

Kickstart the Old Bastardized Panhead Harley

Alex led the way through the house and to an SUV that was idling at the curb. He got in the driver's seat, which felt all kinds of odd, accepted the fob from the human standing there, and waited for me to get into the passenger seat. He pulled into traffic. An SUV was already in front and another eased in behind us. Security for the queen.

I hated it.

Alex drove with excellent precision and confidence, which meant he had likely taken lessons in defensive and offensive driving. But he looked pensive.

"Okay," I said. "I'm listening."

He stared into the night, following the security SUV in front, being followed by the SUV in back. Brake lights lit his face through the tinted windshield. "I wasn't sure what the results meant, even with Dr. Northern's interpretation, and Eli and I didn't want them sent out for interpretation or second opinion. We got the doctors Paquet—Solange and Pierre—to look over them. You know. The ones who took over the fanghead funeral home. They've lived long enough to have studied a lot of everything, and they explained it to me."

"Okay."

"Your DNA and the DNA on your grandmother's robes is human, but both contain some genetic errors that appear and are reproduced on one or both of the X chromosomes. You might remember that the witch trait passes on genes linked to the X chromosome. Skinwalker genes pass through in the same manner. Aya got his Y chromosome from your father. Aya got his X chromosome from your mother, and it had a genetic abnormality."

"My mother couldn't shift."

"No. Something about her recessive genes, though she was from a skinwalker bloodline. Anyway, your mother married your dad, a man with an X chromosome that had abnormalities too, though different abnormalities from her own. Through marriage to your mother, your father became a part of the Panther Clan."

"But they weren't of the same exact bloodline or clan."

"Correct. I posit that the woman you know as grandmother has tracked the bloodlines and made sure that people with the proper traits married out of clan, and then their children, later on in the line, married back into the Panther Clan or were adopted into the clan.

"You got your skinwalker X chromosome from your father and it was in bad shape; you got your mother's normalish X. Ayatas got your mother's abnormal X, with different replications. So you and Ayatas started out with very different replications. Your original DNA, tested from before the rift and the cancer, has more replications than Aya's does. Four times the number."

"Is that bad?"

He made a turn and skirted Bourbon Street, where the night's activities were already in full swing. "The abnormality is actually a doubling or tripling of specific genes, and is passed down from generation to generation, but it's exclusive to one bloodline. So, as I understand it, it's like this. Two sisters receive their genetic makeup and X chromosomes from the same parents, but the sisters' X genes might combine differently. One sister might have nearly

the same genetic reproductions as the gene donors, while
the other might have multiplied reproductions, say two or
four or eight times as many, as the gene sequence"—he
waved his right-hand fingers in the air—"*mutates* isn't exactly the right word because all the genes are the same, just
way more of them, but it will do. These particular sets of
genes don't transfer like normal genes on the X chromosome, but more like a human mutation called Fragile X.
Basically, this means that all skinwalkers are likely to have
different powers and different power levels, even within
one family, and the way the replicated sequence is passed
on is different for each family member."

My first *Tsalagi* Elder, Aggie OneFeather, had raised the
question of clan and my father, so she had known something about genetic lines. "Tangled X chromosomes. Fine.
I get that. So why do you look all intense and upset? Wait.
You said my DNA from *before*. Then I went into the rift. Is
mine the same before and after?"

"No. You have fewer replications than you did."

I wondered if the extra replications had been responsible for my ability to timewalk. And the magical cancer.
And if the current replications were making my shifting
unreliable.

He made a left turn and checked his rearview. "The
DNA also suggests that aging occurs faster in some lines
than others. And aging is the prime cause for becoming
u'tlun'ta."

"Did Ka age more rapidly than me, and therefore that
made her become *u'tlun'ta* sooner? Will I age more rapidly
now that I've been through the rift? Or maybe stop aging?" I looked down at myself. When I came back from the
rift, I looked eighteen. I still did.

"We need Ka's DNA to compare, but I'm thinking your
DNA was repaired more than we thought during your trip
through the rift." His tone said there was more.

"Okay. I can kinda wrap my head around that. How
does Grandmother's DNA fit into all this?"

"Hayalasti Sixmankiller's DNA is in seriously bad
shape. A batch of replicated genes on the X chromosome
is tangled like a hairball." He glanced at me. "Similar to,
but a lot worse than, yours pre-rift. It looks like someone

added DNA with an ice cream scoop and tied it together with yarn. That could be because of someone she ate alive, and the black magic that pulled their DNA into hers. Or not. We don't know."

"Question. Will you ask Wrassler, on the QT, what happened to any samples of Immanuel's blood after I killed him? Maybe blood-stained carpets or rugs or cleaning cloths?"

"If he's got any, you want it tested?"

"Yeah. Let's find out what we have."

"Meanwhile, keep this in your pocket." He handed me a small brown paper bag. "It's a scrap of your granny's sweaty shift. Dr. Northern returned it, and Eli thought you might need it someday." He glanced at me, and I must have looked confused because he added, "*Le breloque* uses blood as a weapon. Maybe it can use sweat too."

And maybe Grandmother could track me by it. But I shoved it into a pocket anyway.

Alex called security. "Alex Younger here. Heading back to the queen's personal residence."

The car in front took a right. We followed.

After the attack that wasn't an attack, I was tense, so I made a pot of strong black tea. While it steeped at the kitchen table, I dragged the trunk of journals close and pulled out an armload I hadn't looked over yet. I flipped open five before I found one in English. I read the first page, handwritten in that old calligraphy style of the classically educated human of European descent. It was simply a name and a date in immaculate penmanship. *Immanuel Justinus Henri Mainet Pellissier, in the year of our Lord, Seventeen Ninety.*

This journal was written by Immanuel.

I closed it, a finger holding my place on the page. This journal was one of the last ones handed down to me by Derek while we were raiding the storage room on sub-four. He had given me this one on purpose, knowing I had killed Immanuel or, rather, the creature masquerading as Leo's son.

Hardly daring to breathe, I reopened the book and turned the page, staring at the words and lines of a diagram, a lineage, vamp style. On one side were physical children—children of the body—written in black ink. On the other side, written in a browning grayish ink, was a vampire lineage. I dropped my nose close to the page and sniffed, getting a whiff of what smelled like old fanghead blood and funeral flowers and ashes. The ink had been made from vamp blood.

Immanuel. The name was like a talisman and a curse. His death had been the origin of everything that had happened in this city since the day I first arrived.

I had killed him.

This man, Immanuel, with blondish hair, an elegant demeanor, and the stink of scorched flesh and rot, was the reason I had come to New Orleans, hired to track and destroy a vampire murderer. Saving the witches was the reason I stayed. And now I was stuck here, queen of the beings I used to hunt and kill. Holding the journal of Leo's son.

There could be DNA on the pages. I got up and went to my room, returning with a pair of gloves. Three-hundred-plus-year-old blood, spit, and sweat from turning and touching pages was probably not useful for DNA, but I wasn't taking a chance.

I turned the pages, reading names here and there. Shopping lists. Descriptions of parties. Names of beautiful human women he slept with. Beautiful vamps. On page 3, Immanuel described himself as a man of leisure, an unashamed womanizer, a rake, a dilettante, and a man of style, which in my time meant he was lazy, a player, and a fashionista. A name jumped out at me, feeling vaguely familiar, as if I had heard the name before. Tsu Tsu Inoli. Russian? Asian? Scandinavian? Probably phonetically spelled.

The cell rang and I flinched just a bit. My honeybunch's face was on the screen. I glanced into the living room to see Alex's feet hanging off the end of the sofa. I hadn't even noticed his soft snores. The Kid didn't sleep enough, so this was either a power nap, or he was crashing and would be down for hours. I picked up my teacup. My voice soft, I answered, "Hey." And sipped. The tea was strong and fragrant, and a sense of well-being moved through me with its warmth.

"Hello, my love," Bruiser said. "Did I wake you?"

"No. I'm just having tea and holding Immanuel's journal. I just found it. It's like a treasure." There was a long silence. "Bruiser?"

"I heard you. Who packed the trunk for you?"

"Derek."

He was silent again, but this time I could hear a chatter of voices in the background. "Derek is missing," Bruiser said. "He was providing a blood meal to Signy, a Scandinavian Mithran who came to HQ this past winter."

A quiet thread of fear twined through my heart. "Go on."

"The furniture is overturned and there is a pool of blood in Signy's room, with droplets here and there in the hallways. Two other Mithrans confirmed by scent that it is both human and Mithran blood. Nothing was on the standard digital security cameras, and it appears there was an *obfuscation* working in use. Wrassler is tracking via the laser monitors and FLIR cameras, but so far we can't prove if he left willingly or not."

I said, "When we were fighting European vamps in Asheville, we knew they sent some fangheads here, hiding among the Mithrans who came for sanctuary. Was she one?"

"It is possible."

"Do I need to come?"

"No. I've called Tex. He's bringing his dogs. One has a nose and he's trained to track. If you see Brute, ask him to come to HQ too. I called because I found the iron witch circle, or where I think it is. Meet me at the Damours' warehouse."

It took a moment for me to place the iron witch circle. We hadn't talked about it since I saw it in the vision of Ka, Adan, and Bethany. I didn't like where this was going. Anxiety wormed under my skin like electric snakes.

The Damours were a vamp blood-family with a witch family linage that had been intwined over too many generations; they had survived the vamp purge in the late 1700s and ended up in New Orleans, where they continued blood-sacrifice of witch children, the most foul of black magic, right under the noses of two of the masters of the city. That magic had involved the blood diamond. Which had been incorporated into the making of the Glob.

"Jane?" he asked, quiet worry in his tone.

I pulled myself back to this moment. "I'll be there in a bit."

"Okay. Be safe."

I hung up. Sipped my tea. My hands were shaking slightly.

Go to place where vampire witches killed kits? Beast asked.

To the place where lots of people were killed, I thought. *We thought we had rooted out all the black magic from that place. Maybe we missed something.*

Take killing steel and white man weapons. And weapons of magic.

Exactly what I was thinking.

I tossed back the tea and silently went to my room to change.

It felt amazing to kickstart the old bastardized panhead Harley and ride through the streets fully human-shaped, alone, the way I had come to this city. Or almost alone. My security team were all around, riding the white crotch-rocket bikes that Leo had bought before he died the second time. I heard the bikes' high-pitched whine all around me, but I could almost pretend they weren't there. Because of traffic, I beat Bruiser to the warehouse and rode around it, taking it in. The front of the place had been subdivided into three businesses, but all the leases had changed since I was here last. I pulled Bitsa off the street into the back parking area and killed the Harley engine, the rumble echoing off the nearby walls.

Setting the kickstand, I swung my leg over, adjusting the hip rig and the nine-mil. I was wearing jeans, a heavy T-shirt, and a leather riding jacket, the Benelli in its original spine holster. Unzipping the jacket, I slid it off, tossed it to the seat, adjusted the fit of the old spine holster, and strapped the helmet to the seat over the jacket. It all felt so normal. So *me*. I opened a saddlebag and pulled out a set of stakes, shoving three wooden ones into my hair and three silver ones into the stake sheath on my thigh rig. I added a glass bottle of fresh holy water, ready for throwing. Shoved the Glob deeper into my pocket, which was jury-rigged with padding against potential magical heat.

I was ready for most anything.

Out of the night, a white blur trotted down the street. Brute. The angel-touched white werewolf stuck in wolf form was showing up, out of the darkness, his movement slightly out of focus with my current reality. Timewalking. I didn't take my eyes off him, but suddenly he was beside my thigh, sitting, looking up at me, panting slightly, tongue hanging out a little to the side of his mouth.

"Crazy wolf," I said. "How did you even know to be here?"

He huffed at me, smiling.

Together we turned and looked at the building. We were at the back-alley entrance off Iberville, and this time there was no vamp scent, no smell of dead human bodies. "I don't think you've ever been here," I said to the wolf.

The warehouse had windows on the lower story at the back and sides, and wide, arched windows on the two top floors. Renee Damours and her husband/brother had used the back half of all three stories; one had been for storage for her long-chained children and her businesses, and the other two floors for living. Unlike in the vamp-owned days, the windows were no longer draped in heavy cloth but blank to the night. No lights shone inside. There were a half dozen security cameras, a single heavy-duty steel garage-style door, and a brand-new steel entry door with a keypad lock.

I wandered up to the door and checked it. Locked. I sat on a low brick wall and waited, Brute stretched out beside me, my security team all around, Quint in the shadows behind me, watching everything. Ten minutes later, Bruiser's SUV and his two-SUV-security team turned in and parked. Bruiser stepped out of the passenger side door and walked up to me, his long legs in an unhurried stride. He took in the bike as he passed it, his eyes raking my clothes and weapons. A tiny smile pulled at the corner of his mouth. "Ready for war?"

"Entering this building has never been easy."

"True." He handed me a headset. Our men surrounded us, four in front at point, two behind at our six. The crotch rockets patrolling the streets moved in closer, the whine piercing.

Brute leaned against my leg, almost as if in comfort.

I put the headset on and heard Bruiser both beside me and through the earbuds, "Clear the building. Reconverge at the lower level."

There were a series of "Roger that" and "Copy" comments as Bruiser punched in a code, and the door unlocked. Four of the unit moved into the dark, two wearing low-light / IR goggles, marking them as human, two vamped out. From the outside, more humans, Kojo, and Thema joined the crew, their low voices letting me know this had been planned, all without me, on the fly. I could console myself that I had helped design the protocols, but in reality, it just let me know how far behind I'd left my Enforcer duties. An unexpected sense of longing filled me about that.

I waited, listening, Bruiser on one side, tense and stiff, Brute on the other, probably getting white hairs all over my jeans. Beast lent me her vision, turning the world silvers and greens, allowing me to follow the action as the point men moved through the dark building. They repositioned with military precision, checking everything with goggles and vamp-eyes, giving reports as they advanced. I knew this building. It was imprinted on the back of my eyelids, the memories full of the dead, the long-chained children, the vamped, and all the horror that had been the Damours. Oddly, Beast wasn't worried. Brute was pressed against my leg. Quint was at my back, covering our six. The security team gave quiet updates as they progressed, and with each statement, my worry increased, though everything they said should have lowered it.

"Hallway, clear."

"Left room one, clear."

"Right room one, clear."

"Entering door at hallway end. Going silent."

"Stairway, clear on this level. No bogeymen noted on first landing. Starting up. Going silent."

I said, "In the Damours' private quarters there was an entrance to a hidden stairway that ran from the top of the building to the garage, providing a secret passage for vamp slavers to move their human cargo. Entrance is in a closet or a wardrobe, if I remember right."

Sweaty Bollock said, "Copy that. Voodoo and I'll check it now."

Thema said, "Checking garage. One interior door for entry to garage is unlocked."

Kojo said, "Garage is clear. No vehicles. Garage exterior door is locked and secure."

Koun said, "Outside fire escapes are clear. No doors or windows open. No movement. Leaving two outside guards and entering level-one door."

Koun was here. Good.

From upstairs I heard, "Stairway clear. Second floor hallway clear."

Sweaty said, "Found entrance to hidden stairway. Going silent."

Then the guard who had entered the room at the end of the hallway said, "Room at end of first floor hallway, clear."

I felt Bruiser relax at my side, and an answering relief washed through me. That room. That was where we had found the long-chained—the insane vampire children shackled to their cots . . .

I didn't smell vamps, except the long-ago stink of the Damours and the Rousseaus. No fresh blood. The building was empty except for New Orleans's ubiquitous roaches and rats, which I could smell, even with a human nose. Fast, the team took up firing positions at the landings, the door, the garage, on the roof, and outside.

Sweaty Bollock said, "Hidden stairway down, clear."

Blue Voodoo said, "Stairway up to roof, clear."

Thema stepped up close and scratched Brute's ears. "The building is safe, My Queen."

I was watching her hand on Brute's head when the words "My Queen" penetrated. Slowly I raised my eyes to Thema. She never called me *queen*. Never offered me her loyalty. She was doing that now. A possibility entered my mind, and I quashed it, not because it was without merit but because now wasn't the time. Yet the possibility was there, nonetheless.

She turned her gaze to Bruiser. "I am the Dark Queen's personal security. You may have chosen another, but I will be the one who keeps her safe." She turned her black eyes on me and her fangs clicked down. The silver piercings in her ears caught the light. "You will stay behind me, My Queen."

It was not a request, but an order. Quint stepped in front

of me, between us, weapons out. Beast bristled at the smells coming off the two women, but I held her down. *Thema's powerful,* I thought to my other half. *Let her lead.*

Beast is not kit to be led. Beast is not prey. Beast does not like where Jane's thoughts go.

Too freaking bad. We're neck deep in quicksand.

Beast does not understand sand that moves fast.

Yeah? You're keeping secrets about our lives. You share all the secrets, and I'll explain quicksand.

Jane is mean.

Yeah, yeah, yeah. Whatever.

Bruiser said, "Quint, take our six. Thema, take point."

Instantly Quint backed up. No reaction this time. No scent change.

We moved forward. Inside, into the dark.

I saw the room as it had been and as it was now, the present overlaid with the past. The windowless room was fifty by forty, give or take, with a fifteen-foot-tall ceiling. The walls were still painted soft coral, but there were no rugs, no leather furniture, no tables or lamps scattered in small groups, as if for playing cards or chatting or drinking tea. The far corner was empty too, where the concrete floor sloped gently to a drain. The ten blackened steel cots that had once held the shackled long-chained vampire children were gone. The room was empty.

There was nothing left to hide any part of the wide concrete floor.

Beneath the spot where the rugs had lain was a black marble square with three concentric circles that touched, like a witch circle made of three parts. The outer ring was twenty feet in diameter, made of wood, the middle was iron, the inner was also wood, sandwiching the iron. The circle was marked along the outer perimeter with symbols that resembled runes, and these were made of stone. The Glob remained inert, not pulling energy into itself, which was a good sign. But Brute went rigid, his body vibrating with a fine tremor, so tight I could feel it through the spot where we touched. He growled low, the sound rumbling, so dangerous that even the vampires went still as statues.

A grindylow popped into view, landing on Brute's neck, chattering. Its steel claws were out. Not a good sign.

"What is it, Brute?" I asked.

And then I remembered another ring in another floor, in the basement of a witch's home, where she had called and trapped a demon. That demon had been eating the two sacrifices. One of the chewed sacrifices had been Brute.

I knelt beside the white werewolf and said softly, "It's okay Brute. You're safe. We're here."

Brute tuned pale eyes to me. He growled low, the rumble like a freight train coming closer.

The grindy put its claws against Brute's neck. It no longer looked like a neon green kitten. It looked like what it was—the executioner of were-creatures who passed along the were-taint.

Inside, Beast tensed. *Madness in Brute brain. Like rabies. No. It's fear,* I thought back. "Is it a demon circle? Smell it. Do you smell brimstone?"

Brute turned his gaze from me back to the ring. He snarled, his lips curling to show his fangs before he huffed, sniffed three times, and sneezed.

I scratched Brute thoroughly under the chin, our noses nearly touching, breathing in and out, sharing breath. Brute's smelled of grilled steak, which was interesting. I wondered who had been feeding him. "It's okay. We're here. You're not alone. You can leave at any time if you need fresh air."

He began to relax. Brute sat and met my eyes, shaking his head no, in the human way. The grindy sheathed its steel claws, chittered at me, and vanished. Like poof. I gave the white werewolf a last scratch behind his ears before standing.

The vamps and humans and my Consort were staring at me. "What?"

"You used to hate that wolf," Bruiser said.

"I used to do a lot of things," I replied. "I'd like everyone to stand back while I check out the circle in case there's some residual power, or maybe a latent working that's only triggered by other magic." Holding the Glob out in front of me, I walked slowly toward the marble square and the circle. I hadn't expected Brute to follow, but he did, sticking tight to my jeans on my left side, which allowed me free access to my weapon on the right. Not that a nine-mil would help much if a demon attacked or a spell went active. I switched the Glob to my dominant hand. It was the better weapon for now.

I bent close to study the construction of the rings. It looked as if the circle had been cut from the marble, the wooden rings put in place, and molten iron had been poured inside them. The wood was heavily charred where it touched the iron. Outside the circle, the cardinal points were etched in the black marble, with north indicated by an arrow. It was an *old* witch circle, from the times when witches and vamps in New Orleans had worked together. It was far older than the demon circle in Evangelina's house, though like that one, this still carried an old stink of sacrifice. Side by side, we walked around the circle once, widdershins. I paused at each stone rune, but the Glob was nonreactive, and Brute didn't seem to smell an active working.

When we reached our starting point, Brute moved ahead of me and stuck his nose against the floor to sniff, moving closer to the circle, working his way in. He made little snuffling and snorting sounds, his lips pulling away from his fangs, his tail sagging slowly. I stayed close to him but out of his way.

Ugly wolf, good nose, Beast thought at me. *Would chase wolf tail if in Beast form.*

Uh-huh. No.

I touched Brute's head, and he stopped snuffling long enough for me to get down on the floor with him again. I stretched out my arm and placed the Glob on the floor, almost touching the outer ring. With one finger, I slowly pushed the Glob closer, until it was lying directly on top of the iron. Nothing happened. I shoved the Glob across and inside the ring. Zilch.

"Okay, Brute. Go for it. What do you smell?"

Brute began snuffling again, and reached the iron ring. His scenting sounds were much more elegant than the sounds bloodhounds make, which are slobbery, lippy snuffling. Brute began to follow the circle, stopping and smelling as he moved.

Ugly wolf, good nose, Beast thought again.

This was the circle I had seen in Sabina's vision. Down here, on the floor, I was close enough to see that the thin cracks between the black marble and the rings were caked with residue. It stank of magic and old blood. "Brute. The stuff in the cracks. Is it blood?"

Brute turned and padded to Kojo, sitting at the vampire's feet, looking over his shoulder at me.

"Vampire?" When Brute didn't react, I asked, "Vampire of African descent?"

Brute nodded and went to a human security guy. Except she was a woman.

"Female, Caucasian, human?"

Brute nodded, came to me, and sat.

"Were you smelling sacrifices?"

Brute nodded.

"Were children, witch children, sacrificed here?"

Brute nodded. He tapped my booted foot. It took me a moment. Then softly I said, "Blood, like mine? Skinwalker blood?"

Brute nodded.

"Is it old? Like over a hundred years?"

Brute nodded again.

Ka. Ka's blood was still here, soaked into the floor, so much of it that it still had a scent to Brute's wolf nose, even after all these years.

CHAPTER 16

It Was Stupid to Use a Handgun as a Club

It was an hour from dawn when we left the warehouse. Bruiser had collected a sample of Ka's blood from the black magic circle, though it was likely contaminated with other blood and unusable. We had walked through the building from top to bottom for anything I missed on prior visits. As we stepped outside, Storm appeared, sitting on top of an SUV. She was wearing armor like I had worn at the wedding and bristled with weapons. All of our weapons were instantly centered on her. Thema stepped in front of me, protecting me with her body. Quint tried to shove me down to stand over me.

I activated my mic and said, "Stand down." The weapons—except for Thema's—were repositioned, but I could smell the intense reactions of my security team. I touched Thema and Quint, each with a single finger, and they stepped aside, their aim never wavering.

Storm's armor was dark amethyst and matched her purple-, lavender-, and grape-colored hair. It was the first time I had seen her wearing anything non-light-dragony.

Check Out Receipt

The security lights limned her with a silver glow, though the light may also have come from inside the rainbow dragon, shining through armor that was less physical and more energy-based than mine. Who knew?

I said, "The Warrior who seeks Peace welcomes Storm."

"This is a bad place," Storm said. "Why do the beings enter and leave? Why do they not destroy it?"

"We may," I said, thinking that a *null* working over the iron circle, topped by a layer of concrete might suffice.

"Why does the Dark Queen allow the fire thrower, the eaters of souls, the burned one, and all her enemies to watch? They are full of malice."

Bruiser spoke into my earbuds, "Get her out of here."

Thema picked me up and raced me toward a second SUV. Like a sack of potatoes. Or a baby. Before I had time to even speak, she had thrown me into the back seat of the SUV. Quint took shotgun. Silent. Weapons out. I rolled to the side. Opened the door. Held out a hand.

"Storm. Join me."

Instantly the arenciel was sitting at my side.

Okay that was weird. A security guy slammed my door, and Thema started the engine, wheeling the armored SUV out of the lot.

"My bike!" I shouted, spotting Bitsa in the dark.

"My mate will bring it to your home," Thema said, gunning the motor, turning into traffic, and then off, slamming me into Storm and back against the door. I pulled off the spine holster that had bruised my back on the turn and buckled in. Thema whirled us again.

"Holy moly, woman. Where did you learn to drive?" I asked.

Thema didn't answer. She just spun the wheel, making a hard left across traffic. This time I was holding on.

Storm was laughing like a kid on a roller coaster.

I replayed what she had said. "Storm, where are the watchers?"

"The burned one is there," she pointed.

To my left I saw Sabina, standing in the shadows. For a bare moment, our eyes met. I somehow had expected Leo. Didn't know which was worse. I caught a glimpse of Brute racing toward Sabina, out of sync with my reality. The SUV swerved again. I could hear Thema talking into her mic, advising the team.

"Where is the Firestarter?" I asked Storm.

"She is preparing to throw fire at the bad place."

I looked over my shoulder. "Dang."

"Do you wish my sisters to put out her fires?"

"Yes." Behind us, I saw a flash of fire. Another. Another. But the spots went dark instantly.

Storm laughed, the sound like bells and wind instruments. "Pearl and Opal enjoy this game. The creature thinks you have found new magic and have stopped her. We will not tell her the error of her ways or show who we are unless she attacks again."

"Okay. Where is the eater of souls?"

Storm tilted her head, frowning. I could have sworn the lights in her hair twinkled. "One is at the bad place." She hesitated. "One is above us, on the air. She is angry."

I craned my head up, seeing a cloudy, dark gray sky. It was nearly dawn. A vamp was driving the SUV. That might not end well. We needed to be undercover soon. And then it hit me. Eaters of souls. One at the warehouse, one above us. Grandmother? As an owl?

I fished my cell out of my pocket and dialed Ayatas.

"FireWind."

"The Firestarter is at or in the warehouse. Gramma is a bird flying over my SUV."

Aya cursed and disconnected.

"You have bad cell phone habits," I said to my dark screen.

Thema spun the wheel, maneuvering the vehicle down one-way streets the wrong way. I held on as she took an alley, knocking over big plastic garbage bins, nearly hitting an Uber vehicle, taking back ways I knew from riding Bitsa and roaming as Beast.

She braked hard in front of the freebie house. The SUV rocked. Steel shutters I hadn't even noticed had been cranked shut over the house windows.

Aya was standing on the second-story porch, buck naked except for a thong around his neck strung with tiny bones. He was staring at the sky, a nimbus of skinwalker magic over his body. Already halfway to a shift. Holding his power still. Waiting.

Two guards ripped open the driver's side doors, one grabbing each of us. Thema and me. Jerking us from the vehicle, standing us on the sidewalk. In a fast exchange, they took off in the SUV. Quint sped to my side.

A light glimmered. Storm, who had been on the passenger side of the vehicle, was standing beside me.

Other guards grabbed us to sweep us inside.

I smelled liver-eater. Heard the flap of wings overhead. Aya leaped into the air, shifting as he did. The sidewalk a story beneath him, only feet from us, cracked and broke, throwing shards into the air as he shed mass. Thema hissed in pain as concrete flew. I smelled her blood. She had stepped in front of me.

I stared. Aya had shifted in middrop. That wasn't even possible. He was a huge bird, a nine-foot wingspan sweeping the sidewalk as he took flight. Not a *Bubo bubo*, but maybe a condor of some kind.

As Aya reached the height of the peaked roofs, an owl hurtled down from the clouds, straight at me. Aya's bird screamed, a screeching roar with elephantine overtones. He whipped his wings and reached for Grandmother. He wouldn't be in time. Thema raised a weapon.

I hit the sidewalk hard. Face-plant. Fire whooshed through my nerves, muscles, skin. For a moment I thought I had been hit by a fireball. The pain sliced and cut, burned and froze. Muscles tore. Bones popped.

When the burning pain eased, I lifted my head and looked along my body. I realized that Beast had ripped through our realities and used my own skinwalker power all on her own. Again. She had added mass to my half-form, taking mass from the concrete sidewalk.

Screams echoed. Gunshots. More SUVs arriving. The putter of Bitsa. Scent of Tex, Koun, Kojo, Thema. My first breath was agony. I whispered a curse.

My cheek was against the broken sidewalk. I stared across the street. Lightning cracked across the sky above me. A momentary brilliance. The stink of ozone and storm. And magic. When the glare cleared, standing on the sidewalk was Adan Bouvier. One arm was up to the sky, lightning still glowing on his fingertips. A cold wind swept down the street. Lightning cracked again, the magic of a weather-witch vamp. Familiar as old, painful memories. A brilliant flash hit the sidewalk at his feet.

No. It hit the body beside him on the sidewalk. It spasmed, curled, and died. The stink of human flesh, cooked and dead.

Two arcenciels dove at Adan, dragon form, slashing claws, tails whipping.

Unexpected strength thrust through me like a fist of might. I shoved upright. Eye to eye with Ka, standing in the shadows across the street. Naked, as she would be after shifting from an animal. Yellow eyes. Black hair. Fierce scowl. A blade in her hand. Then she shifted so fast I couldn't follow it. Still with black hair and eyes, but pale, olive-toned skin. The stench of liver-eater whooshed from her. *U'tlun'ta'*. I knew this one too.

Ka had taken the body and mind and gifts of Aurelia Flamma Scintilla, the Firestarter. Aurelia was—had been— a *senza onore*, a dark Onorio. Ka, a skinwalker, had eaten her while she was alive and taken her power, her memories, and her form. The need for others to fulfill the Rule of Three for Onorio now made sense. Ka/Aurelia raised her hand, and fire began to gather there.

Fury slammed through me. I pulled a nine-mil and a vamp-killer. The world slowed down. From the far end of the street, a vamp strode, walking in the near dawn, his chest naked. The first time in all these days that I had seen him in person.

Shaun MacLaughlinn.

He carried two swords.

All my enemies in one spot.

Not a coincidence.

"Jane Yellowrock," Shaun shouted. "I have challenged you to a blood duel for the rights of this city. We will fight here. Now!"

Kojo and Koun blocked his way, each holding swords high and low. "You will not break parley," Koun shouted.

Ka/Aurelia reared back to throw.

Thema darted in front of me.

My vision, my awareness fractured.

Above us, a dragon screamed. Storm, burning dragon form, dove at Ka. Slow, slow, slow.

The fireball flew from Ka/Aurelia's hand.

Right at Thema. She was a flammable vampire standing in the near-dawn.

Storm's magic reached for the fireball. Her claws slashed at Ka. I tackled Thema and rolled to the side. Avoiding the sidewalk where Aya had left mass. We landed hard.

Thema's arm was on fire. I rolled us into the dirt to the side of the house where large-leafed plants grew and the garbage bins stayed. I crushed her skin into the dirt, smothering the fire. Two other fireballs were extinguished out front. Storm's magic.

I heard a sound like a church bell cracking, a disharmonious, broken gong.

Beneath the broken bell, Ka bellowed in fury.

Gunshots and screams rang out. Fighting sounded from the back of the house too.

"Get inside before the sun takes you out, you stupid vamp," I demanded of Thema. I leaped to my feet. I wasn't wearing the Benelli. It was in the floor of the SUV. I was still holding the nine-mil and a vamp-killer. I sprinted at Ka. Half-form but bigger. Stronger.

I took it all in. A single glance.

Ka was Ka-shaped again. Storm was dragon-form, the coils of her snake body wrapped around Ka. Her dragon fangs buried in Ka's neck.

Ka was holding a blade. In the brighter light, I could see it wasn't steel but cold iron. I was halfway across the street when she stabbed Storm.

Iron was the only thing that could kill an arcenciel.

Storm screamed in agony and coiled away, her liquid-light blood gushing into the street. Ka raised the blade to strike her again. She collected Storm's blood in a cup.

I screamed in rage. Half-form lion scream.

Ka stopped, whirled in Storm's loosening coils. She saw me. I leaped. Midair, I saw Ka's mouth open. Her body shifted into a red-head Caucasian with blue eyes, the shift allowing her to slide from Storm's coils. Fangs clicked down. Vampire fangs. Three inches of vampire strength. Her eyes bled black. Her mouth was aimed at my neck.

I whipped my arms and twisted as if in flight. Leaning back. A move Eli had taught me.

Caught Ka with my silvered blade in her side.

Her iron blade passed above me in the air. Still whirling, I rammed the nine-mil into the side of her head. She fell. I landed as she hit the sidewalk. Found my feet. I kicked her head, making sure she was down and out. Her body rolled into the street, her head at an angle that let me know I had broken her neck. The stench of liver-eater was powerful: scorched flesh and rot.

I had probably screwed up the sights and aim of the gun. It was stupid to use a handgun as a club.

I kicked Ka again.

Looked for Shaun. He, Kojo, and Koun were fighting, my two warriors against one, dueling swords flashing too fast to follow. And Shaun was winning.

A rifle cracked. One of my security team fell. Human. Unmoving. We had a sniper. I ducked behind a car, scanning the rooftops. A second shot. A second human fell.

I spotted the sniper behind partial cover. I'd never make that shot.

An enemy human pulled Ka away. And took the blood cup too.

I searched the air for Grandmother and Aya. They were fighting, claws, beaks, beating wings. But Aya was holding back. He was trying not to hurt his Grandmother. Childhood memories, decades of relationship constraining him.

She wasn't holding back. She was trying to kill him.

Eli was suddenly beside me, breathing fast. He stretched across the side and hood of a parked car. A long rifle in his arms. He sighted. Blew out a partial breath. Held it. Aiming. He fired. The enemy shooter disappeared.

Eli rotated and aimed up into the sky. Waiting. Aya took a claw slash across his chest. A beak peck in his right eye. He dropped, plummeting in the air. Away from Grandmother. Eli fired. Grandmother tumbled, fluttered. Fell. She disappeared behind the house across the street. Aya landed on the hood of an SUV with a deep thump I heard over the battle-deafness.

Eli aimed up the street, the weapon balanced on the car hood. Softly he said, "Koun. Down."

On the far end of the street, Koun dropped to his knees in front of Shaun. Eli fired. Shaun staggered. His people closed in on him and carried him away. Koun stood, watching their retreat. He was bloody. He had been injured. He was breathing hard. And it was near dawn.

Eli said, "Take care of Aya. I'll take out the other target." He meant Grandmother. He sprinted away, weaponed up like an assassin.

Storm was wounded, lying in the street, bleeding but still moving.

The fight was over. We had . . . lost? *Holy crap.*

The maid-servant, Quint, appeared at my side. We raced to Aya, his bird body lying on the pavement. One of our humans was aiming a weapon at him.

"He's mine!" I shouted.

The guard looked up at me and took a step back. Moving his weapon to me. I'd been wrong. This human was not mine.

Two shots sounded. The human fell.

Quint had taken him down. And missed me. Good shot. Maybe as good as Eli. I leaned across to my brother. Aya's wings fluttered. One was broken. One eye was gone. His jaw hung open. His chest was scored, but I had no idea how deep. Bloody feathers all across his chest. I holstered my weapon and sheathed the bloody blade. No extra DNA needed to be around him.

"Cover me," I instructed Quint. Without looking her way, I slid my hands beneath Aya. His bird weighed about thirty pounds. He had lost a lot of mass transitioning to this condor. He needed to shift before he died in this form, before he lost the ability to remember he was human. I carried him to the busted sidewalk where he had left mass, and placed him on the center of the gelatinous, rocky, hard, rubberlike goo. I waited. He tried to get to his bird feet. His head was wobbly on his neck. Panicked. Dying. He wasn't going to change in time. I didn't have my crown. All I had was the Glob. It didn't give power for workings, it stole power, sucking it away.

I looked at Quint. "Can you get my crown out of its protective hedge?"

Quint bent toward me and extended a finger. She wiped

the corner of my mouth. Muzzle. I was heavily cat-faced. Her finger came away bloody. I had been injured fighting Ka. "Alex and I can." Almost vamp-fast, she was gone, through the front door, which was still open.

I cradled the wounded and dying bird in my knobby hands, crooning to it, stroking it, keeping my own blood away from it.

Seconds later Quint and Alex were back, kneeling near me but away from the rubbery, rocky mass.

I accepted my crown from Quint. She wiped her bloody finger off on my clothes, giving me back my unused blood. But I smelled burned flesh. She had injured herself getting my crown. I slapped *le breloque* onto my head. Instantly it sized to fit me. Went hot enough to blister my flesh. The Glob heated in my pocket.

I drew on my skinwalker magics. The silver mist of power rose from my half-form. I had healed vampires before. I had healed myself before. I could do this.

Right. I could also kill Aya trying.

I didn't have time for fear.

I envisioned Aya in his human form. I pushed at the power that was mine. But instead of directing it at the bird, I directed it at Aya's mass on the ground. Somewhere in that stuff was Aya's perfect DNA. And maybe most of his skinwalker magics. *Crap.* Did I leave behind my magic when I lost mass? I didn't know.

I closed my eyes. Eased my power into the rubbery mass, feeling/scenting/knowing chemicals I had no names for. Scenting proteins, things that sizzled with power, things that felt inert but were alive. Felt through them until an electric power met mine. Skinwalker power.

The Glob sought to pull the energies away. I reined the weapon in but kept it ready. I drew on *le breloque*, directing its might into the skinwalker energies. And shoved it toward the dying bird.

Aya, I thought. *Ayatas Nvgitsvle, named for the Nantahala Panther of the Panther Clan. Come to your true form.* Nothing happened. Time passed. Too long. I pushed more skinwalker and *le breloque* power into him, trying the words in the half-remembered Cherokee of his introduction to me, the first time he appeared at my door. *Nv-*

dayeli Tlivdatsi, Nvdayeli Tlivdatsi of Ani Gilogi. Seek the form of Aya. Come back to yourself. Your battle is neither won nor lost. You must be human-form. Come back to yourself.

Inside me, something like longing woke. Something that might have been the memory of abandonment combined with the memory of loss, loss of family. The memory of our father dying. I pushed harder. *Do not make me become a beloved woman to fight in my brother's stead. Alone. I have been alone for too long, without my kin. Without my clan. Come back to me!* I lay across the mass of my brother, cradling his bird.

Come back to me.

God? *You can't take this away. You can't take him away. You can't. You can't, you can't, you can't!*

I was sobbing, shoving my magic into Aya. Tears and snot dripped down my chin. I wiped them on my shoulder to keep from contaminating his mass with my DNA. I hadn't even let myself get to know him. I hadn't tried. I had pushed him away like a kid, out of anger and spite. I had been so *damn* stupid. "Come back," I demanded. And then it hit me. *Rule of Three.* My voice hoarse and shaking, I said, "*Nvdayeli Tlivdatsi. Nvdayeli Tlivdatsi. Nvdayeli Tlivdatsi.* Return to your human form."

Something tingled and quivered beneath my arms. I eased back just a bit. Wiping my face again. Through the trembling sheen of my tears, I watched as Aya's skinwalker energies lifted out of the pile of my brother's mass. I eased back farther. The concrete of the sidewalk cracked and broke again, the mortar used in the construction shattering as the magic tightened, the energies growing thicker, black motes whirling like tornadoes in the midst.

My magic never looked like this.

The mass on the sidewalk drew together. I pulled away from the shape-change, watching, feeling the energies through *le breloque*. A human form began to coalesce out of the rubbery pile and the dying bird and the energies. I crab-walked back, bumping into human legs that gave way for me. A palm rested on my shoulder, fingers warm. Eli. Comforting. I lay my cheek on his hand. Alex was on the other side, hand on my shoulder.

Slowly. Painfully Aya reformed. Solidified out of the boiling energies.

His body was quaking, shuddering, muscles vibrating, curled in a fetal position. And pale, so very pale. I pulled back all my skinwalker energies, the energies of *le breloque*, and shoved down hard on the Glob. Locking it down.

Aya took a breath. I knew that sound. That sound meant his lungs had been in shutdown, and the instinct to breathe had forced his chest to expand.

I stood, leaning on Eli. "He'll be hungry."

"Oatmeal cooked but in the fridge. Three pounds of sliced beef. Twelve boiled eggs. All cold as sin but calories ready to eat. I've lived with you long enough to know what's needed, Janie." His voice was kind, telling me he had my back.

I nodded. "I have to check on Storm."

Eli tensed. "It isn't good."

I shook my head, thinking, *When is it ever?*

"I've called Soul," he added.

Without checking for traffic, knowing without looking that my people had blocked off both ends of the block, I walked into the street and across. Opal and Pearl were in human form, holding Storm in their arms. Storm was unmoving, her dragon form coiled and still. Her sisters hissed as I approached. I ignored them and knelt at Storm's side.

The one thing I knew for certain about *le breloque* was that at some point, one of the two rings that make the crown had belonged to the arcenciels. I drew on the crown again and placed a hand on Storm's frilled face. I had no idea if arcenciels had hearts or pulses or lungs. I moved my hand over her horns and tusks and the delicate skin that frilled out around her head. I moved down her body, touching, shoving with my magic. Nothing was happening. The tears that hadn't dried were dripping down my cheeks, landing on Storm's body. I was sobbing. Tears and snot and boohooing like a child who had been kicked as grief wracked through me. I wrapped my arms around her body and hugged her, praying for my god to heal her, praying for her goddess, if she had one in her world, to heal her. Nothing happened. Nothing helped. Her coils were lifeless. The magic I tried to push into her went sluggish just beneath her snake skin. I reached for the horrible wound. The flesh there was blackened and smelled of hot iron. The magic I shoved there swirled into the wound and bounced back. Knocking me off my feet to my butt. My knuckles scraped the pavement. Ripping off skin to the bone. I rolled to my side, ready to try again with Storm.

And I got a look at the human-shaped body lying nearby. Curled on its side. Burned and blackened where the lightning had struck it. Facing me. Adan's lightning victim.

Bloodied and scarred. Vamp fangs had torn through his throat. His eyes were open and cooked where the lightning had burned him. *Derek.*

Derek. My friend.

Storm.

I raised my face into the dawn. I screamed. Grief shriek. Battle cry. The sound of loss and fury echoing off the brick walls and into the sky. My entire body heated and tore. My joints and bones popped. I sucked in a breath of rage and I *roared.*

I couldn't fix Storm. I couldn't fix Derek.

I didn't know what I was doing. I never had.

Around me, the pavement erupted. Cracking and bubbling and dusting into its component parts. Tarry shards and concrete shot upward. At me. Into me.

The pavement smashed me in the head.

I woke, lying on my side, on Bruiser's fancy rug beside my bed. My face was on his pillow, my body swaddled in blankets. Bruiser was behind me, cradling me. I had been here long enough for someone to wipe the tears and the snot off my face.

Exhaustion weighed me down like lead in my veins. Breathing hurt. Bruiser stroked my hair—which felt different, but I couldn't say why—and down along my shoulder. He knew I was awake. My tears started all over again.

When I could talk I asked, "Eli? Did he shoot Grandmother?"

"No, my love. She got away."

"Aya?"

"He is well." Bruiser kissed my fingertips.

"Storm? Derek?"

Gently, he said, "Gone." When I didn't open my eyes, he added, "Derek's body has been taken by honor guard to the funeral home. His men have gone to tell his mother that her son is gone. Storm was collected by Pearl, Opal, and Soul. I understand that they are taking her to the rift and placing her into it so that her energies can return through it."

"Adan?"

"Vanished when Opal and Pearl attacked."

"Why?" I meant why did Adan kill Derek, and Bruiser seemed to know that.

"We think he's the one who stole Derek from HQ. We think it was a test of the security system, someone to question, and a challenge."

Someone to question meant torture. Derek had been tortured. "Find Adan. Find who he's working with at HQ. Start with Raisin. She smelled wrong." The next part came out as a growl that vibrated in my chest. "They're mine."

Bruiser breathed a soft laugh. "I never doubted that, My Queen and my love."

I was so tired my bones and joints ached. It even hurt to breathe. "Imma take a little nap right here. Wake me when y'all figure out who my enemies are at HQ."

Bruiser kissed me on the cheek, and I felt pelt between my skin and his lips, and the soft scrape of beard. He muscled upright to a knee and toes, his arms on either side of me.

"I failed," I whispered into the air between us.

Bruiser rose to his feet. "You did not fail. We did not know the enemy's strengths and weaknesses and so could not adequately prepare. Now we know, and you will make the Mithran world quake with fear. You *are* the Dark Queen. *Le breloque* has chosen you." With those words, he left the room, shutting the door silently.

I was left with the reverberation of his words and the memory of Derek. Dead. Storm. Dead. The humans the sniper had killed. Silently I cried myself to sleep.

Like a vampire, I woke at dusk. I was pretty sure it was the foundation-rattling snore that woke me. Apparently when I have a muzzle and sleep on my back, I'm noisy. I was utterly certain that the boys would tease me unmercifully, but that thought vanished as the memories washed through me.

Derek. Derek was dead. Storm was dead. I was going to war, starting in HQ.

I tossed the blankets and sheets into the corner because they were covered in cat hair and dried filth. I stripped and showered. Only when I was clean and my pelt rubbed half dry did I look at myself in the mirror. I was . . . interesting.

I had a full golden pelt all over, except from under my chin, my boobs, belly, and along the inside of my thighs. Some parts that had hair as a human were bare. Weird looking. Somehow I had put on thirty pounds of much needed muscle. I was cat-faced, full nose and muzzle, fangs that would do an ancient vampire proud. Claws that terrified even me. I flexed them out. My finger claws were huge and sharp enough to rip armor. I'd have to be careful, or I might hurt myself. I had shoulders like a linebacker. Thighs of solid muscle. Calves that were so well defined it was as if this new body had been chiseled from stone. Or concrete and roadway.

I had a cat face, cat ears sitting high and taller than usual, with unusual tufts at the end, like a caracal cat. My long hair was gone, a fact I had realized when I showered. That was strange. It was now short and kinda mane-like, almost like an African lion, but running down my back to my waist and black as tar. I reached up and tried to get a claw under *le breloque*. I cut my forehead. That sucker wasn't coming off, and my head was bruised from sleeping with it on. Which was a totally unimportant and, considering the loss of two of my friends, irreverent thought. I let my claws resheathe and studied myself again. I was terrifying. In a way that I had never viewed myself, in a way that only another monster would view me, I was dangerous. I was *fearsome*.

When my enemies saw me, they'd poo their pants.

"Okay. Time for war." I blow-dried my pelt, which took way longer than I liked, and dressed in the scarlet armor. But no boots because my paw-feet and claws were bigger than before. I extruded the claws on my toes. Yeah, they'd eat through the boots, even the specially made expandable combat boots. But the paw pads were tougher than usual, so I'd go barefoot.

I weaponed up. Every weapon I had, including the

newer Benelli spine rig and its shotgun, which someone
had retrieved from the SUV and put on my bed while I
showered. I had put on enough mass that I had to loosen
the rigs. I made sure I had my lucky gold nugget in place
and put on the titanium gorget, layering the gold and ci-
trine over it. It matched the crown.

I had never been pretty. But by all that was holy, I was
badder than bad.

I Velcroed the paper bag containing a scrap of the cloth
stained with Grandmother's sweat into a secure pocket.
Debated on carrying the locket. I didn't know what it did
or if it might interfere with the crown and the Glob. I decided against it. Same for the winged lizard amulet.

A soft knock came at the door. I smelled Quint's scent
from beneath. Thema was with her. "Come," I said. Leo-
like.

They entered. Looked me over. Thema started laughing,
approval in the tone. Quint merely nodded and adjusted the
position of my weapons for more perfect draws.

I was starving, especially with the scent of seared red
meat coming through the cracked bedroom door. With my
newer-better-sniffer nose, I could also smell baked potato
slathered in butter, sour cream, and bacon. There was also
something vegetably that smelled of alkaloids and chloro-
phyll, and made me want to gag.

I glanced in the mirror one last time. Satisfied that I
looked like the Dark Queen should, I strode to the partially open door, grabbed the doorknob, and pulled it
open. Ripped it from its hinges. Threw it across the room.
Quint, battle reflexes always on high, ducked fast.

The door hit the far wall with a wham that I felt through
my paws and resonated through the house. It broke the
wallboard. When I looked back out, Eli was standing behind the wall on the other side of the stairs with a weapon
pointed at my chest.

"Sorry," I said.

The minigun targeting me pointed to the floor. "Don't
know your own strength, babe?" he asked.

"Clearly not." I met his eyes, and his face was drawn
with grief. Tears prickled under my cat lids.

"Food?" he asked.

"I seem to find the smell of veggies foul. Meat? Yes. And a lot of it. We have a war to plan."

"Three pounds of sirloin just for you. Rare enough to still be kicking. Sort of. Nice ears, by the way. I think you put on enough muscle to maybe take me down."

I snorted and strode from my bedroom, taking my place at the table, having to half-straddle the chair because of the weapons. The steak was tender; the fangs weren't so big they got in the way of me chewing, which was good, because my throat closed up several times in grief as I ate. I could hardly taste the food. It was sustenance.

When my plate was empty, I was joined at the table by Aya, Eli, Alex, and Quint. I looked them all over as I sipped my cooling tea. Each face, except maybe Quint's, was etched with grief. Aya looked pretty good for a guy who had nearly died as a bird only hours ago.

I set down my mug. "Any news on Leo's whereabouts?"

"Nothing," Alex said. "We sent teams to every known possible lair. No sign of him anywhere."

I grunted and asked, "Anything on the newly installed cameras and microphones, and any recent sensor data from HQ?" When Cowbird Protocol went into effect again, Wrassler and his security crew had installed mics and cameras in areas of the Council Chambers that had previously been off-limits, and they were all accessed into Alex's system.

There was a peculiar silence after my question. Eli got up and served me dessert, which was a side of bacon.

"Yeah. We got stuff," Alex said.

I shoved three crispy bacon slices into my mouth. "I'm listening."

"You're not gonna like it."

"Didn't expect to." I chewed.

Alex talked. The more he talked, the angrier I got. When I saw the video and heard the conversations, that anger went from hot to cold and determined. My nose and the hidden surveillance equipment had finally found our biggest traitor. The lynchpin.

I was Dark Queen. It was my job to make sure justice was carried out. And for once I'd take pleasure in death.

                    *   *   *

As I walked into the repaired airlock at HQ after dusk, my presence was being announced over the building-wide communication system and into my headset. Humans and vamps came out of the woodwork to get a look at me, watching as I walked through the inner airlock doors, my armed entourage behind me. I stood there waiting, the vamp scents rising, floral, herbal, bloody. Letting them look. Letting the vamps smell me. Predator. Top of the food chain. More vamps and humans arrived in the foyer, stopping; the vamps silent, still as stone; the humans whispering, breathing, shuffling into better positions.

The humans smelled of uncertainty and curiosity.

Rising over the vamps' natural scents was the tang of their desire. They wanted to taste my blood. Some of them wanted a full dinner; in vamp terms, they wanted sex and blood at the same time. Once upon a time, that would have offended me, maybe even frightened me. Now it was something I could use to avenge Derek and Storm. I stared them down. I smiled.

The vamps' scents began to alter, morphing from desire to something more acerbic, resembling anxiety. Gently I began to draw on the power of the crown stuck to my head. The crown of power over vamps for the person who could use it. Smelling their unease grow, I stepped forward. They separated, leaving the way open to the main steps. I walked between them, letting them look. Letting them worry. I didn't pull a weapon. I *was* a weapon.

Slowly I stepped up the stairs. At the top, I looked down at the foyer with my crest on the floor, exposed by the flood of people who had arrived and then stepped back. Wrassler was on his honeymoon. The woman standing in the security nook doorway was familiar, Sarah Spieth, a new former military person chosen by . . . Derek.

"Now," I said.

She pulled a massive weapon, a GatCrank, forward and aimed it on the gathered. We had planned this on the way over. "Send the announcement. All the fangheads are to gather in the gym." I swiveled my head around, taking them in. "All of them. Anyone who refuses to *gather* is to be staked with wood and brought down anyway."

The smell of shock and anger began to rise on the air. Not unexpected.

Some of the vamps smelled like fear now too. I snarled, showing my fangs. "I am your queen." Almost as if I knew what I was doing, using the skill I had learned healing Aya, I drew on the blasted crown, yanking the power into me. Gathering it inside myself. Holding it in a loose fist of my will.

So softly it was only a whisper, I said, "Kneel!" I shoved my power into the group.

All around the foyer, vamps fell to their knees. All except a select few. I memorized their faces and scents.

My personal security popped from the airlock into the foyer, vamp-fast, armed to the teeth. Thema and Kojo raced through the crowd, shoving the resistant vamps face-down to the floor. Staking them. I knew who my people were and who my enemies were.

Through the loudspeaker system, an announcement went out. "All Mithrans are to gather in the gym," Sarah commanded. "HQ is in full lockdown mode. There is no way out. You have fifteen minutes."

Satisfied, I turned and walked to my destination, showing them my back.

Leo had taught me well.

Koun was on my tail. He was wearing basic armor in a dull black and carried lots of weapons. And he had both swords out.

I wasn't sure where Leo was, but in this form, I had a very good nose, and he wasn't on the premises. I didn't smell him anywhere. I had thought he might be hiding here and that perhaps I could smell him in this form. I was wrong.

I shoved open the door. It dented the wall where it hit. I was doing that a lot now. I strode into Raisin's office, silent on my pawed feet, the scarlet armor a declaration of war. Two feet in, I stopped.

The old blood-servant was looking at me. Her eyes wide, her lips pursed into dozens of vertical crevices and wrinkles. One hand was beneath her desk. Before she could pull out her hand and aim, Quint flew under my arm and up into the room. Her body twisted in midair, somersaulting and uncoiling. Like a ninja in some old movie.

Time deescalated. I crouched.

The petite blonde crashed into Raisin feet first. A gun fired. Small caliber. It blew out a ceiling light as they disappeared behind the desk. Tumbling.

Quint stood, lifting Raisin by the hair and slammed her facedown onto the desk, breaking her nose. Almost as fast as a vamp, Quint yanked Raisin's arms back and secured them with a supersized zip strip. She smashed Raisin's face down again, leaving a bloody smear on the formerly pristine desktop. "My Queen," Quint said. Not even out of breath.

It was pretty amazing.

Koun laughed in appreciation. He scented of sexual interest.

Raisin spit blood at me.

Quint wrapped a gag around her mouth before shoving her head back to the desk, her cheek pressed into her blood.

I meandered closer. I bent and smelled Raisin, soft little fluttering sounds coming from my cat nostrils. Vamps. Several vamps. I dropped my head to two inches from Raisin's eyes, opened my mouth, curled back my lips, showing her my fangs. I sucked in air through my mouth, over my tongue, across the scent sacs in the roof of my mouth. Raisin was older than a lot of vamps. She would have been around when Ka and Adan were here and when Immanuel became *u'tlun'ta* so long ago. And she had been drinking of Adan. Adan's blood smelled of Monique, the not-yet-dead creature in the scion room.

"Ahhh," I said. Adan had been part of the group I was unable to see while I was in Monique's soul home. I stepped back and sat in the chair that miraculously appeared there, placed by a human, who whispered, "My Queen," and darted out of the room. The chair was leather, comfy, and big enough for my new, wider shoulders. I could get used to this kind of service.

"Ernestine," I said, using Raisin's real name. "You have been accused of treason."

Raisin shook her head so hard her hair smeared into the blood.

"Alex, please be so kind as to play the recording in question," I said into my mic.

Raisin stiffened as if hit with a cattle prod.

"Yeah," I said. "Your sanctuary, which you make certain is swept for devices every day, has been the subject of an internal probe."

Adan's voice came over the speaker system, saying, "There are many of us who will not have a beast as a queen. Many who feel that only a Mithran should have access to *la corona*. That only a powerful Mithran has the right to rule, not an aberration."

"Many of us?" Raisin said, her voice tinny from the recording. "It takes only one brave soul to bring death to a fool. Amaury Pellissier drank blood from a whore who ingested colloidal silver and he died. It is not difficult to kill the powerful."

My eyes narrowed at Raisin's insult. She was talking about Bruiser's mother. The audio continued.

"I always wondered how the human woman acquired colloidal silver to drink," Adan said. The sound of a chair cushion exhaling came over the recording. "In those days it was difficult to acquire in good quality. I salute you."

Raisin closed her eyes as her recorded British voice said, "Difficult. Not impossible for those with the resources. I have always had excellent resources. Leo's uncle was vicious enough, but not wise enough for this city. Leo was much more . . . useful. He was not intended to die. The creature who has the crown was supposed to die in his place."

"And yet she rules. You miscalculated," Adan said. "This time *one brave soul* is not enough. We need more. Will you turn over your people to us and to the one who leads us?"

"You say *us*, yet I see only you. Who is this vaunted leader of whom you have spoken?"

On the desktop, Raisin struggled. Tears and bloody snot ran down her wrinkled face, adding to the smears on her desk.

In the recording, I heard a paper slide across the desk. "These are my people. Our master, the Heir, has been pulling strings for centuries, waiting for the time to be ripe, and though the creature killed many of his players since she arrived in this city, she and this one"—a grunt sounded. Pain. Muffled. *Derek*. Had to be—"opened the way at the end. We have Shaun MacLaughlinn to lead the attack and an amulet that gives him strength and speed. He will kill the creature's protectors. We have a skinwalker to eat her and take her place. Our master, the Heir, will be revealed only after you have proven your worthiness to us, to our cause, and to Shaun MacLaughlinn's power."

"You will be pleased with the assistance that I can provide. The doors that I can open." Raisin's tone was like the snake in the garden, slithering and full of malice.

Adan said, "Immediately Shaun can commit nearly-sixty Mithrans. Shaun is a leader who can destroy the creature. The master has many, *many* more. Together we can hold the States and take back the European cities from the fops who currently rule in the creature's name."

"I accept. You have my loyalty. I shall bow to your leader, Shaun MacLaughlinn, and this heir you speak of. My blood shall be his blood. I so swear."

From behind me, Thema said, "So many Mithrans and blood-servants, each with so many agendas. The curse of our people has always been disloyalty."

Into my earbud, Alex whispered. "Two intruders in HQ, passing laser alarms and cameras, hidden behind *obfuscation* workings, the old spell versions that still let us collect heat sigs. One fanghead, one human. Both are going up the back stairs. They're converging on Ernestine's office."

Softly Alex added, "Another being, possibly human is in the scion lair, trying to free Monique Giovanni."

I had been told several times to end her. I should have listened. "Send a stealth team to the intersecting hallways of Raisin's office and one to the scion lair."

"Closest team has Aya on it."

I sighed softly. "Do it. What's Raisin's full name?" Alex told me. I stood and gestured Koun forward. My Executioner. I had never given him a job like this before. Tonight was gonna suck.

Koun stepped between us, one sword high, the other still sheathed. Behind him, Thema and Kojo turned to face the hallway, guarding us from attack. "Ernestine Frida Bisset. You have been accused of treason. You have, by the words of your mouth, consorted with our enemies. You have admitted collusion in the death of Amaury Pellissier, Master of the City of New Orleans. We hereby condemn you to death, according to the Vampira Carta of the Americas." To Quint I said, "Remove her gag. Sit her up in her chair."

Quint jerked the old blood-servant upright. Removed her gag. As Quint moved, Raisin spat again. This time something flew from her mouth. Midair, it glittered.

"Down!" Koun screamed. With a single downward cut, he batted the thing back at Raisin. With his other hand, he lifted the heavy desk on its end and yanked Quint and me down. His body moving vamp-fast. The desk still rocking over us.

The glittering thing hit Raisin in the face.

An explosion ripped all sound away.

The office shook. Dust and debris flew.

I crawled to my feet. Trying to figure out what had happened. Blinking against the dust and the blood in my eyes. Deaf. In my pocket, the Glob was hot, as if it had pulled energy from the air. So . . . magic?

The memories were splintered and confused but . . . Raisin had spat something from her mouth and Koun had batted it back, yanked up the desk to protect us, and shoved us down. Vamp-fast. Right?

Ernestine's head was gone, nothing of her left above her shoulders, Koun's blade had buried itself in the desk edge and both were still rocking. Koun nodded to me. He was okay. I checked on Quint who was trying to get to her feet. We were all covered in blood, but not our own. Quint and I were coughing against the dust and the stench of whatever had been used in the physical part of the explosion. Koun wasn't breathing, so he was fine. And none of us were dead, thanks to Koun's vamp reflexes.

Time solidified and stabilized. I shook my head as my brain started to work.

Raisin was no vamp. Her body had contained a lot of blood. It still pulsed from her headless neck, though weakly now. It had splattered everywhere. Koun shoved the headless body onto the floor. The blood had drenched everything and everyone in sight. Quint dragged me toward the door. My people had ducked away at Koun's warning. They were racing back. They grabbed at me, searching for wounds. Koun said something and they stepped back. I looked at myself. I was . . . a mess.

That might be a good thing. The blood of the lynchpin between two factions could be a powerful token to vamps. I looked back to see Koun levering the blade out of the wood. He placed it on the desk, palmed a different, smaller blade, and turned to face the door. I touched my crown, and thought about my damaged ears, and how I needed them right away. I felt a tendril of healing flow to them. A hum was followed by a roaring and then by voices as if from a distance. I was able to hear some. That was fast.

Gesturing my people away from the opening, Quint led us into the hallway.

Adan shoved past us into the room, fast, with a little pop of air that sent the dust soaring again. He stopped. His wild hair was flying and patchy. His eyes went wide. This was one time that not having to breathe worked against a vamp. He hadn't smelled the blood in his wild run. Or me.

He saw the body, slumped and headless. Adan reached for his weather magic, but before he could gather it, Quint threw a small blade. It buried itself in Adan's throat.

Adan, who had killed Derek. *Derek*. Who had just become a friend.

In one swift move, I pulled my vamp-killer. Stepped to Adan's side. In a single backhand strike, I took Adan's head. The cut was so powerful his head spun into the air, leaving his body standing.

Quint caught the head. The body crumpled.

From behind Adan, a woman screamed.

CHAPTER 17

Bloody Diminutive Blonde, Dangling Two Heads by the Hair

Ka N'vsita and an unknown vamp stood in the hallway, Ka's amber eyes wide with horror and shock. The vamp old and powerful. I pulled the Glob. It was still hot in my hand.

Ka screamed again. The stink of liver-eater flooded out through her open-mouthed cry. And then she was gone. Simply gone. *Holy crap*, she was fast. And healed.

The vamp drew two longswords and charged me, screaming something, rushing into the small space. Koun stepped in front of me. Batted the opponent's swords away. And in a graceful, single cut, took his head. It flew into the air, blood pumping.

Great. More blood on my clothes and pelt.

In the hallway, three security members raced past, others lying on the floor where Ka had tossed them in her flight.

The Glob cooled in my hand. The blood dripped. Blood spatter was everywhere.

"Nice beheadings," Quint said to us without emotion. "Economical." It sounded like high praise.

"Thanks." Belatedly I said, "Ernestine killed herself in a failed attack on the Master of the City, Jane Yellowrock.

The Dark Queen pronounced judgment and punishment upon Adan Bouvier for treason and the death by murder of Derek Lee, that murder committed within sight of the Queen. And the other one . . ." I frowned and looked to Koun.

"He attacked the Dark Queen and drew swords without challenge. It was necessary to take his head."

"Yeah. That."

The security team gathered in the open door, figures in black on black, weaponed and armored up like a SWAT team. The three who had given chase ran back and joined the group, Aya among them; Aya sniffing, frowning, as if he smelled the same liver-eater stench I did.

Sarah Spieth's voice said into my earbud, "Ka vanished from the cameras, the lasers, everything."

Koun said, "Institute a full search and clearing of the entire building."

"Wait," I said, holding up the dripping vamp-killer.

No one moved.

Ka disappeared? I plucked at the memory of Ka escaping, almost as if she was moving out of time-sequence. Had Ka just done a form of timewalking? The way I used to? And . . . If she had, did Ka begin to eat people as a way to stave off a magic cancer? Ka who was a skinwalker, an Onorio of some kind, and had eaten a red-headed vamp I didn't know and had also eaten the Firestarter.

She had eaten alive multiple kinds of sentient beings and gained their magical gifts. I closed my eyes, remembering the image of Ka stabbing Storm. In her other hand was something else. A cup. Ka had collected Storm's blood.

Seemingly unimportant events clicked into place, and my entire body tightened in something that felt like fury and battle readiness but was more than both.

Long ago, Ka had stood in a witch circle formed of iron, set into the floor, holding a large iron spike. Ka had been killed. Forced through a transition that went beyond mere Onorio. All that took place while Sabina watched. Sabina who could timewalk too, though in a different manner from the one I had used. Sabina with a winged lizard-shaped amulet that incorporated arcenciel blood and scales. *Holy moly.*

At that one single origin point of time, long ago, Sabina, Bethany, Adan, and Ka had been in the same space. They'd had the spike in their possession. Ka had been trying to bend time before Adan stabbed her with a sword.

And then there was the Rule of Three. And we had Monique in the basement scion lair.

"Belay that order, Koun." I pulled my mic back to my mouth and said, "Sarah, tell me what you see on the scion lair cameras."

Sarah cursed and said softly. "The woman in the lair is gone, My Queen. The crew just got there. Checking back over footage and readouts."

I waited. The security crew waited. Blood dripped.

"My Queen," Sarah said, sounding pissed off. "She vanished into thin air."

Crap. "That's what I figured." Ka had timewalked from here to the lair and had taken Monique. There were again, two of the needed Onorios for the Rule of Three for whatever Onorio magic thingy they had planned. All they needed was Bruiser or one of the B-twins. "No one's fault. She used magic. Think of it like a *Star Trek* transporter." Because no way was I announcing to the entire security team about timewalking. "Ka isn't here. Institute internal electronic search, just in case, and check the cameras on the street outside to see if she reappeared there. We need to deal with traitors before I do anything else."

I wiped the blade of my vamp-killer on an upholstered stool in the corner and sheathed it. When I looked up, Aya's eyes were tracking from me to Quint to the bodies and heads. His expression changed from security to law enforcement and back, leaving him looking weirdly indecisive.

"Dark Queen stuff, FireWind," I said. "Raisin was working for Adan"—I pointed to the vamp's body—"who was leading the assault, and she tried to kill a human." I pointed at Quint. "And me. And that guy attacked the Dark Queen of Mithrans. My security dude"—I pointed my bloody sword at Koun—"took care of him. If you have questions, then I recommend you get the State Department and Congress to give us a final ruling on whether vamps who lived most of their lives in the U.S. are U.S. citizens or not. And check the law regarding humans work-

ing for undocumented vamps who try to kill other humans.
But remind the political types that if paras and their ancient blood-servants are counted under U.S. law, they have
to build jails for all the different strength levels, daylight
requirements, full-moon shape changes, and meet the di-
etary standards for us all." I grinned and paraphrased the
old movie *Jaws*: "You're gonna need a bigger police force."

Aya scowled.

Into the mic, I said, "We need a cleanup crew in here,
and put one on standby in the gym. Get the vamp funeral
home people to take care of the bodies."

"Yes, My Queen," The woman said into my ear. Sarah.
Right. Nice raspy voice.

"We need the heads, My Queen," Koun said. He explained why.

"Well, that's gonna make a mess," I said.

Only moments before, we had left the humans and vamps
in the foyer, and now we stood in front of the gym doors
covered in explosive dust and gore. I was sure that I looked
gruesome enough on my own, but this time I was preceded
by a bloody Koun and a bloody diminutive blonde, dangling two heads by the hair in her left hand. Koun had as-
sured me that the display was in keeping with vamp battle
and war and would cause my enemies to quake. Blood was
still dripping from the vamp heads, and I had been careful
to step over bloody tracks and splatters, because gummy
and dried blood would be really hard to get out of the fur
between my toe pads.

We could hear the noise of the vamps and humans inside. Koun looked us all over, said "My Queen," and threw
open the doors. He strode inside, Quint to his left.

She held up the two heads. My lady-in-waiting and personal bodyguard had a gift for the theatrical. Then she
shouted, "Behold the trophies of the Dark Queen and quiver
in fear! Behold her enemies!"

Well. That was a new one.

The gym went instantly and weirdly quiet.

The large space was set up for all kinds of training, sports,
and fighting. It had basketball hoops, rubberized sword

training circles, bleachers, and ways to set up for indoor tennis and shuffleboard. The cameras had been updated. Again. They were everywhere. Right now, the bleachers were full of spectators. Derek's handpicked crew—my heart clenched, and I had to shove the grief down—the remaining Vodka Boys and Tequila Boys were holding weapons on a row of vamps and humans who were lying facedown on the wood floor. The armed crew were hard-faced and grieving, their expressions telling me that they wanted to shoot the entire bunch for just the possibility of being involved with Derek's loss but were holding back. Most of the prone prisoners looked as if they hadn't gone down willingly. I spotted Eli in a shooter's position with a rifle in the far doorway.

Chuffing, I let out a sigh. I spied Bruiser among one of Derek's teams.

"My Queen," my Consort said, and bowed with a flourish that left me distinctly uncomfortable.

The others in the room bowed too, except Derek's team and my personal security, including Quint and Koun, who kept an eye on everyone else.

I wondered what I was supposed to do in response and then decided since I was queen, I could do whatever I wanted. I gave Bruiser what I hoped was a regal nod. "My Consort," I said.

"Behold the enemies of the Dark Queen," Quint said again, which had to be for emphasis since everyone had already seen the drippy heads.

I started to stride closer, but Beast thought at me, *I/we do not run. This is stalk. This is ambush hunt. Beast is not prey. Beast is best ambush hunter.*

Yeah. Right. I slowed and drew the vamp-killer, letting the soft *shush* of steel and silver slither through the air. With a measured tread, like what I'd use if I were still the vamp Enforcer, I walked along the line of trussed prisoners. Sniffing. Flehmen response. Loud. As I walked, the room, which had gone quiet when I entered, became deadly silent. No one moved. I walked to the end of the prone people, turned, and walked soundlessly back toward my starting point. Cat-silent. Making a spectacle of myself and my team, a visual power play, a threat to any who were part of the murders of Derek and Storm.

My heart rate, which had been too fast since the explosion, began to settle. I had a purpose, a job to do. I studied every face. Breathed in their scents.

Quint, bless her heart, walked beside me. Heads dripping. With her free hand, she was holding a sword. I had a feeling she wore her nails unpainted, pared straight with clippers, trimmed her hair with kitchen scissors, and would never ever ask me to go for mani-pedis. She could be invisible yet had a flair for the dramatic. I was starting to really like this woman.

Koun stood at the doorway, a bloody giant of a man, two swords drawn, drying blood on one, his long blond hair loose and bloody too. Quint glanced at him, did a minuscule double take and returned her attention to the prisoners. But her scent changed. Quint might be a sociopath, but she had a strong sex drive. She was interested in Koun.

Back at the beginning of the line, I stopped and said, "In this form, I can smell who drank from Rais—Ernestine and who fed her. I know your scents. Therefore I know your guilt."

The vamp prisoners—already still—froze.

"Yeah," I said, dropping the queenly verbiage. "I know everything." I pointed at three vamps. "These three are lower-level followers. Haul them to the scion lair, lock 'em in cages, and leave them there for a while with armed guards. My most trusted Mithrans will bleed and read them, but they will not be fed. When the enemy vamp prisoners get hungry enough, they can decide if they want to swear to a new master, knowing they will be bound by my loyal vamps and integrated into the households at bottom feeder status. The rest of the fangheads? They smell of Adan Bouvier, Shaun MacLaughlinn, Ernestine . . ."

I stopped. The blood scent was familiar.

In Beast's scent-brain, things, relationships, scent-concepts began to come together. *Ugly dog, good nose,* she thought at me.

I knew that dogs could often scent who was related to whom in a household, and they used that scent to figure out which humans to protect and who to obey and which human was the strongest. They could trace that familial scent. In the same way, the part of Beast's brain recognized whose family this blood odor came from. *Crap*. This was going to be dicey. I waved Quint away. "Alex, are you on comms?"

"Affirmative," he said into my ears.

"You put a surveillance system in Ernestine's office," I said, for the benefit of the gathered. "Will you play a little of the most recent convos over the HQ speaker system?"

Alex said, "Yes, My Queen. They're lined up and ready to play. The most recent, first."

Adan's voice came over the speakers. "Did you find it?"

Raisin answered, "No. But *the creature* did. It was in his desk. She has it at her home now. Using the blood, you can take it from her, you and your Firestarter."

My brain locked up for a second, then flashed into overdrive.

They were talking about the arcenciel blood that Ka collected during the battle, and the locket, which Leo had thought might be important. I glanced at Bruiser and he nodded. The locket was safe. And . . . Ah. The locket was why they had attacked me at my home and not on the road. That and all the other goodies hidden there. Killing Storm and taking her blood must have been an added bonus. But . . . Ka had been bitten by the dying arcenciel, and the venom of the rainbow dragons was toxic. Ka might not be as stable as she once was. And someone had rescued her. Who?

Adan said, "We must have it, as well as the remains of the spike. Sabina hid everything before the fire. We must reacquire it all."

Raisin said, "*The creature* must be removed. Once she is gone, the amulets and icons are ours. Take *her*."

"With the locket and the dragon's blood collected during the battle," Adan said, "Ka will become my weapon. With the spike, she and your Onorios will be able to restore Mithran control of the Council of Mithrans. And when Shaun takes the creature's head, the crown will release and accept Ka as its new master."

I held up a hand, knowing that Alex was watching on the cameras. The audio cut off.

Ka, Adan Bouvier, and Shaun might be able to hold on to the vamp political world if *le breloque* accepted her as Queen. If I let *any* of the twisted, layered, betraying plans succeed, my people would suffer and die. All of the spectators' eyes were focused on me as I let the hush build. The memory of arcenciel fangs in Ka's neck flashed through me. I had to wonder how that was gonna impact the layered vamp / Gramma plans to betray vamps and take my place. A worry for later.

One of the vamps on the floor made an attempt to leap up and run. The closest guard kicked her feet from under her, flipped her over and staked her in the belly.

Though I hated to be one of the monsters, I had to play the part and play it well.

So I laughed. My laughter was part growl, part predator, the big-cat kind that tore into live prey and ate the innards while they still kicked. A couple of the prisoners shuddered. I held up a finger again, twirling it to continue.

On the recording, the Firestarter's voice said, "All our aims have been met except taking the crown and the amulets. We have the outclan priestess. We will not fail."

My heart wrenched.

There were gasps throughout the gym, even vamps taking a shocked breath.

I hadn't heard this part of the recording. There was no way they had Sabina. It was impossible. I had last seen her at the attack on the warehouse. My eyes found Bruiser's, his shocked too. The timelines didn't work unless they took Sabina the instant after I saw her. That . . . that was very possible. *Damn.*

A different voice spoke, Ka saying, "The creature has humans digging at Sabina's chapel. They will find the amulets and the icons, and we will take them."

Adan said, "The old way of life will return, under our control."

"Stop," I said when I could finally speak. The recording went silent.

I closed my eyes, fighting a paralyzing fury. I took three short breaths, rage like a wildfire in my blood. They had Sabina. *Grandmother* had Sabina.

I inhaled deeply and blew out a hard breath, letting the smell of my rage breathe into the room. My fangs flashing, I snarled. Growled. The vibration was like a generator filling the room. *Fearsome. Magnificent.* My rage roared at the vamps, *Choke on the very idea of me!*

I reined back on my anger and pulled on the power of *le breloque* and also on all the knowledge I had about vamps. This was a delicate negotiation, not a violent one. I didn't look at Bruiser. "Consort. Onorio. I ask you a difficult thing. Knowing that the guilty Mithran traitors among us will be judged tonight, are you willing to partially drain and question them?"

"You do not ask me to *bind* them, My Queen? You would leave them free to do you harm?"

Bruiser stared at me, but I didn't look back. I knew how he felt about binding anyone. He had been bound by Leo and had done things that still gave him nightmares, thinking they were good and perfect and Leo was good and perfect as well. But our enemies had Sabina. They had breached our defenses. Bruiser would use any gift to keep me safe.

That said, vamps bound by Onorios were even less independent than humans bound by vamps. Vamps bound by Onorios were clingy and had to be cared for like pets. But . . . these vamps were traitors and murderers, and I was a new predator in a vamp kingdom. I was making a statement. So was he. And I needed to know where Sabina was.

"Not by you, Consort. These are *my* enemies. They're part of a war against this reign. They're part of the group who attacked"—I paused as grief and fury welled up in me, emotions I had no time for right now—"and killed Derek and Storm. They will never be free to do me or mine harm." After an uncomfortable silence, I looked at him and willed him to understand that I hated what I was doing.

"Yes, My Queen," he said, softly.

I met his eyes. They were kind and vaguely amused. *Yeah*. He got it.

"I am Onorio. I will drain and question the Mithrans who resist you. I will not bind them."

"Koun, my Executioner," I said. "When my Consort has taken from the prisoners' minds what he will, and should I deem death a reasonable judgment, you shall behead the guilty, here in this room, to be witnessed by all." I forced the last of the heated fury away into a deep part of me where the frozen grief for Derek and Storm were stored, the fire and the ice coexisting inside me.

"Yes, My Queen. It will be my joy." Koun snapped his

fingers and pointed to a blood-servant. "You. Bring my ax." He returned his eyes to me. "To protect My Queen's most precious floors, it will take two strokes of the ax. This will be infinitely more painful."

I didn't agree or disagree. "Tonight, traitors will be weeded out." I showed my fangs. "And dealt with. One. By. One."

Two other Mithrans bolted and were flipped and staked.

Their blood scent filled the room. They smelled of Ka. They had drunk from her. Fed her.

"Consort," I said.

"I am your servant." He moved into position and paused, looking them over. "And their humans, My Queen?" he asked.

"Where they end up is up to you, Consort."

"I am honored at My Queen's trust."

I gave that regal nod again, remembering the white werewolf nodding, figuring I looked just as stupid.

With a measured step, Bruiser walked to the closest staked vamp, the woman who had tried to run first. Bruiser knelt beside her and put his hand on her forehead. A guard pulled out the stake with the soft sucking sound of wood on flesh. The vamp screamed. She lifted a hand. Dropped it and went eerily still. Bruiser's eyebrows drew together over his Roman nose; a puzzled look crossed his face. Then a lot of nothing happened. It felt as if it was taking too long, but no one moved.

My anger was contained in the dark crevasses of my soul. Breathing was easier. I hadn't noticed how hard it had been to take in air since Derek and Storm died. I hadn't noticed how high my heart rate had been. Now I was doing something. Vengeful Cat. The I/we of Beast. Inside me, Beast panted softly, her energy gathered close, ready for attack.

After an eternity, Bruiser stood, his face still faintly puzzled, telling me he got something from her mind that left him confused. "She will answer your questions, My Queen."

"Who is your Blood Master?" I asked her.

The female vamp said, "My master is Shaun MacLaughlinn, the wearer of the Snake of Snakes."

No surprise. "Why Shaun? Why did you swear to him?"

"He is food for no master," she said with pride. "He drinks from the Heir of the Sons of Darkness."

That caught my attention and Bruiser's too. He frowned hard, his eyes going distant as he did a mental search for such a person.

In my ear, Alex murmured, "On it."

The vamp said, "The Heir gave unto him the amulet called the Snake of Snakes, and from it he acquires great power. He feeds from the Heir, and when the Heir comes, all the world will be restored."

The Sons of Darkness, the creators of vamps were dead. True dead. Deader than dead. And this was the first time I'd heard about an heir. Lucky me. I let my voice become a growl. "The name of the heir, this master that Shaun feeds from?"

"Mainet Pellissier."

I had seen that name recently. Something dark and icy stabbed through me as I recalled where I had seen the name Mainet. Once long ago in the vamp bloodlines, and recently, handwritten in Immanuel's journal, on the front page. *Immanuel Justinus Henri Mainet Pellissier, in the year of our Lord, Seventeen Ninety.*

Immanuel, the *u'tlun'ta*, and Leo's son and heir, had been named after him.

She sat up, suddenly, and reached for Bruiser. I'd seen that expression on a vamp's face before. It was the beginning of Onorio binding.

"This is all that I can do without binding her, My Queen," Bruiser said.

"Stake her," I said to the blood-servant who still held the dripping stake. The wood floors were going to be hard to clean with all this dried blood on them. To Bruiser, I added, "Drain that one," and pointed at the next in line.

It took four vamps before we found another one Bruiser could drain deeply enough to control without binding him. From that one, we learned that this Mainet fanghead was still in Europe. A problem for another day, no matter what he had planned.

I had always wondered who had fed the real Immanuel to a nutso skinwalker *u'tlun'ta* and then put that imposter in place. Who had pulled all the strings? The black magic would have given Immanuel's *u'tlun'ta* memories but not muscle memory, not physical skills, not body movements and emotions. Not handwriting. Who had taught that imposter the minutiae he needed to walk among vamps. Who had provided the teachers?

A freaking dang Pellissier, of course. Why the hell not?

However. Shaun was our problem right now, and he had the fancy snake amulet that gave him some kind of magical power or protection. Snake armbands were common amulet forms, because they could be worn under or over clothes, could be filled with multiple magical workings, and could double as jewelry, which allowed hands-free fighting. I sometimes wore empty snake armband amulets as part of my ceremonial gear.

I asked more questions. Got a lot of jibber jabber gobbledygook.

I looked at Koun. "Stake these vamps. Toss them all into the sub-five basement. Put guards all around them armed with silver blades and shotguns loaded with the special silver-lead fléchette rounds. If one of the vamps so much as twitches, kill the vamp true dead and put the body in the sun. Separate their humans. Secure them in the breakroom The humans will go to new masters for incorporation into any clans willing to accept them. That means throughout the entire U.S."

In the crowd, several humans panicked, and Bruiser's eyes tracked them. "Yes, My Queen," he said.

Loudly Koun said, "Let it be recorded. The Dark Queen has shown mercy to her enemies. My blade shall not be fed. For now."

I thought that was a little too poetic and hopeful, but I didn't say so.

It was an hour before dawn when my team and I left HQ via the front door. Beast lent me her night vision, turning the world silver and gray and vibrant green.

Jane did not let I/we/us drink vampire blood, Beast thought at me. *Jane wasted good strong vampire blood.*

Maybe next time we're in Beast form, I thought back.

We were halfway down the long steps when the Glob grew suddenly, blisteringly hot in my pocket. "Attack," I

shouted, warning. I leaped from the stairs, out of the way.
Midair, Beast-fast, I yanked the Glob from its padded
pocket, pulled open another pocket, and wrapped the Glob
in the hanky I kept there so I could hold it. Raising the
weapon high over my head, I landed in the parking area on
toe pads and one knobby hand, protected at my back by
the building. A familiar place. I'd try not to die this time.
Eli and Bruiser dropped to either side of me. Koun and
Thema in front of me. Lightning flashed from the sky and
exploded in the center of the parking area. Blinding. I
blinked against the retinal burn to see a faint glow in the
center of the parking area.

Ka stood there.

Grandmother was standing at one side, Monique, her
head leaking, was propped at her other side.

"Nice magic trick," I muttered.

Thema laughed.

But the Glob went so hot it burned through the cloth in
my hand. The stench of scorched cotton and *u'tlun'ta* sweat
filled the air. I had grabbed from the wrong pocket. The
cloth wasn't a clean hanky. I had grabbed the scrap of
Grandmother's cloth shift from the sweathouse.

Hayalasti Sixmankiller threw back her head in a word-
less scream. Her back arched. Her polluted skinwalker
magic rushed out of her, toward the heating Glob and her
sweat. She started to shift, changing shape. Grandmother's
hair lit with flames that shot high. Aya leaped at her, the
two forms tumbling into the darkness.

Ka took a step toward me. Her body wavered, shimmered. Shifted. Aurelia took the next step forward. She
wavered. Again she was Ka, and her eyes were wild, like a
rabid fox, trying to hold her thoughts together. But she was
full of arenciel blood. "I miscalculated," she said, as
magic coiled and swirled around her, and once again she
was Aurelia.

The Firestarter was more sane, and this one's magic was
untouched by the Glob, but I could see it, a thick mist of
black and scarlet buzzing with motes of orange power. The
mist of energies was heavy, held protected by a thin layer
of foul green. "I need another host to stabilize my forms,"
she said.

Grandmother stepped in from the dark, looking just fine.

Where was Aya?

"She is mine," Grandmother said.

Ka reappeared. "I need the locket," Ka said. "Join me, sister."

Sister . . . Shock scorched through me. *Turn of phrase? Or some kind of horrible reality?*

"Join us," Ka said.

"No way under heaven," I said.

Everything happened *fastfastfast*.

Fire swirled around Ka/Aurelia's hand as she raised it high. The fire formed into a ball of power so bright it blinded. She whipped back her arm to throw it.

Eli fired. Ka took five shots midcenter.

"Nooo," I whispered, the sound lost beneath the gunfire.

Ka/Aurelia staggered. Healed in Ka shape. She morphed back into the Firestarter. Faster than I could follow, she curled her hands. That waiting magic gathered in her palms. She threw two fireballs. Dead center at us. The fireballs scarcely left her palms when they sputtered and died.

Pearl and Opal dove at Aurelia, who was holding an iron blade.

"Iron!" I shouted.

The two dragons vanished. Eli fired again. And again. He changed out mags. Kept firing. Ka laughed, changing forms over and over. She flung a hand at Eli. A different magic slithered toward him, snaky and twisted.

Opal reemerged for a second and shouted.

Eli's weapon misfired.

Opal's magic batted Ka's away and she disappeared again.

My heart stuck in my throat.

Eli was okay.

Ka walked toward me, closing the space between us.

Opal and Pearl reappeared, their inner light flashing, blinding. Opal thrashed her barbed tail at Ka.

Ka jumped out of the way. Slipped past the barbs and continued toward me, dancing past the tail.

Knowing he would hear even over any gunfire deafness, I whispered, "Koun."

Koun rotated around us all, his body in a graceful, deadly spin, splendid in the night.

Eli pulled two more weapons, but he didn't try to fire, his eyes tracking between Ka and me.

Koun's executioner ax stretched out behind him, a long-sword in his other hand. In a perfect cut, his sword took Ka's right hand. His body spinning, his ax took Monique's head. Opal and Pearl swooped down and caught the head. The two arcenciels flipped again, tails in graceful arcs, throwing rainbow lights against the stairs and the outer walls. The arcenciels vanished. Taking the head with them, like a trophy.

Ka lifted her stump and stared at it. It pulsed blood. A lot of blood.

Monique didn't bleed much. Her body simply folded down into a heap. She was gone.

Koun tripped Ka, slammed his sword hilt across her jaw hard enough to stun her, and watched her head bounce on the concrete. He knelt beside her and applied a tourniquet to her stump. Ka shook her head but didn't fight. She held her stump to her horrified face, the blood still oozing out. With her other hand, she reached over and picked up her severed hand. Koun snapped multiple null cuffs onto her head and each arm. She shimmered and tried to shift, but she had waited too long, the null cuffs doing their job. There was no way she could change shape in the hope of reattaching her hand. Koun used silver plated zip strips to secure Ka's elbows together behind her back, and her ankles together.

From down the street, tires squealed. The stink of vamp rose on the air before weakening as cars pulled away. I knew this smell. Some of the makeshift clan we had fought in Asheville had been waiting for phase two of an attack that hadn't started well. The backup troops were now abandoning ship. Shaun MacLaughlinn and his clan of misfits and psychopath fangheads had been part of the assault. Shaun and I were on a collision course. The day he no longer had a head couldn't come soon enough.

Aya reappeared from the darkness.

Relief scoured through me. My brother was alive.

Grandmother was draped over his shoulder. I smelled

Aya's blood. She had wounded him again. He had not killed her. *Again.* But this time Grandmother was wrapped in null cuffs, six sets of the new cuffs created by the Seattle coven for the military and PsyLED, shackles that stopped all magical activity. The null cuffs were duct tapped in place. Yet, even bound, Granny shimmered and changed shape. Her magic was stronger by far than Ka's. She formed from Hayalasti Sixmankiller into a white female with gray hair. Into a young blond woman. And then she shifted again and again, back to back, so fast I almost missed it. She was . . .

Sabina.

She had killed and eaten Sabina.

I had seen Sabina when we left the warehouse after the attack there. Grandmother had been in the air at that time, a huge bird. She had to have taken Sabina between then and the last conversation in Raisin's office . . . and eaten the priestess. I hadn't kept the outclan priestess protected. The ancient vampire hadn't been safe here in my own city.

Grandmother screamed when she saw me. "You! You are the cause of all of this!" She writhed in Aya's arms. Aya nearly fell back, struggling to hold her. "Kill her, my son!" she screamed.

"No. I renounce you," Aya said, his voice thick and full of history and pain.

Ka began to moan, weeping softly.

Bruiser knelt beside Grandmother in the parking area and wrapped his long fingers around her head. "Shhhh," he whispered. "Shhhh. All is well."

Grandmother whimpered and shook. She became Sabina again. Sabina looked at me. I knew in that moment that Sabina was, in some form, in some manner, still fully conscious within Grandmother, just as Beast was alive in me. Or . . . perhaps just as I was alive in Beast. That was a scary thought.

"I was a fool. I thought I could reason with her as I did so long ago. I let her take me," Sabina said.

"All is well," Bruiser whispered, his lips close to Sabina / Grandmother's forehead, his hands gripping there.

She writhed and shifted again into Grandmother. "All is not well," Grandmother gasped, breathing fast. Her entire body was quivering. "All has not been well since that one"—she looked at me—"killed Tsu Tsu Inoli." She looked at Aya, "He was *mine*. He was in place. Ka and I were ready to return the world to its rightful form." She screeched, "She killed my son!"

"Tsu Tsu Inoli." Aya murmured a translation from *Tsalagi*. "Mark Black Fox. Who is Mark Black Fox?"

"That name's in Immanuel's journal," I said softly. "I didn't bother to read the context."

"I will give you the power I gave to Tsu Tsu," Grandmother said to Aya. "The power I tried to give to Ka N'vsita. Together we can retake our power, can take our rightful places in this land. We can go back in time to the massacre and kill the destroyer. We can restore the power of the skinwalkers. Then we can kill all the vampires," she screeched, "just as your sister and I killed the white man who killed your father."

I flinched. My father had been killed by two white men when I was a child. Grandmother had put a blade into my hand and taught me how to kill, cutting them slowly until they bled to death. Now she wanted to kill vamps. Probably all the vamps. I remembered the drawing in de Allyon's *La Historia de Los Mithrans en Los Americas*, from so long ago: skinwalkers dead all around the powerful vamp. Only one Cherokee skinwalker woman had still been alive, at his feet. Had Gramma heard about the massacre? Or was that drawing of the skinwalker woman actually Hyalasti Sixmankiller? Had she been there? Perhaps that massacre could have been the beginning of her *u'tlun'ta* magic.

"Help me kill them all!" Gramma screeched, writhing in their hands. "Help me to go back and kill the destroyer!"

Yeah. My nutso crazy gramma wanted to timewalk and stop that event.

Timewalking back beyond even a few minutes meant changing everything. In Eli's terms, going back to the fifteen hundreds would be a precision strike, and no matter how careful, the consequences could be catastrophic. I remembered the vision of the dead world, a world without life. Was that the most likely outcome of Ka and Gramma going back in time?

Was that why they needed three skinwalkers?

Aya said, "I remember the tales you told us, Grandmother. I remember the tales of the killing field of skinwalkers, slaughtered by the hand of Lucas Vasquez de Allyon." He turned his amber eyes to me. "I will speak these words aloud so my sister and her court will know them to be true. I heard the old tales. I did not know my Grandmother wished to change that history. I did not understand it was even possible."

"I'm not sure it is," I said. "The potential for a screw-up that changes history way more than she expects is . . . I don't even know how to measure it. The arcenciels haven't gone back in time to fix what they consider the worst crime in all of human history because getting there without catastrophic failure is so difficult. And they're the masters of timewalking."

Aya inclined his head. He continued, "Grandmother, hear me. You cannot control your own skinwalker gifts, let alone a time-jump so far into the past. Even should Jane and I agree to help, even with all the magical amulets you might find or steal, you would not be likely to end up in the right place and time. It has been too many years. You have told many different versions of the destroyer and the killing fields, Grandmother. The exact place and time are lost to you. You do not remember. And worse," he took a slow breath and met her eyes, "you are no longer sane, Grandmother."

She screeched and writhed in his hands, her shape changing over and over. "You will help me! I command it!"

"No. You are *u'tlun'ta*." Aya's words were formal, carefully spaced. I knew he wanted to be speaking *Tsalagi*, but for us, he spoke English. "Not as a law enforcement officer of PsyLED, but as an Elder of The People, I take you into custody. Wrapped in null cuffs, you shall be delivered to the null prison managed by the council of witches, and you shall be judged by your clan before being taken to the top of the mountains and thrown from the high places. Hayalasti Sixmankiller," he pronounced, "you have lost your soul."

He had said something similar once before and I recognized the words as an Elder's judgment. He was going to kill Grandmother.

The old woman sagged in Aya's and Bruiser's hands,

sobbing, and for a moment she sounded almost sane. "I tried so hard. I had everything prepared. All we needed was George Dumas and my granddaughter. With them, we could have avenged our people, destroyed the drinkers of blood who killed all of my people, all the skinwalkers whom I loved. Our people would return to us. *Tsalagi* would rise again, would become our *own*." She stared at Aya. "Do not do this, my child. Do not unmake what I have worked for so long. The *Tsalagi* can rise as a people, today, *now*, under skinwalker rule."

"The Rule of Three," Bruiser murmured. "Three Onorios, three skinwalkers, plenty of Mithrans, and an outclan priestess. Three times three times three, with their power growing exponentially with each of the groups of three. Three icons with arceniel blood and scales. And the remaining slivers and ingots from the iron Spike of Golgotha. And a cup of arceniel blood. They could have done anything. Anything they ever wanted."

"With the fresh arceniel blood from Storm's death," I said, "it's possible that they could have timewalked back to the massacre of skinwalkers. They could have killed the Spaniard vamp—de Allyon."

Grandmother looked at me. Though she was still fighting Bruiser's magic, her eyes were taking on that strange cast of light that an Onorio's mind-bound slave always got. Bruiser was still draining her. I hated Onorio binding. So did my Consort. But to keep our people safe, he would attempt anything that needed to be done.

Grandmother struggled against his hands and said, "Shaun is still here. His plan is still in place. He has not been defeated. He will come for us, for he needs the power we possess. You have not yet won."

"And Mainet Pellissier?" I asked.

"Maaaineeet." She laughed at the name. "The Heir thought to change history to his own desires. I let him think he would win. But we three—Ka, you, and I, granddaughter—together we have the power and the amulets and the place where true power is chained. Only we know where it is."

More crazy talk. Or more angel talk. *Crap.*

"Ka's caught and bound and brought to nothing. And so are your plans," I said.

"We can take Shaun's place and together we can defeat the Heir to the Sons of Darkness."

"Not working with you, old woman. You have no honor."

Grandmother screamed again. Her body writhed and shifted, bones cracking and splitting, partial shapes resolving and sliding away. Somehow the men kept hold of her.

Bruiser, his face white from the strain of trying to control a mad skinwalker, let her go and hunched his body away from Grandmother. Skinwalkers can't be bound—or even controlled—easily, and Grandmother, perhaps, not at all.

Aya stared down at the woman who had raised him. There was pain and horror and a grieving misery in his eyes.

Grandmother shifted to Sabina, who looked at me. "Protect the amulets from the invaders. Keep our kind and your kind and the witches, as well, safe from the place of binding and shape-changing and freedom."

"Where is it?" I asked.

"You will find it," the priestess said. "But you cannot let the one who ate me live. Kill her now. Take and protect the amulets. Save the place of power and the being who is chained there."

Aya said, "Her death is the duty of her clan and her children. But—" He looked at me, his expression shifting through indecision to something harder. "Her trial before the elders will take time to arrange. I am an officer of the law as well as an elder of the *Tsalagi*. I have a duty. May I borrow a vehicle to take them to the witch null prison?"

He couldn't kill her. I got that. It might be a horrible decision to leave her alive, but . . . Gramma was Aya's responsibility. Not the Dark Queen's. I blew out a breath, knowing I was putting off the inevitable. "Yeah."

I addressed the vamp I trusted more than anyone knew. "Koun, will you arrange a security team to help. Eli and I will be . . . ummm . . ." I smiled weakly, "tied up here."

"Yes, My Queen."

CHAPTER 18

Who Knew with Suckheads?

Crap started again at dusk. I rolled over, finding myself in Leo's old bedroom. Mine now. There were people shouting in the hallway and over my earbuds, which were laying on the bedside table. No gunshots, no announcements about being attacked, so that was good.

I was fully human, still with about twenty-five extra pounds of muscle, my head on Bruiser's pillow beside the crown, which had come off again as I slept and changed shape. He was gone of course, because he needed less sleep than I did. I was sweating and miserable and threw off the covers so the AC could cool me. Outside the door, something thumped. Loud.

I hadn't missed all this at the inn, in the mountains, in my place of peace: the constant violence, ornery vamps, and a heat wave in midfall. According to the weather app on my cell, temps had reached ninety during the day and were still in the eighties.

And then I remembered. I flopped over, the horror flashing through me.

Storm and Derek dead in the street. Raisin dead. Adan

dead. Bruiser reading vamps, trying not to bind them, his face showing nothing. Nothing at all of the misery he had been feeling at taking on the burden of such a terrible act. Monique headless-dead. Gramma and Ka being loaded into the SUV and taken to the witch null prison, where they were now, under guard. I had a bad feeling about them, but despite the evil they had done, they weren't mine to sentence. They were the problems of Panther Clan Elders. They were Aya's responsibility, unless they got free and killed witches or humans in my city. So far as I could prove, they hadn't, and until they did, my hands were bound. Once they killed the people I was sworn to protect, all bets were off. I'd take their heads. Kill. Again.

I rolled out of bed, showered, and did the girly things I needed to do in this shape.

Wearing a plush bathrobe, I padded barefoot out of the bath to find my bed had been made while I was in the shower, and my weapons had been laid out on the spread. I figured Quint had been involved, though in this form, I couldn't really differentiate her scent her over the blood and vamp aromas carried on the air system.

The noise in the hallway had decreased as vamps and their dinners paired off, or tripled off, or multiplied off for blood sharing. My stomach growled, and I thought about walking barefoot and robed down to the kitchen, but I didn't want to appear to be presenting myself as a potential dinner to any vamps. I threw open the closet doors, and the first thing I saw was a brand-new set of armor in a gorgeous gold, which hadn't been here before. I no longer knew how many suits of armor I owned. I knew what one set cost. The Dark Queen's fashion and defensive wardrobe expenditures had to be astronomical. I shoved the gold suit aside on its hanger.

Fortunately the clothing in the closet had been replaced and was all stuff I liked—no weird colors, just black, gold, and red—so I could mix and match. I wasn't good with fashion, but I figured even I couldn't mess up with the minimal color choices. The pants and skirts were all black, except the one scarlet dancing skirt that had to be a full circle of the lightest flowing silk. Everything in the closet had slides at the waist with decorative or hidden buttons to give me inches where I needed them. The pockets were mostly faux, so I could always carry concealed. The necklines of the tops were loose and flowing or skintight stretchy stuff. Two shirts had crossover necklines to be worn over a tank or camisole. Each piece had been made with shape-shifting and weapons in mind.

It should be easy to decide what to wear. I started with the narrow cabinets to the sides of the closet and pulled open drawers that held undies and bras in my size, most way too fancy. But I found a few things tucked away that were more useful than lace, satin, and silk, as if someone other than Madame Melisende had snuck them in. Go Quint. I pulled on cotton undies, a Lycra jogging bra, and a body-hugging T-shirt. I had more boobs again, which was nice, but I needed padding to protect my more delicate bits from weapon harnesses. Satisfied with the start, I studied the clothing.

Tonight was the scheduled duello between my executioner and the warrior chosen by the latest invader, Shaun MacLaughlinn, assuming he showed up after breaking parley and attacking us. It was also the date of the execution of the vamps in the basement, which Shaun surely knew, and so he might show up at HQ to attack again and to try and get his people back. Who knew with suckheads? Knowing he had been working with Monique, Granny, and Ka, and that his cohorts were now dead or imprisoned, he might be planning most anything tonight. It was what any self-respecting vamp would do—promise to be on best behavior, cheat, promise again, and then cheat again. I should wear the armor. So maybe this wasn't going to be as easy as I had hoped.

A soft knock sounded on the door, and I heard a voice say, "It's Quint."

Despite only having a human nose, under the door, I smelled seafood and only one person. "Come," I said, unlocking the door, drawing on the robe and palming a throwing knife. Just in case.

The door opened, and the scent of fresh shrimp seared with peppers and homemade bread hot from the oven filled the room. Quint carried in a tray over her head, like a waiter in a fine restaurant, and laid out my meal on the tiny table in the corner. It had drop-down sides, and when they were lifted, it could easily seat three. There was a pitcher of iced green tea with lots of lemon, a green salad, bacon-wrapped asparagus, a bottle of wine, which we both knew I wouldn't appreciate, and the fabulous shrimp.

I placed my chair in the corner, kept the throwing knife in my lap, and sat. Quint watched my every move, and though there was no way she could have seen the small blade, I was pretty sure she knew it was in my lap. Out of the fixins, I put a po'boy together. Though the asparagus was an odd contribution, the bacon made it all work.

"So good," I mumbled through a mouthful.

"Why did you open the door without checking if I was alone?" Quint asked. "You did the same thing at your house when Thema and I were together. Yet you sit with a throwing knife ready to defend against me."

I chewed and swallowed. Took a sip of the lemon green tea. It was pretty good, for iced stuff. "I could smell food. And you. At the house, I could smell you and Thema. And I carry the knife because you're a sociopath, and I'm not one hundred percent sure of you yet." I shrugged.

Quint studied me, her body deceptively lax and loose. "Most people can't tell that about me. My family doesn't know. The only other person who knew is dead. How do you?"

"All animals know. It's in your body language. Small things." I didn't offer to tell her what things, especially in light of the *other person who knew is dead* comment. I was getting smarter in this world of bloodsuckers, other paras, and humans with issues.

Her expression didn't change. She turned her back on me and looked at my closet. "Tonight you have a duello, which may not take place, though you will know soon. And after that, there may be executions. Or not. The prisoners at HQ might agree to go to new masters." She shrugged. "Either way, you must be appropriately attired. Your scarlet armor has been cleaned and is airing out. I can have your black armor or the white armor sent over. But if you don't like the idea of armor again, the black pants, scarlet crossover shirt, and black jacket would be acceptable. With the extra body mass, you no longer look weak and defenseless. The business clothes give an aura of strength, as in, you're so tough and well protected you don't need armor."

"Fine. In which case, you can stand in front of me and take any shots," I joked.

"Of course," Quint said, as if it went without saying. "I'll have your black dancing shoes sent over. Your extra weight doesn't appear to have affected your height or shoe size." She pulled the items out of my closet and hung them on a rack she suspended from the closet door top. "What are you going to do with your hair?"

"Something basic. Tight braid. Tied in a fighting queue at my nape in case I have to armor up after all. I'll do it and my makeup myself." I didn't want her touching my hair again. I pushed away from the table. "Take the tray. Be back in twenty, armored and armed."

"Of course," she said again. Quint stopped. "Your sense of smell is much better than human, even in human form?"

"Yes."

"Can you smell sickness? Emotions?"

"In Beast form and half-form, yes. Not so well in this form."

"I see." She left the room as she came in, tray up high.

When she was gone, I let out the breath I had been holding. Quint was a seriously scary woman. Beast purred deep inside. *Good predator woman.*

Yeah. She is.

"The Sangre Duello will take place as arranged in parley," Bruiser said softly.

"Why?" I asked, my question serious. "They attacked us. Multiple times. Why should we give them opportunity again?"

"Because if there is no official duel, they will continue to attack us, killing our people. If Koun wins, they will likely use treachery, attack after the duel, and then we can destroy all your enemies, who will be gathered in one place. There will be an end to it. If Koun loses, we can use parley and protect our people. Again, there will be an end to it." He smiled at my expression. "The Dark Queen's honor will not be besmirched. I promise. Our people have parleyed the details and announced them to the world."

"Treachery can work both ways," I said.

Bruiser smiled slowly. "Yes. It can. We will be ready. We will be on our home grounds."

Eli, at my side in a rolling chair, said, "We got this, babe."

I sighed and blew out a breath. I kicked off the dancing shoes Quint had messengered over from my home and put my feet up on the big table in the security room, the massive screens overhead. "I'm listening."

"A swordsman named Dovic, no last name, or perhaps no first name," Bruiser said, "is to be Koun's opponent."

Alex, sitting at the main comms station, said, "Dovic is legendary in vamp sword fights. He always fights to the death, no first-blood matches, no tourneys. He's an all-or-nothing kinda guy." He pointed overhead. "Watch."

On the center overhead screen, I watched Dovic fight. Though there were multiple duels, watching them didn't take long. Each ended with Dovic's opponent beheaded in record time. The longest duel was forty seconds. His use and competency with a multitude of weapons was impressive, the fights I viewed involved: two flat Spanish dueling swords (one short, one long), three different weights of cutlasses, axes, hatchets, a dueling pistol and a sword brandished together, a ball-peen hammer and a switchblade, a dull pencil and a butcher knife, and a silver vamp-killer and fillet knife. No matter what weapon or combo of weapons was chosen by his opponent, he won. Even for a vamp, he was freaky fast.

Dovic was blond, blue-eyed, and scarred, including a deep, puckered scar from his right eye, across his cheek, to his chin, which meant he had fought when he was human too. As I watched the matches, I also watched Koun, sitting on the far side of the large conference table, a delicate cup of tea at his elbow, both hands slowly and lovingly cleaning his swords. They were the kind of dueling swords used in the Mithran version of the Spanish sword fighting method known as La Destreza Verdadera, also known as the Spanish Circle, or the cage of death.

I had seen Koun fight in the Mithran La Destreza technique. He was beautiful in motion. But Dovic was fast, intent, and purposeful. And his current master had an amulet that might make his scions even faster. I wanted to say, *Stop this. You can't do this.* But there was no stopping it. And my fighting was sloppy at best, incompetent at my worst, and I was mortal. And my life meant the lives of too many others. So I couldn't take over.

Koun wasn't naked, the way he usually fought. And he wasn't wearing the black armor I had seen him fight in. He was armored in the latest version of Dyneema, Kevlar, and a layer of anti-magic-spelled cloth to deflect spells and spelled weapons. His armor was nearly white, swirled with shimmering, crystalline blue in the same shapes as his blue Celtic tattoos, as brilliant as the pale crystal of his eyes. Magic moved through the tat shapes, powerful energies. He looked spectacular, frozen, like a glacier. Only his hands and his head from earlobes up were uncovered. His blond hair was pulled back into a fighting queue. As if he knew I was watching him, he smiled slightly.

Returning to the screen, I said, "Show me the La Destreza ones again. Quarter speed."

Alex said, "Yes, My Queen." The scenes moved across the screen, one at a time, the endings all the same. Death.

"Eighth speed," I said.

Eli tapped his earbud, slipped away from his chair, and out the door. I watched him go and returned my attention to the overheads.

The scenes played out again, and this time I caught it. Dovic had a tell. Calmly I said, "The left elbow."

"Your eye has improved. And yes. Always, My Queen," Koun said. "Every single time. I tried to teach him better."

I blinked. *Better?* "You were Dovic's teacher?"

"For many years. He was an exemplary pupil, faster than any Mithran or Naturaleza I ever fought. Faster than I am by far."

"So him being here, the two of you fighting. Is what," I said, part question, part demand.

Without looking up, Koun said, "The sad end to Dovic's hubris. I shall claim his swords and his land when I take his head. Fighting your battles has been profitable." Koun lifted a square of chamois and polished his short blade. "Your kind gift of armor is much appreciated."

I frowned and looked around the room. No one was

looking at me. I had a feeling I had missed something. Then it hit me. When I was Leo's Enforcer, my armor had been supplied to me as part of my payment. That meant that I was—or should have been—providing Koun, my chief strategist, with all the high-tech armor and weapons at my disposal. I said, "You're my warrior. There's more where that came from."

The door behind me opened, and Eli entered. He dropped to one knee, holding up a small box, his eyes meeting mine, full of demand. "Forgive me, My Queen. I forgot to retrieve your favor. For your warrior."

I took the box, which was lightweight wood, carved all over in geometric designs. I opened it to see a lace-edged scrap from my closet upstairs. My first thought was that he'd brought me a pair of the fancy panties, but I held in my nervous, shocked laugh and lifted it out. Eli looked from my face to the hanky, kissed his own fingers, and looked at Koun. I put it all together. Fights and tourneys, ancient ways, and the favor bestowed on a warrior who was fighting for his queen. Right. *Crap.* I had forgotten that I was supposed to be using all the formal vamp war etiquette too. Koun wasn't a modern-day European, but he had fought through all the centuries since he was turned. He would understand and expect this kind of stuff, and I never remembered to do it.

Drawing on all my fancy vamp court talk, figuring what I might say, I stood and walked around the table to Koun. "My warrior and executioner." I stuck a hand into my pocket and pulled out one of the small throwing blades strapped to my thigh. I pricked my finger with its tip and a tiny bead of blood rose to the surface of my skin.

Koun went still, his hands cradling the polishing cloth and sword.

I wiped the blood onto the pale pink hanky, staining it permanently. "In you I am well pleased," I said. I kissed the hanky and extended it.

Koun breathed in the scent of my blood. Raised his eyes from the hanky, meeting mine. He slid from the chair to both knees, head bowed. The chamois had vanished, and his hand was bare as he raised an empty palm. "My Queen."

I placed the hanky into his palm. "Be safe. I'll pray for you." I stopped. "And I'll pray for your soul."

His eyes jerked to mine. His entire body shuddered. "My Queen?"

"I don't believe your soul is gone. No matter what you may have seen once upon a time." No. It wasn't gone. It was stored somewhere. Like in a pocket universe, the kind the Glob stored energy in.

Tears filled Koun's pale eyes, making them glisten. He whispered, "My Queen." He kissed the hanky and tucked it inside his armor over his heart.

Behind us, both doors opened, creating a wide gap. Eli pulled two weapons and aimed there. Leo stood in the opening, unarmed, dressed in black, his hands clasped in front of him. Brute, the white werewolf stood at his leg. Something like joy passed through me but was quickly gone. Replaced by a frisson of fear. Was he here to challenge me for his city?

"Hold your positions," Eli said to the security teams on comms. The room went silent. "Alex?"

Alex said softly into his mic, "No sign until now."

That meant Leo had gotten inside without anyone knowing. I had a feeling that Brute had brought him, time-walking.

Alex added, "No weapons. No scions. Not here to take over."

Leo said, "I do not wish to retake this city. Such responsibilities are no longer mine. I am here to say one thing."

Slowly, Eli lowered his weapons, but he didn't holster them.

Koun studied the former master of the city but made no move to go to Leo or to bow to him. He didn't lift his sword either. He just waited, breathing in Leo's scent as if it told him something important.

Leo looked at me. "I am not here to take part in or interfere in the events that may unfold tonight. Such is not my place. But if you need me, you may call. Well done, Jane Yellowrock. Well done."

He placed one hand on the werewolf's head. Light, brilliant, in the shape of a cat's eye, burst out. And they were gone.

"Ooookaaay," I said slowly. "Brute is Leo's . . . trans-porter."

"No sign of them anywhere," Alex said. "No alarms, no monitors triggered."

Eli holstered two weapons. He was armored, which I hadn't noted until now. He glanced at Alex. "If you got that on vid, send it out on the V-web."

I didn't know what that was, but I could wait for info later. "Join me for tea?" I asked Eli. "We need to go over the security for the duello."

"I am honored," Eli said, his dark eyes twinkling. "Thank you. *My Queen*." Together we left the room. As the door closed, I thunked my head. His laughter echoing down the hallway was the best thing I'd heard all day. "Babe," he said, "Leo didn't kill us. And he's right. You did good."

The original form of La Destreza was different from the vamp version. Vamps had added from other longsword fighting systems, calling it the cage of death. They used two swords, usually one long, one shorter; their armor, when they used it, was no longer the original stuff worn in Spain but was updated. And in real combat, they never covered their faces. Matches took place in a fighting circle, and the goal of this one was to wound one's opponent so horribly that taking a head was an easy feat. But I didn't want my enemies inside HQ, so the parley had determined the du-ello would take place elsewhere, and no one had told me the final location. Which was Yellowrock Clan Home.

I hadn't been to the official clan residence in ages. I was pretty sure that the last time I was there was the day I shot Derek. Who was now dead.

The memories of his death slammed into me as we drove up. Memories of his body—scorched by lightning, his throat torn out, lying on the street—cut my soul. Silent, I left the vehicle and entered the front door.

Walking into the house was painful. Even though it had been totally redecorated in white and grays and looked nothing like the original, I could still see Derek fall. My fault. Just like his death. He had been healed that first time and healed all the times after, but not this last. His funeral was in two days. Being my friend was deadly.

"You weren't responsible for his death," Eli said softly, reading my mind.

From behind me, Thema said, "The long-lived lose our people one by one. Grief burrows and plows into our souls until there is nothing within us except that anguish."

I turned from the place where Derek had fallen and looked at her. Really looked at her. She was tall and whip thin, with very black skin for an old vamp. Tonight she wore silver in her ears, around her wrists, and on her fingers, a show of power few vamps could match. Her hair was cut close to her skull, and she was wearing white armor, two steel swords, and a number of modern weapons holstered here and there. She looked deadly. She also looked full of sorrow. Kojo stood behind her dressed in all black, his eyes on me.

"That's why you don't want blood-servants of your own, isn't it?" I asked them, the certainty creeping through me. "Even the longest-lived servants are dead at three hundred years."

"Yes," Thema said softly. "Our blood is potent. We easily bind humans. They do not wish to ever be far from us. It is difficult to be a Blood Master to such dependent beings."

"You and Kojo can stay as long as you like, without taking blood-servants. But you have to contribute. This offer is contingent upon you working with Florence, in her position as Infermieri, to heal all grievously injured humans and vampires sworn to me and to mine. If you agree, I'll make certain that blood meals are provided for you without you having to make them blood-servants."

Thema turned vamp-black eyes to me. "You are always a surprise, My Queen."

"Flying by the seat of my pants kinda does that. Is that a yes?"

Kojo looked at Thema, who nodded. "Yes," she said. Kojo looked away. I wasn't sure if he agreed or not, and didn't really care right now.

I glanced at Eli. "We'll be getting some heavily bound and isolated humans soon. They cared for some crazy vamps in isolation for way too long, and they smoked way too much weed. Once they've been dried out and reintroduced to modern life, make sure they feed a few times from Kojo and Thema and Florence." I looked at the vamps. "The damaged blood-servants and vamps can be test cases."

"Thank you, My Queen," Thema said.

Eli dropped his chin a fraction of an inch in what counted as agreement for him.

"Okay," I said. "Let's tour the house."

It was very different. The decor was now shades of white, shades of gray, and dull gold, with brushed brass pulls on cabinets and doorknobs, brushed brass light fixtures. Thankfully the brass had been used sparingly, because I hated it on sight. Too glitzy. But as a place for events, it would do. I got the grand tour, from the formal rooms and the dueling site on the ground floor to the bedrooms on the upper floor and in the attic. It was functional, if a little cold feeling. And empty. The few vamps who had been living here had found other places to be tonight. I couldn't say I blamed them.

The bedroom that was set aside for me was much more to my taste, done up in shades of warm gray and hints of green. I checked the closets, and sure enough, I had clothes hanging there. Madame Melisende and Quint had been busy. More importantly, there was a set of armor here too. This set was basic black cloth, not leather covered, and it had gold layering around the waist, wrists, and neckline. It looked like something I might wear for formal occasions. It was dang spiffy. I pulled it out and ran my hand over the fabric.

"You would look good in that," Eli said, "especially walking down the stairs after our guests arrive, nice and slow, weaponed up like you intend to go to war. Want to change? Quint is here somewhere, checking out the security measures, determining the potential points of egress should she need to remove you. She can help."

I held the armor up to me and turned, spotting a mirror on a stand in the corner. I walked over and looked at myself with the armor. Yeah. I'd look fantastic in this. Especially if I was half-form. I had been human for over six hours, so I should be able to shift easily and soon. "You like Quint?" I asked Eli.

"No. But she's never broken a contract. She has a reputation to uphold and a contract for five years. Protecting the Dark Queen, keeping you alive, means she can offer her services to anyone at any price she wants when her contract is over. And Quesnel lives at HQ. If Quint is capable of loving anyone, it's him. They play chess and cards, and to all appearances, she dotes on him."

"Mmm. Send Quint and food up in about fifteen minutes. Meanwhile, I'll try to shift into half-form. And send someone back to the house for my black combat boots. And make sure that Quesnel knows he can order anything he wants for his cellars. Let's keep him happy."

"Covering your bases." Eli touched his headset and called for food, Quint, and my weapons as he went out the door, closing it behind him. I stripped and removed the few weapons I had planned to carry. I'd want everything I had for this to work.

Nearly an hour later, I looked in the slim mirror at my half-form in uniform. This armor took badassery to entirely new heights. The red-gripped nine-mils in the black shoulder holster were reminders of blood. The gold on the armor matched the gold gorget. And the crown of silver stakes would glimmer perfectly above the gold of *le breloque.*

Quint handed me a headset and said, "I approve. Your guests have arrived. The duello will take place at midnight."

I put on the headset and adjusted the weapons. Quint made more adjustments until everything was prefect.

"When will Shaun MacLaughlinn arrive?"

"Oddly, he will not be present."

I looked across the room, not really seeing it. Shaun not coming made no sense. This whole duello had been orchestrated by him to take over my clan and my city. Of course, the original backstabbing plan had included Ka, Monique, and Granny as part of the attack at HQ and at my house, and maybe an attack during the Sangre Duello, in total violation of parley agreements. Maybe Shaun was backpedaling to Plan B. I tapped the headset to the private channel and said, "Alex. Eli. Shaun MacLaughlinn isn't coming?"

"Negative," they both said. Eli added, "Odds are he'll show up late and make a scene, but since no one has spotted him in NOLA in the last few nights, we aren't taking chances."

Meaning that Shaun might have lured us here and kept us busy while he attacked us on other fronts. It was a very vampy thing to do. "Precautions?"

"Your people are as safe as we can make them. Ayatas is working in a semiofficial PsyLED capacity with the Roberes, going over the legal papers, and dealing with the governor and the local law enforcement. Earlier today, I sent a team to gather the Everharts into a safehouse and provide protection in the mountains. Liz assures me they have a *hedge of thorns* up around their location and that Shaddock has guards around the perimeter. All security features are up and running at the inn and grounds, and a team is covering it. HQ is locked down with arcenciels patrolling. They seem to be having fun tossing a rotting head in the backyard like a ball game. We have a team patrolling the block around the witches' null prison. All the clan leaders have their lairs heavily guarded. I also sent a squad to the vamp cemetery. The excavation team found some interesting amulets, and they needed protection getting them back to HQ. Our house is under lockdown."

As he talked, I broke out into a cold sweat. That was a lot of places and people who were depending on me to survive the night and kill the Big Bad. But so far, Shaun MacLaughlinn hadn't shown up to his own challenge. He was doing something else, and my people had already figured that out, but they were stretched thin. My friends were in danger again. "Okay. Thanks."

Eli said, "Dovic has arrived. His people are inspecting the arena."

The arena was the main room at the bottom of the stairs. The furniture had been moved against the walls, and a rubberized fighting mat had already been in place when I took the house tour. I also remembered a huge TV screen on one wall. Ugly thing. Big enough to watch films on.

"How many?"

"Twelve, including Dovic. The highest-ranking member of the clan currently on-site appears to be a three-hundred-year-old Russian Naturaleza female named Zariyah. She's wearing a silver earring, the clip-on kind. Thema is staring at her and smiling. If vamps could sweat, Zariyah would be sweating bullets. But the parley was for twenty-four on each side, so I'm not ruling anything out."

"The second string arrived first," I said.

"Except for Dovic. Which means the first string is busy elsewhere or waiting to make an entrance. We have look-outs on the roof and two drones flying, one directly over-head and another one in a wider circle that covers the downtown side of the Garden District. There are spotters at each hotel where our uninvited guests are staying, and we have shooters for three blocks around the clan home."

"Mr. Prepared."

"Always, babe."

"When do you want me to make an entrance?"

"Why don't you be fashionably late. I'll send up tea and a laptop for you to watch the security cameras."

I brightened. "Ducky. And something else to eat? I finished off the burgers, so maybe cucumber and cream cheese sandwiches?"

"You don't eat *cucumber* sandwiches," Eli said distinctly.

"I do tonight. And though I needed the burgers to shift into half-form, I'm pretty tired of protein."

Eli's silence was telling. Because I was never tired of protein.

Tea and cucumber sandwiches were the reason I was sitting in my swanky bedroom at Yellowrock Clan Home when Shaun MacLaughlinn and his small army showed up.

CHAPTER 19

Yada Yada Blah Blah

Thanks to the drones and the spotters, we had plenty of warning, and I even had time to brush my fangs before the action began. Shaun MacLaughlinn's people came racing through the city in Jeeps with no doors, all heavily armed. The police had reports of "armed gang activity" from the time the vamps left Marigny and hit the streets, heading uptown. Thanks to the lines of communication between local and state officials, roadblocks were ready and went up everywhere to keep the city's usual revelers from danger. Cops gave chase from a safe distance, SWAT was already in position in the outer perimeter around the clan home, and Bruiser joined Aya on conference calls to the chief of police—Chief Walker, who owed his life to me—to coordinate the defense of the public.

By the time Shaun reached the Garden District, the invading vamps and their toy soldiers were locked down from a military standpoint, and by the time they pulled up in front of the clan home, they were surrounded, laser targeting sights on all of them. Comms was a screaming chaos, SWAT and Eli's teams were everywhere, working together because they had to. There was more than the number of attackers we had planned on, far more than the additional twelve vamps Shaun had agreed to. He had brought a ragtag army of humans and forty vampires. Not that the vamps fully understood what the targeting lasers meant. Powerful vamps always had blind spots where modern machinery, electronics, and military equipment were concerned.

But the humans with the invading vamps were a different matter. Mercenaries, accustomed to attacking unarmed foes for pay and walking away unharmed, knew what the tiny targeting lights meant. They simply put down their weapons, locked their hands behind their necks, and sat on the street as cops surrounded them at close range, weapons trained on them. I hoped the mercenary group had already cashed their check, because replacing the weapons was going to be pretty pricy. NOLA law enforcement would surely confiscate the high-powered weapons.

That left the vamps who had broken parley and then shown up with armed soldiers to break it again. None of the vamps put up a fight either. Within sixty seconds of the mercenaries quitting, most of them voluntarily disarmed and were lying on the ground under Eli's guard. That was the thing about making a clan out of the remains of disbanded clans and rogue vamps. No loyalty. It wasn't lost on me that I had done exactly the same thing.

When the scene was secured, local cops were allowed to take the mercenaries away, and Bruiser had his team bring all the vamps to the porte cochere, where drones couldn't hover overhead and watch him work. He and his crew went through the vamps, staking the ones not on the invitation list. We couldn't simply behead them in sight of the cops and the neighbors. The uninvited extras would be moved off site, read and bled, and either claimed by a stronger vamp or . . . dispatched. For now, we had a row of staked vamps on the property, which no one liked, because a staked vamp could be unstaked and put back to fight quickly, but it was the best we could do.

Quint laughed at the sight of staked vamps on my computer screen. It was a weird sound, a kind of laughter I both liked and hated at the same time. My feelings about Quint were all over the place. I hoped they settled into something stable soon.

The cameras shifted to inside as Shaun MacLaughlinn and his allowable additional twelve vamps were permitted to enter the house. Following them, I switched the security view to the inside cams.

Even with Shaun wearing his Snake of Snakes armband over a silk shirt the color of fresh blood, it was an ignominious entrance, and the vamps who had been waiting inside looked frustrated and angry, possibly because they had seen their army taken down without a shot fired or a single instance of personal combat. The big ugly video screen had carried it all live. I guessed they would move to plan C now, because no way did they have only one plan for tonight. But until they started something our people could kill them for, everything rested on the outcome of the duel. The futures of the entire city, and probably the entire U.S. Mithran organization, rested on Koun and Dovic. Except . . . They had broken parley. I opened the parley agreement and saw that one type of ammo wasn't among the list of proscribed weapons, an omission—probably accidental—which gave us an advantage.

A smile stretched my face. Quint watched me the way a mouser cat watched a mouse.

I asked Eli over comms, "Were our enemies carrying silver-lead hollowpoint shredders?"

"No My Queen," he said.

Into my mic and to Quint I said, "They broke parley multiple times. If everything goes to crap, silver-lead hollowpoint shredder rounds are not proscribed. No mercy."

"Yes, my lady," Quint said, her eyes lighting with glee.

"On it," Eli said. "I'm also having your Infermieri, Florence, brought here. Things could go bad in a heartbeat."

I could hear Quint changing out mags. Snap, slap, click. Four times. Eli was giving orders. On the laptop, I studied each face as my enemies entered the main room, watched the body language, and concentrated on Shaun as he walked up the few steps to the landing on the staircase. He started an irate monologue about the rights of vamps to command, hunt, and own humans. About how no Mithran or Naturaleza should ever allow a *foul creature* to rule them and how the only way that anyone would pledge loyalty to *that beast* was if they were weak or if some great magic was forcing them. Yada yada blah blah.

Except the great magic he was talking about was the Glob and *le breloque*. The old stories suggested that the corona gave the wearer the ability to force vamps to comply. The stories were right, but only for a limited time and to a very limited extent, at least for this Dark Queen. Those same stories said that the vamps had risen up against the last Dark Queen and killed her, probably because she tried to rule with an iron fist and could only control a few of them at a time. Me running amok and treating them like puppets was not a happy-happy-joy-joy thought being planted in my loyal vamps' heads. By their expressions, it wasn't taking, at least not for now.

When Shaun wound down, Bruiser let a silence build before he walked the four steps up to the small landing to stand beside Shaun. He introduced himself, beginning with his previous title as primo and ending with "and I am now honored to be the Consort of the Dark Queen of all Mithrans." My heart melted.

Shaun sneered.

Politely, Bruiser suggested that Shaun's herald provide the introductions and announcements of titles, but he didn't cede the dais to the herald, which left the enemy's ceremonial vamp standing on the first step, his back to Bruiser, which I could tell Shaun hated. The herald had an amazing voice, deep and sonorous, but since Shaun had no land and no city—which had been turned over to Grégoire when Shaun's *anamchara* Dominique was executed—the intro didn't take long. The herald had little to work with.

Dovic's intro took quite a bit longer, as his intro included all the vamps he had beheaded in battle, personal combat, and duello. It was an impressive list, except it was clear at the end that he had avoided a duel with Edmund and Grégoire, which meant he had been in hiding during the takeover of Europe. The entire time the herald called out his kills, Dovic stared at Koun. His body was positioned so that I couldn't see his face from any camera, but his hatred of Koun was evident in every line of his body.

Koun, on the other hand, looked bored. When the long

list of kills was done, the herald turned back to Bruiser and said, "And your warrior?"

Koun raised his eyebrows, stared at his rival, and said matter-of-factly, "I am Koun. No past kills have value to-night, only the kill I shall register moments from now. This night, I shall be known as the executioner of Dovic, the Arrogant Fool."

Dovic didn't like that. His head came up, and he vamped out, fast.

Koun still looked bored.

"And that's your cue," Quint said.

I slapped the crown on my head, and it tightened pain-fully. Standing, I walked out of my bedroom, down the hallway, and stopped at the top of the stairs.

Bruiser called out, "The Dark Queen of the Mithrans."

Every head turned to me. I exhaled a long slow breath, letting my scent fill the room. I had never smelled like a typical skinwalker, all flowery with spring blooms. I had always smelled like what I was. A predator.

Four of Shaun's first twelve vamps vamped out in reac-tion, uncontrolled, a sign of weakness. All but three of the others shifted body positions slightly, as if to ready for at-tack. My people stood their ground.

Bruiser continued, "She has many titles and land and clans, but nothing can eclipse the crown she wears."

Shaun, Dovic, and three vampires are predators worthy of us, Beast thought at me. *All others are weak.*

We could die, I thought at her. *Let's not start any fights we can't win.*

Inside me, Beast chuffed. *Beast does not fight what hu-mans call fair. Beast is best ambush hunter.*

Quint stepped in front of me, her eyes darting here and there, indicating she was at high alert. She started down the stairs.

Much slower, letting them look, letting my scent fill the room, I started down, one slow step at a time. Beast poured strength and power into my bigger frame, and a kind of grace that only a hunting cat has. She looked through my human eyes, giving them that odd gold glow of my cat. I moved slowly, seeing everything the way a cat does, every inhalation when the vamp should be still, every slight shift of weight. The enemy vamps had never seen such a thing as I was. It made them flinch.

I saw faster than Quint, when Zariyah twitched to draw a throwing blade. The old Russian Naturaleza snapped back her arm. Beast fast, I pulled my own, dodged down and gripped the railing in my offhand. Leaped into the air. Released my blade. Heard the sound of a blade spearing, impacting the wall where my head had been.

Quint's blade and mine pierced Zariyah's throat almost simultaneously, above her gorget. She staggered back. Eli put a round into her forehead. She slumped. Everything went still for a heartbeat, for those of us whose hearts that still beat.

Shaun screamed a challenge that I barely heard over the deafness from the gunshot. "You have broken parley!" He drew his sword and took a step toward me.

Quint shouted back, "No! Your people did!" She pointed at the blade, still quivering in the wall.

"You put that there!" Shaun shouted.

"Cameras!" I demanded.

Shaun shut up.

"All the outclan priestesses sworn to this city are dead," Eli said calmly, his weapon aimed at Shaun's head. "There's no one here to judge a duello, so we placed cameras to prove or disprove parley infractions. Put away your sword, or I'll put a round in *your* brain too."

"Cameras?" Shaun sounded dumbfounded, as if he had never heard of cameras.

"Onscreen," El said into his mic. He tilted his head at the ugly screen on the wall. All heads turned to the screen. Four camera views came up in slo-mo, quarter time. Zariyah's hand reaching down, pulling a blade. Snapping back her hand. Me doing my amazing acrobatics. Zariyah's blade just missing me in the air. My blade and Quint's landing in Z's throat. Eli's headshot.

"Your people have broken parley multiple times in this night alone," Bruiser said. "We will show the world your perfidy."

Eli said, "The footage has been loaded up into the V-web."

Shaun asked, "V-web? What—"

"Think of it like the dark web but for vampires," Eli

said. "The Dark Queen set it up to monitor vampire honor. Most of you have none."

I had done what? I had heard that V-web term before and had found no time to discover what it was.

"Me," Alex said into my earbud. "I did it. You can tell me I'm brilliant later."

Oh. Alex. You brilliant little stinker, you.

In his vampire ceremony tones, Bruiser said, "Your perfidy is known and exposed. All will scoff at you and yours." He lifted one hand to show the screen with the proof. "No one will do business with you. No one will trade blood-servants. All will give you the cut direct." That meant they would be shunned by everyone in the vamp world.

"Enough of this!" Shaun shouted. "Duello!"

Two of Eli's hidden snipers raised up and aimed into the arena. Koun drew his swords. Everyone drew swords. Two shots rang out. Two enemy vamps fell.

Dovic, swords at high and middle positions, raced into the ring. Exactly as he was supposed to. Except Koun wasn't there, I was. Where I had landed when Zariyah attacked. Koun was still at the stair landing. Dovic raced at me, vamp-fast, air popping. I reached for a vamp-killer.

But my blade hung slightly out of place on the new armor. I hadn't given it a final adjustment before I came down the stairs. I was going to be far too slow against the master fanghead dueler.

Koun was instantly behind Dovic. Vamped out eyes wide, fangs down.

Quint was suddenly just *there*, in front of me, two short blades up, two throwing knives clenched in her front teeth. She was tiny. So tiny.

I got my blade free.

Quint ducked, rolled, took out Dovic's legs. Knocking into him. He began a flip, which slowed, slowed, *slowed* as battlefield time took over. His swords swooped down toward me.

Eli bowled me over. Drawing up into a ball. Pushing off the floor with his left foot, that leg behind him stretched out.

Quint stabbed up into Dovic's crotch. Into the small join between Dyneema and plasticized armor. Into his groin. Dovic screamed the ululation of a vamp in mortal peril. He was still falling.

Dovic's longsword cut down, slicing into a seam in Eli's armor, into his thigh. The blade stopped. I heard/felt the blade hit Eli's femur. Blood spurted. Our momentum pulled the flesh and bone free of the blade with an audible *crack*. The sword ripped out. Folding back armor, muscle, and tendons in startling scarlet. Almost as an afterthought, blood pulsed out.

We rolled into the kitchen. Battle erupted behind us.

Before we even came to a stop, I was ripping open Eli's medical pouches and pockets and pulling out supplies. I remembered bits from my medical training. *Don't use a tourniquet on a limb that you hope to save.*

Except in arterial damage cases.

Blood spurted, spurted, spurted.

Around me and behind me, battle had broken out. Screams, the clash of swords, gunshots. Quint and Thema stood over Eli and me, weapons slashing and firing. Kojo covered us from the other side and shot a vamp who tried to get to us there. Raising his sword, he beheaded the vamp. Dovic's head dropped to the floor, followed by his body.

I shut down. No emotion. I gripped the fabric of Eli's armor, tearing it down his leg. Exposing the avulsion. The position of the sword strike started just below his butt, a lateral cut that had impacted the bone, fractured it, then slid down, separating the muscle from the bone, cutting/tearing tendons, muscles, veins, and arteries. Deadly. In seconds, not minutes.

Beast shoved power in to me. My knobby hands were strong as I strapped a tourniquet on Eli's upper thigh at the groin. Yanked it tight.

Littermate, Beast whispered. In addition to the strength, she poured speed into me.

Florence landed beside me. She ripped the flesh of her own arm and her blood poured over Eli's wound. Infermieri blood. "Close the wound," she demanded, her words sharp as glass.

Drenched in the blood of my adopted brother, I slapped the muscle back into place over the fractured bone. Began wrapping rolled gauze around and around. It wasn't enough. Blood still poured through. He was dying. Florence cut her wrist again and held it over Eli's mouth. He swallowed twice. His mouth went slack.

I couldn't save him.

Sabina could. Sabina was dead.

Bethany could save him. Bethany was dead.

Leo. . . . He had said he would come if I called, but I didn't have a number for him. But I had other things.

I pulled a small blade and sliced a cut along the side of my forehead, just above my right temple. Not too deep, but enough to make a big freaking damn mess, my blood pouring over *le breloque*. With my other hand, I wiped Eli's blood onto the crown. In my pocket, the Glob heated and burned, a frigid burn like dry ice applied to my flesh. I wrapped my mind and my will into the Glob. Into *le breloque*. The magic of the Dark Queen was crystalline and bright. With it, I saw all the tiny pockets of time-no-time and space-no-space where the Glob stored all the energies it took when it ripped magic out of the world. All the stored energies I might ever need were contained and stored in the Glob. I let my own crystalline might touch three of the small pockets, emptying them all into the power that was mine. Pouring magic and power into me. *Into me.* With my bright power, I shaped that magic.

I melded it together into a strong net of power that glowed so bright it ached. And it showed everything I was and everything I ever could be. I shoved healing into my brother. But my power was made for war. Nothing happened.

Twisting my power again, I raised my head and screamed, "Leo! Come to me!"

Nothing happened. I applied pressure with my big knobby hands, laying my body across the horrific wound. "Leo!" I screamed.

Nothingnothingnothing.

Except Eli dying. I tried the healing again. And again. "Eli. Come on Eli," Tears and snot ran down my face.

Florence forced her blood down Eli's throat, massaging to trigger him to swallow.

Time and space shivered. Gray and green and red-hot power burst out in front of me. A split like the center of the rift I had fallen into once. I nearly drew back.

Brute wavered into the split in time and space and stepped aside. A hand was on his head.

Beside the white werewolf, Leo appeared.

His black eyes took in everything at once, and he vamped out. His fangs ripped his arm from wrist up to mid lower arm, through his clothing, tearing them away. He bent over Eli, shoved me aside, and poured his blood over the bandages wrapping the wound.

I saw everything at once.

Florence was dribbling her powerful blood down Eli's throat, massaging it.

In the other room, screams, shouts, ululations, gunshots rang out. Positioned over us was Quint. Her short sword dripping. Her nine-mil firing. Precise. Deadly. I didn't have to look to know each shot was a head shot. And that she was using silver-lead rounds.

"Remove the bindings," Leo said to me.

I slipped the tiny blade between blood-soaked fabric and swollen flesh. Slid it gently up, the gauze separating. I heard/felt/knew as Eli's heart skipped a beat. Another.

Leo laid his cut arm on the flesh, his blood flowing. Florence added her blood to his and I bent over as well, letting the blood from my head wound merge and mingle with the vamps. Eli's flesh began to heal. But we were in a spreading pool of blood. So much blood. Too much . . .

Eli's heart . . .

Stopped.

Stuttered.

Beat.

Our blood flowed.

Beat.

Beat.

Stopped.

"Change him!" Alex demanded over the earbuds.

"Leo?" I whispered, begging.

"I am now outclan."

I looked at Florence.

"I am outclan."

Leo said, "You are Dark Queen. *You* have the power to heal him."

"I tried," I said, weeping. "I tried."

Brute padded through the wide pool of blood and stopped inches from my face.

Stinky dog breath, Beast thought. *Good wolf. Follow good wolf.*

Holding Eli's body together with my left hand, I put my bloody right hand on Brute's white head. My magic rose. It shivered and trembled, silver energies whirling and spinning, darker motes whirling. A single red mote coiled and looped. The red mote of evil magic I had thought was gone, not seen in months, was still here. Or was back here, released by the Glob when I opened the tiny pockets of power. The Glob blistered my flesh at my hip where I had somehow tucked it when Eli fell. The red mote circled the Glob, but wasn't sucked into it.

Was I still evil? Or were power and magic just that—inanimate—energy tools needing only the will and might, to be focused and used, making magic not a force with a conscience and principles and morals. Just a tool. Was magic less the might and more the compassion and humanity of the wielder? Even the Glob?

Suddenly we were in my soul home. The temps dropped. The stone walls of the cave were cold and wet. The walls were gray and pale yellow and shades of white. No fire burned in the firepit in front of me.

Eli wasn't here. Was that important? Did it matter? Was he dead?

On my right side, Brute stood. On my left, stood Beast. On the other side of Brute stood Leo. He was looking up. Into the dome overhead. His eyes widened, his mouth opened, his fangs clicked closed on their little hinges. His eyes bled back to human. He dropped slowly to his knees.

I followed his gaze and saw the angel wings draped over and against the stone dome, where they offered protection to my soul home. Hayyel keeping watch.

"Angel," Leo whispered. "Never have I thought to see such a being again."

In my vision, I was female but dressed as a warrior of

my tribe and clan—leggings, long tunic to my thighs, long belt wrapped around my waist. I wore my father's medicine bag on a thong around my neck. "How do I save Eli?" I asked of Hayyel.

"Open the wound," the angel's voice said. The dulcet tones reverberated around the stone room, and Hayyel appeared in front of me. Like a few other times, he was in winged form, but this time his wings were closed over him, hiding his body.

Leo fell to his face on the stone floor. Brute stretched out, belly and head down. Beast chuffed.

"Place your stone of office within his flesh. Pour your blood and all of your power over it. This may heal him," Hayyel said. "Your strongest Mithrans must feed him. Leo, you must use your magic, though it will call to your master. Hurry. And then find where I am. You don't have much time to free me. Your real enemies are close."

"Huh?" I said.

Hayyel looked like he did when I first saw him, black skin, darker than the night sky, and golden eyes. He opened his golden wings, the brown and red spots among the feathers seeming to catch the light. He was wearing a white tunic, golden brown robe, and sandals

Around his waist was a silver chain, bright and glistening and studded with bits of dark iron. Instantly I knew the iron was formed from ingots of the Spike of Golgotha. Somebody had chained an angel.

"Go," he said, snapping his wings over his body.

I was back in the kitchen. "Feed him," I screamed. I yanked the Glob from my pocket and pulled back the avulsed flesh, the heavy part of Eli's thigh. I shoved the Glob inside. I was still holding the small knife and I sliced lengthwise along my arm, as Leo had done to his own with his teeth. My blood pulsed out into the wound. It pulsed and pulsed. All over and into Eli's wound. Hands tried to pull me away. Tried to bind my wound. "No." I stabbed the little knife at the hands. They withdrew. Quickly.

My blood pulsed. Again and again. And nothing happened.

When the world started to go dim, I fell back. "Okay," I said, laying on my side in Eli's blood. I allowed the hands to wrap a bandage on my arm and apply pressure. Other hands wrapped Eli's leg with more gauze, the Glob still inside.

I was laying on the floor with Eli, in his blood. I couldn't hear Eli's heartbeat flutter. His skin was that deep ashen of the dead. I heard ambulances out front, sirens wailing.

Koun landed beside me. He flipped Eli over. Ripped his own flesh with his fangs and fed Eli, massaging his throat. Florence was still bleeding over Eli's bound wound. Leo knelt on Eli's other side, vamped out. He gently bit into Eli's neck. Blue magic flashed out from Leo's fangs, from his hands on Eli's chest. It was a rhythmic cadenced magic, not vamp magic, not the magic of the *gather*. It was like and yet unlike any magic I had ever seen.

The closest parallel was outclan magic. Like when Bethany changed Bruiser from primo to Onorio.

When he appeared, Leo had said he was outclan.

How did that even happen. What the heck did it even mean?

I felt something happen inside Eli. The Glob did . . . something. *Le breloque* did something too, burning my head. Eli's body jerked the tiniest bit. Leo withdrew his fangs. Koun and Leo turned Eli to his side and Koun slapped his back three times. Blood drained out of Eli's lifeless lips. They laid him face up. Leo bit in again and Koun ripped his own flesh again, feeding Eli, forcing down the blood, his fingers near Leo's fangs.

It wasn't going to be enough. I knew it. I was a breath away from telling Koun to change him.

But I reached up and put both hands on *le breloque*, bloody and sticky and cold with all the blood mixed there. I thought about the Glob, its power warm and unexpectedly open and giving, inside Eli. Inside my brother of choice. And I called Eli with all my magic. With everything I had. All that bright and shining power. All that I was. And all that I may ever be. I gave to Eli.

Come back to me. Come back. You will live. Live. Your heart will beat. Beat. Beat. I willed him to live, willed his heart to beat along with mine. *Beat. Beat. Live. Live. Live!*

Inside me, the new magic rose, bright and glowing. Dark

Queen magics. Wrapping around my own skinwalker magics, prism-bright, shining like rainbows, echoing like brass gongs and cathedral bells ringing, brilliant as light through scarlet glass. Warm, sweet smelling, soft as silk yarn. Harder than steel. Blazing forge hot. I focused all that magic, all my own power, and all that power of the Dark Queen onto Eli.

"Live," I whispered.

I heard a heart thump. A long time later, I heard another. More. Eli's heart began beating steadily.

Tears gathered but no longer fell. Couldn't. I didn't have enough fluid left in me to cry, not even for joy. I was empty of blood, cold enough to be dead myself, and exhausted. So tired I could scarcely hold myself off the floor. I didn't have to look up. My power crawled out, snaking into every creature in the building, knowing them all—who lived and who had died.

In the other room were dozens of dead and dying vamps. Some were mine.

"Shaun?" I asked.

Koun said, "His own people turned against him, My Queen. They left their blades in his body, yet he still has his head." Koun pointed to the body against the wall near the bottom of the stairs. It was pinned there by a couple dozen blades. Koun asked, "Will you take his head or shall I, as your champion?"

Bleary, I looked around the room again. The cameras were still rolling, this crazy scene going out to the vamp world and showing us our own actions on the big screen. I had to make this count. For Eli. For all the people who had died here tonight. *Beast?* I thought.

Beast is here, she thought back. *The I/we of Beast is here. Still has some strength.*

We need to behead that vamp.

Deep inside, we growled. The reverberation sounded though the room. I/we forced ourself to our feet and shoved our shoulders back; head high. Padded through the blood and gore to the body pinned upright on the wall, pulling my vamp-killer.

I reached him and he blinked at me. Once. Twice. Focused on me. His mouth moved. He couldn't talk because his lungs and throat were pierced with blades, and he couldn't draw breath.

I turned so I was facing a camera. My image was front and center on the big screen. I was dripping blood. My pelt stood on end. My eyes glowed. My fangs were longer than most vamps. I was as scary as I had ever been. "There will be no more parley. I challenge the enemy who has been pulling strings. I challenge the vampire Mainet Pellissier. Not to Sangre Duello. But to war. I will kill your vampires and destroy any humans who remain sworn to you. I will take your head as I took the heads of the Sons of Darkness. I will feed your head to an angel of the light and your dead body to the sun. Come for me. I will be ready."

I turned and managed not to fall down. I braced my feet and secured the balance of my body. I swung the blade back. Forward. And I took the head of Shaun MacLaughlinn. Bending, I picked up the severed head from the floor and held it in front of me. Darkness spun around me and white pinpoints of light fell in front of my vision like snow.

Bruiser, equally as blood soaked as me, stepped to my side. "Behold," he said to the cameras. "The enemy of the Dark Queen."

"Bruiser," I whispered as all energy left my body. I wavered.

"Cut the feed," Bruiser said. "We are done."

And the darkness took me.

I woke in a strange bed. It still smelled of factory and outgassing, the scents almost hidden by the smell of my blood. So much blood. I was freezing to death, teeth chattering, muscles shuddering. Glorious heat of an electric blanket had been wrapped around me. On either side of me, I smelled vamps—Kojo on one side of me, Thema on the other. Leo's scent was fainter but close by, parchment and pepper. Florence was near my feet. Bruisers' scent came from near my head where he slid my loose crown away. He gently peeled a wad of matted hair off my forehead. Pulled it back behind my ear. Started on another batch. It wasn't necessary. He just needed to be touching me. For a while I just breathed, knowing I hadn't done enough of that lately.

My heart was beating too fast, fluttery, a little weak. I needed to shift into Beast to heal. I hadn't. I tightened one fist, feeling the knobby knuckles. That was the arm I had cut. Yeah. Still half-form-ish. When I released my fist, I felt blood and gauze crackle. But there was no pain. It was healing without shifting. Full of vamp blood.

I managed to get my mouth open. It was so dry my teeth felt like they were wrapped in the bloody gauze, and my tongue felt like a strip of jerky. On the second try, I managed to say, "Eli?"

Bruiser said, "He's in surgery at Tulane. Two Mithrans are standing by to donate blood should it become necessary. Should the change into Mithran need to be finished, Koun is also there. Eli is as safe as we could make him."

"Finished?" I whispered.

"Eli was halfway to Mithran when his human heart began to beat," Thema said from behind me. "It will take little to bring him over."

I thought about that. Decided it was the best that could be done. "The Glob?"

"Koun was delivered a bloody stone from the surgical suite," Bruiser said. "The surgeon said it bit him when he touched it. Koun said he will bring it before dawn."

"Okay. I'm going back to sleep," I whispered.

"And when you wake again, you will shower off the stench of rotting blood," Thema ordered. "You are disgusting."

"Whatever," I breathed. And slept. My last thought was the feel of my heart beating. A little out of sync. As if I heard an echo beating in the background.

CHAPTER 20

Undead Life Sucks

Fall in New Orleans meant that the weather had changed. Again. It was now mideighties, humid, and it was raining, a steady downpour that left puddles everywhere.

Eli and I were sitting on the back porch, alone for the first time, in the old squeaky metal chairs, our feet up on an ottoman from inside the house. We were wrapped in blankets we didn't really need but that were soft and comfy. We had downed two pots of tea, neither of us discussing that Eli was drinking tea and not coffee. By choice. We had chatted a bit about the weather. Mostly we were contemplating being alive, watching the rain fall, not talking much, but knowing we had a lot of ground to cover.

Eli had been home for less than twenty-four hours. His leg was bandaged and swollen. He had things poking up through the bandages. Metal things holding his femur together. There were more metal things inside. He would forever set off metal detectors. He had spent four days in the hospital. He had been given eight units of human blood-bank blood. He had drunk from more than a dozen vamps while in the hospital, several worried vamps lining up each night to donate. Florence had made regular trips to feed him her blood.

Liz had flown to NOLA for five days, bringing healing charms and other Everhart magics. She would be back, also worried about her former Ranger.

I had a feeling that Liz wasn't the only Everhart who would descend on NOLA with the intent to protect Eli and probably tear me a new one at the same time.

Alex delivered a third pot of tea. He was checking on us every fifteen minutes, hovering, even though he could see us from his table-desk. There was good reason for the concern. Even with vamp blood, Eli had nearly not made it.

The doctors had told Eli that with a lot of therapy, he would eventually walk. That he'd limp for the rest of his life. Probably hurt for the rest of this life. That he'd never run again. Eli had raised his eyebrows at the docs and requested to be released. Eli knew about rehab. He also knew about the healing power of vamp blood. He and Florence had come up with a dosage and rotation for vamps that would keep him from being blood-bound or changed. But he'd had so much it was likely he was something other than blood-servant strong, something other than Onorio, but maybe close.

His bed had been moved into my room, so stairs wouldn't be a problem. I had been sleeping in Eli's old room, and would until Bruiser came back and we decided where we'd stay. Bruiser and Koun were off tracking down enemy vamps, unaligned rogue vamps, and taking heads, starting with the most recalcitrant vamps in HQ's basement.

Mercy was a dead concept in my heart right now. Either vamps agreed to be bound to one of mine, swore loyalty, and accepted very junior status in one of my clans, where they could be monitored, or they were beheaded. My executioner had appointed helpers. The Dark Queen had three ax wielders. They traveled with portable chopping blocks, which they didn't bother to clean between uses. Bruiser had opened the trench where Sabina's chapel used to be, drained the water out, and my people were filling it with vamp bodies on a regular basis. No fancy funerals. No nothing. Just unmarked bodies in a pit, the heads tossed into a different pit. My humans watched them burn in the sun with each dawn.

I sipped my tea. As I moved my arm, the charm bracelet tinkled. It was drained of power. The bracelet, her feet, a pile of bloody bones, and a bloody white habit were all that was left of Sabina when they found her. I figured I would give the bracelet to my goddaughter when I saw her again, but for now, I wore it in honor of the priestess.

"What did we do about Derek?" Eli asked.

My heart clenched, which he surely felt. "We had a funeral. A big one. Marching band through the streets of NOLA. Dancing and wailing." Tears gathered in my eyes. "He was in a white casket in one of those glass sided carriages, drawn by white horses instead of the traditional black horses, because his mama wanted them. We gave his family a significant gift. We . . . We grieved."

Eli nodded. Time passed. We sipped, enjoying the quiet and the rain. "So," he said.

"So," I repeated.

"We gonna talk about how I know when your heart beats? When it speeds up and slows down? That our hearts are beating in sync now?"

"We could. Or we could just let it lie and see if it goes away."

Eli made a ruminative sound. "And if I want to talk about it?"

"Stop being such a girl," I said.

Eli chuckled. "Okay. How about we talk about Leo's presence in the city and his change in status. The priest's collar was a shocker."

"He's outclan."

"I got that part, babe. I'm more interested in how that came about and what it means for the future."

"I only know what Leo told me, half of which he guessed about."

"Better than nothing."

"Okay. After the fire, Sabina swam back. It was nearly dawn. She busted through into Leo's mausoleum. The heat had woken him, and he'd been trying to get free, but he wasn't strong enough yet. Or coherent at all. Sabina fed him, but she didn't have much to spare. She was burned badly. She got him to safety in the water pit. She fed him and brought some humans to feed him. At some point, she disappeared and never came back."

I looked down at my hands on the oversized tea mug. The saying on the side read "Undead Life Sucks" and showed a vamp with bloody fangs. It wasn't funny, but the mug held more tea than most. I said, "Grandmother must have trapped Sabina shortly after we were at the Damours' warehouse. According to one of the now true dead vamp prisoners, the *u'tlun'ta* ate her piece by piece while she screamed."

"Not your fault, babe," Eli said.

"Yeah. Right." But we both knew I was blaming myself. Old life patterns, like accepting guilt not my own, were hard to break, no matter the evidence. I picked an easier subject. "I've been reading Immanuel's journal while you lazed around and drank vamp blood," I said.

"And?"

"All the troubles in New Orleans went back to my Grandmother and to Immanuel. To the time in the 1800s when Tsu Tsu Inoli—Mark Black Fox, a skinwalker of Grandmother's lineage, and nearly as old as Gramma—ate him."

"And do you know why?"

"Yeah. And it's the reason Grandmother ate Sabina. To get the artifacts that were in vamp hands. Artifacts, amulets, made with arcenciel blood. So they could change time to suit their needs, and use the powers in the amulets to save the remaining Skinwalkers and bring back skinwalker power. I'm figuring Gramma blamed all vampires for the destruction of our people and wanted vengeance. Instead she and Ka are imprisoned in null rooms."

"Changing time. Seems to be the theme of your life."

I snorted. "And the ringleader—puppet master—is still out there. Leo's *my master*, Mainet. He has a title. The Heir. Which is scary because it means the heir to the Sons of Darkness"

"Leo's outclan now," he said, "and since the outclan can't be bound, technically, Leo has no master, unless it was firmly established before Leo rose again."

"Mmmm."

"The Heir? You challenged him to war."

This time I flinched a little.

"Yeah, I know all about it," Eli said. "Alex showed me the footage. You were pretty pissed off." He gave me a side-eye grin. "You missed an amazing battle while you were saving my life, but that ending was appropriately gruesome and bloodcurdling. Did you know you had blood dripping off your hair? Bet you scared the pantaloons off the old EVs."

"I saw." I had seen the footage too. Once. But I had turned away when Eli died, and I still couldn't talk about him dying on the floor at my knees. Not yet. Maybe not ever. "Leo visited you once while you were in the hospital," I said, changing the subject.

"I remember. Outclan priest," Eli mused. "Never been one of those has there?"

"No," I said. "He had already claimed outclan status, but . . ." I stopped.

"Out with it."

I huffed a breath. I hadn't told anyone this yet. "When we were trying to save you, Leo accidently ended up with me in my soul home, with the angel Hayyel."

Eli frowned. "So that made him a priest?"

"*He* thinks he was a priest from the time he rose from the dead for the second time," I said, my tone saying I wasn't so sure. "Thrice born does mean extra power and gifts, but Leo doesn't want his blasted city back, and being outclan means he's outside of fanghead political structure, and the fact that he saw an angel in my soul home means he's more special than the usual outclan, soooo—." I stopped, not sure what to say next.

"Lucky you, Queen of NOLA." Eli was way too calm for all this. I was freaking out.

I blew out a breath. "Whoopie. The amulet Shaun was wearing disappeared off his beheaded body in the carnage at the clan home. I'm guessing that one of his people took it when they stuck him full of knives and pinned him to the wall like a bloody butterfly. And there's worse."

"Always is."

Alex stuck his head out the side door and said, "Ayatas is here."

"Send him back here," Eli said, before I could answer.

"Copy." Alex disappeared.

I glowered at Eli and continued, "Hayyel is chained, or partially chained, wherever he is. I'm guessing partially chained, since he still manifested in my soul home. There's a silver and iron ingot chain around his waist. He says my enemies are on the way and intend to do something to him. Use his power somehow."

"And you have how many of the amulets with arcenciel blood in them now?"

"A flying lizard, a locket, and one the diggers found at Sabina's chapel." I pulled the ring out of my pocket and extended it to him. "It's a crystal, sealed with silver, with arcenciel blood sloshing beneath. It has power in it."

Eli touched the crystal and yanked back his finger. His mouth turned down just the tiniest bit. "Is this as powerful as I think, or did I get something else from your blood?"

"Beats me. Maybe it's arcenciel blood you feel, something you got from Leo's offering."

"Rule of three," Eli said. "You have three arcenciel amulets. They have one. You have three brothers. They have one—Maniet. So when do we go hunting the location of the chained angel?"

Ayatas stuck his head out the door. "Did someone say chained angel?"

"When?" I asked Eli. "Soon as you can dance, my bro. Soon as you can dance."

CLAN PELLISSIER, ORIGINAL
BLOOD-FAMILY HISTORICAL CHART

Judas, the Eldest Son of Darkness. Sire of:

Claudia Acete, a former slave of, and freedwoman of, Nero. Turned in Rome in A.D. 50. Dame of:

Rufinus Agricola, a centurion in Hispania, turned in what is now Spain in A.D. 125. Sire of:

Cesar and Ordonius Frunimius, turned in Spain in A.D. 400. Traveled to what is now France. They created a large blood-family and returned to Rome, where they fomented a blood feud against the Sons of Darkness in A.D. 950 and were destroyed. Dual sires of:

Alazais Chevalier, turned in France in A.D. 900. Was taken by the Eldest Son of Darkness and forced into his blood-family as a slave in reparation of the blood-feud that killed Claudia Acete. The son felt a strong attraction to the boy and took him as companion, sharing his scions, his bed, and his own blood. This gave Alazais great strength. When his time of servitude was up, he left Roman territory and returned to France, where he became the sire of:

Mainet Pellissier, turned in France in A.D. 1200. Was given rights to start a blood-family in A.D. 1450. In the years following, he turned several of his decedents, including Rudolfo and Amaury Pellissier. Rudolfo did not survive devoveo.

Amaury Pellissier turned his sons and nephews, including Leonard Eugène Zacharie Pellissier, in 1525. Together they came to the Americas and started the Pellissier blood-family under the proprietorship of Clan Pellissier and Mainet Pellissier in France. They became one of the earliest independent clans in the colonies in 1724, and Amaury quickly became Master of the City of New Orleans. He took over the hunting territories of the Louisiana territories. Under Amaury, the territory spread and gained power.

Leonard Eugène Zacharie Pellissier became Master of the City of New Orleans and most of the southeastern United States in 1912.

Immanuel Pellissier was Leo's heir but was sworn to Mainet.

ACKNOWLEDGMENTS

My thanks to:

Teri Lee, Timeline and Continuity Editor Extraordinaire. Thank you for keeping track of all the characters and if they are still alive . . . -ish.

Mindy "Mud" Mymudes, Beta Reader and PR.

Let's Talk Promotions, at ltpromos.com, for managing my blog tours and the Beast Claws fan club.

Beast Claws! Best Street Team Evah!

Carol Malcolm for the timeline update for The Jane Yellowrock Companion.

Mike Pruette at celticleatherworks.com for all the fabo merch!

Lucienne Diver of the Knight Agency, as always, for guiding my career, being a font of wisdom and career guidance, and the woman who pulls me down to earth when I get riled and mouthy.

As always, a huge thank you to Jessica Wade of Penguin Random House. Without you there would be no book at all!

Keep reading for an excerpt from
the first book in the Soulwood series

BLOOD OF THE EARTH

Available now!

Edgy and not sure why, I carried the basket of laundry off the back porch. I hung my T-shirts and overalls on the front line of my old-fashioned solar clothes dryer, two long skirts on the outer line, and what my mama called my intimate attire on the line between, where no one could see them from the driveway. I didn't want another visit by Brother Ephraim or Elder Ebenezer about my wanton ways. Or even another courting attempt from Joshua Purdy. Or worse, a visit from Ernest Jackson Jr., the preacher. So far I'd kept him out of my house, but there would come a time when he'd bring help and try to force his way in. It was getting tiresome having to chase churchmen off my land at the business end of a shotgun, and at some point God's Cloud of Glory Church would bring enough reinforcements that I couldn't stand against them. It was a battle I was preparing for, one I knew I'd likely lose, but I would go down fighting, one way or another.

The breeze freshened, sending my wet skirts rippling as if alive, on the line where they hung. Red, gold, and brown leaves skittered across the three acres of newly cut grass.

Branches overhead cracked, clacked, and groaned with the wind, leaves rustling as if whispering some dread tiding. The chill fall air had been perfect for birdsong; squirrels had been racing up and down the trees, stealing nuts and hiding them for the coming winter. I'd seen a big black bear this morning, chewing on nuts and acorns, halfway up the hill.

Standing in the cool breeze, I studied my woods, listening, feeling, tasting the unease that had prickled at my flesh for the last few months, ever since Jane Yellowrock had come visiting and turned my life upside down. She was the one responsible for the repeated recent visits by the churchmen. The Cherokee vampire hunter was the one who had brought all the changes, even if it wasn't intentional. She had come hunting a missing vampire and, because she was good at her job—maybe the best ever—she had succeeded. She had also managed to save more than a hundred children from God's Cloud.

Maybe it had been worth it all—helping all the children—but I was the one paying the price, not her. She was long gone and I was alone in the fight for my life. Even the woods knew things were different.

Sunlight dappled the earth; cabbages, gourds, pumpkins, and winter squash were bursting with color in the garden. A muscadine vine running up the nearest tree, tangling in the branches, was dropping the last of the ripe fruit. I smelled my wood fire on the air, and hints of that apple-crisp chill that meant a change of seasons, the sliding toward a hard, cold autumn. I tilted my head, listening to the wind, smelling the breeze, feeling the forest through the soles of my bare feet. There was no one on my property except the wild critters, creatures who belonged on Soulwood land, nothing else that I could sense. But the hundred fifty acres of woods bordering the flatland around the house, up the steep hill and down into the gorge, had been whispering all day. Something was not right.

In the distance, I heard a crow call a warning, sharp with distress. The squirrels ducked into hiding, suddenly invisible. The feral cat I had been feeding darted under the shrubs, her black head and multicolored body fading into the shadows. The trees murmured restlessly.

I didn't know what it meant, but I listened anyway. I

always listened to my woods, and the gnawing, whispering sense of *danger, injury, damage* was like sandpaper abrading my skin, making me jumpy, disturbing my sleep, even if I didn't know what it was.

I reached out to it, to the woods, reached with my mind, with my magic. Silently I asked it, *What? What is it?*

There was no answer. There never was. But as if the forest knew that it had my attention, the wind died and the whispering leaves fell still. I caught my breath at the strange hush, not daring even to blink. But nothing happened. No sound, no movement. After an uncomfortable length of time, I lifted the empty wash basket and stepped away from the clotheslines, turning and turning, my feet on the cool grass, looking up and inward, but I could sense no direct threat, despite the chill bumps rising on my skin. *What?* I asked. An eerie fear grew in me, racing up my spine like spiders with sharp, tiny claws. Something was coming. Something that reminded me of Jane, but subtly different. Something was coming that might hurt me. Again. My woods knew.

From down the hill I heard the sound of a vehicle climbing the mountain's narrow, single-lane, rutted road. It wasn't the *clang* of Ebenezer's rattletrap Ford truck, or the steady drone of Joshua's newer, Toyota long-bed. It wasn't the high-pitched motor of a hunter's all-terrain vehicle. It was a car, straining up the twisty Deer Creek mountain.

My house was the last one, just below the crest of the hill. The wind whooshed down again, icy and cutting, a downdraft that bowed the trees. They swayed in the wind, branches scrubbing. Sighing. Muttering, too low to hear.

It could be a customer making the drive to Soulwood for my teas or veggies or herbal mixes. Or it could be some kind of conflict. The woods said it was the latter. I trusted my woods.

I raced back inside my house, dropping the empty basket, placing John's old single-shot, bolt-action shotgun near the refrigerator under a pile of folded blankets. His lever-action carbine .30-30 Winchester went near the front window. I shoved the small Smith & Wesson .32 into the bib of my coveralls, hoping I didn't shoot myself if I had to draw it fast. I picked up the double-barrel break-action shotgun

and checked the ammo. Both barrels held three-inch shells.
The contact area of the latch was worn and needed to be
replaced, but at close range I wasn't going to miss. I might
dislocate my shoulder, but if I hit them, the trespassers
would be a while in healing too.

I debated for a second on switching out the standard
shot shells for salt or birdshot, but the woods' disharmony
seemed to be growing, a particular and abrasive itch under
my skin. I snapped the gun closed and pulled back my long
hair into an elastic to keep it out of my way.

Peeking out the blinds, I saw a four-door sedan coming
to a stop beside John's old Chevy C10 truck. Two people
inside, a man and a woman. *Strangers,* I thought. Not from
God's Cloud of Glory, the church I'd grown up in. Not a
local vehicle. And no dogs anymore to check them out for
me with noses and senses humans no longer had. Just three
small graves at the edge of the woods and a month of grief
buried with them.

A man stepped out of the driver's side, black-haired,
dark-eyed. Maybe Cherokee or Creek if he was a mountain
native, though his features didn't seem tribal. I'd never
seen a Frenchman or a Spaniard, so maybe from one of
those Mediterranean countries. He was tall, maybe six
feet, but not dressed like a farmer. More citified, in black
pants, starched shirt, tie, and jacket. He had a cell phone in
his pocket, sticking out just a little. Western boots, old and
well cared for. There was something about the way he
moved, feline and graceful. Not a farmer or a God's Cloud
preacher. Not enough bulk for the first one, not enough
righteous determination in his expression or bearing for
the other. But something said he wasn't a customer here to
buy my herbal teas or fresh vegetables.

He opened the passenger door for the other occupant
and a woman stepped out. Petite, with black skin and
wildly curly, long black hair. Her clothes billowed in the
cool breeze and she put her face into the wind as if sniffing.
Like the man, her movements were nimble, like a dancer's,
and somehow feral, as if she had never been tamed, though
I couldn't have said why I got that impression.

Around the house, my woods moaned in the sharp wind,
branches clattering like old bones, anxious, but I could see

nothing about the couple that would say danger. They looked like any other city folk who might come looking for Soulwood Farm, and yet . . . not. Different. As they approached the house, they passed the tall length of flagpole in the middle of the raised beds of the front yard, and started up the seven steps to the porch. And then I realized why they moved and felt all wrong. There was a weapon bulge at the man's shoulder, beneath his jacket. In a single smooth motion, I braced the shotgun against my shoulder, rammed open the door, and pointed the business end of the gun at the trespassers.

"Whadda ya want?" I demanded, drawing on my childhood God's Cloud dialect. They came to a halt at the third step, too close for me to miss, too far away for them to disarm me safely. The man raised his hands like he was asking for peace, but the little woman hissed. She drew back her lips in a snarl and growled at me. I knew cats. This was a cat. A cat in human form—a werecat of some kind. A devil, according to the church. I trained the barrel on her, midcenter, just like John had showed me the first time he put the gun in my hands. As I aimed, I took a single step so my back was against the doorjamb to keep me from getting bowled over or from breaking a shoulder when I fired.

"Paka, no," the man said. The words were gentle, the touch to her arm tender. I had never seen a man touch a woman like that, and my hands jiggled the shotgun in surprise before I caught myself. The woman's snarl subsided and she leaned in to the man, just like one of my cats might. His arm went around her, and he smoothed her hair back, watching me as I watched them. Alert, taking in everything about me and my home, the man lifted his nose in the air to sniff the scents of my land, the delicate nasal folds widening and contracting. Alien. So alien, these two.

"What do you want?" I asked again, this time with no church accent, and with the grammar I'd learned from the city folk customers at the vegetable stand and from reading my once-forbidden and much-loved library books.

"I'm Special Agent Rick LaFleur, with PsyLED, and this is Paka. Jane Yellowrock sent us to you, Ms. Ingram," the man said.

Of *course* this new problem was related to Jane. Nothing in my whole life had gone right since she'd darkened my door. She might as well have brought a curse on my land and a pox on my home. She had a curious job, wore clothes and guns and knives like a man, and I had known from the beginning that she would bring nothing but strife to me. But in spite of that, I had liked her. So had my woods. She moved like these two, willowy and slinky. Alert.

She had come to my house asking about God's Cloud of Glory. She had wanted a way onto the church's property, which bordered mine, to rescue a blood-sucker. Because there was documentation in the probate court, the civil court system, and the local news, that John and I had left the church, Jane had figured that I'd be willing to help her. And God help me, I had. I'd paid the price for helping her and, sometimes, I wished that I'd left well enough alone.

"Prove it," I said, resettling the gun against my shoulder. The man slowly lowered his hand and removed a wallet from his jacket pocket, displaying an identification card and badge. But I knew that badges can be bought online for pennies and IDs could be made on computers. "Not good enough," I said. "Tell me something about Jane that no one but her knows."

"Jane is not human, though she apes it better than some," Paka said, her words strangely accented, her voice scratchy and hoarse. "She was once mated to my mate." Paka placed a covetous hand on Rick's arm, an inexplicable sort of claiming. The man frowned harder, deep grooves in his face. I had a feeling that he didn't like being owned like a piece of meat. I'd seen that unhappy look on the faces of women before. Seeing the expression on the face of a man was unexpected and, for some reason, unsettling. "He is mine now," Paka said.

When Jane told me about the man she would send, she said that he would break my heart if I let him, like he'd broken Jane's. This Rick was what the few romance novels I'd read called tall, dark, and handsome, a grim, distant man with a closed face and too many secrets. A heart-breaker for sure. "That's a start," I said. In their car, a small catlike form jumped to the dash, crouched low, and peered out the windshield through the daylight glare. I ignored it, all my attention on the pair on my land, moving slowly. Rick pulled out his cell phone and thumb-punched and swiped it a few times. He paraphrased from whatever was on the screen, "Jane said you told her you'd been in trouble from God's Cloud of Glory and the man who used to lead it ever since you turned twelve and he tried to marry you. She also said Nell Nicholson Ingram makes the best chicken and dumplings she ever tasted. That about right?"

I scowled. Around me the forest rustled, expectant and uneasy, tied to my magic. Tied to me. "Yeah. That sums it up." I draped the shotgun over my arm and backed into my home, standing aside as they mounted the last of the steps. Wondering what the church spies in the deer stand on the next property would think about the standoff.

They thought I didn't know that they kept watch on me all the time from the neighbor's land, but I knew. Just like I knew that they wanted me back under their thumbs and my land back in the church, to be used for their benefit. I'd known ever since I had beaten them in court, proving that John and I were legally married and that his will had given the land to me. The church elders didn't like me having legal rights, and they didn't like me. The feeling was mutual.

My black cat, Jezzie, raced out of the house and Paka caught her and picked her up. The tiny woman laughed, the sound as peculiar and scratchy as her words. And the oddest thing happened. Jezzie rolled over, lay belly-up in Paka's arms, and closed her eyes. Instantly she was asleep. Jezzie didn't like people; she barely tolerated me in her house, letting me live here because I brought cat kibble. Jezzie had ignored the man, just the way she ignored humans. And me. It told me something about the woman. She wasn't just a werecat. She had magic.

I backed farther inside, and they crossed the porch. *Nonhumans. In my house.* I didn't like this at all, but I didn't know how to stop it. Around the property, the woods quieted, as if waiting for a storm that would break soon, bringing the trees rain to feed their roots. I reached out to the woods, as uneasy as they were, but there was no way to calm them.

I didn't know fully what kind of magic I had, except that I could help seeds sprout, make plants grow stronger, heal them when they got sick and tried to die off. My magics had always been part of me, and now, since I had fed the forest once, my gifts were tied to the woods and the earth of Soul-wood Farm. I had been told that my magic was similar to the Cherokee *yinehi*. Similar to the fairies of European lore, the little people, or even wood nymphs. But in my recent, intense Internet research I hadn't found an exact correlation with the magics I possessed, and I had an instinct, a feeling, that there might be more I could do, if I was willing to pay the price. I had once been told that there was always a price for magic.

Ready to find
your next great read?

Let us help.

Visit prh.com/nextread

Penguin
Random
House